THE
ONE CALLED
SAOIRSE

Scott Bowyer

THE
ONE CALLED
SAOIRSE

Scott Bowyer

Published by Two Live Oaks Media, LLC

PART I

1

The boy stood alone leaning against the wall as children hurried to their buses and chattered with one another while they waited for their rides. A black station wagon turned into the parking lot entrance of the school. The boy grabbed his backpack and headed toward the car but heard a cry, "Mr. Stevens. Mr. Stevens. Sir?" When he turned around, a burst of laughter echoed across the school halls. The boy walked grimly on. From behind, a voice murmured, "Well he does walk like him, and he's just as tall and stuffy." Another round of laughter echoed through the halls.

He was not going to let his peers ruin his day. He had some good news for his father. The boy opened the door of the station wagon and slid into the front passenger seat.

"You've got something to talk about, don't you," said the man.

The boy looked at his father with surprise and then nodded.

"Brad invited the whole class to watch *Rebel without a Cause* tomorrow, the new movie by some actor named Dean."

"The Carters' boy?"

"Yes. And he's reserving one of the rooms at Carter's Cinema on Saturday just for us."

The car inched slowly toward the parking lot exit as children swarmed around the cars.

"Everybody at school knows Brad. He watches all the new movies and then tells us about it. Most of the other kids have been to the theaters at least once, too." The boy rubbed his hand hard across his leg and continued feebly. "He sure makes it sound pretty exciting.

I'm surprised he invited me to go. He even invited Wade Pinkerton, so I think everyone's going."

They drove in silence a moment more. Then his father turned and said, "Is the movie about the bible?"

William's face fell.

"Then I don't want to hear about it," said his father.

"But it's just once, dad. It'd be nice to go just this—"

"I didn't move to Grand Grove with your mother so you can play around with fire. I moved here so we can start afresh like grandpa did."

"I know, but—"

"You didn't hear me did you. You're a Churcher, not a Carter."

The boy's face darkened. Then he turned and grudgingly left his father in silence.

On Sunday morning, he met his father at the dining room as usual for his bible study. But the dining table was bare except for a cup of black coffee and a pair of movie tickets.

"Get dressed," said his father, "I'm gonna give you a taste of this world."

The two of them sat in the theater room with the pale glow of pictures dancing across their faces. But the boy's interest in the movie had long since disappeared. Instead, his mind was now wholly consumed by his father's deep displeasure. He didn't have to look over at his father to see his repugnance. He could feel the great divide that separated them, and he could see his countenance in his mind. It was the look he had seen his father give to the inept, the repeated offenders, and the fallen ones. And it was the look his father had often given to his mother. But in his thirteen years, William had never seen it so much as flicked his way. The boy's eyes followed the characters on the screen, but his mind stayed on his father until the look settled in and hardened his features with disgust and deep displeasure. He regretted that he had been so easily persuaded by his peers, and he vowed to never be moved again. But his father did not know his change of heart.

After the movie, the station wagon continued on through unfamiliar, ragged roads and then parked in a motel parking lot. His father had not planned their excursion to end with a movie.

"Get out of the car," he ordered.

The boy obeyed, followed his father through the dark motel corridor, and then waited as he retrieved a bronze key. He walked inside the room and then froze as the lock clicked behind him. Lying on top of a queen-sized bed was a woman with a wilting face and a scarlet blotch for lips. Long, bleached blond hair fell over her barely covered sagging breasts. The woman cooed, "Hey there, big boy," and slid a sturdy leg across the bed.

The boy's stomach turned. He knew what this woman was. William turned to his father, his eyes brimming with confusion, revulsion, and a tinge of fear.

"Dad...."

"You scared William? Don't be scared. She's what you want, isn't she?"

"Dad, Brad's thirteen. He wasn't thinking of—"

The woman drew her leg back. "You're thirteen? You look at least twenty."

Mr. Churcher turned to the woman and spoke in a low, hard voice. "Shut your mouth."

The woman frowned. "I was jus' asking."

"I don't think you heard me," he rumbled.

The woman shut her mouth. The man strolled over to a table and grabbed a case of beer. He pulled a can from a pack and popped open the cap.

"You're right, William. We should start out small with sin. Just a bite-sized sample like the tasters they give you at the ice cream shop. That's why I've got everything here for you, stranger. Chug. Chug."

William's eyes pleaded with his father, but the man growled, "Drink."

The boy tilted the can cautiously.

"Drink. I said drink," his father barked as he tipped the can up and down, spilling beer into the boy's nose. The boy sputtered and coughed as the alcohol burned his lungs.

"Didn't I tell you faster?"

The boy threw his head back and guzzled the beer down with one breath.

"Good. Here's another one. And I want it fast."

The man pressed the boy on one can after another until his belly ballooned and then suddenly contracted from anxiety and distaste. William ran to the bathroom.

"It wouldn't make a difference if you sinned at thirteen or thirty-three," his father called out, "It only matters that you do. First it's the movies, then cursing, drinking, smoking, and then girls. If you're gonna screw sin, you might as well skip to the hard stuff now—in front of me, in front of God."

When William did not respond, his father barked, "Get back here, stranger. I'm not done with you."

William appeared at the bathroom door and wiped the dribble of vomit from his trembling lips.

"Now we get to the good stuff." The man flicked his head toward the woman on the bed. "This is what you envied so much of those boys in school, yeah? Go on now, have your fill and be like the rest of the world, no-son-of-mine."

William stood in front of his father with his head bowed. What he really wanted to do was to cry. To cry and to beg his father for forgiveness. He had been disciplined before, but never in a way where a wedge was driven between him and his father. His father was his life. He knew everything there was to know about God and about life from his father. His father was like God.

"I'm sorry, dad. I—"

"I said sit on the damn bed."

The boy remained still. The man took two quick steps forward, grabbed the boy's arms, and squeezed until William felt as if his arms would crunch underneath. He lifted the boy onto his toes and then dropped him on the bed like a rag doll.

Then he leaned in and growled, "When I say sit down. You sit down."

The boy's eyes flitted back and forth. His mother's frightened face suddenly flickered across his mind. William had always despised his mother for reminding him of a cowering dog, so he hated himself now for bearing that same look of spineless cowardice.

The woman suddenly slid off the bed and slipped on her jacket.

"Where're you going?" the man said calmly.

"I didn't sign up for this mister. I'm not saying I got respectable, but he's a kid. I do have a kid too, you know." She slipped her heels on, grabbed her purse, and headed towards the door. "Sorry guy, but I don't do children."

The man's hand shot out, closed around the woman, and then flung her back hard. Coins and a shoe flipped and scattered onto the carpet as she tumbled backward. The man looked down at the woman.

"That was the wrong thing to say. But I'm going to be merciful to you just this once, so listen closely. As long as I'm here, you aren't going anywhere. Now sit yourself quietly on that bed of yours, and you'll be just fine."

"All—all right, mister. Ju—just don't hurt me. Don't hurt me."

The woman crawled across the floor and then hobbled to the bed. She sat beside William, pushed her disheveled hair aside, and peered at the man towering over her.

"Do it," he said.

The woman turned back to the boy and reached tentatively for his shoulder.

"Do it like you mean it," said the man.

The woman looked nervously back at the man and then massaged her hands sensually into the boy's shoulders and chest. The skin on William's scalp began to crawl. A sticky, unclean thickness settled over him. William hated being unclean. He felt nauseous. Nauseous from the sick ungodly sensation, and nauseous at the thought that his father and God were watching.

The boy's hands shot out suddenly, driving deep into the woman's chest. The woman had the wind knocked out of her, but she sprang to her feet to run for her life. William drove his hands into the woman again. Several times he pushed, yelling and screaming and cursing. He pushed the woman so hard and so many times she stumbled backward, hit her head against the wall on the other side of the bed, and landed on the ground with a thud. The woman was not dead, but she did not get up.

"Don't you dare touch me with your filthy, stinkin' hands!" he screamed, "Or I swear, I'll—I'll—"

Something round and hard bounced against the boy's chest, awakening him from his memories. The boy stood over a man on the ground like a solid, square wall. He straightened his nametag, smoothed his raven black bangs neatly to one side, and then looked down at him.

"Hey, watch where you're going buster," the man sputtered, holding his eye.

He looked up at the boy, and his face reddened. "Willie, you dipstick. Where the heck were you—jacking off in the broom closet?" The man rose and continued screaming, "Twenty minutes ago, I said clean up near room two. Twenty minutes later, the shit's still there. Do your friggin' job you big idiot."

Behind large square glasses, emerald green discs that virtually eclipsed the whites of the boy's clam-shaped eyes glistened. William stretched the line on his square jaw into a tight smile. The little man was hired only a week ago to manage the old theater in the small town of Grand Grove, Alabama. But everyone working at the theater knows the boy doesn't like the words "jacking off" or worse yet, like hearing the two words placed in a sentence with his name. His hand tightened around the necks of the broom and dustpan he held as he stroked the family heirloom that hung across his chest. The ruby-encrusted crucifix glimmered under the dim theater light.

The man snarled at the boy daring him to say something stupid. Behind the thick glasses, two eyes buried deep in the boy's skull narrowed into a total eclipse.

"I'll get right to it, Mr. Stiles," said William.

Satisfied, the little man huffed and pushed passed him, offering a quick, perfunctory smile to passing patrons.

The boy walked over to an overflowing trashcan and scowled. On its lid, stacked popcorn boxes sat beside overturned cups and puddles of soda pop. Trash jutted from its mouth while popcorn kernels and wads of paper napkins lay scattered across the floor. As he stuffed the boxes into a trash bag, a door opened and moviegoers began pouring out. William frowned, put down the trash bag, and began sweeping the carpet as people stacked their trash on top and around the trashcan. Above the murmur of the crowd, a high-pitched voice echoed, "That was such an awesome movie, man."

William's eyes shifted toward the voice. The voice belonged to Tim Connors, a shaggy-haired kid who also attended Grand Grove High. Beside him, a tall, sandy-haired boy with a cigarette stub in his mouth walked with an arm draped across a girl. William lowered his eyes as the group of three walked by.

"That was so awesome, Jake. Did you see the scene before the crucifixion—the part where they tell 'em to identify Spartacus and each slave shouted, 'I'm Spartacus' 'No, I'm Spartacus'."

His taller friend stared at him. "What am I—blind?"

Jake slung his arm off the girl and turned toward the trashcan in disgust.

"Hey you," he called, "The napkins on the floor ain't gonna bother anyone. Why doncha clear out this crap first."

William ignored the boy and continued sweeping.

"Is he deaf?" Jake barked.

"He probably didn't hear you. The guy looks familiar, though," said Tim, squinting. He shrugged. "Nah, don't know him. Just stack your trash on top. He'll pick up."

"Deaf, blind, and dumb, eh? Guess he won't know if I do this then."

Jake dropped his half eaten hot dog on the carpeted floor. Then he flicked his cigarette butt down and crushed it with his shoe. Tim let out a high-pitched cackle. "Oh man, bet he sees you now."

"Let's go," said Jake, wrapping an arm around his girl as Tim rattled on.

When the hallway was empty again, William set the broom aside, snatched the trash bag off the floor, and began shoving the trash into the bag. It has only been four years since his father passed. Three years after his death, William began working in the very industry his father despised. He must be throwing a fit in heaven at this very moment. William popped the lid off the trash can and lifted the bulging bag of trash.

Douglas Churcher was a tall, stately man with steel grey eyes and the same raven black hair he had gotten from William's grandfather and had passed on down to his son. Mr. Churcher was an accountant, a very precise and strict man whose services were sought out by many of the businesses that started out in Grand Grove when it was still a budding town. But the elder Churcher's true aspirations had always remained what it had been when the family first moved in: to pastor a congregation as William's grandfather had done until his death. Thus, after settling in a few years, though he didn't particularly like the idea of strangers milling about his house, he opened his home as a gathering site for people to know God.

For months, William's father posted signs and passed out flyers that threatened eternal perdition. Along with his admonition, Mr.

Churcher had provided curious onlookers with an alternative to hell: a gathering in his home for those who desired eternal salvation. A handful of stragglers had gradually trickled into his house, but none of them had been the kind of clean, god-fearing men and women he had hoped his church would be founded on. Instead, shepherding the stragglers was like caring for a bunch of stray dogs that didn't quite understand or appreciate his perplexing commands. They bit and they growled when he tried to keep them reined in, and they reeked of an unpleasantly foul smell. To his dismay, those who stumbled into his home stumbled quickly back out into the world.

Mr. Churcher's diligence in raising his own son nevertheless produced a vastly divergent and fruitful outcome. From the time William was born, their father-son routine had revolved around their daily bible studies at home and included one monthly visit to a local church. William was an apt pupil, one who by age ten memorized the entire book of Matthew and was able to quickly locate any referenced verse in the bible. But even with his father's diligence, he was not entirely immune to the temptations of the world.

His curiosity for the silver screen had been the one temptation that had driven a wedge between him and his father—a wedge wide and deep enough to make one lasting impression on the unworthiness of sin.

William secured a new trash bag in the can, dumped the contents of his dustpan into the bag, and placed the lid back on top. Working in the theater was more than just an irritation to his spirit, it was an affront to his father and to God. If only his father had married another woman. Things would have been a lot different then.

Since his father's death, William had had to interact with his mother more than he was accustomed to or desired. Mrs. Joyce Churcher was a thin, sallow-skinned woman with a large nest of wiry hair who hardly resembled the young bride in the family wedding photo. Her large pale blue eyes always seemed clouded with a fear that reminded William of stray dogs that steered clear of anything walking on two legs. William's father rarely exchanged more words than necessary with his wife, preferring instead to resolve all spousal concerns behind closed doors. And William's mother hardly ever spoke unless first spoken to. Neither did she ever touch anyone presumptuously—even when it came to her own son. William didn't know why his mother drifted around like a senseless phantom. But it was just as well. He much preferred his mother this way anyway.

Aside from church and a few family routines, Mrs. Churcher rarely appeared with William or his father in public. But when she did appear in her long black dress and shoes, he was always completely mortified. William never understood how a handsome man like his father could ever have become attracted to a woman like his mother. In his eyes, his mother had been his father's one great mistake. A mistake he promised himself he would never make.

Since his father's death, William has had to share a small dilapidated home with his mother, a stranger he did not trust. Though she would be dead soon, her illness had been the reason the family's savings had dwindled away at a time when there simply wasn't much work to be had for a boy his age, so he took the job.

"William!" a voice cried.

William heard but did not respond. The movie theater was not a place he expected to run into friends. He picked up the large bag of trash and then the broom and dustpan. The delicate voice called out again.

"William! William Churcher!"

He frowned. That was his full name. He lowered the broom and dustpan and peered down the corridor. A girl wearing a conservative sundress waved. William took in what he saw with astonishment. Melinda Newborn. What was she doing in a place like this? The girl waved again and then headed his way quickly. Her skirt swished as she jogged, exposing a pair of finely sculpted legs. He blinked.

Melinda was a girl who could not be easily forgotten. She had long auburn hair and blue, sometimes violet eyes. Her lips moved like pink butterflies dancing on powdered snow; and just below her neck hung a golden cross. She was a lily among thorns not only for her beauty but for the way she treated her peers regardless of their circle of friends. Thus, even after three school years have passed, the eyes of both boys and girls never tired of gravitating towards her. William was no exception. Never in his eighteen years had he felt such a potent urge to look at another human being, to just simply stare.

But William didn't forget his father's sensible warnings about women. He had struggled hard not to look her way for years. But it was hard. Very hard. From his memory bank of biblical verses, he could not recall the desire to look upon a woman as being a listed sin. Yet he felt guilty when he stole even a quick, nonchalant glimpse of Melinda. And even when he wasn't looking, his face burned because his mind was staring at her without the help of his eyes. But it was the summer break of his third year now. And he is a grown man seeking for a righteous woman of exceptional beauty. Melinda Newborn was certainly a strong possibility. Aside from a few passing greetings, he had never actually spoken to her. Now, they were in the theater hallway alone. What was she doing at the theater? William wiped his sweaty palms on his trousers as Melinda approached him.

"Melinda. What a surprise," he said calmly.

"I didn't know you work here either, William. It's good to see you."

William felt his cheeks burn. "You too," he said.

"Can you believe this will be our last school year together?"

There was a brief silence as his mind circled around her word "together." Had she ever thought of them together?

"Yes…" he said distractedly, "You know I don't watch the movies here, right. I'm just working here temporarily. I—"

"Melinda! We were looking all over for you," a boy with deep blue eyes called out breathlessly. Three other teenagers jogged over with him.

"Blake," William said darkly.

The boy combed his blond hair away from his face and stared at him. They had attended Grand Grove High together for three years, but the boy looked at him as if he'd never seen him in his life. Then, his eyes widened.

"William, you work here? I didn't recognize you in that outfit, and I never would've pictured you in a place like this. I mean, maybe in a bookstore or something church-related but not here."

A giggle erupted from the red head behind Blake. William's eyes narrowed.

"There were no other job openings, and I needed the money."

"Oh," said Blake.

The group stood awkwardly for a while until Blake tipped his head towards a short, stocky boy with a curly head of hair. "So this is Troy's third time to watch Kubrick's film. Have you watched Spartacus, yet?"

A line appeared between William's eyebrows. "I don't watch movies unless they're reproductions of the bible."

"You're kidding me, right?" Troy laughed as he pushed forward from behind Blake. "What do you do for fun then? Or maybe I should ask, 'you got anyone to hang with?'"

A tall, but lanky boy rested his forearm on Troy's shoulder and said, "Of course he does. He hangs out with priests and usher boys."

Blake caught Melinda's troubled look and barked, "Shut up, Jim."

"What?"

"I said shut up."

"Hey, relax. I was just joking around. Willy understands. Right, Will?"

The line between William's eyebrows deepened.

"Don't mind Jim. He's just being a butt," said Blake as he glanced at Melinda, "Speaking of hanging out…Melinda, Ashley, and the guys were planning on having lunch at Teddy's diner Wednesday. Wanna come?"

Troy and the red head exchanged a look while William's eyes narrowed. Blake had never so much as even acknowledged that he existed in school, and now he was inviting him to lunch with his friends?

"I don't know," he said.

"Aw, come on. You'll have fun. You can stop by my house, meet my family, hang out a bit before I pick up the guys."

"Why don't you come," said Melinda, "I think that's a great idea."

William's chest swelled at her enthusiasm. "All right," he said.

"Great. It's settled then. Wednesday it is."

Blake scribbled an address down and handed it to William. When the group strolled out the theater door, Melinda offered, "That was nice of you."

"Yeah, well, he doesn't seem like such a bad guy. New friend won't hurt you, right? Especially if the guy's pretty much a priest in plain clothes."

****

The light glowed through the cracks of the curtains when he arrived home. His mother was still awake. He wished his mother would stop waiting up for him whenever he returned home late from work. William unlocked the front door, walked through the house, and found her sitting at the dining table in her bathrobe holding a cup of hot tea.

"Mom," he muttered gruffly.

His mother did not reply. She continued to stare straight ahead with dark sunken eyes. He waited a moment longer, but still, she was silent.

"I'm going to bed," he said before disappearing into his room and locking the door.

She turned and looked after him. "Good night, son," she said.

2

His car rolled slowly through the quiet neighborhood. Manicured hedges, rows of trees, and large tracks of land divided one house from the next. William parked in front of a large two-story house, smoothed his navy blue coat, and walked up the long driveway. He rang the doorbell, and a heavy, olive-skinned woman opened the door.

"I'm looking for Blake Blaine," he said.

"Yes? What do you want. We don't buy here."

He frowned a little. "I'm not here to sell anything, ma'am. My name is William. William Churcher. Blake invited me here."

The woman peered at him and then stepped aside. "Come in," she said roughly. William followed the woman to the living room where he was left to himself. He surveyed the room, looking over the elegant and expensive furniture, paintings, and art figurines. A large framed photograph of Blake's family was displayed beside a table lamp.

William drew near, looked over his shoulder, and picked up the picture frame. He studied the faces carefully. They were a handsome family of four. He placed the frame back with annoyance, turned, and then met the suspicious gaze of a Chihuahua. The small dog bared its teeth, growled, and then let its alarm go. A barrage of shrieking yaps pumped into his ears. William hated small dogs. He took a menacing step forward. The dog pulled back but held its fort.

"Dudley, shut up!" boomed Blake.

The dog jumped, looked over at Blake, and then returned to William. It bared its teeth again, barked, and then waddled off.

"I swear Cecilia's training that dog to be as grumpy as she is," said Blake. He pushed the magazines on the coffee table to one corner. "Did he make you get off the couch?"

"No."

"That's good," he said absentmindedly, "You want something to drink? Soda? Juice?"

"No, thanks."

"Well...so....What do you want to do? Take a tour of the house?"

"Sure."

The boys took a quick tour around the large, spacious house; William was introduced briefly to the maid Cecilia; and then they concluded the tour in Blake's room.

"This is it," he said.

William tried not to look too surprised or horrified at the mess. The shelves were crammed full of books, cassette tapes, and trophies with no particular order. Clothing and books were scattered across the room, and a guitar and its pick lay over rumpled bed sheets. Blake stepped easily over the mess and plopped himself on a chair. The room was an aberration from the elegant house, but William found its imperfection comforting, even pleasurable.

"How do you find anything in this room?" he asked.

Blake grabbed the guitar on his bed, swung it on his lap, strung a few chords, and laughed. "You're looking at the master of order. Don't believe me? Test me. Ask me to find anything, anything that is of some significance...so not like pencils or pens. But anything else? I'll pinpoint you its exact location."

Blake closed his eyes and began his announcement.

"Ladies and gentlemen, pick something, anything, and I'll tell you where it is. If I win, I win your dime. If I lose, I'll give you mine."

William spied a pair of scissors and grinned. "Okay, you've only got one pair of scissors right?"

"My man, scissors I can do."

Still with his eyes closed, Blake swept his finger back and forth like a compass until he landed in the approximate area of where the scissors lay.

"I have a pair of scissors hidden beneath three volumes of Encyclopedias, a leather jacket, a striped sock, and two neckties, one navy blue, the other white with black stripes. My man, you've just lost yourself a dime. A whole dime I say. Would you like to try again? Double or nothing? Double or nothing."

"All right," said William. He searched the room again and found an obscure book. "How about the book titled 'Trains.'"

"Another easy one. You're too kind to me, good sir. I do indeed have a book titled 'Trains'. It was a gift from my aunt that I haven't touched since I was seven. It's tucked between two other books 'The Great Gatsby' and 'Funny Things to Think of in the Bathroom' on the shelf closest to my closet. You've just lost yourself another dime, sir."

The secret pleasure that William had in Blake's shortcomings disappeared. The boy was handsome, wealthy, dirty—yes, but a genius with photographic memory. Three out of four was more than what William could hope for himself. If Blake was in any way seriously interested in Melinda, he would have only one card to play against Blake's three. But still, that card would beat Blake hands down unless he was holding that very same card himself.

"You win," said William as he dug into his pockets grimly. A pillow suddenly whapped him on the head.

"What're you doing," said Blake.

William frowned. "I'm looking for the dimes I owe you."

Blake let out a hearty laugh. "You know, the guys warned me that you'd be weird. And of course, you are."

William frowned and opened his mouth to defend himself.

"I was just joking about the dimes. It was a game."

William pulled his hand out of his pocket and smiled grimly.

"Come on, lighten up! You can't be too serious about everything. You're eighteen, not eighty."

William stepped over scattered books and clothes, settled on a chair facing Blake, rested his elbows on its armrest, and folded his fingers on his lap.

"All right, we've played your little happy game. Now we play mine. I like serious games, so I get straight to the point. You and I both know that if we were stranded on an island together, you'd occupy one end and I'd occupy the other. This island is Grand Grove High. You and I have never exchanged a single word in three years. Now you've invited me to your house and then to Teddy's with your friends. What are you up to Blake?"

Blake stared at him. "Aw, come on. We can't be friends just 'cause we're different?"

William gazed at him as if he were a child who had just told a lie.

"Your game's a real downer," said Blake.

William did not move his gaze.

"All right, you want me to give it to you straight then? Fine. I think Melinda Newborn is a nice gal and I like her a lot. You happened to be talking to her at the theaters and she seemed to treat you with a lot more respect than the other kids, so I decided I'd do that, too. There you go."

"So you invited me over so you could pretend to be a nice guy."

"Ouch. A knife right in the gut. I thought you diehard Christians are supposed to be nice."

William's eyes flashed. "You're not a believer?"

"I am, just not diehard like you. I do go to church on Sundays."

William wanted to say attending church didn't make him a Christian, but he kept silent.

"Look. I might have invited you over for the wrong reasons, but honestly, I don't think you're a bad guy when you let loose. A little weird maybe, but not bad. I'm not blind, William, I've seen you at school and I know you exist. Besides, even if I did start out with the wrong intention, if we became friends, the wrong intention would be made right."

To William, Blake was still using him. But two could play the game. This would be the perfect opportunity to know Blake from the inside. If Blake were a bad apple, he'd have everything he needed to dissuade Melinda from getting together with him.

"Maybe you're right, Blake. I apologize."

"Hey, don't sweat it."

"So you like Melinda?"

Blake strummed a tune on his guitar. "What's not to like. She's smart, kind, beautiful. I've had my eye on her for three years, but just never did anything about it."

"Three years? But weren't you dating Stacy Williams, and then there was Rebecca Marsh in the third year."

"Yeah, but my heart was always with Melinda. You know she doesn't take dating lightly, right?"

"She's doing what a respectable woman should do. She considers a person's beliefs and values and dates for the purpose of marriage."

"You feel like a ton of bricks, William," said Blake. He laughed. "Come on, who's thinking about marriage at fourteen. If she weren't as wonderful, I'd almost call her a prude. Anyway, I've been thinking about her a lot lately. Melinda is the kind of gal I'd like to marry, so I invited her to have lunch with us. If everything turns out well…well, you know."

"But what about Stacy and Rebecca?"

"What about them? I've broken those off way back."

"There wasn't anything going on behind closed doors, was there?"

Blake frowned. "What are you—a priest? Should I be confessing my sins to you now, Father Churcher?"

The answer was not as clear as he would've liked, but it was what he needed.

"Just curious."

A voice called out from below.

"It's my mom. Let's go," said Blake. Blake tossed his guitar on the bed and rushed out while William followed calmly after. The boy swung around the steps and greeted his parents.

"Mom, dad, this is William. He's a new friend of mine. William, my mom and dad."

William greeted the adults politely and threw Blake a look. It was strange hearing the word friend coming out of Blake Blaine.

"Would you like to join us for some ice cream? Dad and I decided to be a little bad today. We went on an ice cream run instead of our usual walk in the park," said Mrs. Blaine. Mr. Blaine raised a grocery bag in the air as evidence.

Blake dug into the bag. "Oh cool, my favorite, French vanilla. We still have time for a quick bite." He turned and grabbed two spoons from a drawer.

"I hear you'd like to be a pastor," said Mrs. Blaine, handing the container of ice cream to her son.

"Mom. I didn't say he'd like to be a pastor, I said William will probably be a pastor. And I honestly don't think he wants to talk about this now."

"I don't mind," said William, a little pleased. "I do have hopes to be a pastor one day. It has always been a dream of my father's to be one."

"That's wonderful. I think it's a noble calling," said Mrs. Blaine, "do you have a church you're currently attending?"

Blake dug out a huge spoonful of ice cream and shoved it into his mouth.

"Blake!" Mrs. Blaine cried in exasperation. She snatched the box of ice cream from her son. "That's disgusting. Grab a bowl."

William's forehead wrinkled.

"Mom, William's a walking bible. He doesn't need to go to church. He has everything in his head." Blake smiled deviously at his new friend, "Want a spoon?"

"Blake!" his mother squealed. Mr. Blaine chuckled.

William flushed. He appreciated Blake's compliment and was even a little astonished. When Mrs. Blaine turned her attention back to him, he said, "My father and I used to attend a local church every month or so, but my home church was really just with him. When it came to the bible, he was a very knowledgeable man, more qualified than most pastors I know. But my father passed away a few years ago, and I haven't gotten around to finding a church, but I do study the bible often on my own."

"I'm sorry to hear about your father," said Mrs. Blaine, "I do hope you find a home church. You can always come visit ours. I'm sure Blake can introduce you to everyone there, especially kids your age. And if your mother wants to come—"

"My mother isn't going anywhere," William interrupted darkly.

"Oh," Mrs. Blaine said in surprise. Blake paused, his spoon raised in midair.

"She's very busy," said William.

"Well, we do have services besides Sunday …."

"Got to go mom, we're gonna be late," said Blake. He cocked his head toward the door.

The boys said their polite farewells and then hurried outside.

"Thanks for getting me out of that," said William.

Blake grinned. "Getting you out of what?" he said before he hopped into his sports car. William smiled a little and slid into the passenger seat.

3

The long line inched forward as students pushed their plastic trays from one station to the next. The sweaty cafeteria staff dropped a slice of turkey and ham on each tray, followed by a glop of mashed potatoes. Lukewarm corn from a can came next, fruit cocktail, and then a box of milk. William faced a sea of chattering students hunched over their lunches.

"William!" a voice called out.

He scanned the sea of faces and caught a hand waving.

"William, over here."

It was Blake and his crew. William dragged himself toward the benches where the chattering voices seemed almost deafening, pressing into his nerves like fingernails running over a chalkboard. A few curious heads turned and whispered with one another as he trudged toward the corner of the popular crowd.

"I got you a seat. Sit down," said Blake.

William glanced longingly at his usual corner bench which was now unoccupied, and then he placed a bible beside his tray and sat down. Jim eyed the book as he ripped a piece of fried chicken off a bone. He reached down, fingered the bible, and mumbled, "Whachu got?"

"Don't," said William.

Jim withdrew his prying fingers. "My, are we a little catty today," he said.

William ignored him and bowed his head in prayer. The boys looked at one another, and then Jim lowered his chicken bone while Troy threw an irritated glance at Blake. When he finished praying, William began cutting his ham into small squares.

"So how's your English project coming along?" Blake asked nonchalantly.

Since their congenial gathering at Teddy's Diner, the two boys had gone their separate ways. Blake had tried to include his new friend, but the gathering at the diner had sealed his fate. Even with Melinda there rallying by his side, William was awkward among the group of teens. He didn't find much of what the group found hilarious to be funny; he seemed uninterested with the popular topics of conversation; and Troy, especially, had been so aggravated by his 'condescending, pompous ass' that he threatened that if William were in any way in, then he was out. Though Blake tried to at least greet him in the school hallway, everything still remained pretty much the same. William wasn't surprised at being relegated to his original status of persona non grata. He was actually glad. It would make doing what he was about to do to Blake Blaine a lot easier.

William raised an eyebrow. "We are in the same class, aren't we? I seriously doubt anyone started on it since about, what, two hours ago when they assigned partners. Have you?"

Blake's face colored as he muttered, "I guess not."

"I bet he needs new prescriptions for those," piped Jim, pointing at William's glasses with a greasy finger, "Earth to William. Earth to William. Do you even know that Mr. Salas just paired you with the hottest girl in school? Does Melinda Newborn ring a bell?"

"William doesn't get excited with girls—unless they're ancient and in the bible," said Troy reaching for the book. William's large hands shot out, caught Troy's wrist, and squeezed. "I said, don't touch," he growled.

Surprised at the constricting, almost bone-crunching pain, Troy spoke quickly and tried not to whine. "All right, all right, just let go." William released Troy who withdrew and nursed his injured wrist.

"I'm surprised you allow your friends to speak so unkindly of Melinda, Blake. I would expect someone who just started dating a girl...."

"You're dating Melinda? When'd this happen?" said Jim.

"I'm not dating Melinda," said Blake.

"Weren't you two together at the theater?"

The boys' excitement diffused.

"Melinda was at the movies with Ashley. The boys and I just happened to be there," said Blake.

Troy chuckled. "Yeah, just happened."

"What about Teddy's diner?"

"That was not a date, William," Blake said flatly.

"I don't think he knows the difference between a group date and just a group of people hanging out," said Jim.

"Of course not, he probably doesn't even have enough friends to ever..."

Blake elbowed Troy who let out a surprised cry.

William was glad to hear the news, but he continued darkly, "Look, Blake, I know you didn't ask me over to be chummy with your friends, so what do you want?"

"Uff. Right in the gut," said Jim as he stuffed the rest of his lunch in a brown paper bag.

"He's not going to help you, Blake," said Troy as the boys rose from their seats.

"Hey, where you guys going?" said Blake.

"We're gonna get some soda pop before class. You coming?" asked Jim.

Blake frowned. "Yeah later," he said, turning back to William.

When the boys left, he muttered, "I'm sorry about the guys, but I can't change the system. I told them you're okay, but..."

"What do you want, Blake."

Blake's brows furrowed. "I was gonna ask if you could put in a good word for me when you're working with Melinda. Anyway, forget it, it's stupid. Thanks for joining us," he said as he rose from the table. William smirked and forked a piece of ham into his mouth.

4

The morning sun flooded into the spacious living room. The living room had the kind of order and neatness William appreciated, though the colors were too bright and cheery for his own tastes. There were flower-filled vases in several corners of the room and the walls were painted pale green, white, and a shade of olive. If this were a living room he and his wife shared, he would be sure to add more gravity to what he saw as a feathery fluffiness to the room.

William peered at Melinda from underneath his eyebrows. She was working diligently coloring the backdrop for a two-person skit. They were finally alone. Melinda's mother had stepped out for a quick grocery run so now was the perfect time.

"I like your living room. It has a lot of order to it," said William.

Melinda looked up and glanced around the room. "Thanks! Mom just changed the color scheme. She loves everything green. It's my favorite color, too."

He smiled a little. "I expected something like this from you, though. I guess order would be too much to expect from Blake."

"Blake? Oh that's right, you were at his house before Teddy's. How'd that go?"

"The house was nice and clean overall, but his bedroom was hellish."

Melinda laughed. "Yeah, I hear most guys aren't too good about being clean."

"Thank God I'm not like most guys," he said frostily. His eyes flicked towards her. "Do you like Blake?"

"Blake? Of course. Jim and Troy are all right too, though Troy can be a bit snippy."

"No. I mean. Are you interested in him as more than just a friend."

Melinda stared at William and then her face colored.

"Blake dated Stacy and Rebecca, you know. You know that don't you?"

"I've seen them around at school."

"You know what a good-looking man does when he's all alone with a pretty girl."

"I...I'm not sure what you're trying to say, William."

"I'm saying this for your own good, Melinda. If you're thinking of ever dating Blake, you need to know the facts. What a man does to one or two girls, he'll do to you. A man who claims he's a Christian but is no better than a heathen. I think you deserve better, Melinda."

Melinda looked down at her work. "You know, Blake thinks you're all right."

"Like hell he does," growled William, his voice rumbling like thunder, "And I really don't care what he thinks of me. I care about what God thinks. God and only God." He steadied his voice. "The thought of you being with Blake makes me mad. I care about you, Melinda. I want to be with—"

"Hello! Hello! I'm back," Mrs. Newborn called from the hallway. The teenagers turned to her as she walked into the room with a grocery bag.

"Got the flour and a few extras, too. How're you kids coming along?"

"Fine," Melinda mumbled.

Mrs. Newborn rested the grocery bag on a chair. "Something wrong?" she asked.

"Not really. Just plugging along."

"All right, I'll be in the kitchen then," she said.

When they were alone again, Melinda turned to William. "I'm sorry William, but I see you as a friend and nothing more. As for Blake, he's never said anything, so I'm not going to make any assumptions. But he does honestly like you. And I think you should give him a—"

"Why should I?" he hissed, his broad shoulders looming over her as he drifted closer. "You want me to give him a chance, don't you? Then what about me? You hardly even know me. I bet you don't even know that we share the same beliefs, the same values. And that I'm a real Christian, not like Blake or most everyone else in Grand Grove."

Melinda shrank back as his blazing green eyes drew near.

"You're making me feel uncomfortable," she said.

William was not listening. His large fingers closed into a fist and his shadow fell over her like a dark cloud. "No, you listen to me...."

Melinda recoiled quickly and popped onto her feet.

"We're done," she said firmly.

William frowned, flustered by her unexpected initiative. "What do you—you mean with the project? But we're not even halfway through."

"I'm sorry, William, but I don't feel comfortable working with you anymore. I'm going to request a new partner or work on the project myself."

His face darkened. Melinda Newborn was not what he expected. She didn't know her place as a woman. He rose.

"Fine, suit yourself. You'll be sorry. I guarantee you will."

****

A desk lamp lit the dark room. William knelt beside his bed and pressed his forehead against interlaced knuckles. His head was still spinning and his breast burned at the knowledge that he had been thrown out of a house by a woman. No. Not even a woman. A girl. He wondered what he would've done if Melinda were his wife. The lines on his forehead deepened at her lack of submission. What should be done to those who were rebellious and stiff-necked. What would his father have done. But Melinda was not his wife. She was not even his fiancée. There was nothing he could do now, but to pray for her. And then he would pray for himself to know the way.

PART II

5

The old, rusty car shuddered and coughed down the road, its engine hot from the long hours of driving. It wasn't used to being driven more than twenty miles at a stretch, but in the last thirteen hours, the driver had ridden it hard, stopping in the cities and towns it passed only when the gas ran low. In the last hour, the driver had been staring ahead at the long winding road seeing and yet not seeing. The tears on her cheeks had long since dried, leaving a trail of salt crystals that snaked down her neck. Her mind was on autopilot as she maneuvered the wheel and shuffled her foot between the brake and accelerator. The hand on the gas meter rested on the empty line, but the driver no longer took notice. She had passed a small town with the only gas station miles back but she hadn't noticed that either. Somewhere along the way, the world had stopped mattering. The car continued to roll down the road until it sputtered and died.

The driver stepped out of her car and continued on. The woman walked for a long time. She walked until the skies above began to choke with clouds that swelled like thick smoke. From a distance, the sound of thunder rumbled. Still, the woman walked, unknowing and unseeing. She took a turn off the main road, meandered through gravel roads and grassy terrain, and then ambled onto more streets, more pathways, and more roads. The heavy clouds hovered over her as she walked these directionless paths. They followed her until droplets of rain like tears burst from their cheeks and fell on the woman below. The woman took no notice. She continued to walk on.

When the rain slowed to a drizzle, the grey skies blended into the dark night and shrouded the moon and the stars that twinkled above. Not many drifters and vagrants ventured into this part of northern California. There were not enough people living on the land, leaving it too barren for most to subsist in for long. The lack of familiar structures of civilization left roaming itinerants with only the moon and the stars as their guiding lights at night. But on cloudy nights like these, they walked as blind men.

Two approaching headlights illuminated an empty road. The purr of an engine drowned the faint sounds of the night as the car rumbled quickly through. A woman with luxuriant blond curls that cupped her face and her pearl earrings gripped the back of the driver head rest nervously. She leaned forward.

"Tony, you're driving too fast. You're not wearing your glasses. It's dark. And I just know you're weaving over the divider. Why don't you let your sister drive," she complained.

"There's nothing wrong with me driving without my glasses. I barely even need them. Luz's got twenty twenty. That's exactly why she's beside me," said her husband.

The woman in the front passenger seat remained silent, peering down the dark road.

"I know Luz's got twenty twenty, but if there's such a thing, your reaction speed is two thousand twenty. Besides, it's black as pitch out there."

"Two thousand twenty, eh?" said the man. He tilted his head toward her. "The only person around here who might possibly drive on this road at this time of night is my sister, and as you can see, she's right here beside me. Everyone in Restwood is asleep and the girls always call a couple of weeks before they come. Neither you nor I have received such calls. Furthermore, if you hadn't insisted on staying so long at the party, I probably would have been in a better mood to let Luz drive. Heck, I might have even let you drive."

"You see how rudely he talks to me, Luz? You see?" said Betty, "It's just like you to never listen to me when it's for your own good." Betty folded her arms and settled back into her seat.

The man glanced at his rearview mirror.

"I know you're tired, Tony, but it is especially dark tonight. It would be dangerous if we hit a deer or a large animal," Luz said quietly.

The car rumbled on.

"Oh, all right," he said, slowing the car significantly.

While he did give in, Tony was not about to let his wife get away with putting him in this predicament. He grumbled about how it was hours past their bedtime, that good thing tomorrow was a Sunday, and about how he never wanted to go to the party in the first place. Then he repeated that if they hadn't left so late, he wouldn't be in such a hurry to get home. Complaining was not something Tony did much at all. But the stiffness of his tie and the prim and proper decorum of the party had gotten onto his nerves.

Betty stared at the back of her husband's head like she would an alien. Though she had taken on the Silvan surname for more than thirty years, Betty still sometimes wondered how they could have ever fallen in love. Tony owned a construction company and often worked all day under the hot sun. Though he kept himself clean-shaven, his tanned face was angular and rugged, unlike the husbands of the women in her circle of friends. And even at the age of forty-nine, his strong, muscular build stretched the trousers and long-sleeved shirt he wore tonight like a gorilla would a suit.

Luz Ekklesian, who was five years younger than her brother, was just as strange. Luz never went to beauty salons as Betty did. Instead, she wore her brown wavy hair short and allowed her wild tufts of hair to curl as they please. Her jewelry consisted of bold, exotic pieces of hand-carved wood, strangely shaped metals, beads, and what looked like braided strands of leather or twine. These contrasted with Betty's shiny baubles and the jewelry pieces of almost every other woman in town. And like her brother, Luz always wore comfortable and casual clothes, never quite fitting into Betty's small-town but stylish crowd.

Tony shifted his eyes to the rearview mirror as if he sensed his wife's disapproving gaze boring into the back of his head.

"What now," he said.

"Nothing. Just focus on the road."

Luz frowned as the car continued to approach a dark irregularly shaped figure on the road. She leaned forward.

"Tony," she said hesitantly.

Tony looked from the rearview mirror to his sister.

"Tony, look out!"

Tony spun around and caught sight of the dark figure. In another split second, the headlights lit its face. The dead eyes of a pale faced woman stared back at them. Luz screamed for her brother to turn the wheel. Tony slammed on the breaks and jerked left. The car flew off the road, skidded in a circle, and came to rest by an oak tree. The three sat in the dark trembling, listening to the quiet purr of the car.

"Are you all right?" Tony asked, his white-knuckled hands still gripping the wheel. Luz nodded. "Betty?" he cried, turning anxiously.

"I'm fine," she said.

Tony breathed a sigh of relief and touched his wife.

"I'm sorry. I'm so sorry."

"It's all right," she said, rubbing his forearm, "We're safe. That's all that matters."

Luz pushed open her door hurriedly.

"Where are you going?" asked Tony.

"I'm going back to the road. I'm almost positive that was a woman we saw."

"Wait. It's dark out. Let me swing the car around and use the headlights."

"A woman? There was a woman on the road?" cried Betty.

"I'm not sure. I would have said the figure was a ghost if I believed in such things," Tony mumbled. He swung the car around and directed the headlights on the road. Before them, a body lay crumpled on the ground.

Tony murmured. "My God."

****

Luz shut the door quietly behind her as she balanced a bundle of wet clothes and muddy, ragged shoes on one hand. She walked downstairs and into the dining room where Tony arose from his chair.

"Is she all right?" he asked.

Luz nodded. "She's asleep. She's dehydrated and it's likely her blood sugar is low but her vital signs are normal. There were scrapes on her legs and her feet were covered with fresh blisters. She must have walked a long way to get here. I changed her into some dry clothes, bathed her feet, and then bandaged them. She pretty much slept through it all."

Luz glanced at the bundle she placed on the dining table. "I'm guessing she got caught in the thunderstorm that passed."

"Any I.D. on her?"

"No. She had nothing with her," said Luz, "Where's Betty?"

"She's tired. She fell asleep on the living room couch. You all right? You look a little shaken." Luz gave her brother a weak smile. "Sit down. I'll get you a cup of tea," he urged.

Luz sat at the dining table and rubbed her face with her hands. She was tired, but she could not stop thinking about the eyes staring at her through the windshield. The dead eyes bothered her.

As a nurse, she had seen those eyes before on patients who were confined to their beds or shuffled around in empty shells of flesh. "They're like dead men walking. You'll only find those eyes between these hospital walls," a young doctor had once remarked. Luz knew that wasn't true. She had seen the very same pair of eyes on those who did not suffer from sickness or injury. She had seen them on those who otherwise appeared healthy and normal but were condemned to die by the law, by their circumstances in life, or by their own minds. As long as the eyes remained on these, every one of the few that she had known personally had passed away soon after. To Luz, the dead eyes, regardless of their color, shape, or size, had been a premonition of death. Her mind had been fixed on the dark brown eyes buried in the pale hollow skull of the woman, playing them over and over like a broken record.

"She's too young. Too young to be walking around with those eyes," she murmured. But the woman's eyes had only been the tip of the iceberg.

They were only ten minutes away from Luz's home when they had come upon the stranger. The close proximity of the house was not the only reason they had decided not to bring her to the hospital. They had tried to rouse the woman. But when Betty had insisted urgently that the woman be brought directly to the hospital, the woman had awakened momentarily, gripped Tony's arm and said, "No. Please. No hospital. No police. I just want to sleep. Just let me sleep." Despite Betty's insistence, Tony complied with the woman's wishes after consulting with his sister. After a quick examination, Luz followed her instincts. The woman had appeared sentient enough to have made those statements, and Luz was sure she must have had good reasons for making them, so they brought her home.

At the house, Luz performed a second, more thorough examination in the guest room upstairs and proceeded to change the woman into some dry clothes. When the woman's long grey dress was unbuttoned, Luz had drawn back in horror.

Carved with repeated horizontal and vertical slashing strokes, bloody crucifix-like gashes approximately six inches long and four inches wide marred the woman's flesh just above her sternum. Just beneath the gashes were dark shadows of similarly cut wounds. These were wounds that had healed but left sinister reminders of the woman's past. Luz hoped and prayed that there was no more pain she would have to uncover, but as she peeled the dress from the woman's body, she found that the woman was riddled with destruction. Purple and blue bruises mottled the woman's ghoulishly white skin. And like the carvings, all the bruises had been inflicted in discreet parts of her body, concealed under the conservative grey dress. The shock of what the woman suffered reverberated within Luz. What had happened to this woman?

She stared blankly at the wall as her brother moved about in the kitchen grabbing mugs and tea bags. The wounds were convincing reasons for the woman to be walking so far and so late at night. The woman must have been walking so late at night because she was running, running from something or someone who had inflicted such destruction on her body and no doubt her mind. The chaos must have been what had gotten her lost and kept her hovering in the middle of a dark road like a ghost. The chaos must have been why she hadn't flinched or even so much as batted an eye when the car had come so close to hitting her. Luz ran her hands across her tired face again.

"Here. Drink this. It's Chamomile."

Luz took the mug and murmured a word of thanks. She watched as steam rose from the hot tea.

"Tony, I think we should keep what we saw tonight and the whereabouts of this woman to ourselves. At least until we sort things out."

Tony nodded as he swallowed his tea.

"Will you tell Betty?"

"Of course. But you know Betty. She's not exactly good at keeping secrets."

"I know," she said in a low voice.

"Why? Did the lady say anything?"

Luz hesitated. The woman didn't actually speak to her, but she did speak. She had flinched in her sleep when Luz was dressing her blistered feet. When Luz had asked if she was all right, the woman did not respond. Instead, her eyes had popped partially open. The bottom half of her deep brown irises had stared straight ahead.

"I tried asking for her name when her eyes opened, but she didn't respond. She kept mumbling instead. Said she was sorry over and over again. She did say something else. Something like 'I didn't mean to do it' or 'I didn't do it'. When I tried speaking to her again, her eyes glazed over and she fell asleep."

Tony waited for his sister to continue.

"I saw some wounds on her body too, wounds that don't look like they were done by somebody nice. That's why I want to wait. Give her some time to recuperate and decide for herself what's best. Something just doesn't feel right about reporting this to the sheriff or to anyone else."

"Nobody is going to report anybody. I'll make sure to tell Betty not to fan any flames. I'll bring Betty home and come back first thing tomorrow morning. We'll see if the lady is all right to speak and then go from there."

Luz looked at her brother gratefully and nodded.

When they finished their tea, Tony left the room and then returned with Betty a moment later.

"Did the lady say anything?" asked Betty.

Luz's lips parted and her eyes lingered on Betty. "I let her sleep. Her body is weak, but nothing food, water, and rest can't cure."

Betty covered her mouth as she yawned. "I still say we should bring her to the hospital. She might need the medical care you simply can't provide."

"Luz can handle this," said Tony.

Betty opened her mouth, but Tony led her gently toward the door. "What I think is that we all need to get some rest tonight. Luz, if you need anything, call me. I'll be here tomorrow morning to check on you."

"I'll come too," Betty added.

"You my darling, will stay home and sleep. I'll wake you up when I get back."

Luz smiled. "Thank you."

6

A persistent breeze gently pushed aside the curtain, allowing the morning sun to illuminate the room with brief bursts of light. Blue jays twittered in a tree outside the window. Inside, the body of a woman lay like a corpse on a bed. Only the faint rise and fall of her chest indicated she was still alive. The birds continued, slowly wrestling her away from the haunted dreams that imprisoned her. She flinched but did not awaken. The wind pushed through the curtains again, swirled around the room, and then settled its cool lips upon her face. The woman's eyes flickered partially open. She gazed at the ceiling. Slowly, she stirred and propped herself up.

The woman looked drunkenly around. A neatly folded towel and washcloth was placed on a dresser in a corner. Beside the dresser, a long-sleeved grey dress hung on an open closet door. A pair of ragged black flats was placed on the floor below. The woman frowned. She looked down at herself. She was wearing a cotton nightgown that hung loosely over her thin frame. She stretched out her bandaged feet and then looked back at the pair of shoes in bewilderment.

Where was she? The woman leaned against the headboard of the bed. A dull pain throbbed against her temples, and the muscles of her body, especially her legs, burned. The woman let her head drop drunkenly to one side. A pitcher of water and an empty glass stood on a night stand beside her bed. She opened and closed her dry, cracked lips, but she did not touch the pitcher. Instead, she slid to the side of the bed and swung her legs off. Her feet landed on a pair of slippers on the floor. She curled her toes back quickly, and then stepped over them onto the cold hardwood floor.

The woman walked cautiously to the dresser and stood in front of the mirror. A pair of sunken dark brown eyes encircled by black stared back at her. She touched her face. The stranger in the mirror touched hers. Blue-tinged, faded lips merged into a ghostly white face. Long, black hair draped over the stranger's hunched shoulders like the hood of a nun. Observing the stranger's wretched condition was enough to awaken the woman to a pain that radiated from her head to the tip of her tailbone. She stretched her aching spine, but it resisted and subdued her until she resigned herself to a stooped, almost cowering phantom.

The journey to the dresser had tired the woman already. She pulled aside a chair and settled in like a weary, old woman. A picture frame caught her eye. The woman pushed aside the towel and washcloth, picked up the frame, and examined a man and a woman in a warm embrace. She squinted, trying to think, to remember something, anything. Who were these people? Her grandparents? Her parents? Friends? Nothing surfaced.

The woman looked up and was startled by a large wooden cross that hung on the wall behind the bed. The body of a man was secured on the cross by nails that had been driven into his hands and feet. The man's head was tilted. He had been watching over her as she remained in the dark oblivion of her sleep. Watching her without her knowledge. The woman rose from the chair and drew closer to the man. The man's body was marred with gaping wounds, and a ring of jagged thorns had been buried in his skull. The stranger gazed down at her with the eyes of a dying man.

The woman shivered. She backed away from him, back to the dresser and back behind the chair. Then she turned away. Surely, this man was a strange, almost distressing adornment to display in a room. Had she hung this very piece on the wall?

The hardwood floor outside the room creaked. The woman drew her arms close and curled her fists upward, covering her abdomen as if her belly ached. Three soft taps on the door echoed in the room. The woman did not move. Again, the tapping repeated. Slowly, the knob turned and the door cracked open.

A voice whispered. "Hello?"

Luz stuck her head in. She looked at the crumpled blankets on the bed and then turned to see the woman standing behind a chair near the dresser. Her eyes brightened as she greeted the woman with a smile.

"Good morning."

The woman still looked almost translucent like the ghost Luz thought she had seen several nights earlier, but her dark brown eyes were not dead. They were lost, but they were not dead. She breathed a sigh of relief.

"Brought you a little something," she offered as she pushed open the door and carried in a tray of food. The woman's eyes followed Luz as she moved into the room.

"Did you sleep well, sweetheart?" she asked.

The woman's heart pounded in unsynchronized beats with her throbbing headache. Was this lady her mother? The stranger looked too young to be her grandmother. The woman wanted to speak, but her lips refused to move. Luz slid the tray halfway onto the nightstand.

"Brought some breakfast for you. You should eat and then rest," she suggested, transferring the glass from the nightstand onto the tray. Luz picked up the pitcher and slid the tray onto the nightstand.

"You should drink more water, too," she said, pouring a glassful. "Your body is still dehydrated. I was only able to get a few sips and bites of food down your stomach these two days." She walked to a bookshelf by the door and placed the pitcher on top.

Two days? The woman burrowed deep into the grayness of her memory. Still, there was nothing. She had never seen this short, middle-aged woman in her life. Her eyes flitted in confusion.

"I'm sorry, dear. You must be wondering who I am and how you got here," said Luz. She took a few steps toward the woman but stopped when the woman recoiled with her dark brown eyes wide and alert.

"It's confusing to wake up in a stranger's house, but you're in safe hands," said Luz. She took a step back and sat at the foot of the bed.

"My name is Luz, Luz Ekklesian. Two nights ago, my brother Tony and his wife Betty and I were driving home on State road. You were crossing the road. It was dark and we almost didn't see you, but thankfully, Tony turned just in time. We were going to bring you to the hospital because you had fainted…."

At the word hospital, the woman's eyes clouded over with apprehension. She wasn't sure why she was afraid, she just knew that she was. She didn't want to be discovered. She wanted to hide. She pressed her arms closer to her body.

"But we didn't," Luz added quickly, "You awoke briefly and didn't want us to take you to the hospital, so we brought you to my house. I'm a nurse, a retired one anyway. After a quick check up, I let you sleep, waking you only to get some liquids and light foods in you. You look like you had come a long way."

The woman's eyes flitted to the grey dress and shoes.

"Your dress has been washed. And your shoes too. Though it looks like we might have to get you some new ones," said Luz.

The confusion within the woman grew. Why wasn't she able to even remember whether she had ever owned such an outfit?

"Are you hungry?" asked Luz.

The woman's stomach growled.

"I'll take that as a yes. I should have a bed tray somewhere. You can eat in bed," offered Luz as she rose and walked to the closet. The woman slunk further behind the chair as Luz stuck her head into the closet, frowned, and then brightened. "The storage room. I brought it down to the storage room. I'll be right back."

"Please don't," the woman squeaked. She paused as if she were surprised at the sound of her voice, but continued, "I'd rather eat on the dresser." She looked over at the finely painted furniture and added, "Or the floor."

Luz looked at her in surprise. "Oh sweetheart, you can't eat on the floor. It's too dirty. The dresser table is fine if you feel comfortable sitting there." Luz walked toward the nightstand.

"I placed a basket of amenities by the sink in the bathroom just down the hall. If you need anything else, just let me know." She picked up the glass of water, placed it on the dresser, and then returned for the tray of food.

"I know you don't know me well, but I hope that doesn't keep you from making this house your home," said Luz as she turned to leave, "And when you're better, I'll get Tony to help me carry a desk to your room. Eat and then get some rest."

When she was alone again, the woman allowed her tense muscles to fall. She was exhausted from the exchange and wanted to sleep, but her body had begun to quiver from the smell of food. Fluffy, golden eggs, browned sausages, and freshly baked muffins. The woman was famished, but she did not move. She waited until she could no longer hear the floorboards creak outside. Then she spun around, huddled over the food, and grabbed at the plate with trembling hands. The eggs slipped through her fingers as she tried to aim the food towards her mouth. When she had gotten enough down her stomach so that her hand had stopped trembling, the woman was able to quickly wolf down the rest. Within minutes, she had eaten everything in sight and gulped down the tall glass of water. The woman sighed.

As she wiped her lips with the back of her hand, she caught the stranger in the mirror staring at her. The woman blushed and pulled her hand away. She lowered her eyes, averting the stranger's gaze. The woman picked up a napkin and wiped her hands and mouth. Then, as if someone had scolded her for eating while she was standing hunched over the tray, the woman sat abruptly down on the chair. She stared sluggishly at the empty tray, uncertain what to do next. Her stomach gurgled satisfactorily, but her body felt exhausted and her mind more clouded than ever. The woman wanted to return the tray, to be courteous and polite, but she was afraid to leave the room. In her indecision, she remained sitting in front of the dresser. Her head lolled to one side, her eyes fluttered, and soon she was asleep.

7

The house was quiet, but the woman awoke abruptly as if a train had rolled passed the window of her room. She found herself curled on the bed in a dark room. She peered into the darkness. She was still in the house of the woman named Luz, but somehow, she had moved from the chair at the dresser to the bed. The woman's fingers fumbled for the lamp beside her bed. She squinted at the clock. Three thirty six in the morning. Her eyes flicked towards the dresser with alarm. The tray. The tray was gone. In its place stood a basket of fruit, a Ziploc bag of muffins, a bag of beef jerky, and a pitcher of water. The woman slid off the bed, stepped on the pair of slippers, and walked towards the dresser. She plucked a note from the basket. "Tried to wake you for dinner but didn't want to force you up a second time. You looked so tired. Left some snacks for you. There's beef stew in the refrigerator downstairs. Help yourself with anything else in the kitchen. Sleep tight, Luz."

She remembered breakfast, but she didn't remember waking up for lunch. It troubled her that she didn't remember until she looked over at the basket of food. The woman sat down and crammed a muffin into her mouth. Then she rammed down beef jerky, fruits, another muffin, and gulped down the food with two glasses of water. Though the beef stew downstairs was more desirable, it was not an option. She was too afraid. The woman read the note again as she chewed. Why was this stranger so kind to her? Her kindness only made the woman feel more nervous and ill at ease. She wasn't used to such kindness, and she wasn't sure if she quite liked it. It made her feel as if she did not belong. When she finished eating, the woman arose, walked to the window, and pushed aside the curtain.

A full moon glowed outside her window and stars glimmered in the open night sky. The woman gazed across the grassy landscape dotted with a few solitary trees. At a distance, a forest covered the land. There was not a single neighboring house she could see. The woman closed her eyes to think. Now was the perfect time to leave. If she snuck quietly downstairs and out the front door, no one would know. But where would she go? The woman opened her eyes and stared into the night. There was a dull knot in the pit of her stomach that told her to hide. But if she left now, sooner or later, the police would find her. They would approach her and question her. They would know that she was lost. They would be able to read it in her eyes. She had no choice.

The woman laughed at her stupidity. She laughed and laughed until she cried, but she allowed herself to cry for only a moment.

"Stop crying, you pathetic dog. You make me sick," she snapped.

The woman stopped crying. Her wet eyes glazed over, the life in them gone. She stared out into the night for a long time, mumbling to herself. Then she turned her head slowly from side to side. "I don't want to be bad." She moved her head up, down, and then slowly back up. "I want to be good. Very good. I want to be a good girl."

The house groaned underneath. She flinched at the sound, and then life flickered back in her eyes. The woman scratched at her cheek and then studied her fingers. They were wet with tears. She frowned. She didn't remember crying.

No choice. That's right. Even though she'd rather not, she had to stay. She needed Luz's help. This was a place she could remain hidden until she knew who she was and where she was going. Hopefully tomorrow. Hopefully her memories would return tomorrow morning and all of this had just been a bad dream.

8

The woman bent over at the top of the stairway and peered downstairs. She could see only a sofa, a section of a coffee table, and the bottom half of a large window. She stepped cautiously down the stairway with her eyes fixed on the window. Outside, clouds floated like tufts of cotton candy in clear blue skies. A soft drizzle had left the carpet of grass glistening under the morning sun. As the woman continued to descend, her eyes flitted nervously back to the living room and then widened in surprise.

The living room was furnished with a few pieces of rustic furniture: a sofa, a square coffee table, an armchair, and a bookshelf. A small vase of fresh cut daisies brightened the coffee table, but the woman was not staring at this either. Her eyes had gravitated instead toward the flat, low-lying shelves that occupied the peripheral space of the room. Colorful pieces of intricately designed pottery lined these shelves, each piece different from the other. The woman drew close to the pottery like a fascinated child. On the shelves were a bowl, its thin clay walls undulating like sea green waves; a vividly brilliant copper red vase; an indigo teapot attached to a cane handle; Raku-fired vessels with black crackling over a sky blue surface that bled into brown; and more. The woman moved from one side of the room to the other until she settled on a gold-rimmed royal blue vase. The beauty of this piece drew her in. She stretched out a hand.

"Watch out!"

The glow in her eyes disappeared. She recoiled at the sound of ceramic shattering across the floor.

"Oh great," muttered a man.

"Careful. You'll cut yourself," said a woman.

Luz. That was Luz, the woman thought. She listened like a frightened child as the voices continued in another room.

"Don't use your hands, Tony. Here. Use the broom."

In the other room, Tony swept the broken pottery and cookie pieces into the dustpan.

"Need some help?" asked Luz, wiping her hands on her apron.

"No, I got it. You just finish what you're doing."

Luz returned to hulling strawberries, and then she checked the stove. The eggs were still sizzling nicely beside the bacon on the pan. She picked up the bowl of strawberries and set it on the table. A plate of hot sausages and a cold pitcher of apple juice and one of milk were already sitting on the table. A coffeemaker gurgled in a corner.

"You're preparing a feast not breakfast for three," said Tony.

"I thought Betty would be coming today."

"I thought so, too. Even after thirty years of marriage, I never know what'll set her off like that. All I said was you didn't want her to go blabbing around town about the girl like she always does with everything new under the sun."

Luz threw her brother a you-didn't-actually-use-those-exact-words-did-you look. He wrinkled his eyebrows guiltily.

"Okay, maybe I should have chosen better words. Still, it is a blessing she made that silly vow of not seeing you until you apologize. I mean, having Betty mill around the girl and then telling her to keep quiet is like trying to stop a balloon you keep filling with air from bursting. It's bound to happen. Besides, you and I both know she won't be able to stay away for long."

Luz sighed. "You're probably right. You think she'll keep what she saw so far to herself though?"

"I think so. It's when the news gets too juicy that she can't help herself." He popped a strawberry into his mouth. "I hope the lady upstairs is hungry. Is she feeling better?"

"She seems better. Her appetite has been good. She still looks very thin though."

"Maybe you should check on her."

"I'll do that," said Luz as she turned off the gas stove. She picked up the frying pan, slid the eggs on a plate, and scraped the bacon on another. "Here, place these on the table, will you? And can you set the table while I'm gone?"

"Sure thing," he replied.

Luz slipped her apron over her head and hung it on a cabinet door. As she did so, her eye caught a glimpse of a pale figure hovering in the shadows of the dining room entryway. She let out a startled cry. Tony looked at his sister in alarm and then followed her gaze. A hunched-backed woman with long, black hair that merged into her grey dress stood partially hidden behind a wall. Luz placed her hand over her heart.

"Oh sweetheart, I'm sorry. I didn't see you standing there."

The woman held her arms protectively over her abdomen and shifted her eyes to the ground. An awkward silence separated her.

"You're just in time for breakfast," said Luz, "Tony here was about to set the table."

The woman's eyes flickered over to Tony's feet.

Luz laughed. "I'm sorry. This is my brother, Tony Silvan."

Tony approached the woman with an outstretched hand. "Nice to meet you," he said. The woman stared at his hand until he withdrew it awkwardly.

"I may have mentioned to you about Tony and Betty…," said Luz.

"But you probably don't remember me," said her brother, "The whole day was a blur for me, too. But it's good to see you feeling better."

The woman remained silent.

"I hope you're hungry," said Luz, pulling aside a chair.

"Yeah. Let's eat," encouraged Tony.

The woman's sunken eyes darted from the chair to the plates and utensils on the counter and then back to the chair. She took a few steps toward the counter.

"Oh no, sweetheart, Tony will do that," reassured Luz.

The woman stared hard at the plates and utensils until Tony removed them from the counter and began setting the table. She stood stupidly near the entryway, watching like a lost child. Luz placed her hand on a chair and encouraged the woman with a smile. The woman moved towards her with her arms still covering her abdomen and sat down.

"I'm glad you joined us today. We made a lot of food," said Luz. She slipped a pair of mittens on, pulled open the oven door, and dragged a muffin tray out. The woman's eyes followed her as she arranged the hot muffins in a basket, but flitted nervously back to Tony when he sat down at the table.

"I'm thirsty. I'm gonna have me some juice first," said Tony, reaching across the table. The woman cringed as if she were afraid that he might accidentally touch her from more than a foot away.

"I'm sorry. I didn't mean to startle you. Would you like some apple juice?" he asked, lifting the pitcher. The woman lowered her eyes, glanced sideways at Luz, and then stared at the table. She shifted in her seat, but did not reply.

Uncertain of what to say or do, Tony placed the pitcher down without pouring himself a glass. "You're free to have whatever you like," he offered. The woman continued shifting and staring. Tony cleared his throat and returned to his seat wondering what he did wrong. He wasn't going to try to figure women out today. He threw a quick look at Luz, pleading for her to take over.

"I hope you brought your appetite. I made food for four. Betty was supposed to join us but cancelled," said Luz as she set the basket of muffins and a plate of butter on the table. She placed her hands on her hips and beamed.

"There, now this just looks good," said Luz. The woman's stomach grumbled in agreement. Luz laughed and sat down. "I guess I'll have nothing to worry about this morning. Sounds like you could eat for two. Would you like to say grace, Tony?"

"Sure," he offered, bowing his head. Luz caught a glimpse of the woman staring at the table before she, too, bowed her head.

"Amen!" he announced, "Now—let's eat."

Tony helped himself to sausages and eggs as the woman watched hungrily.

"Aren't you hungry?" he asked.

"There's no need to be polite when it comes to food, sweetheart. This is your home as long as you need one. A person living in her own house is never polite when it comes to food. So please, eat as much as you like," Luz encouraged, pushing the plates of eggs and sausages towards the woman.

The woman hesitated. A thin arm gradually rose from beneath the table, fumbled with a fork, and then slid some sausages and an egg onto a plate like a furtive cat dragging its food to a secure hideaway. The woman skewered her sausage, studied it, and took a small bite. She took another bite and then another. Soon, she was grinding and tearing at the juicy bits of meat and sucking eagerly at the runny egg yolk. Within minutes, her plate was empty again. The woman was still starving, but her hand was too afraid to reach for more. She stared hungrily at the food. Tony and Luz, stunned at the speed at which the woman ate, were still working with the sausages on their plates.

Luz passed the muffin basket to her brother. "Here, take a muffin," she said. Tony grabbed a muffin and boasted, "Luz makes her blueberry muffins from scratch. They're the best in town." When the woman grabbed a muffin for herself, Luz encouraged her to take another. "They're smaller than the ones in the store. You should be able to eat at least two." The woman snatched another muffin and placed them on her plate.

"Muffins aren't as tasty without butter," said Luz, pushing the plate of butter towards the woman. The woman picked up the butter knife, measured back and forth, peered at her hosts, and then cut a slab and spread it over her muffin. When she ascertained that her hosts appeared to be concentrating on their food, the woman quickly cut another slab, slapped it onto her plate, and balanced her second muffin on top, keeping the butter well-hidden. She looked at her hosts. Both appeared to still be concentrating on their food. Satisfied, she placed the knife on the plate and calmly pushed it away.

"Would you like some milk or juice?" Luz asked. The woman looked over at the milk. Luz picked up the pitcher. "Some milk?"

The woman gave her a crooked smile and pushed her glass forward. Luz filled the glass to the brim. The woman ate and drank greedily as her hosts chattered. Their preoccupation with one another relaxed her. Gradually, she allowed her eyes to wander. From where she sat, she could see that the kitchen was connected to a pantry room where fruit preserves, sacks of beans and rice, glass jars containing pasta and pickled vegetables, and canned and boxed foods filled the shelves. Like the living room, the dining room and kitchen were also furnished simply. But in these rooms, every piece of pottery was put to use for a particular task. The tall cylindrical vases contained wooden spoons and spatulas; the flat V-shaped bowl served fruits; various jars contained cookies, dried beans, and other goods; and the sugar bowl served sugar.

The woman studied the white sugar bowl on the dining table. The petite bowl was plain in color but its handles, body, and lid were delicately shaped. The woman reached out and touched its long, curvy handles with her fingertip. She did not notice that the conversation over breakfast had ceased. Luz spoke softly.

"Do you like it?"

The woman looked at Luz and drew her hand quickly back underneath the table.

"It's okay. I set it on the table to be used," said Luz.

The woman's hand did not return.

"It's actually a reproduction. I made the original for a special person, but I never had the chance to give it to her," said Luz.

The woman remained silent.

"I have a pottery workshop in the back of the house. Would you like to see it?"

Tony winked at his sister. "I'll take care of breakfast."

"Thanks," said Luz as she rose from her chair.

"It'll just be a moment and then we'll be right back," she reassured.

The woman hesitated but rose and followed her, walking a few steps behind. At the end of a long hallway, Luz pushed open a door and flipped on a light switch.

"Come on in," she said. The woman stepped into the room and looked around the large studio. "Might as well give you a short tour," Luz offered.

Luz pointed to the various equipments and gave a general explanation of their purposes. Then she pointed to the pottery pieces sitting on the racks waiting for their next stages. The woman's dull eyes flickered alive as she moved from one corner to another. Her curiosity kept her so absorbed that she nearly forgot how her bones ached as she moved about the room. But the pain did not leave. It crept quietly and gradually, starting with the joints of her knees, and then her hips and lower back, and climbing through each vertebra until it reached the base of her skull. It started as a vague dullness and then graduated to a pulsating affliction. The fascination in her eyes wavered like a flame in rough winds.

"Have you worked with pottery before?" asked Luz.

The woman shook her head, wrinkled her forehead, and then spoke in a quiet voice, "I'm not sure."

"You're always welcome to join me in the workshop if you'd like. It would be nice to have company."

The woman's eyes brightened and then glazed over. Blood drained from her face, leaving her pale with a tinge of grey. The bones of her spine had begun to throb with sharp splinters of radiating pain. The tour had temporarily distracted her, but now she felt as if ice picks had been jabbed between the vertebrae of her spine. The last of her energy reserves that had kept her standing relatively erect were draining quickly. She gritted her teeth, walked stiffly to a nearby chair, and gripped its back until her knuckles turned white. Tiny beads of sweat formed on her forehead and down her back. She could not prop herself up much longer. The woman longed to return to her room, but she was afraid. She was afraid to interrupt Luz; she was afraid to ask permission to retire to her room; and she was too embarrassed to sit down. The woman glanced at a clock on the wall. She counted the number of hours in her head to determine when she could finally retire to her room.

"Are you okay?" Luz asked, noticing how pale the woman had become.

The muscles around the woman's jaws flexed, but she did not reply. Luz did not need the woman to tell her it was time to go. In her previous line of work, she had seen the bodies of women that were as thin and as pale and abused as this stranger's body was. They were young bodies that ached and screamed like the bodies of the aged and crippled. These bodies could not stand or sit for long, and they hunched over because of the heavy secret burdens of cruelty they bore. She understood.

"I'm rambling again. It's time we get some rest, especially after such a big breakfast. When you're ready, I can teach you the whole process. You'll be making your own pieces in no time," said Luz as she ushered her out.

When the women returned to the kitchen, the table was cleared and wiped clean. Tony had donned on Luz's gloves and apron and was working on a pile of dishes in the sink.

"You're back. How'd it go?" he asked.

The woman smiled a little. Tony's eyes widened. He had directed the question at Luz with the assumption that the woman would not respond.

"Why, that's great. Luz makes some of the most unique pottery pieces I've seen. She's very popular at the trade shows, and she runs a shop in town selling the pieces she makes."

"My brother always makes me look so good. I quit working as a nurse after my husband passed away, so I had to do something with my free time. Anyway, enough talk about me, we're going upstairs for a while. You okay being me for a day?"

Tony looked down at the apron and grunted.

"As long as it's just for one day," he said.

Luz smiled and then the woman followed after her. They trudged up the stairway, and then at the door to the guestroom, Luz reminded the woman to treat the house as if it were her own. "Get some rest, honey," she concluded.

"Thank you," said the woman "For everything."

Luz continued down the hallway and into her bedroom and then headed toward the open closet. She stood in front of her closet thinking. The woman was at least four to five inches taller and quite thin. Most of her own clothes would be too small to fit her. She looked at her watch. The nearest clothing store was forty minutes away. If she left now, she would not be able to return home before lunch. She remembered how the woman had left the beef stew several nights ago untouched. The woman just might skip lunch if she found herself alone in the house. Luz closed the closet door. She would prepare lunch and leave a note for the woman to help herself. She would just have to hope that she would do so. She returned to the kitchen downstairs.

"Have you come to thank me before I leave?" Tony said gravely. The light in his blue eyes danced as he stuffed muffins in a Ziploc bag. His voice brought Luz back.

"Oh, you're leaving?" she asked.

"Betty just called. I don't think she wants you to know, but she wants me to sneak home some of your muffins. Something wrong?"

"No. You go ahead."

Tony sealed the bag. "Stop worrying. The girl will warm up. Give her a few days."

"I know. Did you take enough?" she asked.

Tony raised a full bag.

"Good. Tell Betty I said hi."

"I will," he reassured, letting himself out the door.

Luz put on her apron, walked to the pantry room, and looked over the shelves of food. She had moved to the small town of Restwood after much prayer and some convincing from Tony and Betty. Though she lived alone, Luz continued her habit of stockpiling enough food to feed a houseful of children. Her husband of ten years, Paul Ekklesian, was the man responsible for instilling this habit in her. Paul was raised in a family that consisted of a Catholic father, a Baptist mother, three older sisters, and a younger brother. A large family was his father's contribution and a Protestant upbringing was his mother's. Even before they had met, it had been

Paul's dream to raise a brood of children after establishing his medical practice. Luz, who had been raised in a family of four, was more doubtful of her maternal capabilities to care for so many. Nevertheless, their Christian faith united them.

Even after the Ekklesians discovered that they would never be able to give birth to a child, Paul had remained undaunted. It took two months for him to convince Luz to open their home to the children in foster care. If they couldn't bear children, Paul reasoned, they could still become the parents of many. Since then, their home had never been devoid of three things: a Christian upbringing, the voices of children, and a pantry full of food. Every child that stepped into the Ekklesian home became a part of the family, and when it came time for the child to part, each child received a pottery piece designed and hand-crafted by Luz as a reminder that he or she is loved.

But when Paul passed away suddenly from a heart attack, everything changed. Luz withdrew from participating in the foster care system, and their large, vibrant home grew silent as grief filled the rooms. Luz couldn't understand why the man she loved so dearly and the same man who adored the God they both served had to pass away so soon, but she did not bother to ask such questions. Luz knew no explanation, even if perfect, would have been reasonable enough to make her husband's death more understandable or comforting enough to make her feel any less miserable. It was in her greatest sorrow and suffering that she walked away from God.

For two years, Luz remained alone in her home. She allowed the food in the pantry to dwindle, giving away almost everything and disposing the rest. And by the time she heard from God again—on a day she stopped by a local deli—the pantry room had long been in a state of disuse.

Luz had walked along the street outside the deli many times, but she had never noticed its branching alleys. On a wintry afternoon, something within nudged her, prompting her to stop. She was familiar with these promptings, but they had all but disappeared when her husband passed away. Luz didn't want to listen, because she knew who it was who moved her. Only the urgency of the prompting made her think twice. She peered into the darkness.

Men and women were huddled in the alley with trash bags and cardboard boxes spread over their bodies, sheltering themselves from the light rain. The stench of alcohol, sickness, and death hovered over them. A few pairs of eyes stared back as she stood at the mouth of the alley.

Luz took a step to leave when the urgency pulled at her again. She knew that who she was about to see was much loved, so much so that God would ask her to come out from her own misery and fear for this moment in time and would give her the strength and the love to do so. She faced the alley and took one tentative step after another. The eyes in the darkness faced her, and the air grew tense from her intrusion, but she continued walking until something within told her to stop. She paused and turned to the body curled beneath a blanket. Then she bent down and waited.

A head wrapped in a woolen cap stirred. Then as if he or she sensed that someone was near, the drifter's eyes popped open and their eyes connected. The drifter cursed and leapt up, gripping a metal rod like a batter ready to swing. Luz jumped and stepped back, afraid but resolute. Wrapped in thick layers, the drifter looked like a squatty snowman with a small head and stubby arms that moved above its bulky torso. Splotches of purple bruises were splattered like leopard spots across one side of a pale face, and one eye was swollen shut. The drifter shouted at Luz, threatened to beat and rape her if she came near, and then hacked and spit out discolored phlegm.

Luz did what words alone could not do. She offered her bag of sandwich. The drifter stared at her with the good eye and then swiped the bag. Luz stood by as the drifter wolfed down the sandwich with one hand while the other hand held the metal rod ready.

Of all the bodies that lay in the alley, this one was the one God drew her to.

She filled her pantry with food that very day. Luz visited the drifter every day thereafter, dropping off food and blankets while she tried unsuccessfully to coax the drifter to get medical attention. Still, the pale face grew thinner and the circles around tired eyes grew darker. Only the energy the drifter used to spit, to threaten, and to hurl curses when Luz spoke of God's love did not seem to diminish. On the tenth day, Luz found the drifter curled beneath a blanket with a shock of matted brown curls scattered about. She gasped. The drifter she had been visiting was a girl, a teenager. Luz called out to her, but the body on the ground remained still. She touched her, thinking that she had been too late. The girl opened her eyes and then smiled as if she had been waiting for her. She raised a hand and touched the silver cross of the necklace Paul had given to her. Luz understood and rocked the girl like she would her own child until she closed her eyes one last time.

Luz stood absentmindedly in front of the pantry shelves holding a can of corn. She knew now why the eyes of this woman had bothered her so much. They were the same sunken dark brown eyes she had seen in the drifter who had died in her arms: the same color, the same shape, and the same premonition of death. Luz put the can down and took a deep breath. She walked out of the pantry room toward the kitchen counter where she placed the sugar bowl.

She had designed and created the original model for the girl in the alley. She had worked late into the night to perfect its beauty and had excitedly and carefully set the delicate white sugar bowl on the kitchen counter. To this day, she could not understand how what had happened happened. She had stepped into the living room to retrieve wrapping paper when she heard the high-pitched cry of a fragile piece being destroyed. She had rushed back into the kitchen a second later, hoping that somehow she had imagined everything. But she had not. Though she was alone, a thousand white fragments were scattered across the floor several feet from the counter. The day she had returned to the alley empty-handed was the day the girl had passed away.

After the drifter's burial, Luz recreated the sugar bowl as closely as she could. Though the second bowl did look similar to the original, it did not feel the same.

She picked up the delicate sugar bowl. She would make sure this one lived.

****

The clock downstairs chimed three times. The woman yawned and opened one eye. Then she sat up abruptly and looked over at the clock. She had only intended to take a short nap, but that was more than four hours ago. The woman slid from underneath the covers, fixed her bed hurriedly, and rushed downstairs. Except for the ticking grandfather clock, the house was quiet. The woman continued cautiously into the dining room where waves of aroma washed over her. She took a deep breath. Cooked meat. She was sure. Blood drained from her head and circled around her empty stomach like hungry wolves. The woman followed her nose and found herself alone in the kitchen standing in front of the oven. When she pulled open its door, plumes of aroma filled her. The woman's hand quaked as she stood staring at the trays of meatloaf and potatoes like a ravenous dog.

She squeezed her eyes shut and closed the door. No. She had no permission to touch the food. She turned and kneaded her fists into her stomach to quiet its angry snarls. A piece of paper taped on the refrigerator door caught her eye. "Will be back late. Meatloaf and potatoes in oven. Salad and dressing in fridge. Eat as much as you like. Luz." The woman read the note once and then twice. There it is. Permission to eat. But Luz was not there. That should be okay, shouldn't it? As she contemplated this question, the refrigerator and kitchen walls suddenly flipped to the ceiling and then dropped to the ground. The woman shut her eyes and raised her hands to brace herself as her head spun. The weight of her arms was surprisingly heavy. She forced her quaking hand blindly forward, swiping at the air until she caught the whirling refrigerator door handle. Her whole body was now shaking uncontrollably from hunger. The note would have to do. She must have food. And she must have it right away.

The woman pulled open the door, grabbed the bowl of salad and dressing, and set them on the kitchen counter. Then she slid out the trays of meatloaf and potatoes and carried them to the counter, trembling. The woman sliced a wedge of meat, skewered it with a fork, and shoved it into her mouth, almost swallowing it whole. Then she cut another piece, shoved that in the same way, and lapped up the potatoes she spooned in a bowl. By the time she swallowed the potatoes, her quivering body had calmed. She sighed as color returned to her cheeks. Though she was still hungry, she could think now.

The woman studied the meatloaf greedily as she chewed but cut out a slice that was smaller than desired. A more reasonable quantity of potatoes was ladled onto her plate. She hoped Luz would overlook how much she had already eaten.

The woman did not notice Luz's return until she walked into the dining room, catching her with a mouthful of food and looking like a stray dog that had stolen a slab of steak.

"You just started eating?" said Luz looking at the sliver of meatloaf on the woman's plate. "Can I join you? I didn't have much for lunch while I was out shopping."

Luz grabbed a plate. "You know. Your goal when eating should be to make sure you're full. That sliver of meat will only make you hungrier. It certainly would for me." She cut out a generous slice of meatloaf and said, "This is for you."

The woman stared wide-eyed at the large piece of meat. "That's a lot," she said.

"That's good. I'd rather you have more than be hungry," said Luz, plopping the meat on the woman's plate. "What's applicable to meatloaf is applicable to salads and to all foods," she said, handing the clamp to the woman. "Now, you try."

The woman clamped a few leaves and a tomato and dropped it into her bowl.

Luz shook her head. "That won't do for a woman your size. More. You've got to take more." The woman clamped sparingly into the salad. "More please," sang Luz.

The woman clamped down again and pulled out a generous helping. "Now that's about right," said Luz. The woman let out a giggle but stopped abruptly. Luz smiled and then bowed her head for prayer. The woman stared at her in question but waited quietly. When Luz finished, she spoke about her day as they ate.

"I got some clothes for you. I hope I've got at least the size right with the ones I chose. You can try them on after lunch."

The woman paused with her fork stuck in her mouth.

"You can't question me on this one. A woman must have her clothes. Besides, you can't wear the same dress day after day," said Luz, drowning her salad with dressing, "When you're better, we can go together. Then you can pick the styles you like. Can you believe it took me almost an hour to get to the nearest department store?"

The woman did not respond.

"When I first moved out here, I thought it would be busy. This is California after all. Where my husband and I are from, there were always people. We surrounded ourselves with a rowdy bunch back then. Kids, I mean. We were foster parents. Did I mention that to you?"

The woman shook her head.

"When my husband passed away, I took a step back. But I never stopped thinking about the kids. I'd like to work with them again someday, but somehow God says this is where I'm to stay for now, where there aren't many children let alone people. I wonder why every day."

As she finished speaking, she knew. Her eyes lingered on the woman. She had been sent here for this one.

9

The smell of fried chicken, glazed pork, grilled vegetables, mashed potatoes, and fresh bread mingled into the afternoon air. The woman set the eating utensils beside two plates and then stepped away from the table. She had forgotten who she was, but she hadn't forgotten how to cook. Lunch was ready to be served.

The woman jumped when the doorbell rang. Luz had not spoken to her about guests. She stood in the kitchen, nervous and confused. As the ringing continued, she flitted here and there and then ran straight into the pantry room. This would be her excuse for not answering the door. The doorbell couldn't quite be heard in the spacious room. The ringing continued as she pushed jars of preserves from one end of the shelf to the other. Then, it stopped.

Luz called for her. "Sweetie, come and meet Betty. Tony is here too."

The woman took a deep breath, walked calmly out of the pantry room and past the dining and living room to the front door where her eyes gravitated towards Betty and then remained there. Tony, dressed in a flannel shirt and an old pair of jeans and boots, blended easily with the house. But Betty, Betty sparkled like a five-carat diamond. The woman stared at her prim and proper dress, the color of sunshine, and her white high-heeled shoes. Large clusters of pearls hung around her neck and down her ears while soft curls framed her pretty but aging face. In her gloved hands, she held a freshly baked pie.

"Good afternoon," said Tony.

"Hello," the woman said quietly.

Luz placed a hand on the woman's arm. "This is Betty, Tony's wife, my sister-in-law."

"Good afternoon, Mrs. Betty."

"Oh that sounds so old. Just call me Betty. And hello to you, too. I bet you didn't expect any visitors today. I suppose that's why it took a while for you girls to answer the door."

The woman's face reddened.

Betty offered her gift. "I brought you some homemade pie. Do you like pumpkin pie?"

The woman was silent as her face continued to burn from embarrassment. Betty threw her husband a strange look and then repeated the question slowly and deliberately like she would to a child.

"I think she heard," Tony said with annoyance.

Betty ignored her husband. "Something smells really delicious," she said.

"We were just about to have lunch," said Luz.

"Oh, well, Betty just wanted to drop the pie off. We'll let you girls eat," said Tony.

"You shouldn't rush me. I haven't seen this woman since the day we almost ran her over. This girl needs company. She must be bored to death to be locked in a house without a single visitor. You should come to my house sometime. I always have guests over for tea."

The woman hunched forward, clutching her elbow with one hand. Luz looked at her sister-in-law with amusement. Betty had not spoken to her for more than a week. Now, she had invited herself unannounced and had recommended herself as a social consultant to a woman Luz frankly sensed she distrusted.

"That's nice of you, Betty, but I think she needs more rest."

"Rest? This woman doesn't need rest. People who get too much sleep end up even more tired. It's a vicious cycle you know."

Tony applied some pressure on his wife's arm.

"Well, it's true. Cheryl Hortman says so and her husband Roger is one of the best physicians in town."

"We should go now. I'm sure Luz and…and you women are hungry," said Tony.

Betty threw her husband a look and turned back to the women.

"I'm sorry for barging in like this. I do hope you enjoy the pie," Betty said with a smile. She hooked a hand around Luz's arm. "We need to talk. Walk with me to the car, will you?"

"Go ahead and start. I'll be right back," said Luz.

When they stepped outside the house, Betty leaned in and said, "I don't understand why you still haven't asked the woman about herself. Something. Anything. For Pete's sake, Luz, you don't even know her name. I was calling her honey and dear and just tripping all over myself speaking to her. Besides, have you even considered that she might have family who are worried sick about her? And God knows what she's doing in that house while you're working. You're simply being reckless."

Betty whipped her head around.

"And you, yes you," she said, narrowing her eyes at her husband's wide-eyed look. "You're not helping your sister by playing along in this game."

Luz patted her sister-in-law's gloved hands.

"I know you mean well, but I'm sure there's a good reason she hasn't opened up yet. She just needs some time. That's all."

"But why not ask something as simple as her name. It would drive me crazy if everyone were always calling me honey this and sweetheart that. If you just get her name, you'd be able to find her parents. Heavens, this woman might even be married with children."

Betty turned to her husband for support. Though they were complete opposites, Tony was perfectly in tune with his wife's timing as he looked innocently down at his watch.

"Oh my, we should go. The women will be arriving soon for your pies."

Betty glanced at her watch. Her eyebrows rose. Then she made one last plea.

"Luz. Will you at least consider my advice? It's for your own good. That woman might be an escaped convict for all you know."

Luz's face scrunched at the idea.

"It is possible you know. Don't say I didn't warn you," she said.

As Tony held the car door open, his wife slipped into the passenger seat, raised her forefinger, and wagged it at Luz.

10

As the days turned into weeks, the woman's hollow cheeks began to fill and the dark circles around her eyes lightened by a few shades of grey. Layers of flesh began to swell across her body, cushioning her skin from the ribs of her long, lean torso. The woman still walked with lowered eyes and a hunched spine, but time did seem to be reversing for her. Still, it was not until she agreed to cut her hair that a beautiful discovery was made.

The woman's hair had hid her face like the closing curtains of a show, merging her features into shadows thrown by the long, black drapes. Cutting the drapes removed a veil. For the first time, Luz realized that this woman who was once composed of dry, aged skin and bent, protruding bones was young, possibly only in her early twenties. And even more shocking yet was that the woman was truly and remarkably beautiful.

Changes that dealt with the woman's mental wellbeing took longer to accomplish, however. Even after multiple assurances, it was difficult for the woman to grasp the freedom that Luz had given her. Having the freedom to help herself with food or the freedom to roam about in the house sounded foreign to her. The woman would inevitably ask for permission even after being reminded time and time again that she didn't have to. The woman was not quite sure why she was afraid Luz would suddenly become mean or ugly over an intrusion. She only knew she was afraid.

So for a long time, Luz reminded the woman that the books in the library room were there to be read, the radio was there to be turned on, and the tools in the workshop were there to be used until the unknown but deeply imbedded reason that made the woman so afraid gradually faded. The only activity that the woman seemed to be able to do without permission was to clean. Cleaning was like eating or breathing for the woman, but even this task was performed only within the public confines of the house. And when Luz told the woman that she would share in half the chores, again, it was as if she had spoken in a foreign language.

What finally brought the woman out from her shell was when she worked with clay. The woman absorbed the techniques of pottery making quickly. When Luz encouraged her to create her own pieces, the woman did so without restraint, allowing her normally rigid body to loosen and flow. And it was here in the workshop that she took her first steps into the past.

The woman was working on a ceramic design at a desk while Luz was centering clay on a wheel nearby. Her attention had returned to the picture frames that hung before her again. She had found similar photographs displayed throughout the house. "They're my kids," Luz had said when she first asked, "Kids my husband and I cared for under the foster care program." The woman studied the children surrounding the smiling couple. So many, she thought. She couldn't imagine caring and loving so many. Just one. One would be enough for her.

"How did you manage?" she asked absentmindedly.

Luz drew her hand back from the clay and looked up.

"Did you say something, honey?" she asked.

The woman faced her. "How did you manage to take care of so many children?"

Luz allowed the spinning wheel to slow and then stop. "It was pretty much God, some Paul, and I guess a little bit of me. Paul always jumped into everything with enthusiasm. I was the more careful one. I couldn't picture myself taking care of so many children, especially children who carried burdens no child should ever have to carry. I just didn't have the faith at the time," said Luz, "I'm glad my fears didn't stop Paul though. My understanding of God and of life would never have been the same if I only did what I knew I could."

The woman studied the photograph of a beaming curly-haired girl holding a vase. Flattened dandelions and dried flowers glued on sky blue construction paper bordered the photograph.

"That's Anna. Anna Wood. She was only ten when we took her in. Anna designed and put together that picture frame all by herself. She just loved dandelions. She used to make a wish whenever she blew on one. She said the wind would carry her wish in a hundred seeds of prayers to heaven," Luz said with a smile.

The woman's eyes traced over the long dark scars that ran across her left cheek and the twisted skin on her forearms. The injuries on the girl were much worse than the bruises and cuts she had found on her own body. Hers had healed so that only the dark vertical and horizontal blemishes had remained. At least she had been able to run from whatever had caused so much pain. This child had nowhere to go. Her heart constricted, and she looked away.

"Did her parents hurt her?"

Luz hesitated. "Her mother's boyfriend set her arms on fire when she wet the bed. The scars were from her mother. Neither of them take care of her now. A wonderful family has taken her in."

The woman met the little girl's eyes again. Her own mother. Anna's smile was as bright as the morning sun, so full of joy and peace that the woman would've guessed that the scars were caused by an accident instead of by those she loved. The Ekklesians' home had been good for her. The woman fiddled with the eraser tip of her pencil. Luz had never once questioned her about the bruises and cuts, though the woman knew she must have seen them on the day she arrived. She had allowed the woman to stay and to recover without any questions asked. She turned to her.

"I want to thank you for—" she croaked, "for helping me. I'm sorry I stayed so long."

"Oh sweetheart, I had an extra room and so much food. If you hadn't stayed all the extras would've gone to waste."

The woman's eyes lingered on her.

"What's wrong?"

"Luz. My memory is gone. I can't remember anything. Not where I came from, whether I had a family, or even who I am. The only memories I have began in your guestroom. That was why I never spoke about myself. I was waiting. I was waiting for my memories to return, but they never did."

Luz rose, walked over to the woman, and sat across from her.

"I know I can probably go to the police, but I'm afraid. The scars and bruises, the nightmares of faces and places I've never seen. I'm afraid. I'm afraid of going back to what I might have tried to run away from. And I'm afraid of going crazy. I'm not crazy, Luz, I'm not. You believe me, don't you?"

Luz squeezed the woman's hand. "I believe you. You don't have to go back if you don't want to. You can stay here."

"I can't stay here. I've already taken so much from you. I need to find a job and a place to stay."

"What for? What good is an extra room when it's unused? And all that food in the pantry will just go to waste without you. Plus, I'll let you in on a little secret. Since your arrival, my ceramic pieces have been flying off the shelves. I've sold more in weeks than I have for months. So if there's anyone benefiting in this little arrangement of blessings, it's me."

The woman looked into her kind eyes and then studied her sturdy hands. Here was a complete stranger who had provided food and shelter and who had taken her in without question or a desire for remuneration. The woman found it difficult to believe that there were people in this world such as Luz Ekklesian. She felt a tinge of regret. What if she had loved ones just as wonderful who were looking for her while she remained hidden because of her unfounded fears? She shook her head to dismiss the thought.

"Why would you do this for someone you don't even know? You don't know where I've been or what I've done. Aren't you afraid I might hurt you, or worse yet, infect you?" she exclaimed.

Luz looked at her tenderly. "I just feel like you won't hurt me. And you don't look sick enough to infect me with anything. Are you feeling unwell?"

The woman reflected over her words. That did sound peculiar—even to herself.

"No. I—I don't know why I said that," she said, even though the word 'infectious' was bouncing in her mind like a ball pinging against the buttons and switches in a pinball machine. The woman touched her head and squeezed her eyes shut.

"Are you all right?" Luz asked.

The woman nodded.

"And even if you were contagious, which I honestly doubt that you are, it's a little late now for me to worry," said Luz.

Fear continued to quiver in the woman's eyes.

"Before I married Paul, I knew it was his dream to have a big family. To tell you the truth, I was afraid. Then, when Paul spoke about caring for children from broken homes, some that knew a pain and a sorrow I would never understand, I was afraid. But if I had listened to fear, I would never have come to know and love Anna; I would never have agreed to marry the most wonderful man I've ever known; and I would never have experienced the second greatest joy in this world."

The dark trembling in the woman's eyes shifted and began to fade.

"What's the second greatest joy in this world?"

"To love and to be loved by another."

The woman reflected over these words in silence. To love and to be loved by another. The pinging noises in her mind stopped as she tried to think and understand.

"Can I ask—what's the first greatest joy?"

"To love and to be loved by God," said Luz.

The woman squinted as if she were pondering over the strangeness of these words. To love and to be loved by God—a phrase that was far more peculiar than the word that had escaped from her own lips. Far more bizarre and outlandish than the word 'infectious.' The woman said nothing. She didn't know what to say. She knew the defined meaning of the word God, but she knew absolutely nothing about him. There was a grappling in her heart as she debated whether to ask about this God; but in less than a second, it was gone.

"So you will stay?" said Luz.

The woman let out a short laugh. "I would love to stay. Thank you. Thank you for everything."

"Wonderful," said Luz, "Now, there's only one thing left to do."

"What's that?" asked the woman.

"Find you a name."

"But—I don't remember my name."

"You don't have to. I've got books that'll help. Baby names from A to Z. You can pick a new name, redefine yourself. Paul bought the books before we even tried to conceive. I never got to use them, but I always believed that I would someday. Today is the day."

The woman smiled. "Will you help me look for one?"

"You didn't even need to ask. I'll go get them right now," said Luz, slipping off her apron, "Will you grab some cake from the kitchen? I'll make coffee and meet you in the living room."

The women scurried out of the workshop, and within minutes, the vase of red roses was pushed aside and the cake, forks, cups of hot coffee, and books were placed on the coffee table.

"They're a little old, but I don't think we'll miss too many new names," said Luz, handing her a book. The woman opened her book, smoothed her hand across its face, and began studying the names.

"Paul bought three because he thought one wouldn't be thorough enough. We picked out a name for a boy and a girl months before we even tried to conceive."

"What were the names?"

"Actually, it was just one name. We both loved Saoirse, which means freedom or liberty in Irish. We had planned for our first child, whether boy or girl, to be named Saoirse."

The woman repeated the name to herself but moved on. They discussed the names of famous people and how their names may have been connected to their destiny; and they scanned through picture books and read biographies of women. But the woman was quick to focus on a list of a select few.

Luz took a sip from her coffee cup and made a face. "Cold."

"I'll get you a new cup," said the woman.

"Thank you, sweetheart," said Luz.

The woman picked up the cups and headed toward the kitchen.

"Will you grab the sugar bowl, too? Thank you, dear," said Luz. She was glad that soon she would be calling the woman by her chosen name.

The woman brought two cups of coffee and then returned to the kitchen for the sugar bowl. She held the sugar bowl with both hands and set it carefully on the coffee table. As she drew back, her elbow brushed the vase of roses. The vase tipped and wobbled precariously. Wide-eyed, the woman swung around and gripped its neck, thrusting the teardrop-shaped vase into the air. The vase kicked the delicate white sugar bowl hard, causing it to slide across the smooth table surface. The roses, red as blood, spilled from the mouth of the vase, and water splattered across the coffee table. The woman watched in horror as the sugar bowl and cap slid off the table edge together, separated, and then struck the floor with screams of splintered porcelain.

Luz glanced at the broken pieces and then turned to the woman who was standing barefooted on the hardwood floor. She was staring at the pieces with her hand still gripping the neck of the vase.

"Don't move honey, you'll cut yourself," Luz warned.

The woman did not hear. Her eyes had glazed over and the life within had disappeared. She placed the vase on the coffee table, walked around its corner, and bent down. White grains of sugar were scattered across the floor like hard crystallized snow. The woman cupped her hand to the ground and pushed the sugar into a small white mound.

"No, you'll cut yourself," cried Luz.

The woman continued, lowering and pushing her hands. A scarlet flow burst through the folds of her skin, staining the sugar and hardwood floor. Still, the woman continued. "Stop," said Luz, placing a hand on her forearm. The woman stopped, but her eyes stared dead ahead.

"I broke it," she murmured as she picked up the sugar spoon and set it slowly on the table.

"Please stop," Luz said softly.

The woman continued picking up the pieces, placing them gently in her palm. Luz rested both hands on her arms. "Stop. Please stop. It's just a sugar bowl." The woman turned and faced her with dead eyes.

"I broke your sugar bowl," she said.

Luz cupped the back of the woman's hand with her own, led her to the coffee table, and gently tipped her hand until the broken pieces tumbled onto its surface. She examined her hands and then met her eyes.

"Just stay here, alright? Don't move. I'm going to get you a pair of slippers."

The woman stared straight ahead as Luz scurried off, returned, and then squatted down.

"Here put these on before you cut yourself."

The woman mourned. "I broke your sugar bowl. The one you like so much. All in a million pieces." Tears welled up in her dull eyes, but she did not squint or rub them. Luz rose and cupped the woman's face in her hands as she would a child.

"Look at me, honey, look at me." The woman's eyes blinked twice. A thin layer of dullness receded.

"It's all right. Do you hear me? The sugar bowl isn't important. You are," said Luz, "Now I need you to put these slippers on, will you do that?"

The woman stood motionless staring at her. Bewildered, she watched as Luz bent down and coaxed her to lift a foot. The woman stared at the foot as if it belonged to a stranger but lifted it. Luz held on to the woman's heel and guided her foot into the slipper. When she persuaded the woman to raise the other leg, she found a spreading pool of blood. The woman swung her foot across the sides and top of the slipper, bumping drunkenly against it.

"Stop. You're bleeding. Just keep your foot up."

Luz rose, took a hold of the woman's left arm, and slid it across her shoulder. The woman complied absentmindedly.

"I want you to hop to the sofa with your good foot."

The woman looked down at her foot.

"Good. You ready?"

The woman hopped and fell onto Luz, nearly toppling them both over. With the woman draped across her petite, but sturdy frame, Luz heaved the woman until they both slumped over the sofa. She unhooked the woman's arm from her and helped her to sit up. Then she lifted her legs and placed them gently on the coffee table. She examined the left foot. Blood gushed from between the folds of flesh and the porcelain shards wedged within. Luz winced.

"You're cut pretty badly. I'm going to go get the first aid kit," she said.

The woman stared catatonically at the porcelain pieces on the coffee table as Luz hurried off. The grandfather clock in the room continued to tick, lulling her to sleep with her eyes wide open. In her awakened stupor, something unseen crawled from its cave deep in the recesses of her mind. The thing unseen whispered a few words of command. Then, the wrenching began.

It was a wrenching within her ribcage, turning and twisting like a crocodile in a river with the head of its prey caught inside its powerful jaws. Most victims would immediately recognize the heavy drag that began in the chest, constricting the ribcage, and then reaching for the shoulders, striking the heart, and then finally the brain, dragging and pulling and twisting the head in murky waters, drowning the victim in a river of sorrow, anger, and hopelessness. Those who were sentient, though trapped, would know that something was deeply and terribly wrong. But for the woman, her mind was too far gone to know. Her eyebrows turned up as if she felt not quite right, but she never moved. So the thing unseen experimented with a deeper impression. It spoke to her, whispering softly into her ear with a voice that sounded like her own.

What have you done, Mara. The woman remained motionless with her mouth parted. The voice tried again, this time, pressing its accusing words harder against the ridges of her brain. *You deserve to die for what you've done.* The woman stirred. Her eyes shifted from side to side. She hadn't actually heard anything, but she did feel as if she were no longer alone in the room.

She called out. "Luz?"

No one responded. A shiver moved through her spine as the clock continued to tick. The woman closed her eyes. She wouldn't see whatever it was that frightened her here, she thought. But it was in the darkness that she saw what the thing unseen had wanted her to see: the glint of a blade slashing across her chest, moving with smooth precision. The visions slipped into her mind as with a magician's sleight of hand. The thing unseen tugged at her like a puppet master, moving her as desired, spreading its fingers further as the blade moved closer to her throat.

"I'll be right there," Luz called.

The visions slipped out as the thing unseen retreated into its cave. Disappointing. The images had no time to settle.

Luz set the water basin down and swung the first aid kit onto the coffee table. Then she reappeared with a pitcher of water and set it beside the water basin. She removed a pair of tweezers from the first aid kit, placed it on the table, and then sat on a nearby stool. Gently, she lifted the woman's injured foot. The woman's eyes closed and then opened like the shutter of a camera. Suddenly, she was wide-awake and sentient. She drew her foot back.

"Oh! My foot," she cried.

"Don't move. You're cut pretty badly."

The woman looked over the bloody splinters embedded in her porcelain white hands, bleeding her like hungry leeches. She pulled her foot towards her and then winced in pain.

"You're going to hurt yourself. Stay still," said Luz.

"What happened? How did I? Your—your sugar bowl. I'm so sorry," she whispered.

"Sugar bowls are replaceable, but you aren't. Now stretch out your left foot."

"It's dirty."

"A dirty foot doesn't bother me as much as a foot embedded with porcelain. If we don't clean and wrap that soon, it'll get infected. Then we'll have a lot more to worry about than just a dusty foot."

The woman extended her foot towards Luz who submerged it in a basin of water. When she lifted it, blood was still spreading from its wounds and mingling with the dirt on her skin. Luz cleaned the wound and then poured more water from the pitcher. She carefully plucked the pieces of porcelain with her tweezers and then went to work on the woman's hands. The woman winced as the porcelain grated against her flesh, stubbornly refusing to let go. Luz poured more water and prayed silently as she dressed her wounds.

"I'm really sorry I broke your sugar bowl," said the woman.

"Everyone makes mistakes, honey. God knows I've broken many, many pieces. And my kids? A lot of them break more than just ceramic. Some even break things intentionally. It doesn't make me love them any less. They're still my babies."

The woman looked at the pieces that lay scattered on the coffee table. Unlike the bowl, the lid still remained intact. She picked up the cap and examined its chipped corner. A long hairline crack ran from one end of the cap to the other.

"But you'll never be able to reproduce the original," she said.

"Sweetheart, you are so much more important than this sugar bowl. Infinitely more."

The woman considered these words.

"I guess you're right. If I had a child, I wouldn't stop loving my child over a cracked bowl. I wouldn't love my child any less. No matter what happens."

Luz took the lid from the woman and said, "Stretch out your hands." She fastened the bandages over her wounds and then sighed. "There. Now I feel much better."

The woman smiled. She could see that Luz cared for her. Really, actually cared.

"Thank you, Luz. For everything."

Luz patted the woman on her calf and rose. "I've got a pair of old crutches in the garage. I'll be right back with them. And don't forget to wear your slippers when your foot gets better. I got them for you. They're yours."

"Luz," she called when Luz turned to leave, "I think I'm going to add another name to the list. Mara—I think."

"Mara. Did we look at that name? It sounds familiar."

"I don't know."

"Well, if you like it, it's all right with me."

"I'm not sure though."

Oh, but you are.

"Then take your time, honey. You'll know what name is right for you."

The woman nodded. She did want to pick the perfect name. Her name would redefine her, erase the fears of her past, and bring her new life. She added the name to her list.

11

In the far corner of the large library room, sketches, photographs, and magazine cutouts of pottery designs were secured on a drafting table. Framed photographs of children hung on walls around the room. Several children frowned; a few looked adrift; but most flashed the camera with bright, toothy smiles. An old desk and chair in another corner of the room was also unoccupied. Near the entrance, tall bookshelves lined the walls. A coffee table was set above a Moroccan carpet that blanketed the floor by the bookshelves, and square pillows were placed around the table.

The woman was hunched over the coffee table scrawling on a pad with a color pencil while Luz was nestled in a beanbag nearby. The sole of the woman's left foot was still bandaged, but the rest of her body had undergone a significant transformation. She had filled nicely and the grooves that furrowed her once sallow skin were gone. She radiated instead with a rosy pink glow. The woman smiled more too and allowed an occasional laugh, though she always stopped short as if shocked by its strangeness. And more and more often, Luz found her huddled in the library room reading and sketching away. At first, the woman would stare wide-eyed like a child caught in the midst of transgression. But lately, she would look for assurance in Luz's face and then resume with her work in the room. She was beginning to grasp the meaning of freedom.

The woman moved her color pencil over the long neck of a bulbous pottery piece soaked in shades of red, orange, and sky blue. A flickering flame captured in clay.

"It's beautiful," admired Luz, "The colors swirl together like a flame of living fire."

The woman blushed. Weeks earlier, she would not have known what to do with such compliments. Such words sounded foreign to her. Weeks earlier, she would have looked down at her feet and remained silent until the awkward moment passed. But now, she knew to say "thank you." The words sounded strange coming out of her mouth. She felt gratefulness and a sense of humility for such honor. The woman placed her pencil down, turned to Luz, and kneaded her knuckles into her leg.

"I've settled on a name," she said.

"Really?" said Luz, "You have my full attention."

"I chose Mara. I feel like I'm supposed to be a Mara."

"Mara is perfectly fine as long as you like it."

The woman didn't actually like the name. She just knew that she belonged to it just as an animal belonged to the hand that held its leash. The feeling of being tethered to a name annoyed her so she moved on to the real reason for her excitement.

"I would also like to take on your last name, Ekklesian. At least until I get my memory back—and as long as it's all right with you."

Luz smiled. "Mara Ekklesian. You would be family by name. It would be an honor."

Mara's heart skipped when the doorbell rang.

"Oh, I almost forgot. Tony is helping us carry the desk to your room today," said Luz as she rose with Mara following after her. "I don't want you working on the dresser table anymore. You'll get a bad back."

Luz walked through the hallways, approached the front door, and swung it open.

"The handyman has arrived," Tony boomed.

The woman hunched over at the sight of the tall, broad-shouldered man.

"Hello there. Haven't seen you in a while. Looks like Luz has been taking good care of you."

Mara said hello, smiled, but remained silent.

"So where's this desk you wanted me to carry?" he asked, turning to his sister.

Luz's eyes sparkled. "First, I'd like to introduce you to my daughter, Mara Ekklesian."

Tony looked at the women and then scratched the backside of his head. He was tempted to burst into one of his candid-but-not-always-tactful questions but cleared his throat and said, "You're daughter?"

Luz suddenly realized she had a lot to explain. She turned to the woman apologetically.

"I'll have to explain one day, but I'd rather you do it now," said Mara.

"Come with me then," said Luz, leading her bewildered brother to the living room.

"I can't stay long though. Betty is afraid the bathroom sink'll explode if I don't fix a leak soon," said Tony, plopping down on the couch.

"Well, if Mara is willing, you might be able to let Betty in on this, too."

"Oh, well Betty would definitely want me to stay for this."

The woman nodded and Luz proceeded.

"Mara has amnesia. She can't remember anything before we brought her to the house, including her name. Mara Ekklesian is just a name she'll use until her memories return. And for me, because she's an Ekklesian, she's now family."

Tony leaned forward, ignoring the mother-daughter discussion completely. "Amnesia? She's got amnesia? Shouldn't you take her to the doctor?" he blurted.

"She's not ready yet."

"Not ready? But what if there's a problem?"

Mara folded her arms and held them rigidly in front of her belly.

"A doctor probably won't be able to bring her memory back any sooner. But the decision is completely hers."

Tony looked over at the woman who was now staring at the ground, waiting for his reply. "Well then I support that decision," he said, "Mara Ekklesian. That would make you what. My niece?"

Mara grinned a little and said, "I guess so."

"All right Mara, you ready to get the desk?"

The woman nodded.

The trio carried the desk from the garage to the bottom of the stairway. As they lugged the desk up the steps, the women pulled from the top while Tony pushed and pretty much carried the desk from below. When it was finally squeezed through the doorway, Tony lumbered toward the dresser and collapsed onto a chair.

"You filled the drawers with rocks, didn't you," said Tony as he wiped his forehead and fanned himself with his hands.

"Nope. Just a couple of Encyclopedias," his sister teased.
Tony nodded.

"I'll get some lemonade," offered Mara before she disappeared.

"How's she coming along?" asked Tony.

"Wonderfully. She's opening up slowly but surely."

Tony wiped his forehead and nodded. "She's talking to me, so that's good. She looks prettier with some weight on, too. I almost didn't recognize her."

Luz handed tissue papers to her brother and threw open a window.

"Have you taken her around town, yet?" asked Tony, wiping himself with the tissues.

"She didn't seem ready."

"Not even to church?"

"I don't think she's Christian."

"You haven't spoken to her about Jesus yet? That's not like you."

"It didn't seem right just yet."

"There's a right time to do that?" asked Tony.

Luz shrugged.

"So she's always home? She must be bored to death."

"She keeps herself busy with books and art supplies. I taught her some basic pottery making techniques, too. She's already making some pretty impressive pieces, so I don't think she's particularly bored."

"You're lucky she hasn't got Betty's habits," said Tony, tossing the wad of tissue into a nearby trashcan. As he did so, a sheet of paper caught his eye. Tony bent down and pulled out the wrinkled sheet and a crumpled wad beside it.

"Tony, you can't dig into someone's...."

A sketch of the woman's unsmiling face, painted with a sickly yellow that bled into shades of blue and grey was slowly unraveled.

"I never knew she painted. And that sketch...."

"…Is really, really good," continued Tony as he began unraveling the crumpled wad, "Imagine what she could do on canvas."

"Tony, you shouldn't…" Luz said absentmindedly as she marveled at a pair of hands extended heavenward.

"They're so lifelike," she murmured.

"Yeah, and they look exactly like yours, too. Why would she throw this?"

Luz studied her hands and then returned to the sketch. Sections of the paper had been rubbed thin by an eraser, but the sketch exactly mirrored her hands. Tony bent over, pulled another wad from the trashcan, and began unraveling the sheet of paper.

"You can't dig into people's things, Tony."

"I'm not digging into her things—just her trashcan," he argued.

As he flattened the third sheet of paper on his knees, the floorboard creaked. Tony looked up and found Mara staring at the sheets of paper in his hand. She was holding a pitcher of lemonade and clutching two empty glasses against her chest. The siblings exchanged an awkward glance.

"I'm sorry, I shouldn't have gone through your trash. Luz had nothing to do with this. It's just a bad habit I've got with my girls."

Mara shuffled into the room and placed the pitcher and glasses on the desk. She filled the glasses with lemonade, handed one to Tony and Luz, and declined one for herself. Tony gulped his lemonade awkwardly and placed his glass on the dresser table.

"They're just drafts," said the woman, "I keep the final ones in my folder."

Tony brightened. "But they're great. These hands look exactly like my sister's."

"They are her hands," she said with a smile.

Tony held up another sketch of a pair of hands that clearly belonged to a man. A fleshy palm with closely trimmed fingernails rested on a table like a spider. Beside it was a hammer-like fist.

"This one's good, too. Are these mine?" he asked.

Mara shook her head. "Your fingers are much longer and the bones of your hands more pronounced."

Tony opened and closed his hand. She was right.

"The sketch is very detailed. Whose hands are those?" asked Luz.

"I don't know. Maybe someone from my past or maybe no one at all. I don't like this sketch as much as the one I did for Luz though."

Tony nodded. "Would you like to save these?"

"No, I keep the final drafts in my drawer."

Tony placed the sheets of paper back into the wastebasket.

"All right ladies, I got to get back. The missus is waiting," he said as he rose, "By the way, what happened to Karen's housewarming gift?"

"What housewarming gift," said Luz.

"The crucifix she bought from her trip to Chile or wherever it was. The one you kept in this room when she insisted you hang it somewhere."

"I hung that…"said Luz, looking at the empty nail, "I could have sworn I did."

The woman walked to the dresser, slid open a drawer, and removed the crucifix. She carried the cross so as not to touch the carving of the man and placed it on the bed.

"I took it down. I couldn't sleep. It was hard for me to stay in the room with him watching me," she mumbled.

Mara didn't say that she felt a consuming remorse for the murder of a man she did not know. He was merely a household adornment. Yet, the stranger on the cross had pursued her with his eyes relentlessly, haunting her for the blood she had shed.

Tony cleared his throat. "I wouldn't blame you. It's hard for me to see such suffering, too. I'm sure Karen would understand if we moved the cross."

The hairs on the back of Mara's neck rose.

"Who is he?" she asked.

The siblings exchanged a look of surprise. They had assumed that the woman had at least heard about the man even if she were of another faith. Luz's heart leapt at the realization that her curiosity had opened the doors to a restoration she could not provide. A wholeness that required God: a restoration of the spirit, body, and soul. Luz wanted so much to see this one whole.

"The man on the cross is Jesus Christ," said Luz.

Luz explained that the sins of man resulted in the separation of God and man. God gave his chosen people commandments to obey so that they might remain pure and acceptable to him; but regardless of their efforts, none could fully and without fail comply with the law. Thus, when his people sinned, a lamb was sacrificed so that the people might be purified and reconciled with God once again. Despite human weakness and sin, God still loved the world and his desire was to be reconciled with his people forever. Because of his great love, Jesus Christ, the Son of God who was a sinless and therefore unblemished lamb was born as a man. Through the shedding of his blood on the cross, he took on the sins of the world. This sacrifice was provided so that anyone who received Jesus Christ as his or her Savior was reconciled to a holy God through his grace and mercy and not by man's own efforts at keeping the law.

"We are then reconciled with God not by our own striving, but because he loves us and by his love, grace, mercy, and Spirit, we are able to love and follow him," said Luz.

As she spoke, the woman studied the face of the stranger. She tried to find what Luz had described about this Jesus on the man, but nothing in his hand-carved face struck her as loving and kind. Even in a crowd of three, the man's blank, expressionless eyes still haunted her.

"Are you a follower of Jesus Christ?" she asked.

"Yes. Tony and I are Christians. So were my grandparents and parents. God loves you, Mara. And he can help you and heal you more than any man or woman."

The woman suddenly felt herself being pulled away, separated from Luz, Tony, and even herself. She wished Luz would stop speaking about this man. Her head, which had begun to throb, felt light. She dug her nails into her skull as a piggish squeal echoed in the back of her head. She wondered if it was this god, Jesus Christ, who had come to punish her for her skepticism. She wondered if he had come to punish her for her desire to hear no more. *Yes Mara, he has come to kill you.* Mara felt the room spin. She saw Luz's lips open and close, but the hot, angry squeals drowned her voice. A moment later, the earth tilted. The woman caught a glimpse of Luz's horrified face before her knees buckled and darkness swallowed her whole.

12

Mara heard the distant voice of a woman calling her name. Her eye slit open. Dark, obscure shapes moved in the foreground of a bright light. She closed her eyes. She wanted to stay in the darkness, to remain in the void where she no longer seemed to live. The distant voice called out to her again, pulling her from the consuming vortex. Her eyes fluttered half open, and her mind followed drunkenly after, moving like a man running underwater. She stared at the shapes until they refined into the features of Luz and an olive-skinned woman with kind but penetrating eyes. A stethoscope hung around the stranger's neck. Mara stirred and found her body wrapped underneath a blanket. Her tired eyes flitted past the women and rested on a figure that gradually morphed into a man. It was Tony.

"Where am I?" she asked.

"You're still in your bedroom, Mara. You fainted. I'm sorry dear, but I had to call a doctor," said Luz, "Doctor Bollai is a friend. You can trust her."

Mara glanced at the doctor and then returned to Luz. She pushed herself up from the bed, but her stomach growled in protest.

"Are you hungry?" Luz asked.

She was hungry. But Mara was always hungry. She had gained quite a few pounds since her arrival, but she couldn't stop eating, and she became agitated when she tried. She glanced at the clock. It was too early for dinner.

"I'm fine," she lied.

"Your stomach disagrees. I'll fix you a bowl of soup, but before I do, Doctor Bollai would like to ask you a few questions. Are you well enough to respond?"

Mara nodded.

The doctor turned to Tony who said, "Excuse me ladies," and exited the room.

"I just have a few questions and then I'd like to give you a test. Is that okay?" she said. Mara folded her hands and nodded.

"When was the last time you had your menstruation?"

Mara's face reddened.

"Doctor Bollai just wants to find out what caused you to faint," urged Luz.

"Probably two months. I haven't had one since I got here. I don't remember anything before that."

"Doctor Bollai is going to give you a test. I'll bring some soup for you. Then I'd like you to rest," said Luz.

Mara nodded. She was exhausted. If her stomach didn't persist as much as it did, she would've pulled the covers over her head and gone straight to sleep. But she kept herself awake until the test was administered and a bowl of hot soup brought to her.

"Get some rest, honey," said Luz before she stepped outside with the wooden crucifix.

The man on the cross. She remembers now. That was why she had fainted. When the door was closed, she felt an immediate relief at having rid herself of the stranger, followed by remorse at having rejected the God that Luz seemed to love so much—Luz who had exhibited the kind of love that she had testified this God was all about. It wasn't completely her fault for feeling this way, though, was it? Mara just couldn't see what Luz had described about her God in those vacant, lifeless eyes. In fact, the man's hand-carved face frightened her. She dipped her spoon into the soup gloomily. Maybe she was just tired. She'll eat and then sleep. Tomorrow, she may see and think differently of this God. Tomorrow or maybe a month or so from tomorrow.

****

She was awakened by a sick uneasiness that rolled in her belly. Mara opened her eyes and found herself staring at a full moon that glowed eerily just outside her window. Her stomach continued to turn as she lay in bed. She shut her eyes and took deep, long breaths, but the breathing exercises did not help. They were not able to stop the muscles that contracted from the pit of her stomach to the base of her throat. Another series of contractions sent her rushing out of the room. She scuttled as softly as she could down the hallway and into the bathroom, locking the door behind. The woman dropped to her knees and pointed her mouth over the toilet bowl. Within seconds, her stomach contracted violently in rapid successive episodes. She felt as if she would explode as vomit poured out of her mouth like sewage from a rusted pipe. Tears rolled down her cheeks. She gasped for air, but the stench of her vomit choked her lungs and her stomach contracted again. This time, nothing more could be brought forth.

As she waited with her head over the toilet bowl, a soft tapping reverberated on the door.

"Are you all right?"

Mara sat back and called out, "I'm fine. Just using the bathroom."

There was silence on the other end. Mara rested her head on the cool wall, waiting for Luz to press her with questions, but none came. She waited until she was sure that Luz had gone. Then she grabbed a wad of paper towels and cleaned the vomit that had dribbled on the floor. She flushed the toilet, washed her hands, and brushed her teeth as she watched herself in the mirror. She had changed so much she hardly recognized herself.

The hallway was empty as she had hoped, but as she approached her room, she noticed light streaming through the door cracks. Her heart sank. Luz had been waiting for her in her room. Mara opened the door and found her sitting in front of a window. The skies outside were still dark, but the moon was no longer in sight.

"Join me for a sunrise? I probably can't stay awake that long, but we can sit for a while," Luz said with a yawn.

Mara sat down beside her, drew her legs close, and then wrapped her arms around them, looking like a butterfly still wrapped in its cocoon. She was staring into the dark horizon, waiting for Luz to speak.

"I was planning on speaking to you about this in the morning, but I heard you throwing up and I didn't want you to worry. You're going through some symptoms of wonderful news," said Luz.

Wonderful news. Mara braced herself.

"You are with child."

Luz continued on, but Mara no longer heard the words that came out of her mouth. She stared at Luz's lips until they stopped moving. Then she turned and stared into the night. She didn't know how long she sat gazing at the horizon, and she didn't know if

Luz had retired to her room or still sat beside her. She remained with her arms wrapped around her legs in a hollow cocoon shell seeing and hearing nothing.

In the horizon, a soft glow penetrated the darkness, slowly stripping shades of grey from the early morning sky. Light crept onto the edges of the woman's chair and then broadened its reach, touching first her toes and then spreading to her feet, her legs and arms, and then resting upon her face. The brilliance of the sun forced the woman to squeeze her eyes shut. When she opened them again, she heard birds chirping. The sun had awakened the woman to her fatigue but had not removed the confused despair she felt as one who had lost her memories and was now with child. Her head ached and all she wanted to do was to sleep. She looked around somberly.

"Luz, wh—what are you still doing here?"

"I was worried about you."

"You should have gone to bed. I can't believe I kept you here," said Mara as she unraveled her arms and legs. A sharp tingling numbness shot through her legs. The woman winced and stiffened. When she was able to move again, Luz spoke.

"Do you remember what I said to you?"

The throbbing in the woman's head worsened. She pressed her fingers into her skull.

"Are you all right?" Luz asked.

"I'm just tired."

"We'll talk about this after you get some rest."

Luz helped the woman to her bed where she slid underneath the covers and promptly fell asleep. She looked with concern at the face of the woman who even when asleep still bore the troubles of her mind.

****

In the darkness, a voice neither man nor woman spoke.

You've forgotten about me already, haven't you.

Except for the black void that had swallowed her whole, the woman could neither see nor feel a thing. She wondered who spoke to her from the dark.

You have forgotten me, I'm hurt. Let me refresh your memory, said the voice. The woman heard a grating sound and then a hiss. The tongue of a blood red flame licked the tip of a matchstick. *There. Now do you remember me?*

The woman peered at a face that glowed in the dark. There was only enough light to see that the speaker possessed the strong features of a man. She wished the stranger would hold the flame closer to his face but was too afraid to speak.

You don't have to be afraid of me, Mara. I won't hurt you. I won't hurt you unless you've been a bad girl. But you haven't been a bad girl, have you? The flame danced wildly as the stranger pulled the burning matchstick closer to his face. *There.*

The woman stared at a large, whittled face of the man on the cross. A crown of jagged thorns was embedded in his head, and black, viscous blood ran down his face. A pair of green, clam-shaped eyes glowed. The woman turned and ran. As she ran, the voices chased after her until she was swallowed in the black crevasse.

13

She stared at the ceiling in bed. It was one in the afternoon. She had awakened refreshed from a deep sleep, one in which the many dreams that had penetrated her mind had been forgotten. Her thoughts lingered instead on the revelation she was with child. Mara had no recollection of the child's conception, no memory of ever loving or being loved by a man. But within months, she would give birth to a child, a human from her flesh and bone. She could not imagine the demands, the stress and strain she would bear as the protector, caregiver, and mother of a being so utterly at her mercy. She shivered. Last night's confusion had worn off. Now, she was simply afraid. Afraid of her own weaknesses as a human being. Afraid she had no one to share the responsibilities with for such a daunting task. Did her decision to escape from her past save her child? Or was it a mistake that would deprive her child of a father. A mistake that resulted from an unsound mind. She brooded over everything. Still, one thing was certain. She was in a safe place now. So was her unborn child. Mara burrowed her hands underneath the covers and rested them on her belly.

Her thoughts drifted to the heavenly being that Luz had spoken of. He was a perfect and sinless man who bore the sins of the world. He was the Son of God whose sacrifice reconciled a fallen world to a holy and righteous God by invitation. Mara ruminated over this concept. A concept of redemption. But why did she possess so great an aversion towards this man? From the very moment she laid eyes on him, she had been afraid. When she slept, she had slept close to the edge of her bed, preferring not to sleep directly in front of the man as he gazed down at her. When she dressed, she did so in the closet with the door shut behind her. As long as the crucifix had hung on the wall, she had been afraid to even stay longer than necessary in her room. Why would she be so frightened of a man who had brought redemption to this world?

But Luz. Luz was the fruit of such a God. Mara had tasted God's love through the hand of this woman and her brother, and the love had stirred her. She wondered if there were many Christians in this world. She wondered if her child would like to be raised a Christian. She wondered if this God would be able to give her what he had given Luz. As she pondered, hope stirred within and a peace settled over her.

Her mind drifted back to her child. She did notice that her body had made significant changes. Her ribs no longer protruded and her arms, legs, and belly had grown fleshy. All this time, she had chided herself for being a greedy eater. And all this time, it had just been a baby. She chuckled to herself. Just a baby. Never did such a thought ever occur to her.

A teardrop slid down her cheek. Surprised, she wiped the trail with her fingertips, but another droplet formed. Mara dabbed at it and studied the globular bead on her finger. Her chest contracted from the honesty of the solitary drop. She tried to push them back, but her efforts were futile. More crystalline beads rose and escaped from the corners of her eyes. The drops of liquid crystal that sheathed her pain and sorrow refused to be swallowed, so she let them fall. She didn't remember when was the last time she had allowed herself to let go. It was a good feeling. It was liberating.

Serenity gradually comforted her. She wiped her face with her hands and arose. As she walked to the closet, the woman caught a glimpse of herself in the mirror. She faced the mirror with curiosity. Then she turned aside and touched her belly shyly. She could not believe the woman in the mirror was her.

"You are me," she whispered, "and I am you. I'm glad to be you."

The woman placed a hand on her neckline and then slowly unbuttoned her night gown, exposing her upper sternum. The scars had healed, and only dark shadows of the cross-like blemishes remained. She smiled and breathed a sigh of relief.

"Things are going to get better," she murmured, "I know it."

By the time her child is born, she would be well. Well enough to give her child the very best.

14

Fridays and Sundays were church days in New Day City. She had never been invited to attend the services, but Mara was relieved that Luz had never done so. She wasn't ready to mingle with strangers. But if Luz had asked her to, she would have gone. There would have been no option to decline after having received so much. Mara would have pledged her allegiance to any god or religious tenet if Luz had asked her to, but she never asked.

For months, she watched discreetly as Luz prepared for church, following her from behind walls and doorways until Luz exited the house and backed her car from the driveway. But the weekly surveillance only served to whet her curiosity. In the last three months, she had accompanied Luz a few times to her ceramic shop, and to her knowledge, the trips had not raised too many eyebrows in town. Luz's church, which was located in a large city, should be even safer. She would be a stranger among strangers, the perfect place for Mara Ekklesian.

Mara was also beginning to see herself less as a mindless itinerant and more as Luz's daughter. So if there really was a good God, she would give him a chance. Then of course, secretly, there was more. Mara wanted what Luz had: the peace, the love, the joy, and if possible, the feeling of never being alone in this world. There was a large, cavernous hole, a bottomless pit that not even Luz seemed to be able to fill. Mara wondered if this God might just be the one to seal it.

Since the removal of the crucifix, she had been thinking increasingly about God, but Luz never approached the subject again. The lack of discussion about Jesus only served to frustrate her. Whenever Luz left for church, Mara would pace anxiously about. When Luz returned, she would mill around her hoping she would speak about her day. But Luz only gave enough details to feed her curiosity. Her frustration continued until one Sunday, dressed in a long navy blue dress, she descended the stairway as Luz was searching for her shoes nearby.

"Oh, Luz, I didn't see you there. Where are you going?" she asked coolly, knowing that Luz knew she knew the answer. Her face colored.

"I'm going to church," Luz replied with a smile. The woman held her breath and pleaded silently for her to ask.

"Would you like to come?"

Mara smiled. "I would love to come."

"It's a two-hour drive from here to the city. You should bring some snacks," said Luz.

Within minutes, Mara packed a bagful of snacks, slipped on her shoes, and hopped into the car. As they drove, the women chatted and Luz pointed out buildings and towns along the way. When they were quiet, Mara listened to the radio. She smiled under the morning sun as her hair whipped in the wind. She was beginning to dread less and less the times she spent outside of home.

The truck rumbled on, passing tall, opulent buildings, and then rolling through ragged streets where metal bars secured rows of graffiti-scrawled buildings. Mara stared at the people begging on the streets as drifters pushed trash-filled shopping carts along. When the car slowed to a crawl, an unpleasant smell permeated her lungs. Her face crinkled.

"Are we near the church?" she asked, sticking her head back into the car.

The car turned into a crowded parking lot beside a brick building. The sign above the building door displayed the words "God's Grace."

"We're here," said Luz.

Mara took in the strange sights of the city and then the strange smells. She covered her nose and ducked quickly into the building after Luz. The room was packed full of sweaty bodies. The crowd was already singing and clapping to a gospel tune lead by a young black man. In a corner, a woman slid her fingers across the keyboard of an old piano while a man dressed in an untucked shirt and jeans plucked his guitar strings beside her. Mara and Luz scooted into the last row of chairs and stood beside a man dressed in rags. The old man brought back memories of the stench Mara smelled in the streets outside. Fear and repugnance crept up her spine as he flashed a toothless grin.

"Hello!" said the man, blowing a puff of air into her face as he spoke. Mara controlled her instinctive urge to recoil but said nothing. The man tried again. "Hello! My name is Chuck. Welcome to God's Grace, sister," he cried. Mara smiled grimly at the man, trying not to throw up, and then scooted closer to Luz. The man shrugged and continued belting out a tuneless hymn.

Mara surveyed the plain room. On stage, a student desk served as the pulpit, and a large wooden cross hung directly behind it. Beside the cross, the words of a hymn were projected on the wall by an overhead projector. A rusted air conditioner hummed while dusty ceiling fans whirled above. Rows of foldable chairs, two hundred in total, were parted into two sections.

When the worship ended, a man rose from the first row.

"That's the pastor, the person in charge of the church," whispered Luz.

The young man, dressed in jeans and a shirt with its sleeves rolled to his elbows, was not the type of person Mara expected to lead a holy proceeding. Then again, she didn't quite think the attire of more than a few congregants were appropriate when worshiping the God of the universe.

The pastor preached about God's reconciliatory love for prodigals from an open bible on the student desk. The man didn't seem to mind being interrupted as he preached. A person in one corner would shout, "Hallelujah! Praise the Lord!" In another, "You got that right, pastor!" would then erupt. Then there were others Mara watched nervously from the corner of her eyes. A few seats in front, one man cried and cried. A few seats to her right, a woman giggled under her breath from time to time. Yet, the pastor seemed to not be bothered by it all. As the novelty of the church began to wear off, Mara gradually found herself drawn to the God spoken of by the man behind the pulpit.

When service came to an end, people slowly filed out of the church. A black woman spotted Luz in the crowd, waved, and then moved towards her.

"Paige! How are you?"

"Just fine. And what happened to you last week? This woman left Tommy with a bag of cookies and then disappeared on me," the woman complained. She turned back to Luz. "Come here and give me a hug."

Luz laughed and hugged the woman who said, "My goodness, you never even gave me a chance to say thank you."

A little boy scuttled to the woman and embraced her thick legs with both hands. "Speaking of little Tommy…," said Paige, looking down at the boy, "What should you be saying to Ms. Luz." Paige raised an eyebrow as the boy peeked at Luz from behind her leg. "Tommy, you can't gobble down those cookies and not have something to say."

The boy popped his face out. "Thank you, Ms. Luz. It was real yummy," he chirped.

Paige nodded. "Good boy. Now who is this beautiful friend you brought today?"

"This is Mara Ekklesian."

"Ekklesian. You family?"

"Not by blood. But she's family," said Luz.

"Well, nice to meet you, Mara. My name is Paige. Welcome to God's Grace, sister," said the woman, giving her a sturdy hug. Mara's eyes popped open and her shoulders stiffened. She did not like being touched by strangers, but she did not draw back.

"Thank you," she mumbled.

The little boy tugged at her dress. "Can I give you a hug, too?" he asked.

Paige laughed. "You want to give Ms. Mara a hug, too?"

The boy nodded. "Hugs are good."

Mara glanced hesitantly at Luz and then bent down. The little boy threw his arms around her neck, rattled off, "Jesus loves you," and then scuttled away.

Paige laughed and then sighed. "Silly boy. Just like his mama was."

"How's Jessie?" Luz asked in a low voice.

"Much better. He really hurt her bad the last time. Real bad. I keep praying dear Lord help her to see. God works miracles. He does, I seen Him. But Jessie's gotta want to take his hand. It can't just be him. She's gotta want to take the Lord's hand, too."

Luz gave Paige a hug. When they pulled away, Paige wiped a tear and laughed.

"Thanks. I needed that."

"Keep me updated, and let me know if you need anything. I'll keep praying, too."

"I will. It's so good seeing you, and it was nice meeting you too, Mara. You stay with Luz. You'll be mighty blessed if you do."

****

Mara mulled over the morning's events during the drive home. She didn't remember ever attending a church service, but this was not what she expected. A church building was supposed to be more immaculate and well-furnished. And if that wasn't possible, the churchgoers were at least supposed to be more appropriately dressed and serenely pious. The atmosphere just didn't seem clean or holy. God's Grace looked just like a dilapidated building with people gathered straight from filthy city streets. Mara was shocked that a holy place of worship would permit some of the strange-looking people she had seen. Still, the members of the church did seem to fervently want god. And though the pastor looked as young as Mara did, the message he gave possessed the depth of spiritual maturity and power.

"I didn't expect a church to look like that," she murmured.

"We get that a lot. It's a young church. And it serves a rough neighborhood."

Mara stared into the distant mountains.

"Do you ever feel like you don't want certain people to touch you or be near you?" she said.

Luz glanced at her. "Which ones are you talking about?"

"The ones that don't look like they have God in them. The ones that look unclean."

Luz thought for a moment. "No honey, I've never felt that way," she said gently.

"So you're not afraid of catching what they have?"

"I'm not sure I understand you."

The women drove in silence for a while.

"Nevermind. It's nothing," said Mara. She wasn't sure what she meant to say either.

The trip home was a long and quiet one.

15

Winter had arrived. A cold wind blew across the land and whistled through the window cracks into the warm house. Inside, Mara peered out at the grey clouds. A partially painted canvas stood before her. She lowered her paintbrush and rubbed her bulbous belly with her free hand. Her belly had grown quickly and unusually large. The doctor had confirmed that she would be blessed with a gift of two instead of one. The news about the twins elicited a squeal of delight from Luz and stunned silence from herself. But fear no longer held as strong of a grip on Mara as it did months before.

She was almost self-sufficient now. Her resolve to venture from the four walls of the house had been strengthened since her visit with God's Grace. She began looking forward to attending church, to getting acquainted with this God called Jesus, to praising him alongside Chuck, and even to shaking his hand. Mara eventually became baptized in a portable pool. And gradually, she was introduced to the people of Restwood. Many already knew as much about the woman as Betty did. And though the people often whispered about her mysterious pregnancy and her strange arrival, no one faulted Mara for her memory loss or her hesitancy to return to a past that may not be good for her or her unborn child.

There was one thing that everyone at Restwood did agree to with Mara Ekklesian though. When it came to mastering the skills of pottery making, Luz had taken on a worthy pupil. Mara's artistic pieces had received an eager crowd of buyers from local residents, and those from distant cities had begun trickling in from reports of her remarkable dexterity with clay. Her gift had even sparked in Betty the possibility of matching a beautiful face and such skilled hands with a respectable man in town. But fortunately, like all things new, Mara's novelty eventually wore off and the local residents soon regarded her as they did themselves.

"I need a break," she mumbled as she stuck her paintbrush in a jar of water and heaved herself off the high chair.

Mara grabbed a pile of books and waddled out of the workshop toward the library room. The heater in the room hummed. She was alone. Luz had gone out to run errands and would not be back for a while. Mara waddled to the shelves and began placing the books back into their slots. When she finished, she stuck her hands on her hips and looked around. Only months before, she could not step into this room without feeling as if she were trespassing. She smiled as she remembered Luz's patience at encouraging her to see the house as her home.

Luz had gone beyond just opening her home. She had taught her everything about her ceramic business and had allowed her access to all her bookkeeping files. She had completely trusted a stranger who had done nothing to earn her trust. When Mara asked why and how she could possibly trust her, Luz's answer was simply not something she could understand.

"It's true I don't trust everyone as I've trusted you. But God sees you. He knows you. And I trust that he speaks to me," was all Luz had said.

God sees me. As Mara pondered over these words, her eyes came to rest on the crucifix that Luz had removed from her room. It was propped against the wall by the drafting desk. She had seen it many times in passing, but her attention had never been arrested by it as it was now. Her heart skipped as her eyes locked with his. The man was staring at her again with reproachful eyes. She wanted to look away, but the spell held her, and voices inserted themselves in her consciousness, whispering words of disapproval, reproach, and disgust. More and more flittered through, skittering in deep like hungry newborn roaches, each claiming a right to a piece of her mind.

A draft of air blew past her, startling her. Mara hunched over and took a step back.

"Luz said I could come in," she said in a quiet voice, "I didn't take anything."

The wooden statue glared at her. Mara frowned and turned away. "God sees me," she said out loud, "And Jesus loves me. You're just a carving made by a man. You're not God."

She received no reply, but the swelling cloud of voices stopped. Mara stood trembling, still trying to recover from the violation of her mind. A voice suddenly spoke. *I will reclaim you. You haven't won, Mara dearest.* Her mouth parted with surprised concern. Unlike its previous attempts at infiltration, the voice of this one had not been impeded by the confusion of her mind. This one had gone straight through. She searched the room for the speaker. Were these her own words? They couldn't be. But the voice did sound like her own. Maybe she was tired and mumbling to herself. Mara wasn't sure, but she did not want to find out. She walked out of the room calmly but quickly. At the door, she turned and looked at the crucifix. The accusation she saw in the eyes of the man had disappeared. What she saw now was simply what it was: a hand-carved man on a crucifix. Her eyes blinked in surprise. She turned and waddled out the door.

When Mara returned to the workshop, her desire to continue painting had diminished. She stood in the room wishing someone were with her now. As loneliness bore down on her, she felt sudden thrusts of little feet within. Mara touched her belly. From inside, a foot pressed against the layers of membrane and met her hand. Her eyes moistened. She smiled and whispered, "Thank you. Mommy can't wait to see you both either." Her mind drifted.

It was lonely times like these when Mara wondered about the man she had been intimate with. Did he think of her as often as she thought of him? Was he still searching for her? Did he love her? Mara felt as if her heart would break at the possibility of such unanswered questions. The longing for a man who would love and protect her was so deep and so—no. She won't do this to herself. The paintings and sketches had spoken. She shook her head and wiped away her tears.

Mara walked towards her private corner where painting canvases were stacked against walls. In this corner, watercolor paintings hung on wires strung across the room while books of sketches were piled high on tables and chairs. Every piece of art in this corner derived its conception from her dreams. Each piece was different but somehow connected to another like the pieces of a puzzle yet to be completed. There were paintings of parts of a building with a tall steeple built on an expansive lawn, a large two-story home built with stone, and filthy city streets with stragglers milling about. The sketches contained pieces of furniture, a pair of hands, large square eyeglasses, knives streaked with blood, broken beer bottles, and more.

These were the ethereal images Mara had quickly caught on canvas or paper whenever she awoke with the images still intact. She had waited patiently for these dreams as they visited her in the night. So far, they were not images that assured her that she would be safe if she returned to her past. As long as nothing in her memory provided this assurance, she would remain where she was regardless of her lonesome desires.

16

Beads of sweat dotted her forehead. A few globules connected with one another and slid into her eyes, stinging them. Her gown was drenched with sweat. She gasped for air. She had been pushing for what seemed like an eternity and the pain was growing unbearable. Her children seemed to be clawing the insides of her womb, refusing to enter the world.

Doctor Bollai called out to her at the foot of the bed. "Push, Mara. You're almost there." Mara squeezed Luz's hand, closed her eyes, and pushed.

"The first one's coming out," the doctor cried. Mara gasped, gritted her teeth, and pushed again. "That's good. That's good. She's almost out. I see the other one, too."

Puffing and wheezing, she gritted her teeth and pushed once more. "Wonderful. Good. Wonderful. Keep—" The doctor's voice drifted off.

Hard breathing echoed in the room as the doctor and her nurse stared at the child. A sudden shriek pierced the silence.

"It's out. The child's out," said Doctor Bollai.

Luz squeezed her hand. "You're done." Mara breathed a sigh of relief and smiled. "Rest now. They'll have to cut the umbilical cord, and the nurse will clean the child first," said Luz. Mara nodded. A moment later, the nurse carried the child quickly to another room.

"I'd like to speak to you in the other room," Doctor Bollai said gravely.

"Doctor Bollai wants to talk to me. I'll be right back," said Luz.

"Will I get to see my babies?"

"Of course. We'll be back. I won't be far."

Mara laid her head back and closed her eyes.

Luz followed the soft cries into a room. Her smile disappeared when she saw the doctor and nurse bending over the crying child with their backs facing her. They were studying the child from a distance as if it were a strange specimen.

"Is something wrong, doctor?" she asked, startling them. The doctor spun around and the nurse looked up at her with wide eyes betraying all her fears and disgust. The doctor took a step toward her.

"Mara didn't give birth to healthy twins."

"What do you mean? What happened?"

"One of the twins didn't form correctly," said the doctor. She stepped aside.

Luz looked down at the bloody child still writhing and squirming on the cold metal tray. Her mouth parted in shock. A smaller fetal-like creature lying above the child was clinging to the baby like a tick with elongated arms and legs. The doctor picked the baby up and carefully loosed the creature's fingers and toes from the child. The small mass arched its back and fell backwards, jutting out like a tree limb. Its pelvis was still connected to the baby's abdomen, and layers of loose skin sagged around its belly. The head of the creature was slightly shrunken and the left side of its skull was twisted, as if it had been crushed, beaten, burned, and then had healed imperfectly within the womb. Thin, almost translucent skin stretched across the damaged portion of its skull, revealing a web of grey veins. The other half of the creature's head was normal, an exact replica of the cherubic face of its twin. Its eyes and mouth were closed tightly shut. And it did not move or cry. The doctor placed the baby back onto the tray.

"I can't understand. How did this happen?" Luz murmured.

"The smaller child is likely a parasitic twin, a twin that is incompletely formed or wholly dependent on the fully formed child. It does appear to possess most of its body parts, so I wouldn't have thought it to be parasitic if it weren't for its small size and its lack of response. The skull looks crushed, but I don't believe it's caused by physical trauma. My knowledge in this area is limited, however. We would have to perform several tests, but from the way they're connected, the twins probably share too many vital organs to make a separation possible."

The nurse erupted. "That's not a child, Ms. Luz. I've helped with many births, including babies that were not formed properly. But that thing? No ma'am. No newborn has fingers and toes that can grip another child like that. That creature's the devil. When I carried that child into this room, I saw that thing—"

"That's enough."

"But Ms. Luz has got to know."

"I said that's enough. You're imagination is affecting your work, and I won't have you talking such nonsense."

Mara's voice echoed feebly. "Is everything all right?"

Luz retreated from the room and then returned. "Can we bring the child now?"

"I'm worried about Mara, Luz, I think—"

"Where's the baby?" Luz interrupted, startled by the silence of the room. The women turned and found the child watching them. Luz smiled with relief. "We left you all alone, didn't we? I'm sorry." Gently, she scooped the child into her arms, fussing over it.

"I'm concerned about Mara, Luz. I'm afraid she may reject the child. She's been through a lot of trauma. The child's deformity might shock her."

An anxious cry rose from the other room. "Where are my babies?"

"Just a moment longer," Luz called out.

"This is Mara's child, Doctor Bollai. We can't guess how she'd react. We need to get this child cleaned."

She turned to the nurse, but when the nurse shook her head, Luz cleaned the child herself. When they returned to the room, Luz greeted Mara with a smile.

"You have a beautiful baby girl," she said.

"Doctor Bollai said I would have twins."

"One of the twins didn't form properly. They're still connected with one another, but only one of them is able to respond."

Mara pushed herself up. "Connected? Isn't there something we could do?"

"We're not sure yet," said the doctor, "But judging by the way they're joined together, a separation may be a high risk for both. A thorough exam must be done before surgery can be recommended."

"I'm not risking my child. Give me my baby. Let me hold my baby," she cried, stretching her arms out. Luz drew near and placed the child in her arms. Mara gazed at her child, touched her cheeks, and then whispered, "Hello there." The child stirred and then fell back asleep. She touched the parasitic twin next with her little finger, but it did not move.

"Why doesn't the smaller child move?" she whispered. The doctor leaned forward. "The brain of the smaller twin may not be fully developed. But with tests, we may be able to surgically…."

"I said no surgery. This thing stays if it means my daughter lives."

Doctor Bollai straightened and smiled. "You're the mother."

Mara gazed at her baby and then turned to Luz. "I've decided on a name for her. I chose Saoirse. Saoirse Ekklesian."

Mara smiled at her daughter. She could stay in bed forever, gazing at her newborn child. She marveled at the smallness of her nose, her eyes, and her ears. She marveled at her tiny fingers. She was in awe of the beauty of her child.

17

A vase of freshly cut roses, bright and yellow, was placed on the coffee table. Four plates of sliced pound cake remained untouched on the table. The teacups beside the plates moved with more frequency. The guests sitting on the couch sipped their tea quietly. Mara had baked the cake from scratch and brewed the tea herself for the special occasion. She had anticipated a lively discussion where Betty was involved; but now, only Saoirse cooed and giggled on Luz's lap. Tony, who sat a little ill at ease beside his wife, waited for her to initiate the social exchanges. But for the first time, Betty was at a loss for words. She raised her teacup again and pulled her lips into a thin smile.

"Delicious tea," she offered.

"Thank you," said Mara.

The baby giggled at the short exchange and waved its chubby arms as foamy saliva dribbled from her mouth. Dangling in front of her with its back arched backward like an outstretched arm was the other twin. Betty watched as its deformed head swung upside down to and fro. Mara had apologized, explaining that she could have tied the parasitic twin to the child to prevent it from being so much of a distraction, but Saoirse had fussed until she finally just allowed it to hang as it did.

"But most of all, I thought it would be nice for you to see Saoirse just as she was," Mara said sheepishly. Betty kept an aching smile on her face and reassured her that she and her husband had come for that very reason and that of course they wanted to see the child just as she was.

Though the parasitic twin had remained as it was, small and emaciated, Saoirse had grown to be a strong and vivacious baby. She was a beautiful child with emerald green eyes, creamy white skin, and soft brown hair that curled delicately around her face. Even Betty, who by proper decorum tried as much as possible not to stare, could not keep herself from doing so. But as many times as she gravitated towards Saoirse's cherubic face, Betty was just as equally tempted to gawk at the face of her ugly twin. She sighed quietly as she placed her teacup back onto the coffee table. It was a pity that such a beautiful child would be destined to go to waste.

"I'm so glad to see Saoirse. She's very adorable," Betty fibbed.

The baby squealed and lunged at her with chubby hands. Betty shrieked and pulled away as Luz restrained the baby who giggled and blew more bubbles from her mouth. Tony stifled a smile as he watched his wife color under her heavily powdered face.

"I think she likes you. She's never been this aggressive," said Mara as she watched the baby wave excitedly.

Luz chuckled. "Yes. I think she's flirting with you."

"It's the shiny jewelry. If I were Saoirse, I'd want to grab those things myself," Tony reasoned. Betty flashed her husband a look of displeasure. He reached for his teacup and brought it to his lips. "Just a thought," he muttered.

"So how is everything with the baby?" asked Betty.

"Busy, of course," said Luz when Mara did not reply, "You know, changing diapers, feeding the baby, keeping her busy. Saoirse's a curious child and surprisingly mischievous. A few days ago, she insisted on sleeping on the blanket we placed on the floor. So Mara, who had been sitting on the armchair, let her lay there as she read. You'd think that a baby who had been playing all day would be sleeping soundly. Well, not Saoirse. I checked on her before I headed towards the library room. Her eyes were half closed, so we both thought she had fallen asleep. But sometime after I left, the baby made a quick, and I should say silent breakaway, crawled down the hallway and into the library room, and sat herself behind me in her diapers. I'm not sure how long she was there. All I heard was Mara calling frantically for her. When I turned around, there she was observing me at the drafting table with a silly smile."

Tony chuckled as Saoirse released another delightful squeal.

"How cute," Betty offered. As Luz launched into one story after another with Mara adding to them as desired, Betty wondered how the child managed to crawl around the house with an extra appendage hanging around her abdomen. She wondered how they could all sit back and laugh as if the creature before them was a completely normal child. She wondered if Luz and Mara planned on bringing the child around town like a circus attraction, or if they planned on keeping the child hidden in the house as they did until now. She hoped they would choose the latter. When the hearty laughter died down, Mara said, "Yes. She's certainly more adventurous than I could ever be. I'm not sure where she gets that mischievous spark, her father I suppose."

"Her father? You know who he is?" said Betty.

Tony cleared his throat, picked up a plate of cake, and offered it to his wife. "Would you like to try some cake, honey? Luz said Mara made this herself."

"Tony," she reprimanded, "Can't you see I'm talking?"

"I think you'd like some cake, honey."

"No, I would not. If I wanted some cake, I'd have some."

Tony's eyes flicked to his sister, but she shook her head. He sighed, plunged his fork into the cake, and popped it into his mouth.

"No, I don't," said Mara.

"Well, why don't you find him then? We can do a paternity test. Go to the police. If he's anything like Saoirse he would certainly be a decent fellow. A child needs a father as much as her mother."

"Thank you for your concern. But I've decided to start a new life here. Restwood is my home now."

"What about everyone from your past? Your parents or your brothers and sisters? They're probably worried sick about you and your child. I would die of a broken heart if my girls disappeared and never came back. I would absolutely die."

"She already said she wants to start a new life here," Tony said with a mouthful of cake. His wife ignored him. "You can't hide in this house forever. It's absolutely unhealthy for you to do so. You'll be sick. I'd be sick. I haven't seen you for months since you gave birth."

Mara nodded. "You're right."

Betty gave a hard nod and then stopped abruptly. "Wait, what do you mean I'm right."

"I've been thinking about this for a while and I've decided, for Saoirse's sake, I'll have to interact with more people in town and have Saoirse do the same so she can make new friends. I thought I'd start by inviting you and Tony over for tea."

"Mara knows how to drive. When she's ready, she can get her license. I've got another car that sits in the garage except when I go grocery shopping. Mara can use that or she can buy her own. In a few months, she'll make enough selling her pottery pieces to buy any car she wants. She's that good. By then, she'll be able to come and go as she pleases," said Luz.

Betty stared at Mara. The reality that everyone in town would soon associate this woman and her strange-looking illegitimate child with Mrs. Betty Silvan now sunk fully into her consciousness. She picked up a plate of cake and smiled weakly as she cut a tiny piece with her fork and forced it into her mouth.

"That's great news," said Tony, "Maybe you girls can stop by my office so I can introduce you to my associates."

Betty threw a sharp glance at her husband.

"Thank you for the kind offer, Mr. Silvan. I'd like to wait until Saoirse is a bit older, but we'll certainly visit you when the time comes," said Mara, "I want to thank you both for your support. I'm really looking forward to living a normal life again."

Betty swallowed her piece of cake and smiled feebly.

18

When Saoirse turned five, Mara took her measurements and began sewing a pink and white floral dress for her big day in town. The short-sleeved dress had a hole in the abdomen area that slipped easily over the parasitic twin. For the twin, Mara made a separate outfit: a dark blue long-sleeved dress, the bottom of which she eventually sewed together with the dress. When Mara was done, she hung her own outfit, a grey long-sleeved dress that fell to her ankles, beside the floral dress. Below, a pair of black flats was placed neatly beside petite brown shoes. The outfits hung on the closet door untouched for weeks until the morning before Saoirse's first day in town arrived.

Luz stood at the doorway watching Mara do a fitting for her daughter. A plastic bag hung on the crook of her arm. "She looks beautiful," she murmured.

Mara turned and blushed. "I've got butterflies in my stomach. You'd think it was my first trip to town instead of Saoirse's."

Luz walked into the room and sat on the bed. "I bought Saoirse a little something for that beautiful outfit of yours," she said, pulling out a box from the bag.

She removed its lid and Saoirse's eyes widened.

"New shoes," she chirped, "and a hair ribbon!"

"Try these on and see if you like them" said Luz, handing the ribbon over to her mother. Mara secured the ribbon on Saoirse who then ran to the dresser mirror.

"It's pretty," she chirped.

"It's pretty because you're pretty," said Luz.

Saoirse sang her words of gratitude, bounded back to Luz, and then threw her arms around her. Luz hoisted the little girl onto her lap.

"We're going to have fun tomorrow, right?"

"Right!" she chirped.

"Do you remember what your mommy and I said about those who might be hurtful to you?"

The memory of her mother taking a bubble bath together with her drifted into Saoirse's mind. As she piled bubbles onto her own head, Saoirse had asked why her mother didn't have something growing out of her belly as she did. Saoirse remembered seeing the joy disappear from her mother's dark eyes. And when she finally spoke, it was with a tense restraint. "It doesn't matter why, Saoirse. You're not any less of a person because of it. You just stand tall and know that you're my baby and I will always, always love you. You understand?"

Saoirse remembered feeling an underlying fear as she nodded.

"But remember, as much as I love you, I don't ever want you talking to this thing or treating it like it was human, because it isn't. You understand?"

Saoirse nodded again. She had stopped scooping bubbles onto her head after the exchange.

Since then, her mother had been more composed when she spoke about the parasitic twin, even explaining to her about its biological development, but Luz had been the one who had taught her how to respond to those who would be hurtful to her.

Luz pushed aside a curl from Saoirse's face and repeated herself. "What would you do if someone is mean to you or laughs at you?"

"I forgive."

"And what matters most is that?"

"Jesus loves me."

"And who else?"

"Mommy and you love me."

"That's right. We love you, too."

The next day, Saoirse skipped about in her new dress as her mother opened the rear passenger door. With an arm hooked across the neck of a stuffed bunny, she slid onto the car seat and secured her seatbelt. Mara double checked her handiwork and then slipped into the front passenger seat. As the car rumbled down the road, Saoirse stuck a hand outside the window.

"Don't stick your hand outside the window, Saoirse," her mother warned.

"Okay," she replied, snapping her hand back into the car.

"We're going to stop by the shop first," said Luz, "The streets there are lined with stores. We can shop a little and then grab lunch. You like burgers and fries don't you, Saoirse?"

"Yap—but I not sure about Sara," she said before slapping a hand across her mouth. Her mother looked back. "Who's Sara? Is she your little friend?" Saoirse wrinkled her nose and then shook her head vigorously. "No—I not sure her name Sara. She say Saoirse, but Saoirse is my name. So she must be Sara." Mara stretched her arm back and ruffled the bunny's head. It was only natural for a child to see a stuffed animal as an imaginary friend. Mara understood this but hoped her daughter would find some real friends soon.

"Is Sara tired?"

Saoirse shook her head. "But she can be hurtful."

"Hurtful? Has Sara ever hurt you?"

The little girl frowned and then shrugged.

"What is Sara doing now?" she asked.

"Nothing."

Mara studied her daughter's face. "Is Sara hurtful because she's hungry? Maybe a burger will make her happier."

Saoirse made a face. "I never see her eat. I hear her once and I tell her, 'Go away!' And she never talk again."

"What did she say?"

The little girl kissed the forehead of her bunny. "I not remember."

Mara looked at the bunny. "Maybe it's good you ignore her if she's hurtful. You'll make some new friends in town soon, all right?"

"Okay," said Saoirse.

When the car stopped, Saoirse released her seatbelt and waited eagerly for her mother to open the door. As soon as she did, Saoirse hopped out of the car, ran to a store window, and glued her face to the glass, sandwiching the parasitic twin between the glass and her upper torso. Inside the store, a gray-haired Asian lady standing behind a counter glanced at the girl and then returned to her newspaper. The little girl sitting on a high chair beside the lady continued watching the girl at the window and then spoke to the lady.

"Saoirse," her mother called, "Saoirse, let's go. Luz's shop is a few stores down."

The old lady snapped the top half of her newspaper down and then peered from above her glasses. Then her lips parted in horror. What she had thought was an ugly rag doll was the body of a deformed child. The girl at the window waved enthusiastically at her, and the girl inside waved slowly back. The old lady, still stunned at the grotesque humanlike head that dangled in front of the strange girl, did not wave back. She stared at the girl as she followed the women and disappeared from the window frame.

"You've met Mrs. Ming Hua Chen briefly before. That's her granddaughter, Ellen Hong," Luz said to Mara, "We should visit them later. Ellen is a sweetheart. Mrs. Chen is very direct, but if you look past her words, she really means no harm. Most people in town have gotten used to her candid style, and she's an excellent seamstress."

"She's funny with her mouth open," added Saoirse.

When they arrived at the shop, Saoirse clapped and squealed. The store was filled with colorful pottery pieces. Luz unlocked the glass door, and they stepped inside.

"You remember the pottery from home, don't you? Aunt Luz brings them here to sell at the shop. I don't want you touching anything, okay?"

"No touch. I won't touch," said Saoirse.

Mara took her daughter's hand and explained the process of pottery making as they admired the displays. Saoirse listened attentively and asked, "Where's yours, mommy?"

"You'll have to follow me to the front of the store for those," said Luz.

When they reached the storefront displays, Luz bent over and hoisted the girl in her arms. "These are your mother's creations. Aren't they beautiful?"

Saoirse stared at the shelves of artistic pieces. "I want to buy— everything!"

Luz chuckled. "What are you going to give your mother in exchange?"

Saoirse thought for a moment, turned to her mother, and offered her bunny solemnly. Mara nuzzled and kissed her daughter who squirmed and giggled with delight.

"You silly girl, mommy would never take a single penny from you."

A quick rapping reverberated abruptly at the window. Mrs. Chen was staring through the glass with both hands cupped around her eyes as her granddaughter stood quietly beside her. Luz set Saoirse down, opened the glass door, and greeted the grim-looking woman. "Good morning, Mrs. Chen. How are you?"

The old woman bent to her left and peered at the strange girl behind Luz. She had seen Mara a few times, but she had never seen the little girl.

"They customer?" she asked with one eyebrow raised high.

"They're my friends," said Luz moving aside, "You've met Mara before. This is her daughter, Saoirse. They stay with me at my house. Mara, Saoirse, this is Mrs. Chen and her granddaughter Ellen Hong."

The salutations were one-sided as the old woman continued to stare until her granddaughter responded, "Nice to meet you." The old lady looked down at her granddaughter and then back at the strangers. She leaned forward and then whispered loudly to Luz. "What's wrong with her?"

Luz explained Saoirse's condition and reassured the old woman that she was a completely normal child. The old lady eyed the little girl and then leaned in again. "You tell your friend her daughter will scare people. Cover the extra head. Tell her to come to my store. I make her a covering—no charge. Your friend will be happy."

Luz looked over at Mara. She was sure Mara had heard every word, but her face remained undisturbed.

"Thank you, Mrs. Chen. I'll let her know."

Mrs. Chen peered at the little girl again and then marched her granddaughter out the door. Before Luz could say another word, Mara reassured her that she knew that the old woman was just trying to help. Luz was glad Saoirse's first introduction had been a relatively positive one.

Many of Restwood's residents were already well-acquainted with Mara and had allowed her to pass undisturbed in their midst. But Saoirse's company with her mother recast her as a person of interest. The mother and daughter duo drew stares when they ate their burger and fries, when they window shopped, and when they visited a local park. Mara hunched over increasingly as the day wore on and her lowered eyes flitted left and right only when Luz pointed to something of interest. Despite her discomfort, she held on to her daughter's hand and continued on. Saoirse, on the other hand, was oblivious of the stares and whispers that occurred behind their backs. She smiled at everyone and when they did not smile back, she simply walked on with no concern. When they returned to the car, she had yet to have a stranger take away the joy of her first day out. She was happy, and she was free.

But the days that followed were not as pleasant as they began to accompany Luz more often to work and to various tradeshows. They began to do their shopping and errands around town, and they visited the local park and other recreational sites. These daily activities exposed both mother and daughter to more people, which often resulted in unpleasant verbal and nonverbal exchanges from strangers and acquaintances alike. Saoirse gradually grew to understand the meaning of these mannerisms so that her cheery demeanor became more tempered as she grew. Her ecstatic outbursts of delight, which frequently startled and even frightened people, were soon confined to the home or to the time spent with her newfound friends Ellen Hong and Charlie Strong, a pudgy freckle-faced boy whose parents owned a bookstore across from Luz's shop.

Fortunately, like everything new or strange that had become familiar, Saoirse's physical deformity was soon largely ignored by the residents of Restwood. Her exposure to ridicule was further alleviated by Mara's choice to home school her daughter. Saoirse was a quick learner with an innately curious nature and was often found poring over volumes of books. She loved to read and she asked questions about everything, everything except her mother's mysterious past.

Her silence was a result in part of having once witnessed her mother's rare episodes of relapse. It was the only one her mother had had since her birth. She had found her mother wandering in the backyard among the thorny rose bushes mumbling about sin, purification, and death. This encounter, along with her mother's collection of painted dreams that seemed to emerge, grow, and spread like a poisonous weed—dreams that her mother had confided in her were likely snapshots of a forgotten past—had been enough to keep the young, loquacious Saoirse from digging into her past. That is, they were enough to keep her from doing so until she turned seven. When she turned seven, Saoirse finally believed her mother well enough and the timing safe enough to broach the subject of her past. Saoirse didn't need to know everything about her mother's past. She just wanted to know everything about one person: her father.

19

Grey clouds loomed overhead and covered the afternoon skies like a swarm of locusts. A few cars splashed through soggy streets, and fewer shoppers ambled along wet sidewalks. Mara was inside the shop sitting on a stool carefully unwrapping layers of old newspapers that had been secured around the pottery pieces. Behind the counter, Saoirse was studying her mother as she sat sprawled across its glass surface. She moved her pencil across the paper accordingly and then raised her sketch before her. She made a face. Saoirse tapped her pencil on the counter and then finally spoke her mind.

"Mom, what do you think dad was like?"

The rustling of newspapers stopped. This was the third time in the past month Saoirse had asked about her father. Though their prior discussions had produced nothing; here she was, pressing her mother again for what she could not provide.

"I thought we discussed this, honey."

Saoirse planted her chin on the counter and stopped tapping her pencil. The room remained devoid of rustling newspapers. Mara knew her child. Saoirse was not one who gave up easily when it came to unanswered questions. She waited as the pencil hovered over its sketch.

"But even if you don't remember, what do you imagine him to be like?"

Mara sighed. She finished unwrapping the clay jar and arose. With her chin still resting on the counter, Saoirse rolled her emerald green eyes up at her mother as she sat across from her.

"Your father, I imagine, must be a persistent, unshakable man. A person who presses on and on and who refuses to give up without a fight."

Saoirse popped her head up. "Why would you think that?"

"Because I have a persistent, unshakable daughter. You certainly didn't get those traits from me."

Saoirse whined. "Mom. That's not true. You're persistent and unshakable, too. You didn't give up on me when you found I wasn't born right."

"That's different. Mothers never give up on their children," said Mara.

Saoirse smiled and poked her mother's arm with the tip of her eraser.

"So maybe he's persistent and unshakable. What else?"

"Your father is probably a handsome man with wavy light brown hair and kind, emerald green eyes. I imagine he loves to give lots of hugs and kisses, is quite bubbly, loves to read, and probably bakes a mean blueberry muffin."

Saoirse whined again. "Mom. Aunt Luz is the one who bakes a mean blueberry muffin."

Mara thought for moment and then agreed. "But you do like to help Aunt Luz when she's cooking and baking, so I bet you can make a pretty mean blueberry muffin soon all by yourself." Saoirse giggled. "Besides, cooking and baking is not something I particularly enjoy, not the way you seem to. So I imagine your father is a good hand in the kitchen. And he's probably got a mind like a sponge, too. Mine's leaky."

"That's not true, mom," Saoirse argued, "You're a sponge too. You just don't know how smart and wonderful you are."

Mara touched her daughter's face tenderly. She was often astonished at the words that came out of such a small child. Saoirse was lovely in so many ways. Her face radiated a natural beauty that drew the eyes of strangers like the splendor of wild ocean waves. In her seven short years, Saoirse had also developed an affable charm and wittiness that had been able to disarm the few who looked past her deformity. Betty Silvan was one of the few. It took a few years until she finally opened up to the child; and Mara suspected she even secretly loved her to be visiting so frequently. She smiled. What a priceless gem she had been blessed with from her splintered past. She wasn't sure if she wanted the pieces put back together again.

"Do you regret not having a father?" she asked gently.

Saoirse thought for a moment. "I don't know. It depends on how my father is as a father. If he's hurtful—no. If he's not—then—maybe. I'm just curious I guess."

The raindrops that had plunked hard one by one suddenly quickened, scampering across the rooftop like a herd of running feet. Thunder cracked overhead, startling both mother and daughter. Mara placed a hand on her chest and muttered, "Goodness. That was loud."

Outside, thick clouds had completely covered the sky, an unusual sight for the summer months of Restwood. Heavy rain fell onto roads and slapped against the window. Mara stepped off from her high chair and walked to the window with Saoirse following behind. She glanced at the clock and then stared into the darkness. The store will be closing soon, but Luz had not yet returned. She had left for the bank more than three hours ago.

"I wonder why Luz hasn't come back yet."

Saoirse looked up at her troubled mother. "Don't worry, mom. God will take care of her."

Mara nodded as she continued peering into the darkness, and then she berated herself silently for being so easily frightened. She turned and walked towards the back of the room. She needed a cool splash of water to refresh herself.

"I'm going to the restroom, Saoirse. If anyone comes, just call, and I'll be right out."

"Okay," she chirped.

A moment later, the bell at the entrance jangled. A man holding a limp newspaper over his head ducked into the store. The man threw Saoirse an impatient glance and tossed the newspaper into a nearby trashcan. He brushed raindrops off his black priestly garb and then straightened his collar. A silver cross fell across his chest. The man combed his blond hair with his fingers as he watched Saoirse with a pair of pale blue discs buried deep in his skull. Saoirse stared back, mesmerized by his eyes. They were beautiful, and they reminded her of the eyes of wolves. She placed her pencil down and greeted the man.

"It's raining cats and dogs out there, huh. I have some paper towels you can dry yourself with."

The man's eyes searched the store cautiously.

"Where's your mother?" he asked with a deep voice.

"Mom? She's in the back. I'll go call her."

The man took a step forward. "You do that. And hand me the paper towels."

A draft of cold air prickled Saoirse's skin. She shivered and mumbled about the sudden drop in temperature. Then she reached for the roll of paper towels behind her.

"You're a priest, aren't you? I recognize the white collar."

She turned around with the paper towels and paused.

"Sir, did you know your cross is upside down?"

"My what?"

She pointed at the silver cross. "Your cross. It's hanging upside down."

The man responded with an icy smile. *She's keen.*

"What's your name?" asked Saoirse.

"Bedlam. Father Bedlam James. And what is your name, little girl."

"Bedlam. I've never heard of a name like that. My name is Saoirse. Nice to meet you, Bedlam."

The man's eyes narrowed. "Saoirse. That's a pretty name. It's a shame your parents never taught you some manners to match that pretty face. A horrible shame. Do you go to church my dear?"

"No—I mean, yes," she replied, wondering what she had done wrong.

"So you do know there is a god and god demands that you respect those whom he has placed over you."

Saoirse stared at the roll of paper towels in her hand. A flame of hatred was kindled in her breast, but she remained silent. *Yes. That's it. That's what I want from you.*

The man smiled.

"It's good you are silent, my child. I'm going to teach you some important lessons. The first lesson for you is that I may wear my cross any way I please. The second is this: I'm not your little brother, I am a priest. So your unconsecrated lips are never to touch my first name. To you, I will be Father James. Understood?" The man's pupils widened, virtually swallowing his pale blue irises.

Saoirse allowed the man's words to sink in as she reflected repentantly upon her error, but she couldn't help but shrink away from the man. Aunt Luz had also once explained the importance of referring to the pastor at God's Grace as Pastor Tom instead of Tom. Saoirse had not been upset by this exhortation to respect pastors and priests, so she couldn't quite understand why she felt anger and possibly even hatred for this stranger. She wished the man would simply go away. There was something not quite right about him. Something not quite right.

"Yes, Father James," she murmured.

Saoirse climbed down her chair with her shoulders sagging and her eyes lowered. As she circled around the counter with the roll of paper towels, the man recoiled from her with horrified delight. Saoirse followed his eyes, which now looked like steel blue rings, to the creature that dangled before her.

"I was born like this, sir. I mean, Father James, sir. I'm just like everyone else except for this," she said defensively. Saoirse did not see the eyes on the creature's head open. Its bright green eyes searched for the man's steel blue rings. The man trembled as he tried not to smile.

"Don't touch me, you filthy girl."

The eyes on the shriveled head snapped shut. Saoirse cringed and took a step back. "Mom," she called out. For the first time, she felt very much afraid. Slowly, she backed into a chair, which tipped over and knocked a bowl off its display, smashing it to a million pieces.

Mara rushed out and cried, "Saoirse! Are you all right?"

Saoirse whimpered as she rushed towards her mother and buried her face in her leg. Mara comforted her daughter and then looked back at the man. The man looked at her grimly.

"Is this your child?" he demanded.

Her eyes moved across his slick hair and over his broad shoulders that towered over hers. His clam-shaped eyes, thin lips, and wide and square jaw startled her. The man looked very familiar.

"Did you hear me?"

"Y—es," she stammered, "I'm sorry, sir, but do we know each other?"

Good. That's good.

The man frowned. "No, and I'm not from this town. I was just stopping by to get directions."

Both mother and daughter shivered from an icy draft when the man took a step forward.

"What's your name?" he asked.

"Mara Ekklesian. This is my daughter, Saoirse."

"Mrs. Ekklesian," he said calmly, "I would like to ask you a question that is more important than the exchange of mere pleasantries."

Mara blinked.

"Do you know Jesus Christ?"

"Yes. I'm a Christian. So is my daughter"

The man nodded grimly. "That's good. Very good. Have you ever read verse thirteen and fourteen of proverbs twenty-three?"

"I've read the whole bible, sir, but I don't remember those particular verses."

"Let me help you, then, my child. Verse thirteen and fourteen exhorts us to correct our children, to even beat with the rod, for their salvation. For the rod does not kill, but hell—" He chuckled. "Do you believe in beating your child, Mrs. Ekklesian?"

"If Saoirse does anything wrong that requires her to be spanked, I would do so. But I've never beaten my child with a rod, no."

"Fair enough. Many prodigal children require more than just the distastefulness of iron to return from their wanderings. Some have been rebellious unto death. Judgment comes to those who flaunt their sins. It would've been better that these prodigals be beaten within an inch of their life if it means they don't burn for an eternity. But my next question for you is—can you see what it is that your child has done wrong? Or is there something that is preventing you from seeing? Maybe something that you've done wrong in the past? Only when your eyes are opened will you be able to apply the most appropriate punishment, am I correct?"

Mara's heart began to pound as confusion swirled in her breast. A sense of desperation to reply appropriately to this man clenched her throat. "I—I don't know. I might use a rod if—if it would save my child. I would use anything to save her. But Saoirse has never done anything to require such punishment. Has she?"

"I don't know. Has she? I pose this question because of what I see. Your daughter's deformity isn't a birth defect. I sense something darker, something sinister. I don't want to frighten you. But I would rather you and your child be saved than to go to hell, so I will leave you to consider my words and to inquire from the Lord. That is all."

The man looked out into the darkness.

"I must be going now," he said.

"No! Please. Stay. Help me—I mean, I thought you needed directions, sir. And it's raining hard out there. Won't you wait a while?" she pleaded.

The man scanned the streets outside as if he were looking for someone. He shook his head. "I must leave now," he said. Without another word, the bell on the glass door jangled and the man disappeared into the night. A moment later, it jangled again when a woman with an umbrella entered the store murmuring about the strange weather.

Saoirse erupted, "Aunt Luz!"

"Sorry I'm late girls. I bumped into Mrs. Toori at the bank, and she invited me for tea. You know how that goes. Anything exciting happen?" she asked.

Luz followed Mara's frozen gaze and then looked back at her. "Mara?"

Mara was still staring outside. "Did you see a man walk out just as you were walking in?" she asked.

"There wasn't a single soul anywhere around the store. Was he a customer?"

"He was a man of God," said Mara.

Saoirse scampered to the trashcan by the door and looked in. It was empty.

****

Weeks passed but neither Mara nor Saoirse could shake the man from their minds. Saoirse had been teased and ridiculed by adults and children alike, but no one's words had ever bore into her soul as the words of the stranger. Her ordinarily cheery demeanor disappeared, and she shied away from both friends and strangers, something Luz had never seen her do before. Although she missed playing with her friends at the store, Saoirse often made excuses to stay home to avoid running into the man again. Saoirse didn't quite follow the words exchanged between the stranger and her mother, but she knew that the conversation involved her physical deformity and some kind of sin and punishment. She also knew that the words of the stranger had muddled her mother enough that she suffered an episode of relapse shortly after.

Mara was also bewildered by the stranger's suggestions about her child and herself. And like her daughter, she had also avoided going to town for fear of running into the man. There was something very familiar about the man, too. Mara was sure she had seen him once before. She was thinking constantly of him now, replaying the events of that day over and over like a broken record. The confusion of his words swirled in her in the daytime. And in the night, it brought on a torrential flow of dreams, dreams which she spent more and more time in the workshop capturing on canvas and paper.

Luz had also been troubled by the strange behavior of both mother and daughter. But Mara's silence about the matter had left Saoirse hesitant to reveal her own confusion to her.

Saoirse sat cross-legged on the floor of her room looking for some release from the chaos in her mind. She studied the creature on her lap. Her mother would not want her speaking to it, but she was alone now. It would be harmless for her to talk to it just this once, wouldn't it?

"Mom has gotten worse. She's been sitting on her bed at night staring like she did with the rose bushes. I wish I never brought dad up." She paused as she considered the events. "You think that man might have been my father?" She studied the creature's motionless face, and then her own face slowly twisted with anger.

"I hate you. It's all your fault. You mon—"

Her heart stopped. The creature's eyes had rolled underneath its eyelids. She was sure of it. Saoirse examined its face for further movement. There was nothing. She rose abruptly and ran, but the creature would not release her. It would never let her go.

20

Saoirse wrinkled her forehead as she scooped her spoon into the soggy cereal. Her mind had followed after Luz when she left the dining table to check on her mother. Saoirse had no appetite, but she served herself a bowl of cereal for Luz's sake. When Luz returned, her face was clouded.

"Your mother's door is locked. She's probably still in bed. Let's skip service this week."

"But we haven't been to church for three weeks, Aunt Luz. And weren't you supposed to meet with the youth group today?"

"I know, but I'm worried about your mother."

"I'll stay with her. Mom'll be okay. And Uncle Tony and Aunt Betty are just around the corner."

A subtle uneasiness flitted across Luz's mind. And then she sighed. "Maybe you're right. Worrying will do us no good. You have Uncle Tony and Aunt Betty's number, don't you?" Saoirse nodded. "Call them if you need anything. Anything at all. I'll come home right after the meeting. Maybe all she needs is rest. Having me hover over her wouldn't help."

Saoirse gave her a smile of assurance.

****

Her eyes fluttered open drunkenly. Her mind was heavy and her body ached with exhaustion. She looked down at her bloody hands. Crimson paint had stained them and soiled her bed sheets and comforter. So—she had visited the workshop again. Today was the sixth straight day she had been awakened after an endless barrage of nightmares. For six straight nights at the hour of three thirty-six, Mara had felt called, almost compelled, to assemble in the workshop below. There she would spend her morning hours moving pencils and paintbrushes in chaotic, frenzied strokes, capturing her dreams. Then, at the exact hour of six, she would be released. Though Mara vaguely remembered rising from bed, she never remembered the dreams she captured in her lost hours. She never remembered her dreams until she returned to the workshop and removed the bed sheets that covered her artwork. Mara had kept the artwork of her last six days well-hidden, though she didn't quite know why. Luz was not one to pry.

She yawned and ran a stained hand across her blood-shot eyes. The summoning of the night was taking a toll on her body and mind. She propped herself up on the bed.

"Saoirse," she cried weakly.

No one responded. Mara slid off her bed and staggered to the dresser, reaching blindly before her. She grabbed a hold of a chair, sat down, and massaged her head until she realized it was Sunday. Then she forced herself to rise, unlocked and opened her door, and then shuffled back to the window. Luz's car was gone. She dragged herself back to the dresser, sat down, and closed her eyes. She reprimanded herself. How could she have slept straight through service?

That's because you hate going to church.

Mara frowned. Her mind had not been very clear lately though she had been in silent prayer when she was awake, when she ate, as she moved, and when she slept. Unceasing prayers of penitence for some sin she had yet to discover but that she knew must be the reason for her exhaustion and despair.

Hello, Mara.

Her mouth had not opened, but she was sure the words were spoken in her own voice. "Luz?" she whispered with her eyes tightly shut.

No, Mara. I'm much better than your precious Luz, and even more precious than your beloved Saoirse. You haven't forgotten me, have you?

Mara opened her eyes slowly and peered around the room. No one was with her except the woman in the mirror. The stranger in the mirror opened her mouth.

You can't hide from me, Mara. I can make you see me even with your eyes closed. You will see who I am, because I am you. The real you.

Mara dug her fingers at her skull and grabbed two fistfuls of hair.

"Go away," she growled through gritted teeth.

Mara. Mara. Mara. You know you can't hide from god forever. God knows everything. He sees your past. He knows your sins. I have to commend you though. You've buried them well. So well you've even erased the god you sinned against.

"Who are you? Why are you doing this to me?"

The stranger in the mirror crooned. *Mara, I'm here to help you—to remind you of who you really are. After becoming a born again Christian twice, you must want the truth, don't you?*

Tears welled up in her eyes and dropped onto her hands. She no longer resisted the stranger. She did want the truth. At all costs, she wanted the truth, because she loved God.

There's really nothing to be afraid of if you know who I am. I'm here to help you. I'm here so that you might be purged of your sins. Sins you had wiped clean from your memory.

"What do you want me to do?" she whispered, loosening the grip on her hair.

There now. See? That's better. I don't want to hurt you. Just close your eyes and relax. Mara obeyed. *Relax. Will you let me take you to where you need to be?*

"Yes," she whispered.

At her consent, the darkness of her mind quickly permeated the pores of her skin and the orifices of her body. She opened her mouth to scream but was choked by a thick, black liquid that seeped down her throat. A moment later, the light within was extinguished.

When she opened her eyes again, she found herself standing under the soft lights of a church building, trembling. Though she stood in the back pews long enough to be noticeable, the pastor continued preaching as if she were not there. Mara sat awkwardly down and then searched the building for familiarity but found none. As she scanned the sea of faces, she suddenly recognized an eighteen-year-old girl sitting on the same pew a few spaces away.

The girl was dressed in a white long-sleeved blouse buttoned to her neck and tucked neatly in a skirt that fell to her ankles. A gold plated cross hung below her collar.

"That's—that's me," she whispered.

She had known God as a child after all. The girl peered at the pastor from beneath long, dark hair. When the next verse was read, she turned the pages of her bible, glanced up at the pastor, and then returned her gaze to the man sitting several pews before her. Mara followed her gaze to a dark-haired man who was watching the pastor from behind large square glasses. The man was tall, broad-shouldered, and bore a strong, square jaw that complemented his formidable presence.

The sea of heads suddenly tittered, startling her. She looked at the pastor who was recovering from a joke and then returned to the girl. The girl was chuckling, but when she stole a quick glance at the stern man, her smile faded.

The voice that sounded like her own spoke. *Do you see anyone you know?*

"I see me," said Mara.

Indeed, you do. But she cannot see you. The voice pressed her again, *Do you recognize anyone else?* Mara shook her head. *Keep looking my dear,* said the voice.

The girl suddenly rose and then walked down the aisle through the sanctuary doors. Mara stood up and quickly followed after her down the hallway and into the women's restroom. The girl placed her bible aside and stood in front of a mirror. Mara watched as the girl's reflection morphed. Her clothes turned into rags and her arms and neck were covered in bruises, her wrists slashed. The girl in the mirror spoke. *You can't hide. He'll know you for who you are.*

"But I'm not what my father says I am," the girl argued, "I'm a new creation in Christ, and I did what I had to survive."

Really Mara, you never have to do anything. You could have looked for a job or begged for bread. You could have stayed, but you chose to run away.

The girl remained silent.

You ran and became what your father knew you to be. You sold yourself to every man on the street, just like your mother.

"But I got off the streets, and I found a job, and—and I've accepted Jesus into my heart."

The girl in the mirror giggled hysterically.

A leopard can't change its spots, sweetheart. You are what you are. Man never forgives. And man never forgets. He'll know.

"I don't believe you. Jesus died for me. If God forgives me, then so will William. He'll see me for who I really am. I love him, and I don't care what you say."

Mara frowned. She loved him?

Angry tears covered her face as the girl rushed out of the bathroom. Mara hurried after her, but the girl had already entered the sanctuary. She quickened her steps, but as she raised her hand, the double doors suddenly parted. She drew back in bewilderment as the eyes of the congregation turned towards her. Then, in a slow, rhythmic flow, Mara took one step after another into the sanctuary. She looked around in a dazed stupor. The sanctuary seemed to have shrunken in size, allowing enough room for only two hundred faithful believers. Clothed in black and shades of grey, the grim-faced congregation gazed at her. They were different from the churchgoers she had seen earlier. They seemed to loom over her like a shadowy mass of human bodies.

Mara looked down at herself. She was wrapped in a lacy white wedding dress buttoned to her collar, and her hands were secured around a bouquet of roses. A melancholy wedding hymn drifted from an organ, driving her steadily down the aisle. She was unable to let go of the bouquet; she was unable to speak; and she was unable to stop herself from moving forward. She rolled her eyes around its sockets looking for the girl, but the girl was nowhere to be found. When she reached the end, she remained frozen as the pastor shared some words and then turned to the groom. "You may kiss the bride," he said somberly. The body she was held captive in turned to face the groom. Their eyes met, and in a moment, all the dreams she had captured in her artwork came alive. Mara suddenly remembered everything.

She remembered being beaten by her father. She remembered her father's frequent drunken rages about her mother's imaginary whoredom and secret infidelities that occurred every hour of the day while he was away at work. She remembered her father's indifference to the sudden and strange disappearance of her mother. She remembered running away from home at the age of thirteen and selling her body on the streets for food and shelter. She remembered being beaten and left for dead by both men and women. She remembered being beaten and cut by razors with her own hand when everyone had stopped beating her. She remembered being invited to church by a stranger, committing her life to Jesus, and trying to climb out of the gutters. She remembered working as a maid at cheap motels and saving all her money to buy a new bible, a gold-plated cross, and a new conservative wardrobe. And then she remembered marrying the love of her life: William Churcher. A man she had watched from afar when she was still a girl. A man she had never divulged her past to before she had said "I do" for fear of losing everything she had wanted. Mara looked into the emerald green eyes of the man, and blood drained from her face.

"My love, you didn't think god would let you forget who you are, did you?"

The man's words released her from her spell. Her mind suddenly connected to the cells of her body. She turned to run, but the man was quicker. He closed a hand around her arm and jerked her back. *"You snake of a demon, did you think god was smaller than your lies? He always reveals the truth to me,"* he hissed.

"Let me go. You're hurting me," she pleaded.

The man laughed. *"I'm hurting you? You brought this on yourself. Shall I refresh your memory?"* Mara fell to the ground when the man let her go.

"I didn't do anything, William. Honestly, even years before we met. The baby is yours," she cried, crawling to her husband, "You have to believe me. I'm your wife."

The man bent over and hissed, *"Don't touch me."*

She cringed.

"You're good, Mara, I have to say. You are very, very good. No one suspected you to have done such sick, vile things. Not little Miss Mara with her sweet smile, her neatly ironed dresses, her passion for the bible, for passing out tracts, and even for helping with the children in Sunday school. You couldn't keep the lie in your own church, could you. You had to follow me to mine. Well you sure did fool me, Mara. You sure did. If I hadn't bumped into one of your old clients, why, we would have gone on living that lie forever. I've always wondered why you had so many scars on your body. Now, I know. You deserve every one of them."

"I didn't lie to you. I told you my past wasn't right, I just never told you the details, and you never asked so I thought you wanted the past to stay there. That's why I never asked you about yours. I would've told you about my time on the streets. I would've."

"So you're putting the blame on me now, are you? That's just like you to point the finger at everyone else but yourself. You did this. Not me. You. You belong in hell with your mother."

Mara grew quiet. "But Pastor Tom—Pastor Tom and Luz said Jesus died so we might be reconciled with God."

"Pastor Tom will say anything to keep his flock happy. And Luz is a liar. She's a liar and a whore like you."

"No, she's not," Mara retorted, "Luz helped me. She helped me stand up. You don't even know her, how can you say she's a liar?"

Mara began to wonder if the man who stood before her was really William. No. This is a dream. This isn't real. She was having another nightmare.

"*Stand up*," said the man.

"I can't."

The man's eyes narrowed. "*You don't have a choice. I'm ordering you to stand up*," he growled. Mara forced her quaking legs to stand as she whispered, "This is a dream. This is only a dream. I'll wake up. Everything will be fine."

"*I want the truth from you. Did you sleep with another man while we were married?*"

"I'm—I'm sure I—"

"*Don't play with me. Did you sleep with another man while we were married?*"

"I—"

Had she slept with another man and simply forgotten? Was Saoirse another man's child? But whose child was she? Her mind searched for an answer. She wanted to give him the truth. He was a man of God after all. If she lied, he would know.

"I—I don't know. I don't remember."

"*You lie. You were a whore. That kind of perversion never leaves. The demons can be reined in like wild dogs, but never removed. The bruises and cuts on your body are proof. You knew what you kept in that bag of skin, but beating it and cutting it wasn't enough. That's because they come back. They always do.*"

William was right. Why else would she have wanted to die for as long as she could remember? She had tried to free herself from her past, but she could not erase the memories. She could not erase her father. She could not erase the men. And she could not erase death. Death haunted her. She had tried hard to be free of her demons, but they always came back, so she had had to rein them in. She had beaten them and cut them, so she might save herself. They were evil, the demons of her sin. And they deserved to be punished.

But nothing seemed to ever be enough. Mara had reduced the cutting considerably when she married, but the compulsion continued. It continued even when she read her bible and attended church religiously. It continued even when she was married to a godly man. It took the complete erasure of her memories and a new life with Luz to be free. But now, she remembered everything. She was back to where she came from. William was right about her, just as her own father was, too. She could never run away from who she was. It was God's punishment for who she was.

Mara fell to her knees and cried hysterically, "Then save me. Save me from myself. I'll do what you want me to do, I'll say what you want me to say, I'll beat myself harder. You can lock me up if you have to. Just help me. God help me."

The man looked at the sobbing woman with disgust. *She's exactly where I want her to be. It won't take much now. Just one gentle push.*

A voice suddenly pierced through the darkness.

As the song about God's love continued, golden flecks of light fluttered in and drew near the man. The man frowned as the flecks of light settled on his shoe. The thick, black liquid the shoe was composed of ignited and smoldered like the embers of a fire. Mara's crying gradually subsided into quiet sobs. She listened as the sweet, melodic voice pierced through the deep recesses of her mind.

"Saoirse," she whispered.

The man turned to her and spoke calmly, but quickly. *"My love, if you listen to me, I will tell you how you can save yourself."*

Mara turned from the light. "Please, tell me how I can be truly saved and set free."

"Then do this. Get rid of Saoirse."

"Get rid of Ss—saoirse is my daughter. She's—she's your child," she cried.

"Saoirse is not my child. You ran didn't you? You ran because you knew she wasn't mine."

"I—"

"*Mara, Mara, Mara. Why do you keep lying to me? Are you saying that you didn't run?*"

"I—I don't know."

The man's eyes burned with green flames. He gripped her arm and squeezed it hard. "*Stop lying to me,*" he snarled. Mara cringed. The embers on the man's body flickered and began to spread, eating the black liquid with fire. The man lowered his voice but spoke quickly as the melodic voice continued.

"*You want the truth, don't you? I alone possess the truth. Saoirse is not mine. She's the diseased fruit of your adulterous affair, a child born with a demon woven into her flesh because of sin. The doctors can only explain what they see, but they can see very little of what truly lies in this world. Get rid of her. Stop her from singing. Or not only will she burn in hell, you will too.*"

Mara covered her ears and shut her eyes. "I don't believe you. This isn't real. Get away from me," she sobbed.

As she cried out, the man burst into flames.

The singing stopped. A muted voice floated into the darkness in which Mara drifted.

"Mom?"

Her heart skipped a beat.

The voice spoke more urgently. "Mom! Are you all right?"

"Saoirse?" she called out. Mara opened her tired eyes, and the light stung them. She held the swollen side of her throbbing head. Saoirse showered her mother with questions. "Mom! Mom! What happened? Why are you on the floor?" Mara did not answer. She dragged herself to the foot of the bed and propped herself up on the bedpost.

"I'm going to call Uncle Tony," said Saoirse.

"Don't. I'm fine. Really."

Saoirse could see that her mother was not fine. Everything in her screamed to call Tony, but she knelt beside her mother instead.

"Why were you on the floor? And why do you have paint on your hands?"

"Paint? I was sitting on the chair by the dresser and then—I must have fainted and hit my head. I thought I heard your voice. Was that you singing?"

"Yes. I was in the bathroom. Did I wake you?"

She smiled weakly. "You did. But it was good that you did. I was having one of my nightmares again. I had a dream about a man, but it was only a dream."

Mara looked tiredly up at her child. "What time is it? Has Luz returned? I need to speak to her." Saoirse looked at the clock on the wall. As she did so, her mother's eyes settled upon the misshapen head that lay on her daughter's lap. She frowned. And then her face grew pale. The eyes on the misshapen head were open, and they were following her. Mara screamed.

Saoirse's eyes grew wide and then filled with tears when her mother drew back.

"It's me, Saoirse."

Mara tried to dodge its gaze. "Stop following me. Get away from me," she cried.

Saoirse began to cry.

"It's true," Mara whispered, "My dreams. They were all true. I remember everything now. Those eyes. They belong to a demon."

Saoirse looked down at the creature, but its eyes were already closed.

"Mom," she whimpered.

Her mother's face darkened. She was a different person with her memory back. She rose and pulled her daughter roughly to her feet.

"We have to get out of here before Luz comes back. I have to do what god wants me to do. Pack your bags," she ordered.

Saoirse whined. "I don't want to go."

Mara grabbed the little girl and shook her like a rag doll. "How dare you. I'm your mother. You do what I tell you to do."

Saoirse was too afraid to cry. She met her mother's wild eyes and gave a frightened nod. Both mother and daughter packed quickly. Clothes, shoes, blankets, and other necessities were thrown into bags and loaded onto the car in the garage. Saoirse packed her sketchbook and art supplies and hid them underneath the bags. When she returned to the house, her mother ordered her to stay in the car.

Mara ran up to her room, grabbed her envelop of savings, and dropped some money for the old car along with a note. Then she ran downstairs, locked the door behind her, and slid the house key underneath.

****

The car rolled onto a maze of freeways and roads, passing unfamiliar cities and towns, but Saoirse remained quiet and submitted to her mother's every request. Almost two days have passed, and she wondered if Luz and the Silvans were looking for them. Saoirse studied the creature that lay peacefully on her lap. She felt a growing urge to stab her fists into its head. She wanted to rip the creature out of her. She wanted it to suffer. This vile, loathsome creature had destroyed her happy life. She could kill it with one blow. Just one. But she was too afraid. Their fates were interwoven into a twine of misery. With its death would come hers, and she didn't want to die. She wanted to live.

Saoirse peered at her mother from the corner of her eyes, afraid that any sudden movement might revive the strange behavior that had taken over her days ago. Maybe the long drive would change her mind. She hoped and prayed that her mother would remember everything good she was leaving. Luz Ekklesian. Tony and Betty Silvan. Ellen Hong. And Charlie Strong. The happiness and joy of family and friends. The peaceful, settled life of a small town. The love of a kind and merciful God. She didn't understand why her mother would leave everything good for something that looked very, very bad. She wished she had never encouraged Luz to leave her alone with her mother. She didn't think something like this would ever happen.

As Saoirse prayed silently, Mara swerved the car onto an off ramp and exited the freeway. The little girl's heart leapt with hope. She waited for her mother to turn the car around, to say that it had all been a big mistake, but her mother did not do so. The car continued down a winding road and took one last turn onto a narrow roadway that led to an old, whitewashed house. Mara parked the car and muttered, "Stay in the car."

The soil of the front yard was cracked dry. Patches of weeds grew underneath what little shade the house and a few solitary trees offered. Mara walked up the steps of the house and knocked on the door. No one answered. She thumped harder and called out for a woman. The woman would be able to provide her a place to stay, a place to think and to decide what to do next with Saoirse. They had been friends before she married, but Mara had not spoken to her for years. She thumped the door again; but still, no one answered her call.

She walked to a window that was cracked slightly open and peered through. The house was empty except for pieces of broken furniture. A ghostly layer of dust covered its insides. She turned and leaned against the wall. The money she had saved would not last if they continued staying in motels when night fell. This place will have to do. She turned around, grabbed the handle of a window, and yanked hard. The old, decaying frame groaned underneath her pressure. Flakes of rotting, whitewashed wood crumbled onto the floor; but still, the window would not budge. This one was secured well. Mara walked to another window, took a hold of its handle, and yanked. The window shifted, permitting a slit of entryway. Just her luck. She tugged and jerked at the frame until it gave way. The old dilapidated house exhaled a breath of stale air, and then Mara climbed in and unlocked the door.

21

Hand-sewn curtains were drawn over locked windows all around the old house. Inside, two white bed sheets that hung on wires divided the one-roomed house into three sections: two bedrooms and a common area. A cheap wooden cross hung over the door frame of the house, overlooking the rooms. Behind a bed sheet, an old mattress lay on top of the dusty floor. A folded blanket was placed on one end of the bed while Saoirse's clothes, sketchbook, and belongings were placed at the other end.

The bed sheet across from Saoirse's room was partially drawn. This room also contained a mattress along with Mara's clothes and personal belongings. A body occupied the mattress with its pale feet pointed heavenward. A cloud of flies circled above.

In the kitchen, the pantry door was chained and secured with a lock. A small voice called out from behind the door.

"Mom?"

And then it was silent.

22

The night air seeped through the cracks of the door. Saoirse lay on her side staring at the feeble flame flickering on a stub of wax. She didn't need the light to see, but the flame comforted her. Only a few more hours of light remained. Saoirse knew she should be saving the candle, but she couldn't help it. She felt so alone, and she missed her mother.

They had lived together in the house for three months. When the envelope of cash had run out after two, her mother was still somehow able to support them both. She never knew what her mother did or where she went in the midnight hours to raise the money to feed them. She only knew she hated seeing her mother return home with her hair disheveled and her dresses wrinkled and sometimes torn.

One early morning, Saoirse had heard her mother whispering through the door as she pretended to sleep. A man who she guessed worked with her mother had followed her home. The man had pleaded for something more, but she had dissuaded him, and he had left. Saoirse couldn't quite hear what the man wanted. She only knew that she was afraid for her mother, and she was afraid for herself. She didn't want her mother to work anymore. She felt as if she recognized the woman who returned in the early morning hours less and less.

On their last day together, her mother had possessed a serene lucidity that had cheered her and yet somehow unnerved her deep inside. Mara had prepared beef stew, her favorite dish, and purchased sliced fruits and fresh baked French baguettes. She had set the food on a blanket she had laid underneath a tree outside, and they had shared the meal together as mother and daughter. In the months they were together, her mother had been afraid of touching her, treating her like a person who had contracted an infectious disease. But not on their last day. On their last day together, Mara had caressed her face as an adoring mother, and Saoirse's heart had ached at having forgotten what it was like to be loved. She had missed her mother so much, even while they had lived under the same roof and even while they had shared the same room.

When evening came, Mara had taken her daughter's hand and led her into the empty pantry room. She had explained to her that because of work, she would be gone for a few days and that the pantry room was the safest place to hide. Saoirse didn't question her mother. There were days when her mother did not return home from work until the following night. She also remembered the stranger who had followed her mother home. Saoirse knew her mother was doing what she could so that they might survive. She did not question her when she found a roll of tissue and a tin bucket inside the room. And she did not question her mother when she set a box that contained some food, a jug of water, candles, and a matchbox inside the room. Saoirse was simply glad that she had her mother back for a day, and she resolved not to do or to say anything that would upset her. She had watched her mother close the door and secure it with what sounded like metal chains. But she was not afraid. She knew her mother had done so to protect her. She knew she would be back to unlock the chains.

The flame had shrunken to a small, oval glow. Melted wax bled from the stub and merged with a plateful of wax puddles. Tomorrow, there would be no more light. Saoirse had run out of food two days ago, and now only a cupful of water remained. She hoped her mother would return soon. She was hungry and the stench from the tin bucket had grown unbearable. She would try calling to her again. Maybe her mother had simply forgotten. She hoped her mother was just outside. She hoped her mother was home.

23

The fiery sun beat down on the old house, scorching its dry, rotted timber. The air in the pantry room grew thin from the summer heat. Beads of sweat connected and dribbled down Saoirse's emaciated frame as she lay curled near the door. Strands of hair, wet with perspiration, clung to the angles and curves of her face as she sucked greedily at the air. The body of the creature lay cradled in her abdomen. Its eyes were wide open. And it was waiting.

"Mama—help—God."

Your mother is dead, Saoirse. Soon, you will be too.

"No. Go—mama."

Her lips opened and closed like a fish gasping for water, but no sound escaped.

24

The muffled sound of a deep voice echoed in her mind, followed by muted thumps.

"Hrrruuuuu. Hruuuuuuuuu. Mms Bttteeee rrrruuu errrre."

"Hrrruuuuuu."

Saoirse did not open her eyes. All she wanted was to sleep. She fell drunkenly back into the darkness where the thumping disappeared.

25

The police broke through the door but rushed back out as quickly as they rushed in. The stench of decay from inside choked their lungs. An officer staggered to the end of the porch and heaved. "Dead body in the house. Looks like a woman," someone yelled. A short, thin man who had been speaking to an officer holding a notepad turned and stared wide-eyed at the speaker.

"No—no that can't be. Mara and I were together about a week ago."

"If you say your relationship was what it was, how did you know where she lived?"

The man looked absentmindedly at the officer.

"I—I followed her home about a month ago. I was hoping for more, more of a relationship than, you know, what I asked her to do for money. Mara was beautiful, and she was someone you could love. She made me promise to never come here again, but I couldn't help it."

"So why did you follow her again."

"I didn't follow her. I just hadn't seen her for a while. I was worried. Her car was here and I called out to her for a couple days, but she wouldn't open the door, so I called you guys."

An officer shouted, "Check and see if there's anyone else around. A child maybe."

Inside, a burly officer pounded on the pantry door.

"Break the lock will you, Jack?" he said.

A young officer snapped the lock, removed the tangled chains, and opened the door. Light flooded into the room.

"My god," said Jack.

The burly officer knelt down and turned Saoirse around.

"She's still alive. Hey there sweetie, can you hear me?"

"Wait, Matt. There's something on her."

The officer lifted the creature's limp body and examined it. "It's attached to her. She was probably born with it. We need a medic here now."

The burly officer turned and frowned. "Stop staring and move your ass."

The man turned back to Saoirse. "Can you hear me, sweetie?" he said.

Saoirse's eyes fluttered like frantic butterflies. "Dirsty—Waddur—Mama—"

"We're gonna take good care of you, sweetheart. Just stay with me, all right?"

Saoirse focused on the man.

"What's your name?"

She moved her mouth, but her jaws felt like jelly, "Maaa. Where—Ma."

"You're looking for your ma?"

She blinked.

"We'll find her. What's your name?"

"Ss—saoirse," she slurred.

"Saoirse. That's a pretty name."

The medics secured her onto a stretcher and rolled her outside. Saoirse was tired, but she forced herself to stay awake. The curtain to her mother's room was partially drawn, and several officers were examining a woman dressed in her mother's navy blue dress. A pale hand was sprawled on the floor with its fingers curled heavenward.

Saoirse whispered, "Mama."

As the stretcher rolled across the room, she could hear the men conversing.

"Looks like she died swallowing acid. Pretty much burned everything inside."

"Well she deserved what she got, locking her child in the room."

"She's a whore, Hank. What do you expect? Did you see the girl, though? She's got this thing on her that looks like a monster from a sci-fi flick. Her ma probably thought she wouldn't make it without her, so she tried to take her along."

They were the last words Saoirse heard before she closed her eyes.

Outside the house, the officer concluded his interview.

"Never knew she had a daughter," said the thin man, "I was planning to check on her a little later, too. Guess someone up there was looking out for the kid."

PART III

26

The streets in the sparsely populated neighborhood were empty. Everyone in the small community was still sleeping. Underneath a wooden board propped against a tool shed, a large but emaciated stray dog nosed a blanket aside and emerged from its hiding place. The dog stretched, yawned, and then trotted toward the open window where it last saw its most recent benefactor. It let out a low woof at the rendezvous and waited. The benefactor stirred on her bed but did not reply. The dog released two more signals: woof-woof. Still, there was no reply.

The incessant scratching on the walls outside finally woke her. Saoirse did not want to get up, but she knew that if she didn't, animal control would soon be called. She wished she had never offered the dog her Bologna sandwich the morning before, but she couldn't help it, it looked so sad. She had been afraid of the dog, a German Shepherd that possessed all the intimidating attributes of a pure breed, but it had been quite clever, lowering itself to the ground, crawling to her, and then rolling about and wagging its tail. She had offered the dog half her Bologna sandwich, and for that, it had followed her home. Saoirse built a shelter for the dog by leaning a board against the tool shed and then covering it with a blanket. Now she wished she had never done so. She knew her parents would never let her keep the stray. She would have to convince the dog to leave tonight if it still wanted its freedom.

Saoirse rubbed her eyes and leaned over the window sill. "You're gonna get me in trouble if you stay here," she lectured, "Wait here." The dog sat dutifully and waited.

The floorboards of the house creaked as she snuck into the kitchen. Saoirse opened the refrigerator door and looked over its contents. The roasted chicken tempted her, but her mother would notice and she didn't want to risk being questioned and thereafter disciplined. Saoirse stashed slices of bread and rubbery meatloaf in a plastic bag and tiptoed to her room. She looked outside. The dog was still sitting dutifully, waiting. Saoirse grabbed her house key, climbed out her window, and gestured for it to follow. The dog trotted behind her as she crept from shadow to shadow. At the front of the house, she walked briskly on the brightly lit road, hoping her parents would not awaken and see.

When she reached an empty crossroad at a comfortable distance from her house, she sat down and presented the bag of food. "Sorry, doggie. This was all I could take without getting an earful from Alice," she said. With its head lowered, the dog padded toward her, sniffed at the food, and began slurping the portions into its mouth. She studied its frame as it ate. The dog stood just below her hips when she stood, and though it was thin from a lack of nourishment, its frame was sturdy and wide. The dog must have once stood regal, bold, and strong. But now, it quivered at everything. She wondered what it had gone through to be afraid of an eleven-year-old child.

"You can't stay. They'll call the pound if you do. You'll have to leave right after you're done." The dog licked its lips. The food was delicious, but it had come to Saoirse for something more. She stiffened when it lowered its head and crawled towards her. Saoirse had kept a safe distance from the dog since they met, so its slow crawl toward her brought fear and uncertainty. She kept her arms raised like an apprehended criminal, but when the dog was close enough to nose her thigh, the soft parts of her heart triumphed. She lowered a hand and stroked its head.

"I know how you feel," she said quietly, "I know how you feel."

Saoirse carried on a conversation with the dog until its eyes grew heavy and closed. Then she said, "I have to go now, doggie. I'll get in trouble if they know I'm out." The dog opened its eyes and raised its head. She picked herself up.

"Time for you to find a real home now. Shoo."

The stray dog stood motionless, waiting for her. "Go. Scat," she cried, waving at him. The dog cowered, scurried a distance, and then looked back. Saoirse repeated the process until it finally complied. The dog had gone through this before. It understood.

Saoirse moved furtively within shadows as she approached her home. She searched her parents' window upstairs for any sign of movement, but the lush green vines that snaked around the stone walls in front of the house made it difficult for her to see. Saoirse slipped around the back of the house to her bedroom window. She jumped, caught the ledge, grunted as she pulled, and then let go. She tried a second and third time without success. She would have to enter through the back door. Saoirse tiptoed through the back door and across the living room and then froze. She could see the silhouette of a man in the dark shadows.

"Where have you been?" said the man.

She stopped breathing. Her lips quivered, but no words came forth.

"I only like to ask a question once. Where did you go."

"I went out for a walk, sir."

The man unraveled his fingers and rested his hands on the black leather armchair. "A stroll in the middle of the night. Were you alone?"

"Yes, sir."

The man studied her face.

"Straying was a weakness of your mother's, and rebellion her greatest sin. I intend to make sure you do neither as long you live in this house. You're my responsibility now, Saoirse."

Her heart quivered from dread and a flicker of fury, but her face remained somber and remorseful. It was what was expected of one who had sinned.

"Go to your room," he ordered.

Saoirse walked to her room, closed the door, and let her breath tumble out from her quivering throat.

The man in the living room was still thinking. He was troubled by Saoirse. Sneaking out in the middle of the night was a step towards rebellion. He rose, trudged up the stairway, and walked into his bedroom. His wife was patting her rollers in front of the dresser mirror. She spun around when she saw her husband's reflection.

"Well? What was she doing running around like a shameless woman."

"She was taking a walk."

"Taking a walk was she." The woman sneered, "You and I both know she wasn't taking a walk at three o'clock in the morning. That girl was with someone."

"I didn't say she was alone."

The woman's eyes widened with salacious interest.

"Really," she said, "who was she with then?"

"What not who. She was with the stray I was going to get rid of today. She walked the dog out and returned home alone."

The woman peered at her husband. "I doubt that was all, William. She must have been wandering around with someone, you know, like Mara."

Her husband's face darkened.

"Alice," he said.

The woman shut her mouth. William Churcher was not a man to be trifled with.

Alice and her parents had been faithful, upstanding members of their church, a congregation of two hundred, for as long as she could remember. When William Churcher first arrived, he was in his mid-thirties and still single. Though his parents were both deceased when they were introduced to one another, Alice knew from what she saw of him that he was a man with moral character, someone who would fit very well with her background and needs. But Alice could not compete with the mysterious and now infamous Mara Mergos, the woman who had "found" her way into their fold after William had visited another church for a few months. Alice never liked Mara. She was one of those women who looked good on the outside but was rotten on the inside. There could be no other reason why a person's past remained so mysteriously vague as hers did. Alice knew she could not win as long as those skeletons remained hidden. She watched miserably then as Mara snatched away the man she loved. Now, she has had to raise a child birthed from the same sordid woman she despised.

At first, she could not understand why her husband would ever want to raise a child that was not of his flesh and blood. When the authorities approached him, he had accepted the child without question and without a paternity test.

"This is about God," he had explained.

Alice knew, for her husband, it had always been about God. William pitied the moral failings of his first wife. He reasoned that if he could salvage any goodness through the child's redemption, it would be worth the trouble of taking her in. He would set rules and he would make sure those rules were followed. Then he would raise a godly child from the ruins of sin. The idea of caring for a prodigal sounded godly and reasonable, so Alice had agreed reluctantly, though this had all been decided before they had actually seen the demon that accompanied Saoirse.

The child's introduction into their lives had been especially hard for Alice. She had believed that as long as she provided food, shelter, an education, discipline, and prayerful exhortations for the Lord to continue disciplining the child where she had been deficient, she would have exceeded her duty. Saoirse had been relatively simple to care for when she was young. She had been reserved and largely compliant, completing her schoolwork and chores while Alice visited around town. But Alice had grown annoyed at seeing her face every time she returned home. She shuddered whenever her eyes fell across the strange half-smile on the face of the creature. And she was especially afraid that Darren Churcher, the son birthed from her husband and herself would be infected from living with the child of an adulteress.

Both Alice and her husband knew that Saoirse was born defective because the blood that carried the sins of her mother flowed in her veins. But only her husband believed that such evil could be controlled. Alice did not. Alice could not imagine the lifetime burden of standing as a watchman over a child whose veins coursed with pure rebellion. All she desired was for Saoirse to leave the Churcher home, or even better, for her to be forced to leave without the option to return.

She looked away from her husband and mumbled a quick apology.

"Unless I bring her up myself, when I say I never want to hear that name in this house, I mean it."

"I'm sorry," said Alice. Tears of angry humiliation covered her face. She wiped at them with a trembling hand.

William looked down at his impetuous wife, a woman who was quick to anger, quick to laugh, and quick to cry, not unlike the weaknesses of too many women he knew. This flaw had been one of the reasons why he had initially not considered her as a suitable partner despite her excellent moral upbringing. Until the discovery of Mara's sordid past, his first wife had simply been more compatible.

Though reserved, Mara was calmer and possessed the compliant nature he required. Moreover, while William had never been very intimate with either one of his wives, he still recognized beauty. He had been denied of beauty once with Melinda Newborn. Everyone had laughed at him, taunted him, and ignored him. No one had ever believed that he would ever marry, so he prayed. William prayed daily that God might bestow upon him a wife worthy of his godly devotion. Thus, when Mara came into his life, he believed her to be the one and received her without question. The deception.

William had lamented over his folly since then. He had resolved not to ever relive his father's greatest mistake, but had done exactly that with Mara Mergos.

He waited patiently for his wife to calm down, and then he wrapped a hand around hers. This rare gesture of affection startled her. Her heart quivered and swelled with a longing for more. Though she yearned for her husband's touch, Alice had learned to restrain herself. Anything more required her husband's invitation. Her eyes fell across his chest, and she trembled with anticipation as he leaned in. "I know what you're thinking," he whispered.

Her face grew hot. William was a man who received revelation from heaven. She was always afraid he could read her thoughts, because her thoughts were not always pure.

"You do?" she squeaked.

William withdrew his hand. "Of course I do. Saoirse will be disciplined. Proverbs twenty-three, thirteen commands us to."

Alice stared at her husband. He had taken a turn somewhere in their step towards intimacy.

"I know you want what's good for this child. But you don't have to carry all her burdens just because I'm at work. Tell me, has Saoirse done something to upset you?"

Tears welled up in her eyes as she nodded with painful agreement. Her husband knew her so well, even better than she knew herself. Alice leaned against her husband's chest and cried.

"I'm just tired of homeschooling her," she said, wiping a tear away, "She's slow to understand, and I can't make pie out of rotten apples. I can't handle her myself anymore, William. She needs the church's covering."

William frowned. "We've been through this before, Alice. The church will know when I feel it's time."

"But when will it ever be the time? I can't even discuss her with my parents. They can't even come over unless she's locked in her room. I'm being driven mad here. She's not normal. That monster on her isn't normal. And I don't have any experience casting away such spirits."

"Saoirse is not demon-possessed."

"Possessed, oppressed, haunted by, draped over. Does it really matter what word I use? I see what I see on Saoirse. And what I see scares me."

William had to agree. The doctors had been wrong about Saoirse. They understood only what they could explain. But there was more to this world than what could be seen with the human eye or understood with the human mind. Though he did not believe Saoirse required an exorcism, the creature was clearly not normal. But his wife irritated him.

"You don't trust me? I'm your husband. I may not be a pastor, but the church depends on me," he snapped.

"I do trust you. Completely. But Saoirse will be a woman soon. And it'd be nice to have the church help keep an eye on her. It's Darren I'm worried about. Darren is our son. Ours."

William's face was grim. He had delayed Saoirse's introduction to the world so that she might be disciplined and trained to overcome the curse of her mother's blood, and he had kept his eyes on the creature all the while. Though the creature did appear to have grown some, it had remained motionless and silent, a good sign she was still clean. If Saoirse obeyed him, then she would be safe. The church would know that he had done well as a spurned husband, a compassionate father, and most importantly as a man of God.

"I'll keep my eye on her. And God will help me. You've warned Darren, haven't you?"

"Every day. He's never to be near her even when I'm in the room."

"Good. It won't be long. I promise."

****

When she could no longer hear the muffled voices upstairs, Saoirse clasped her teddy bear close and curled on her bed. She wished she hadn't gone out so late at night. She had upset her father again. And she had seen in his eyes the familiar look of unsurprised revulsion—a look that consumed the most fragile parts of her inside. She had seen the same pair of eyes among strangers and among the children in the group home she had lived with as the authorities searched for her father. The children had been particularly nasty, descending upon her like a pack of wolves, wolves that squabbled with one another prior to her arrival. Saoirse had learned to grow calloused from the eyes of strangers and the fists of her peers. She had even grown to expect them. But she wasn't prepared to receive them from the family that took her in.

The group home supervisor had reassured her that her father and his new wife were upstanding citizens with a child of their own. She had informed her that she was one lucky girl, renewing in her a hope that she would once again know what it was like to be loved. The ecstatic delight of her expectations bubbled over so much so that when the supervisor waved at the arriving family, she had raced to them with the quick sprint of a baby gazelle, eager to bestow a hug. She did not see her new mother gasp with horror and search her husband's steady gaze for assurance. And she did not see her new parents grip the shoulders of their son. She only saw her mother flash a rigid smile, a smile that seemed to invite her for a warm hug.

As she raced toward her brother, the shock of a girl with a hideous creature bouncing on her belly frightened him. Saoirse heard the little boy scream, "Get away from me, you monster!" And then a pair of hands drove into her chest. She tumbled backwards on the grass as the boy ran screaming and crying to his mother. She lay on the grass, stunned and speechless. Tears from a deep well of sorrow filled her eyes, but a voice spoke harshly to her then. *Stop crying. Do you want to go back? Is that what you want?* Saoirse stopped, bewildered. Her eyes flitted around, and then rested on her parents. They stood before her grim and unmoved. Saoirse wiped the tears that escaped, swallowed the rest down, arose, and dusted her pink and white dress. The first day she met her new family was the last day she saw her mother's handmade clothes.

That evening, Alice had gone into her room, removed all the clothes that had allowed the creature to hang freely and replaced them with a wardrobe of baggy clothes and cloaks. Saoirse did not want to part with her mother's clothes, but she had a father and a new mother now. She wanted them to like her and eventually to even love her as her own mother once did.

For weeks, she sought to engage her new family. She was always following one person or another with her presence or gaze. She smiled often and frequently tried to engage Darren in games and conversation, but Alice had cautioned her son to keep his distance. Darren did not need to be warned however. The little boy was already dreadfully afraid of the fiend that hung on Saoirse. After he screamed "no touch" a few times, Saoirse simply stopped trying to befriend her brother.

Weeks after moving into her home, Saoirse's ardor dissipated. She became quiet and reserved, withdrawing from her family unless her presence was requested. She confined her leisurely activities to her room and passed her days within the house like a phantom. The

Churchers much preferred Saoirse in her reticent and subdued state as they no longer felt the burden of expectancy hovering over them.

Saoirse wiped her tears into her stuffed animal and pulled it close.

You should have seen this coming, but you only think about yourself, don't you—selfish, selfish little girl.

Her face wrinkled. Did she just say that? The voice did sound like her own. She touched her lips with her fingers. They were clamped shut just as she thought they were. It was definitely not her who had spoken.

You should pay more attention to what I say.

Saoirse pulled her blanket to her nose and peered into the shadows of her room. Beads of sweat sprung across her face. She was terrified, but screaming for her parents was not an option.

Don't be stupid Saoirse. I'm a part of you.

Saoirse withdrew to the headboard of her bed and pulled her pillow before her like a shield. The voice giggled, bouncing off the walls of her room. Saoirse was not sure whether the laughter echoed in or outside her head, but she was sure now the voice was not hers. She squeezed her eyes shut and began to pray, hoping that God would actually answer. She had stopped praying with such expectations long ago. God might have once found her worthy enough to answer, but that had been a past with her mother and Luz, a past of innocence and goodness where she loved God instead of questioned his very existence. She was no longer the same Saoirse; but in her desperation, she clung to just about anything.

"Please don't let it hurt me. Please."

Stop that, the voice commanded in a tone six octaves lower.

She stopped praying.

The voice spoke to her tenderly. *I'm here to help you. You must trust me.*

"Who are you?" she whispered.

There was no reply.

"Why are you hiding from me if you're here to help."

The voice giggled. *Look down.*

Saoirse searched the wrinkled bed sheet in front of her pillow.

"I don't see anything," she said.

Move the pillow away from you and look down. Saoirse pushed the pillow aside and looked down.

Finally, said the voice.

She lowered her legs that were folded close and stared at its impish face. Its emerald green eyes and wet parted lips gleamed in the bright moonlight.

You're not afraid of me now are you? I've been with you all your life.

Saoirse stared at the creature in astonishment. Its lips had remained motionless even as it spoke. The voice laughed.

You should be pleased I haven't moved much. Your life would be hellish if I did.

The floor above groaned and creaked. Saoirse glanced nervously at her ceiling and door, wondering if her parents had heard the voice.

They can't hear me. I only have an audience of one.

Her eyes flitted to the creature and then returned to the door.

You should trust me. I would never lie to you.

Gradually, Saoirse straightened her legs underneath the creature, shifting it about like a rag doll. Its arms hung limply to the sides of her legs, and its legs remained straddled across her torso. Only its eyes moved.

"Wh—what do you want from me?" she whispered.

My dear Saoirse. Is this how you speak to someone who knows everything about you, your father, your mother, Alice....

"You knew my mother?" she whispered.

The skin around the creature's beady eyes crinkled as if it smiled, but its lips remained still.

Indeed, I knew your mother very, very well.

"And my father, too?"

I know everything about you. I know your past, your family history. I was there when you rose and when you fell asleep. I watched you very carefully when you were born.

The creature held her complete attention. What was this thing? An angel? An alien? Surely it wasn't God. God would never present himself in such a grotesque package. Besides, he would never rest in her anyway. She was always making mistakes and always sinning. Her chest tightened at the thought. She wasn't going to think about God now. He was always angry at her. And he had ignored her all these years. She had performed her customary prayers and she had confessed her sins before she slept. This was her time now.

Saoirse considered her mother. Had her mother been mistaken when she ordered her to ignore the creature? It had been so long ago. She had forgotten her mother's reasons for ordering her to do so. The creature lured her in with more sweet and curious treats.

I know your real father, too.

"My real father? William Churcher is my real father."

The skin around the corners of the creature's eyes crinkled. *Is he really? Let the truth in when it comes. You are quite the beautiful child, Saoirse. Very much like your mother.* The voice smiled grimly. *He just loves that smile of yours.*

Saoirse smiled shyly. Did the creature mean to say that underneath her father's stern exterior, he loved her smile? Or was her real father a man she did not yet know?

"What do you mean my real father?" she asked.

In time, Saoirse, in time.

The creature shut its eyes and the voice spoke no more.

"Hello?" she whispered. The creature did not reply.

Saoirse wanted to awaken the creature. The creature had whetted her appetite. She reached out, touched its arm, and then drew back in astonishment. Her finger had pressed into the arm of the creature as if it had pressed upon her own. She felt it. This had never been true before. For years, she had bathed the creature and dressed it daily without feeling any tactile sensations on herself. But after their verbal exchange tonight, this no longer held true. Every stroke and every puff of wind that touched the creature's body touched her own.

The change made no imprint of concern on Saoirse though. There was only one thing on her mind now. Her father. She tried again. "Hello? Are you asleep?" The creature remained silent. Saoirse waited a moment longer before she finally curled onto her bed. She studied the creature and then rolled on her back, allowing it to lie on her belly as she pulled a blanket over them both. She reviewed tonight's events. Maybe she had imagined the conversation in her fatigue. Maybe she was dreaming. Gradually, her eyelids grew heavy and closed.

Cricket chirps and night sounds floated into her dreams. She wrinkled her brows and tugged at her blanket until the head of the creature was exposed. The creature lay peacefully listening to her heart beat with its green eyes wide open.

27

The Churchers rarely brought Saoirse out in public, but when they did, it was always to a city or town where they didn't risk seeing anyone they knew. When Saoirse turned twelve, her father brought her to Lottie Wright's tailor shop. That was when her world changed.

Ms. Wright was a skilled seamstress and an old family friend of the Churchers. When her only son, Jed Wright, had gotten in trouble with the law, she had borrowed a sum of money from the Churchers when her son had moved back home. "Bad friends will bring Jed a slow death," William had warned as he handed her the money, "Sin is a disease, easily caught from one infected. Jed needs a father figure in his life. Let me speak to him."

Ms. Wright had accepted the proposal gratefully and arranged for the two to meet. Their first meeting at the church met with failure when Jed slipped away just as the choir began their second hymn. Their second meeting had been held at the old woman's home. While Ms. Wright was preparing refreshments, William had preached about an eternal damnation that awaited the young man if he did not repent. When she returned, she found William sitting grim-faced and alone.

"Your son is in more danger of being forever lost than I had previously believed," William had said, "The only way for him to be saved now is for him to fall. When he's in the lowest pit eating pods that are fed to pigs, he will remember."

Ms. Wright watched her son fall into the pit of hell as he shuffled in and out of jail until, at the age of twenty-two, he simply left home and disappeared.

At the second lowest point of her life, William had been by her side reassuring her. "You did what was right, Lottie. There was nothing you could do but to let him go." Though, at her lowest point, when the police requested that she identify the body of her son, she had been alone.

"Get on the apple box, Saoirse," Mr. Churcher ordered.

Saoirse stood on the apple box with a cloak draped across her shoulder. Ms. Wright studied the child as she hobbled around the apple box. The Churchers were gathered loosely around Saoirse while Darren sat in a corner of the tailor shop reading.

"She's a beautiful girl, William. I see no flaw on this child, except for this ugly rag," clucked the woman as she flicked the black fabric.

William smiled grimly. "Looks can be very deceiving."

The old woman raised an eyebrow and stepped aside as William drew near the girl.

"Pull aside the cloak," he ordered.

Saoirse lowered her eyes and pulled the cloak aside. Underneath, she was dressed in a long-sleeved blouse and skirt. The creature, dressed in a separate outfit, was bound securely to her torso with leather belts and twine. The eyes of the creature were closed, but its mouth was parted and wet in the corners. The old woman recoiled.

"What in the world—"

Saoirse flushed crimson red.

"She was born this way. The doctors say it's a twin that never fully formed," said William.

"It doesn't have a life of its own though," Alice added, "It's like an extra arm or finger."

The old woman stared wide-eyed at Saoirse and the corners of her lips plunged in disgust. She was not a fearful person, but there was one thing she very much dreaded: those who carried demons within and those who bore them on their backs. She did not believe what the doctors said of this child. Saoirse was a carrier.

Ms. Wright had seen many of them in this world. But she could count in only one hand those she had seen in her church over the years. Her church, the same congregation the Churchers attended, was a safe haven. Carriers rarely ever stayed there for more than a day. And she could always tell who they were. They were covered in tattoos and strange piercings. They were prostitutes who had no shame. They were killers, liars, cheaters, and simply put, heathens. They were bleary-eyed men and women with blood saturated with liquor and drugs. And they were the children born of these people. They were prodigals, all of them carriers, because they looked and smelled of the sickness of sin.

The old woman pitied these people because she remembered her son, but pitying a prodigal did not mean consorting with one, subjecting herself to possible infection. She had barely escaped the clutches of death by the bottle at one time. It was a time when the wrath of her husband still ravished her home and a time before she had joined the church. No one at the church knew. She would bring her sins to the grave.

The old woman looked at William from beneath furrowed brows. "I'm—I'm sorry, Mr. Churcher, but I can't help you," she mumbled.

William was surprised, and then he burned with indignation. The old woman had never rejected his requests.

"Does the child's deformity bother you?"

"You know I would never take your requests lightly. It's just—"

The woman looked at the child. Saoirse was not aware that William was not her real father, and the old woman had been instructed to keep this to herself, so she chose her words carefully.

"Can I speak to you privately?"

William followed the old lady to a dressing room in the back of her shop.

"Well, what is it?"

"I'm sorry, but I think that—that there's something spiritually crooked with that child. I know what the doctors have said, but they're wrong."

William's eyes flicked toward the woman.

"I know you took her in," she added, "but like you said, she's Mara's child, not yours. Can't you return her? Tell the authorities you made a mistake? You're a good man, William, and I know you've taken her out of the goodness of your heart. But as for me, I'm not as strong as you and Alice. My heart isn't as good. And— and I'm afraid of being infected."

William knew this would happen, but he hadn't expected it to occur so soon. He knew by his encounter with Jed that Ms. Wright had been more familiar with the ways of the world, so he didn't expect her to react as the rest of the congregation would. His anger subsided. He looked at the old lady patiently, almost sympathetically. He couldn't blame Ms. Wright for steering clear from the child.

She was only reacting as any God-fearing Christian that he knew would act. He spoke patiently to the old woman.

"Saoirse's deformities were caused by her mother's adulterous affair. But even so, I took her in because I believe the Lord wanted me to save her, to keep her from repeating her mother's sin. That's why I've come to you. Until now, I have spoken to no one at the church about the child or her deformity. I believe there's no need to do so just yet. Saoirse has remained clean under my watch. I believe I've disciplined her well enough for her to know that she must stay away from sin. But we can't keep Saoirse locked in the house forever. I want to bring her under the covering of the church, but it wouldn't be fair if she were judged without the opportunity to prove what lies in her heart. That's why I want the creature hidden. It may just be that the time and money we have poured into disciplining this child will keep her in the straight and narrow path for good. "

Ms. Wright mulled over these words as he continued to speak.

"I wasn't able to help Jed overcome his demons, but I hope to succeed with Saoirse. I want to make sure this one is done right. All I need is something that will keep the creature secured tightly around her so that it remains hidden."

The old lady remembered her son. "You're a good man, William. I'll help you."

They returned to the front of the tailor shop, and the old woman reexamined the girl.

"The creature is quite small and can be pressed against her body. What she needs is a corset. She'll appear slightly heavier in the midsection but will look pretty much like a normal child. As she grows, I'll have to make new corsets." She unraveled the measuring tape. "I'll have to take her measurements."

The old lady completed the preparatory steps quickly, trembling as she came within inches from the creature's deformed head. Then she excused herself and retreated to the bathroom where she scrubbed her hands with soap and hot water until they were raw. When she returned, her mood lightened.

Alice thanked the old woman and then invited her for dinner, but the old lady declined. "I'd like to get started on this right away. I couldn't save my son, but maybe I can help Saoirse. Every day that child is away from church is another day of temptation."

William rose and then dipped his head with a slight smile. As his family headed toward the door, he spoke to her in a low voice.

"Keep this meeting to yourself, and treat the child as if you've never seen her when I bring her to church. There's no need for anyone else to know about her deformities just yet. The time may come when it must be laid bare, but I'll be the one to decide."

"My lips are sealed," said the old woman.

William nodded, turned, and exited the store.

28

Alice poked through racks of dresses and coats in their various stages while Saoirse stood awkwardly on the apple box with a hand hooked to her elbow. When Ms. Wright returned with the corset, Alice was already sitting comfortably reading a magazine.

"This is just a sample. The others will be made if this one fits," said the old woman.

Alice sighed and placed her magazine aside. She took the corset from the old woman and stretched its fabric. "It's strong. Why is there a hole here?"

"Saoirse will probably be wearing these several hours a day. I know you said that thing doesn't eat or breathe, but frankly, its head looked too human for me to ignore. The hole is large enough to fit around the face of the creature, but small enough so the elastic fabric is still able to secure its forehead and chin against her body."

"This is great. William will be ecstatic when he sees this," said Alice as she handed the corset back.

The old woman cleared her throat. "I think it'd be better for you to secure the corset. Especially since you'll probably be the one doing so," she said quietly.

Alice opened her mouth to protest but the old woman pushed the corset back.

"I'll guide you," she reassured.

Her face darkened. Alice had been fortunate that she had been able to perform her responsibilities with Saoirse at a comfortable distance. This new task would force her to touch what she had avoided for years. She felt almost violated.

"Remove the cloak, belts, and twine, child. Then, lay the creature's head to one side and wrap its arms and legs tightly around your torso," said the old lady. She turned to Alice. "When she's done, you can wrap the corset around the creature. The elastic section around the opening must be positioned over its face and the laced section wrapped behind Saoirse. Always remember to keep the creature as flat as possible."

When Alice shifted the corset around, the elastic fabric caught and pulled at the creature's eyelids and lips.

"No Alice, the face must be positioned within the hole," said the old woman.

"I'm trying, but it's not working."

"You might need to move its face with your hands. The hole is quite small."

Alice glared at the old lady. "Excuse me, but I've only got one pair of hands." She turned and spoke shrilly, "Don't just stand there like an idiot. Move that ugly head of yours."

A little to the right.

Saoirse looked anxiously down at the head and shifted it to the right. The side of its face fit perfectly in the hole.

"That's good. Now lace the strings up and secure the corset tightly against her body," continued Ms. Wright. Alice laced the strings and pulled. When the creature did not cry out, she gritted her teeth with a smile and pulled even harder. Saoirse gasped.

"That should do it," said Alice, pushing a strand of hair from her face.

The old woman handed the dress to Alice who tossed it onto her daughter and said, "Put these on." Saoirse slipped on the dress, and a smile spread across the women's faces.

"Well now, that's not too bad. Her belly's only slightly thicker, and the dress still hangs loosely," said Alice.

The old woman grunted. "Not bad at all. What'll you say if someone asks?"

"We'll tell them the truth. Birth defect. They just won't know how hideously ugly she really is," said Alice. She looked thoughtfully over the child. "You know—if you could make the corset so that the strings can be secured in front of Saoirse or by her side, then she could do this herself. I can't be expected to take care of the child forever."

"I'll see what I can do," said the old lady.

"Wonderful. Where's your bathroom? I need to wash my hands."

"In the back."

Alice left the tailor shop with a newfound hope that Saoirse was one step closer to leaving home. With her husband's permission, she purchased a new wardrobe of clothes for Saoirse that was a shade lighter and a size larger. "Cloaks would only attract unnecessary attention," she reasoned with her son, "especially during the summer. After everything I've done for Mara's spawn, I'd die if anyone branded me as the evil stepmother."

The day the corsets were brought to the Churcher home was the very day Saoirse wore them.

"As long as you plan on stepping outside your room, you're to wear them," her stepmother had ordered, "Make sure it's tight. And I don't want you picking at it when you're in public either."

But Saoirse hated wearing the corsets. The strings had to be secured so tightly that it was difficult to breathe. The corners of the contraption poked at her, and during hot, summer months, the corset was almost unbearable. Saoirse always looked forward to the evenings when she could free herself from its rigid structure. Fortunately, as time passed, she grew accustomed to the corsets so that she hardly noticed they were there. By the time she arrived at the church, the corsets had bonded comfortably to her every curve.

29

William sat with his head turned aside and his right arm hooked on the wooden pew behind his son. He was surveying the parishioners as they pushed through the heavy double doors. His eyes flitted around the sanctuary and then came to rest on Saoirse who was sitting at the other end of the pew a comfortable distance from her mother. Saoirse was dressed in a navy blue dress that fell to her ankles. Her wavy hair was secured in a bun, and her delicate hands were clasped together as if in prayer. He frowned at the thought that she looked almost pure.

"Hey there stranger," said a man, clamping a hand on his shoulder. Startled, William turned with displeasure toward the presumptuous offender. He did not like being touched when he did not know who was doing the touching, even at church. A young man wearing a crisp lilac shirt with a purple tie stood over him, grinning.

"Morning Alice," said the man before he reached over and ruffled Darren's hair. The little boy frowned. "Good morning, Pastor Rick," said Alice.

William rose and turned toward the man. "Colorful outfit you have on."

"You mean this? Cheryl bought this last week. She says I should try brightening up the church a bit." The young man lowered his voice. "The wife wants me to convince people here there are clothes beside a black suit and tie and a starched white shirt."

The young man drew back and laughed. William hated the man. Rick Darton was the young newcomer who had slid into the position he had coveted for years: the church youth pastor. And though the junior pastor, Henry Keene, and William had both put aside their differences temporarily to prevent the young man from joining the leadership team, the senior pastor's decision had prevailed. William had always hoped that he would finally be found worthy of the position. He certainly had given the old pastor enough suggestions of his aspirations. So he wondered if he was bypassed simply because he had never gone to seminary school and thus was presumed to be "unqualified." Whatever the reason, William still felt the sting of rejection even after almost two years have passed. He waited patiently for the young pastor to explain himself.

"Speaking about colors…," Rick mumbled as he moved his head back and forth. "Ah. There she is. How're you doing down there, Saoirse?"

Saoirse bent forward. "Fine, thank you."

"Good. How are those sketches coming along?"

"Sketches?" she said feebly.

"I saw the sketch you did of Ms. Goodman last week. It was very good."

Her shoulders drooped. The pastor had seen her sketches? She had never shared her artwork with a single soul since her mother's death. She stole a nervous glance at her father who was looking down at her for answers. Pastor Rick looked at William and then back at Saoirse.

"Oh—well Saoirse wasn't drawing during service. A piece of paper slipped out of her bible, I picked it up and just assumed it was hers. As a matter of fact, I have it right here," said the pastor, taking a folded sheet of paper from his pocket. "Is this yours?" he asked.

Saoirse looked at the folded paper with the doodles of thunderbolts on top.

"Yes," she said weakly.

The young man nodded at her encouragingly, but William pinched the folded sheet between his fingers and said, "I'll take this."

The young pastor released the sheet of paper. "Saoirse's very talented. Her sketches are remarkably lifelike, but I'm sure you already know that," he said.

William smiled thinly.

"I, um, also discovered not too long ago that Ms. Goodman's daughter Billie is quite the artist, too. My wife and I had dinner at their house and we got to see some of her artwork. You know Billie Goodman, don't you, Saoirse?"

Saoirse turned and caught sight of the Goodman pair. Martha Goodman was wrapped in a dress that fell below her knees but could not quite contain the fullness of her breasts or its phoenix tattoo. Her face was covered with too many colors, and she was smiling eagerly at parishioners who greeted her with equal discomfort. Beside her sat her grim-faced daughter.

Billie Goodman was what every parent at the church had warned their child not to hang around with. She was a prodigal who sported spiked jet black hair, a heavy metal t-shirt, ripped jeans, and Converse shoes. A tattoo draped over her right forearm and wrapped around her left wrist. Billie reminded Saoirse of one of the group home girls who had torn all her sketches and given her a black eye. The girl glanced at her short, black fingernails and then looked up to catch Saoirse staring at her. Saoirse whipped her head back and then leaned forward.

"Not really," she mumbled.

Everything she knew about the Goodmans came from over the dinner table. The Goodmans were new to their church, and they were one of the rare ones who stayed. Martha Goodman was a divorcee and a waitress who worked in a neighborhood that parishioners avoided. Being new in town, Rick and his wife had wandered into a café, and Ms. Goodman had been their fortunate server. She had been irritable due to a persistent pain in her wrist. The young man inquired about her wrist and then offered to pray. Ms. Goodman had joked that if God was able to heal her, she would give her life to this Jesus and attend the pastor's church as long as she and her daughter remained in town. The pastor prayed over her, she felt a burning sensation, and then the miracle happened.

The very next Sunday, Ms. Goodman took her first steps into the church. The miracle made her an instant celebrity at the church. "But when the buzz faded," Alice clucked over the dinner table, "She and her daughter were left looking like what they were: strange fruit."

Pastor Rick pressed her again. "So, do you want to meet Billie?"

Saoirse looked to her father. His face was grim, but he moved his head faintly down and then up. She had once heard her father warn Darren that he was to be courteous and polite to the Goodman girl but was never to associate with her, so she was surprised when he gave her his approval. She turned back to the pastor and said softly, "Okay."

"Wonderful," said the pastor, "We have about twenty minutes before church starts, why don't I introduce you now?"

She looked to her father again but saw no response, so she rose and met the pastor at the end of her pew.

The parishioners greeted the young pastor, and a few boys stared at Saoirse as she walked by. Less than a year ago, they had tormented and teased her. But lately, she had the strange sensation that the same boys appeared to now be eyeing her with anticipation.

The boys are looking at you, Saoirse. Why do you suppose they're staring?

Saoirse bent her arms across her abdomen as she continued down the aisle. When they reached the last pew, the pastor said, "Good morning, Ms. Goodman. Hey, Billie."

The heavyset woman broke into a broad smile, rose, and greeted the pastor. Then she thumped her daughter's arm with the side of her fist. The girl dragged herself up and leaned against a pew.

"You know the Churchers, don't you?" said the pastor.

"Yes. This is their daughter—Saoirse, right? She's so adorable. You can't miss this one in a crowd."

Billie rolled her eyes.

"I thought you girls might like to get to know each other better. Saoirse has a good eye. You should see her sketches. Perfectly precise would be how I'd describe them."

Billie's eyes flickered toward Saoirse, but she remained silent.

"Billie used to have a group of art friends before we moved here," said Ms. Goodman. "They'd hike, go to the beach, or stay at the house and paint a model or scenery they chose. Then they'd compare their artwork—it was like some kind of game."

"Art is not a game, mother," said the girl.

"You're being rude, Billie. I'm talking."

"He was talking to me not you."

A steely silence settled over the Goodmans.

The young pastor coughed. "That's very interesting, Ms. Goodman. Maybe Saoirse could join Billie in her art expeditions, or maybe you two can just hang out, watch a movie. I'm a movie buff myself. You watch movies too, don't you, Saoirse?"

"I'm not allowed to. They corrupt your mind," she said quietly.

Billie threw her a strange look and then smirked as the young pastor turned a shade of red.

"Oh. Well. It's true that some movies aren't good for the spirit. But you don't really have to go to the movies. There are many things I'm sure you both will enjoy. How about it?"

"Sounds like a great idea," chirped Ms. Goodman, "Billie made some new friends in town, but none that I know who share her passion for art." She turned to Saoirse and continued, "In fact, why don't you come over to the house next week? You girls can paint or draw or do whatever it is you like."

"I—I'm not sure. I have to check with my father first."

"Oh, well your parents and Darren can come too, of course. I'd be glad to have them."

Saoirse threw a quick look at her father. He was watching her from the far corner of the sanctuary.

"Thank you, Ms. Goodman. I'll let him know."

30

She stood in front of a door, turned, and looked down the hallway at Ms. Goodman. "Not that one, sweetheart. That's her bedroom. She's in the next door down."

Saoirse walked to the next door and then looked back.

"That's it. Just knock."

Saoirse balled her hand into a fist and raised it. She wondered whether she would sound too eager if she knocked and called out a friendly hello or too aloof if she knocked and just waited silently until the door opened. Fragmented images of Ellen Hong and Charlie Strong flitted across her mind. She didn't remember making friends to be this complicated, or this stressful, but then again that had been many years ago. She wondered if the proper etiquette for making friends had changed since she last had one. She looked back at Ms. Goodman again.

"Go ahead, Saoirse. Knock. She's inside."

She pasted a smile on her face and knocked. Saoirse waited, but no one answered.

"Knock harder. She might be painting. She doesn't answer sometimes when she's painting."

Saoirse knocked again and waited. A muscle around her rigid smile twitched. Still, no one answered. Saoirse released her smile and moved aside as the portly woman stomped towards her and then pounded on the door.

"Don't you disrespect my guests, Billie. Open up this damn door right now."

A voice inside spoke. "Turn the knob."

Ms. Goodman turned the doorknob and stepped into the room. A girl dressed in a black shirt, faded jeans, and old hiking boots was standing in front of a painting, studying a wooden clock. She glanced at her guest. "Come in," she said. Saoirse stepped into the room.

Ms. Goodman surveyed the room and frowned. "I thought you were going to clean your room before the guests arrived."

Billie turned to her mother. "I thought Saoirse and I were supposed to get to know each other through our artwork. I've got a canvas there, a sketching pad here, all the paint, paintbrushes, and anything else she needs over there. Everything is in its perfect place. Saoirse is an artist. She understands, right Saoirse?"

"No, I mean, yes, yes, this looks fine," she mumbled.

Ms. Goodman peered at her daughter. "Fine, then. If this is the kind of mess you people work best in, then there's nothing I can say."

Saoirse bit her lip.

"I'll be downstairs with your parents, Saoirse. If you need anything just holler."

When the door closed, Billie brushed her nose with the back of her hand and sniffed. "It was clean before you came," she said, "Well, pretty clean anyway."

Saoirse stood by the door as her eyes swept across the chaotic room. Paint-stained newspapers were scattered across the floor and tabletops. Jars filled with paintbrushes, charcoal pencils, and pens were set alongside tubes of paint, paint-smeared books, and sketch pads on tabletops and chairs. Stacks of canvases leaned against the wall, and several strange but beautifully dark paintings hung before her.

Saoirse looked down at herself. She had arrived at the Goodman home dressed in black flats and a long plum-colored dress with her hair weaved into a tight braid, a stark contrast from the girl that stood before her. She studied the girl from where she stood. She's so honest, she thought. She hides nothing of herself.

You're the imposter, Saoirse, you.

Saoirse frowned. It was true. She was the imposter in the room. She was familiar with the destruction in the paintings. She knew them very, very well. She knew them as one would know an old enemy: an enemy without form or substance but that was rising with power and momentum since her mother's death. She could feel it in her, screaming, digging with its claws, prying itself to her surface. She had flashes of its thirst for destruction and had heard it giggle from her own lips once. There were times she imagined she could even feel it spreading into her cells like an infectious disease, eating her insides like leprous snow.

Who are you, Saoirse. You can't hide yourself from God. He knows.

The girl turned to Saoirse as she stood awkwardly in the far corner. "Guess you need a canvas, a palette, paint, the works." She pointed at a high chair with her pinky. "Grab the chair if you need to sit. I'll get the canvas and paint."

Saoirse looked absentmindedly at the girl. "I don't need a canvas. I've brought my sketching pad and pencils."

"All right, grab what you need then. The clock is the model. You can do whatever you want though. I almost never paint what I see. I paint what I feel when I see what I see. Sometimes the model is included, sometimes not. There are no rules. You can even paint the time on the back of a mad dog if you'd like."

Saoirse placed a chair a reasonable distance away from Billie, seated herself, opened her sketch pad, and began to draw. Though she desperately wanted to contribute more than just the few words they exchanged, she worked in silence. She had forgotten how to make simple conversation. Forgotten what it was she was supposed to do when making a new friend. Billie had been standoffish at church, but she was not like the girls who snubbed her entirely. The congregation seemed to be afraid of Billie, often treating the strange, grim-looking girl like a person with an infectious disease behind her back; and yet, still welcoming her like a guest in front of her though she had attended the church for months. Saoirse understood why they did so, but she couldn't quite get herself to treat Billie with the same aversion when she saw so much of the girl in herself. She hoped their afternoon together would result in some form of friendship. She actually kind of liked Billie.

As she moved her pencil in large strokes over paper, her thoughts of Billie, herself, her peers, and the church gradually faded. Soon after, the sights and sounds around her disappeared. Her eyes focused in on the clock, following every corner, curve, groove, and line like a skilled marksman. Her hand moved gracefully but still complied with the precise commandments of her eyes. *Follow the lines, Saoirse. God hates mistakes. He'll punish you if you fail. Follow the lines.*

For a long time, Saoirse disappeared into another world that consisted only of herself, the clock, and a voice that sounded like her own.

A muted sound murmured from a distance. Saoirse did not reply. The sound murmured even louder, piercing her silent, colorless world. She turned and stared blankly at the source of the noise. "Hello, earth to Saoirse," repeated the source. The world began to materialize before her. She wiped her hand over her face and peered at the source. This time, she saw Billie.

"I'm sorry. I must have drifted off somewhere. Did you saying something?"

"Yeah, for the last five minutes. Were you in a trance or something?"

"I'm sorry. I must have been daydreaming."

"Some daydreamer. I've never heard of anyone who could daydream and still sketch with such precision."

Saoirse looked down at her artwork and her face wrinkled. She was surprised she was almost done.

"Anyway, I was just saying art reveals a lot about its creator. It's kinda like an open portal into your soul," said Billie, "Hope you don't mind me looking. Guess that'll only be a problem if you did shitty work, but that's not something you need to worry about. You're good."

Saoirse looked down at her sketch and blushed.

"So did you hear anything I just said?" Billie asked.

Saoirse shook her head.

"I was just saying that you don't have to be so polite. You can use my canvas and paint if you want. I mean. I've got a lot of paint, and I can always buy more canvases. You're really good with a pencil. I'd love to see what you can do with a brush."

"Thank you, but I don't know how to paint. And—it looks too hard. I would never be able to reproduce the colors perfectly."

"You're kidding me, right?" said Billie, dropping her paintbrush on the bare floor. She swiped the paintbrush and muttered "Jeeezzuh...." but stopped short when she caught Saoirse's look of uneasiness. "I didn't say it. Almost disrespected your god, but didn't. Look, what I'm trying to say is no one is asking you to be a photographer, just a painter. You've sketched things without a tangible model right? Created things just out of your mind?"

Saoirse wasn't sure if she wanted to go any further in this conversation.

"Yes," she said quietly, "But just once."

Billie stared at her and then pushed no further. She returned to her canvas, dabbed her brush into azure blue, two strokes of white, and a touch of black.

"You're not like the rest of them, Saoirse. You're different," she said. Long broad strokes coated the untouched portion of her canvass. "You're more like me."

She dipped her brush into a glass of murky water and swirled.

"But you've got too much shit in your eyes. You're like—blind. And deaf, too."

Billie wanted to slap Saoirse over the head as much as she pitied the poor but awfully dumb girl. She looked at her with irritation. The girl was just trying her best to be a good Christian, but damn can't she see she's miserable trying to pretend she's one of them? The misery was all over her. It was bizarre that she was completely oblivious to this truth.

Her parents find her as disgusting as they find me and she can't even see it. The damn hypocrites. If there ever was a heaven and hell, I'd rather go to hell than see the likes of them in heaven.

"What do you mean I'm blind?"

Billie shook her head. "How old are you, Saoirse?"

"Fourteen. I'll be fifteen next month."

"Fourteen." She added another layer of color and smirked. "It's just so crazy for me to see someone your age be so naïve. But I can't blame you for being you. Being blind has helped you survive. You'd be eaten alive out there if you did what I would've done."

She jammed her paintbrush into a second glass of water and swirled. The clear, pristine water turned grey.

"I don't understand."

"You've been living with your parents for like fifty years. Don't you ever listen to anything that goes on around you?"

Saoirse stared at Billie as if she were searching for the answer on her face. Billie frowned, walked to her door, opened it, and looked down the hallway. When she found it empty, she locked the door, turned on her CD player, and resumed painting.

"We can talk, but just keep your voice down," she said in a low voice. Saoirse nodded. "There's been a lot of talk about you and a boy."

Saoirse's eyes flicked over to her.

"I don't normally listen to that crap, but with so many people talking about it, it's hard to ignore." Saoirse moved her pencil but remained silent. "They're saying you're getting too close to Brad, talking to him more than what's normal."

Saoirse stared at Billie. Then her eyes widened. "You mean Brad Schroeder?"

Billie shushed her. "Keep it down. The doors are thin. And yes, I mean the Schroeder boy. But that's not the important part."

Saoirse frowned. That seemed like a pretty important part to her. The thought that people believed she was interested in Brad shocked her. She tried to think of all the times she came into contact with him. She remembered exchanging a few words with him, but she didn't remember about what. She wondered if her parents thought she liked Brad. They would be her main concern.

"Go on," Saoirse said calmly.

"A few days ago, I heard Pastor Rick mention about Brad possibly taking an interest in you. Mrs. Schroeder was there along with your dad. Rick seemed to find it cute, but your father wasn't happy at all. He mentioned something about a family secret that will have to be made known if you made a single slip-up. Do you know what he's talking about?"

Saoirse thought about the creature but said nothing.

It's time, Saoirse.

"Your father really does have a good hold on them you know," she said grimly "If Mrs. Schroeder ever liked you before, you're the Black Death to her now. The way he spoke about this secret—I would've thought it was you who nailed Jesus to the cross. You aren't the only one who's clueless though. Rick was just as dumb. For me to know about this when he has been in that church longer? And a youth pastor?" She shook her head.

Saoirse stopped breathing but shrugged and continued to move her pencil.

"Look, Saoirse. I'm just gonna give it to you straight. Your dad pretty much told Rick your mother is Judas in a dress. He said your mother was a prostitute but tricked him into believing she was clean. How a man could be that dumb is beyond me. Anyway, he said she cheated on him even while they were married and then ran away. In plain words. William Churcher isn't your real father."

William Churcher is not your father. You are a child of an illicit affair.

"Your father thinks you got passed down some 'infected' sins from her. So if you're wondering why they treat you like a communicable disease, there you go. That's the reason why you've been feeling pretty much like shit. You're no different, Saoirse. When your parents see you, they see your mom, they see someone like me. You must have sensed at least some of their negative vibes."

William Churcher is not your father. You are a child of an illicit affair.

Saoirse's hands trembled as she attempted to follow the lines of the clock.

"Sorry if that hurt you, but it's better to know the truth than to live a lie. Besides, now you know, it's not you. It's them. They're the asses."

The pencil in her hand stopped. "Are you sure?" she said quietly.

"That they're asses? Hell ya. But if you're talking about whether I heard things right, Mrs. Clovis told my mom first about your story. The conversation I overheard just confirmed what I already knew. You don't have to believe me though. You can check things out yourself. But take my advice if you want to stay out of trouble, stay away from the guys."

Saoirse wanted suddenly to run—to run far, far away from her family and from the world. Voices swirled around the clear waters of her mind: crimson red with a dab of white, a dollop of black, and a drop of emerald green. *You've got sin in your blood. Obey me, and in time, I'll purify you. Then, when you're clean, I'll love you.* Hadn't she obeyed her parents all these years? Wasn't that obedience to God? How much longer was she to be purified. When would she be free and finally loved. She looked at Billie and envied her. *What would it be like to be free from the incessant demands of God. Billie is so true to herself, not an imposter like you. You're a wolf in sheep's wool, Saoirse. Let the truth claw its way out. Let it spread in you like leprous snow.* The voices clamored for her attention. *You disgust me, Saoirse. You disgust all of us. You aren't trying hard enough. Try harder. Try harder. Try harder to be good.* All the colors merging, bleeding, muddying the waters until it turned into a cloud of grey. Saoirse could no longer discern who was speaking in the grey, the grey that was quickly turning into black. *Run away, Saoirse. They hate you. They won't miss you if you're gone. Your father is not your father. You are a child of an illicit affair. Run, Saoirse.*

Saoirse cried out, "Stop! Stop! Get away from me!"

The pencil in her hand detached from her sketch pad and then she awoke as if from a dream. Billie stared at her. "Whoa, I didn't mean to freak you out this bad. I just thought the truth would help."

Saoirse touched her head. "I'm—I'm sorry. I didn't mean to yell at you. It's not you. These—voices. I do want to know the truth. I always want to know the truth."

"You sure?"

She smiled weakly. "Yes. I'm sure."

****

The ceiling fan rotated lazily, barely cooling the living room. A desk fan swung a half moon forward, shuddered spastically, and swung a half moon back. Books, art supplies, and rolls of paper were piled high in a corner. Canvases smeared with shades of macabre leaned against walls. From the couch, Alice surveyed the room with distaste, sighed, and then stuck a forkful of pie into her mouth. Her husband was studying the paintings while their host sat on the edge of her chair, unnerved by the silence of her guests.

"How's the pie?" asked Ms. Goodman.

Alice held up a finger and swallowed. "I didn't think I could fit in a single bite after your finger sandwiches. Thank you, but you really shouldn't have, Ms. Goodman. Really. We did already eat before we arrived."

"Oh, it's no trouble at all. The pies are leftovers from the diner. I bring them home every night. It's a waste to be throwing them when they're only a day old."

Alice placed her plate of pie on the coffee table.

"Do you mind if I join my husband? The paintings look very intriguing."

"Oh no, go ahead. Sorry about the clutter. Billie usually keeps her paintings in her art room, but I made her clean it before you folks came. Bad idea. She started yesterday, moving all her things into the living room. She got half way and then started doing something else. When I got home from work, it was too late. We had a spat after. I had her clean as much as she could this morning, and I tried helping her, but Billie doesn't like anyone touching her paintings."

Alice stared at her in disbelief and said, "How horrible." She peered up at the empty staircase, left her husband's side, and then sat by Ms. Goodman. She placed an understanding hand on her host, startling her with its sudden intimacy.

"Did you discipline her?" she whispered eagerly, "When a child talks back—that needs to be dealt with right away. Billie needs to know what she did was wrong."

Ms. Goodman remembered the fight clearly enough. She had screamed at her daughter when she returned home. Billie had screamed something back about her kissing the Churchers' great big behinds. And then she had slapped her daughter hard across the face with each hand. Ms. Goodman had waited for the cursing, or even for a mother-daughter brawl, but neither came. She did not know that deep in her child's mind, the violent red rage had exploded into tens of hundreds of thousands of voices pushing and clamoring in unison against the walls of her daughter's skull for blood. Her blood. She did not hear the shrieks of Legion. Billie was only sixteen, but she was more than capable of hurting a woman or even a large man in such madness.

Billie turned, and for a split second, she caught sight of a framed photograph she had taken with her mother. In the photo, a five-year-old Billie wore a crooked but happy smile. She was sitting on her mother's lap with Band aids covering her knobby knees, elbows, hands, forehead, and chin. She was supposed to be sitting on Santa's lap that day, but Billie had adamantly insisted that she sit on her mother's lap while Santa was to stand beside them both.

She remembered in flashes that just before the photograph was taken, her mother had carried her bloodied into the public restroom. She remembered her mother cleaning the wounds and band-aiding her. She remembered feeling confused, embarrassed, and pleased at her mother's rare expression of tenderness. She remembered her mother's words, "You're lucky I keep these band aids in my purse. Next time you go running off like that, you can take a picture with Santa in your own bloody red suit, you hear?" She remembered giggling tearfully at her mother's words. She remembered.

The woman in the photo was the same woman who had driven her strong, solid palms into her face. And the woman in the photo was the same woman who stood before her now. Billie forced the clamoring, screeching, clawing voices back into its cave and bolted the doors. But Ms. Goodman didn't know what her daughter had done. She didn't know that someone eventually had to shed blood for the voices to be appeased. She didn't know that if she were not sacrificed, it would be her own daughter the voices would go after next. Instead, she had simply screamed, "Did you hear what I said? I'm talking to you."

Billie had slowly turned to face her mother. When she did, Ms. Goodman had met her dead eyes: two vacant balls buried within the sockets of a lifeless body. She had felt her heart quiver in fear. And she had opened her mouth to scream. She had wanted to get something familiar from her daughter. A string of invectives. An impulsive fist smash through walls. Or even, if at all possible, remorseful, apologetic tears. Anything to show that her daughter still lived. But she had received nothing. Not a single word. When Ms. Goodman raised her hand a third time, Billie had not even flinched. Instead, she had stared straight ahead with the pair of dead eyes. Eyes that had frightened Ms. Goodman enough to put her hand down. Billie had turned then and walked back into her room. Yes. Ms. Goodman remembered the fight as clear as day, but she never knew what had gone on in her child's mind. She only knew that she hoped to never see those pair of eyes again.

She looked up at Alice grimly. "I did. I let her have it when I got back. But I think I might have pushed her too hard. It's not easy with Billie. She's got a hard head."

Alice cradled Ms. Goodman's weathered hands in her soft, supple palms and squeezed. She looked tenderly at the weary woman and spoke to her as to a child.

"Oh, but you've got to be strong," she said, "Billie is not the parent. You are. You can't let a child step all over you like that. Obedience to the Lord begins with obedience at home."

Ms. Goodman looked away. It was true. Alice was the one who was still married. Alice was the one who had the respectful children, one of which she didn't even give birth to. She was the woman with the perfect marriage, the perfect children, and the perfect life. She was the perfect wife and the perfect mother. And she walked so long and so well with God. A tinge of jealousy rose within her breast. She felt so stupid and small before this woman. Her shoulders drooped, and she looked down at her gnarled hands. She would have to try harder to be a better parent. For Billie's sake, she would try.

"It's hard to do the right thing, I know. I hate disciplining my children, too, even if a particular child is really not my own. But the fact is I do have to discipline Saoirse much more than Darren, so I do. The discipline has kept her in the straight and narrow path. You know her mother's history and what she's susceptible to. But look at her now. You've got to discipline Billie until she obeys you without question. If your child can't obey you, then they certainly won't obey God. And you and I both know that God values obedience over anything else in this world."

Ms. Goodman nodded gloomily. Alice released her and then wiped her hands with tissue papers. "Good. I'm so proud of you," she said.

****

Saoirse rubbed her thumb over her pencil nervously as she listened to Billie chatter. "I doubt we'll be in town much longer. At least I hope not. Mom says we're just here until we get the house sold," said Billie. Saoirse looked around the room. "I didn't know this was your grandmother's house."

"We sold a lot of grandma's furniture and gave away most of the other stuff. Mom put out some furniture we brought from Texas so we'd have some kind of a home."

"Is that why you've got Texas up there?" asked Saoirse.

Billie turned and looked at a collage of license plates hanging on the wall. Photographs were pasted around and on top of each plate. "Oh that. Yeah, it's an art project on all the states I've lived in. The photographs are of the friends I've made in each state."

"Can I take a look?"

"Go ahead."

Saoirse stepped off her chair and walked over to the wall. She studied the license plates and photos with awe.

"Mom could never stay too long in one state. She always moved when she found a new boyfriend or when she dumped an old one. I don't mind her moving so much though. I kind of like moving around myself."

Billie took out a cigarette from a desk and placed it between her lips. "Oh, don't look at Missouri. It's bad for you," she mumbled.

Saoirse couldn't help sneaking a peek at the one photograph pasted on the Missouri license plate. Her eye caught sight of a young man hidden behind one large middle finger raised high. She wrinkled her face. She wasn't quite sure what it was that Billie wanted to protect her from. When she turned around, her eyes widened.

"Relax, I'm not gonna light it. I just need to smell the tobacco. Besides, the door's locked." She walked to the door and jiggled the knob. "See?"

The tension that Saoirse felt with her new friend gradually faded. Saoirse marveled at Billie's honesty about her life without God. There seemed to be no secret too reprehensibly shameful for her to divulge. Drugs, sex, alcohol, brushes with the law, brawls. Though she barely knew Saoirse, Billie did not bother to hide anything or to make anything more or less than it was. She seemed free, free of pretending to be someone she was not, free of the expectations and the striving of being good, free of all the rules. She envied Billie's freedom to be who she wanted to be and to do what she wanted to do.

The truth shall set you free, Saoirse.

Billie clipped the cigarette with her thumb and forefinger and removed it from her mouth. "So tell me something about you," she said.

"There's nothing interesting to say."

"Aw, come on, you're being stupid."

"It's true. I don't go out much, I'm homeschooled, and—"

"You're what?"

"Homeschooled."

"What's that?"

"It's where instead of me going to public or private school, I get an education at home."

"Damn. Sounds like heaven. Who's your teacher?"

"My father and Alice. But mostly Alice because my father is usually at work."

"Alice? She hates your guts. Wait. They both hate your guts. Damn, your heaven just turned into hell," she said with a hearty laugh.

The questions about Saoirse's books and curriculum and about what it was like being under constant supervision continued. Though Saoirse was glad she could amuse her new friend, she chose her words carefully, keeping her remarks about her parents and the home school program on an even tone. Billie had been honest and open with her, but Saoirse didn't quite know if she could trust her. The two girls chattered on until they heard a knock. Saoirse froze.

"Billie, open up," Ms. Goodman called.

Billie slipped her cigarette from her mouth back into the drawer. Another round of rapid blows followed by a doorknob jiggle brought her to the door.

"What'd you lock the door for?" Mrs. Goodman asked, entering the room with two plates of pie. Billie's face twisted. "I locked the door?"

"Yes you locked the door."

"Oh. Didn't know I did."

"Well you kept Saoirse at least five minutes from a warm apple pie. You hungry Saoirse?"

"I love apple pie. Thank you."

"Good. Now if I could just find a place to set these down."

Billie wiped her hands on her apron and reached for the plates, but her mother withdrew them. "You're filthy. Go wash your hands. Both of you." Billie frowned but complied. She led Saoirse down the hallway, chatting and pointing to the rooms as they walked. The girls washed their hands and returned laughing, eager for some apple pie. As they entered, both girls stiffened.

Ms. Goodman hissed. "Where are your manners, Billie?"

Billie smiled thinly. "Good afternoon, Mr. and Mrs. Churcher."

Mr. Churcher's green eyes narrowed as he returned the smile. *I know your kind. You don't fool me one bit. If you were my child, I'd rip that rebellion right out of you.*

"Good afternoon," he said.

William surveyed the room, trying to conceal his disgust with its chaos. "You have quite a room here and such artwork. Your mother showed us some of your paintings downstairs. I was very intrigued," he said, exchanging a look with his wife. "My wife and I were both intrigued, so I thought we'd see how Saoirse is doing under your tutelage."

Billie looked grimly at her mother.

"Looks like they used the clock as their model," said Alice. William studied the painting with his hands clasped behind his back.

"Your work is very different. You use a lot of black, dark blue, brown, and blood red. It's very dark. Almost violent. Is this what you actually see?"

"Apparently," Billie murmured.

Ms. Goodman hissed. "Billie."

William smiled as he closed his fingers on the back of a nearby chair. The knuckles of his hand turned white. No child who belonged to the church had ever spoken to him without respect and gotten away with it. Any child whose lips went astray knew that no parental protection would be provided for defiance. *By my rod, you shall save her.* But William could not touch Billie. She had not received Jesus into her heart yet.

"I'm fine, Ms. Goodman. Billie doesn't understand yet," he said. *But she will in time. She will know that there is a God.* William clasped his hand behind his back and strolled to an open sketch pad on a chair. He picked up the sketch pad.

"Is this your work, Saoirse?"

"Yes, father," she mumbled promptly.

William studied the clock and then looked over the drawing.

"What do you think?" he asked, turning the sketch pad toward his wife.

"You drew that?" said Alice.

Saoirse continued staring at her feet. "Yes."

"I'm surprised. I never knew you could draw."

William looked at the sketch. "I never knew she could draw either."

"Your daughter is very good with a pencil and paper, Mrs. Churcher. I've never seen someone her age have the ability to copy what she sees with such precision," said Billie, "But what I'd really love to see is for her to use some color. To paint and to feel. To express her opinions in color. But of course—as her mother—I'm sure you would too." She turned abruptly. "Can we have some pie now, mom?"

Ms. Goodman handed a plate to each girl while Alice folded her hands across her chest. *You little imp. She's not my daughter and you know it.*

Alice threw a quick glance at her husband who was too busy frowning at the Missouri license plate to notice the look on her face. She took a deep breath and let it out slowly. Patience. She would have to conceal her aversion towards Billie if she wanted to achieve her ultimate goal.

"Well, I think we had a wonderful time today, Ms. Goodman. And Billie, you are an intriguing young lady, just like your paintings. I'm so thrilled that Saoirse has found a friend in you. It would be nice to see them go out together more often," she chirped.

"Why, of course," Ms. Goodman exclaimed. "Saoirse can stop by anytime."

"She's old enough now and we've taught her well. She should get out and explore. And once in awhile, maybe, Billie might come over to our house, too." William threw his wife a strange look. "I mean. It would be strange to have Saoirse over at your house all the time. So, what I mean is, once…in a while, Billie could play in Saoirse's room. Don't you think, William?"

William peered at his daughter. In a few years, she would become a woman. It was time to let her go now to see what lies within her. Billie would be her first test.

31

The voice of her stepmother echoed from the living room as Saoirse walked down the hallway. She paused and waited in the shadows with a change of clothing in hand.

"She's not going to make it, you know," Alice said in a quiet voice, "She has too much of that woman in her. She will fall."

"Then we'll just have to discipline her as we do with anyone else who sins," said William.

"What if she still rebels?"

"She won't. But if she does, she'll leave just like the others, or we'll force her to leave. But I doubt she will. She won't be able to survive out there on her own."

"What happens when she's eighteen then? You can't keep her with us forever, William. We still have Darren to take care of. I spend all my time taking care of her I don't even have time for my own child."

William was silent.

"And what about college? You know we can't afford to put her through."

"She's not going to college."

"What do we do then. I'm not going to take care of her until I die. I'll lose my sanity."

"Alice, I want you to stop."

The house was quiet.

Saoirse continued down the hallway to the bathroom and locked the door behind her. Her muscles had grown rigid as she stood listening to her parents. She let the hot water run. She would take a bath instead. She slipped off her clothes and removed her corset. Then she pried the fingers of the creature from her back and draped a washcloth over its head. Slowly, she immersed herself in the water. She sat up and laid the creature on her hand, keeping its head above water. She scrubbed it while voices clouded her mind like a misty steam.

I'll lose my sanity, William. We'll just have to discipline her the way we do the others. She will fall. She won't be able to survive out there on her own. Leave Saoirse. They hate you.

Saoirse stared at the white tiled walls. In the midst of her distraction, a hand rested on hers and pushed it away. She continued to stare straight ahead, listening. When she realized she could no longer feel any weight on her hand, she looked anxiously down. Her hand was empty. She found the creature, instead, lying against her, clutching her back with its fingers and toes. Half its face laid beneath the waterline, but its skin was still a lively pink.

She giggled and wiped her tears of pain. How ridiculous that she had panicked, thinking it had drowned. But then she was given a soft reminder.

Our lives are inextricably intertwined, Saoirse. I die. You die.

Saoirse slipped her hand onto the creature's chest and pushed it back impatiently. The creature did not move. She frowned and turned aside. Its fingers and toes were still clamped on her back, and they had grown thick and strong like that of a large monkey. Grey-tinged blood vessels snaked through its hands and arms. Saoirse pried the creature off her body, untangled its legs from her waist, and laid it back on her hand. She thought hard. Wasn't the creature lying on her left hand? She could have sworn that she hadn't moved it towards her. The creature had grown fleshier, too. And its arms, legs, fingers, and toes had grown muscular and hard. She shook her head. That's impossible. She must have simply not noticed she had moved the creature back towards her. She must have been daydreaming again.

Saoirse finished taking her bath and climbed into bed, placing the creature as far from her as possible. She wanted to have nothing to do with it tonight. It had caused her so much grief and yet she had had to keep it close every day. Saoirse pulled a blanket over them and pushed it down in between, creating an illusion of two separate beings. She had not slept separately from the creature for a long time, but it felt good to do so.

****

A pinching sensation awakened her. Saoirse reached behind sleepily and touched something cold, hard, and yet a part of her.

Her eyes popped open, and she jerked her blanket off. The creature was wrapped around her like a python. She was not a person who moved when she slept, but the creature had. Saoirse flipped on the lamp switch and turned to look at her back. New sets of crescent-shaped fingernail marks marred her skin. She remained sitting in the moonlit night. The creature had a mind of its own. It was moving. And now, it wanted more. More of her until there was only one mind: its own.

32

Billie peered into the skies from the driver side window of her forest green Chevy truck as it puttered up the driveway of the Churcher home. A few raindrops plunked onto her car and then pitter pattered onto her coat as she stepped out. Inside the Churcher home, Saoirse sat quietly on the sofa waiting for her friend while Alice glanced repeatedly at her watch.

"She's late. It's twenty past five. She said five, didn't she?"

Saoirse looked up at her stepmother. "Maybe the rain slowed her down," she offered. But Alice reprimanded her with piercing eyes.

"First time she comes over, she keeps me waiting," she muttered.

Though Alice was very much annoyed, she would be forgiving. She had been secretly delighted at the progression of their friendship, especially now that Billie was allowed to drive. Saoirse's increasing absence was worth the sacrifice of being civil, even if it meant inviting the rebellious girl to visit their house at least once.

The girls' activities had revolved mostly around Billie's home or the church for the first year. Though Billie still dressed in the same dismal attire she had always worn, the congregation saw her increasingly regular attendance as a good sign she would soon turn from her wayward ways. They did not know, however, that between the two girls, it was not Billie who was changing.

When Billie was finally allowed to drive her grandmother's old truck, the girls' adventures expanded to a few unapproved avenues. Alice would first drop Saoirse to the Goodmans' or to the library where the two would meet. Once she was gone, Billie's unsightly friends would appear and then pile onto the truck. The group would then drive to the nearest movie theater, watch the latest flick, drive back, and then disappear before Alice arrived. Still, even during these deviant escapades, Billie was careful to forbid her friends from smoking or drinking while Saoirse was around, and she even threatened a lusty male friend or two who had a few extra special plans for her friend.

Saoirse eventually learned how to drive, to take the bus, and to walk to nearby destinations under the tutelage of her friend. She was beginning to enjoy spending her time outside her bedroom. And she had even begun to speak to strangers with a new sense of ease. Saoirse realized that as long as the creature remained hidden, she was just like everyone else. She was normal. And to many who noticed her maturing features, she was even beautiful. But none of these personal changes, however, went unnoticed by her father.

The doorbell rang. Saoirse arose and walked to the door with Alice following after. She opened the door and said hello.

"Hey," said Billie before she muttered a greeting to Alice.

"Hello, sweetheart. Wet day, isn't it. I bet you had a hard time finding the house," Alice said with a smile, "Come on in."

Billie stepped into the house and removed her coat.

"Here, I'll hang that for you," said Saoirse, taking the coat.

"So, where do you girls want to stay?" asked Alice.

"My room will be fine."

"You read my mind. You girls can stay in the living room, too, of course, but I'll be coming and going, and that'll probably bother you," said Alice. She looked at Billie and then back at Saoirse. "Well then, I'll see you girls later. It's so great to have you, Billie."

Alice waited for a similarly courteous response, but when Billie responded to her with a strange look, she walked away reminding herself about the virtues of patience.

"Come on, let's go," said Saoirse.

Billie followed her friend down a long hallway and then stepped into her room. She was caught off guard with its stark contrast from her own. A few pieces of furniture occupied the room: a squatty book shelf, a desk, a chair, a twin-sized bed, and a trashcan. The room was neat and organized, but skeletal. Not a single piece of artwork adorned the white walls of the room.

"This is it? This is your room? It's so naked. Where's your artwork?"

"In my closet. I'm not allowed to tape pictures or hammer nails on the walls."

"In your closet?" said Billie. She laughed incredulously, "What is this place—a sanitarium?" Saoirse placed a finger on her lips. "But the living room wasn't like this. I saw paintings out there. And what's that about not including you in the family portrait?" Billie whispered hotly.

Saoirse shrugged. "I was probably sick that day."

"You're parents are screwed up."

Saoirse looked away from her friend, walked around her bed, and sat on the floor. Billie followed her friend and did likewise. The bed stood like a barricade, hiding the girls from unwelcomed guests. Saoirse pushed aside a blanket and slid out a tray of brownies and two cans of cola from underneath the bed. Billie's eyes brightened and then darkened.

"Why do you have food underneath your bed?" she asked.

"They're clean. I'm not allowed to bring food in my room, but I know you won't go out there because of Alice, so I had to sneak these in."

"You're weird," said Billie, grabbing a brownie and taking a hungry bite. "Whoa. This is good stuff. Real good." She put a hand on her friend's shoulder. "You are pardoned for your weirdness."

"Shut up," Saoirse said with a slight smile. Billie put a hand to her mouth.

"Oh—my—god. You said a bad word. Saoirse said a bad word everyone."

"And I'll say it again. Shut up."

Billie flashed her friend a brownie covered smile and popped open a can of soda.

Saoirse walked to her closet, grabbed a box, and set it down at Billie's feet. She removed a few books and pulled out several sketch pads and folders.

"I don't have much. I throw most of my sketches away and keep only the perfected ones. I haven't looked at these a while myself."

Billie nodded, took another bite from her brownie, and flipped open a sketch pad. "These are good. Real good."

Saoirse peeled off a piece of brownie and placed it neatly in her mouth. "Thanks."

The girls continued to critique the artwork and laugh as they munched on brownies. As Saoirse handed her friend another sketchbook, a folded piece of paper slipped from between its pages and dropped to the ground.

"What's this?" Billie asked, picking up the paper. "The paper looks old. Is it a very old, well-kept secret?" she asked, peering at her friend with mischievous eyes. Saoirse wrinkled her face, and then her eyes widened in disbelief.

In her first years with the Churchers, Saoirse had kept the folded piece of paper concealed in a picture frame, sandwiched between a magazine cutout of a forest and the cardboard backing that secured the picture in its frame. The paper was removed and viewed only when her bedroom door was locked.

One night, as Saoirse was removing the paper from its hiding place, her father had jiggled her doorknob, rapped furiously on the door, and demanded that she open her door at once. Saoirse had panicked and slipped the paper among her belongings. After opening her door, her father had barged in and demanded that she explain why she locked her door. When she tried to do so, her father had pushed past her instead and searched her room, even peering outside her window into the dark night. When he was satisfied, he had shut the window and locked it.

Saoirse remembered her father placing his face up close to hers. "Don't you ever—EVER lock this door again, you hear?" Her lips had trembled at the fear that a mistaken response would bring his fists crashing into her face. When her father finally retreated, her muscles had wilted, so she crawled straight into bed. Two months passed before she was able to summon the courage to look for the piece of paper. She searched everywhere, but was never able to find the sketch again. That had been years ago.

"What is it? A secret love letter?"

Saoirse laughed nervously. "You're crazy."

Billie pinched the corners of the paper and cracked it open. "Can I?" she said with a devious smile. In their two years of friendship, Billie was the one person Saoirse could trust in the most. And yet, she still had never revealed to her friend the most important or most shameful parts of her life. She glanced over her bed at the closed door and then turned to her friend.

"You promise you won't tell a single soul?" she whispered.

"I promise," said Billie.

Saoirse looked into her friend's eyes. "All right. Go ahead."

Billie removed the outer layer of paper, unfolded the sheet inside, and gently flattened its creases. The face of a young man, drawn with the elementary skills of a child, was scrawled on the paper. She wrinkled her face. She had expected more for her oath of secrecy.

"Very cute. Was this your childhood crush?" she asked.

Saoirse took the paper gently from her hand and turned it around. Billie arched an eyebrow. The kind eyes of a handsome, young man gazed back at them. Dark tufts of thick black hair fell over a strong, angular face beaming with a toothy smile.

"Wow. This guy is fine," Billie whispered, "He's kinda old for you, he's what, in his mid-twenties? You're not secretly dating him, are you?"

"It's not like that. He's not who you think he is."

"What then? Give me the scoop."

"All right, but it might sound a bit strange, so don't laugh. When I was eight, I dreamt of this man seven nights in a row. My drawing skills were still undeveloped then, so I sketched multiple versions of him, but none of them turned out right. When I stopped dreaming about him, my memories of him faded. I saved the drawing that most accurately represented him and tore the rest. A few years later, the man reappeared, but this time, while I was awake."

"What? You mean you saw him in person?"

"No. I was fully awake when I saw him. He was standing in front of me like a projected image."

"You're screwing with me."

"I'm serious. He just stood there while I made a sketch of his face on the back of the paper. When I was done, he disappeared."

"You've been watching too many sci-fi flicks, girl. No sci-fi movie for you."

Saoirse frowned. "I'm not joking, Billie. This actually happened." When Billie saw that her friend was serious, she looked at the man again.

"You got any idea who he might be?" she asked.

"For a long time, I didn't. But now that I know William isn't my father, there's no other reason for this person to be recurring in my dreams and visions. He has to be someone really important.

Like a person I'm destined to meet. I think he's my father—my real father."

Billie looked skeptically at the man and then back at Saoirse.

"I don't know, Saoirse. You don't look like this guy. Your face isn't as angular. Plus, he's got straight hair, not wavy hair like yours. I mean even if this man is who you say he is, so what? He definitely doesn't look like this now. He probably doesn't even know you exist."

"He'll know if I find him," said Saoirse.

Billie frowned. "Are you crazy? This guy could be anywhere. He might not even be in America. He might be in Canada or Beirut. Heck this guy might even be some actor you saw on a commercial but you just forgot."

"I'm not allowed to watch T.V., Billie."

Billie stared at her friend. "You're not…Whatever, that's not my point. My point is that it's stupid to go looking for someone you aren't even sure is your father, especially if he's probably got his own wife and kids. I'm telling you, Saoirse. If you leave home to look for him, you'll be screwed over. Your parents will kill you and you're setting yourself up for a whole world of hurt."

"You'd leave if you were in my shoes," Saoirse argued.

"Yeah, but that's me, Billie Goodman, in your shoes. I'm a lot more capable of taking care of myself than you."

"Calm down. I wasn't really planning on looking for him," she lied.

Within minutes, the flame of hope she had protected for years was extinguished. She lifted her can of cola and sipped her drink slowly as they remained in silence. Billie knew she had hurt her friend, but there was no chance in hell she was going to soften her stance. She did not want to be responsible for encouraging Saoirse—at least not now. To do so would be like egging a five-year-old to jump into a raging river. Though Billie hated the Churchers, they were much safer than what was out there. She knew. She patted her pockets. "I need a cigarette. You got one hidden underneath your bed, too?"

Her eyebrow arched when Saoirse said, "hold on," groped underneath the bed, and pulled out her hand. She opened her balled fist. A large grape-flavored lollipop.

"Surprise. Got it at the convenience store. Thought you might like it. It'll keep your mouth just as busy, and it only causes cavities."

Billie grabbed the stick of candy. "A lollipop?" She laughed heartily, choked, hacked, and then laughed some more. "How in the world did we become friends, Saoirse. I swear. In another life, I would have avoided you like the plague."

"I feel so honored," said her friend.

"Oh, I'm sorry. Not!" said Billie with a laugh, "You're just so like me and yet so not like me, too."

Saoirse smiled. *You're very good. You've fooled even your best friend. Why don't you show her all of who you are? Show Billie the true you. You're exactly like she is. No. You're worse.* Her smile disappeared as she crossed her arms over her belly. In the years they had known one another, Billie had never noticed anything particularly unusual about her friend. Saoirse had wondered often if Billie would still accept her if she bared her most hideous parts, but she wasn't about to test their friendship. She didn't want to lose her best and only friend.

Billie unwrapped the lollipop, popped the candy in her mouth, and pushed the ball to one side. "Look Saoirse," she said, taking the candy out of her mouth, "I'm not saying you shouldn't look for your father. If finding him is important to you, then do it. But not yet. The problem is, without me, your whole world is composed of a five mile radius around your house. You go to the library, the church, and on occasion a nearby convenience store. Whoopee. If you run away from home now, people are going to see right through you and take advantage of you. Remember that shady guy

who flashed you on the street?" Saoirse wrinkled her face. "Exactly.
I still don't get why he ran when I whistled. I look pretty decent.
You think it was the nose ring?"

Saoirse's eyes narrowed. "Billie."

Her friend grinned. "Anyway, the guy acted like he didn't even
see me, but he sure made a beeline towards you. Imagine what'll
happen if my friends and I weren't around." Billie stuck the candy
back into her mouth and crunched down hard.

"Takes too long to get to the chewy middle," she mumbled with
her mouth full, "What I'm saying is—get dirty. Open your eyes to
what's out there. Do things apart from your parents. Most importantly, get a job and save as much money as you can. There are
worse things than living in the dumps if you run away without
money. I'll help you while I can. Mom says the house will probably
sell this summer. That'll be enough time to get you functional."

Saoirse looked gloomily at her friend. She didn't want to think
about Billie moving.

"All right," she said, "Thanks."

33

Black leather seats in the corners of the room encircled low-
lying rectangular tables. In the back wall of the waiting room, soft
lights showcased bold brass letters of a company name. Saoirse sat
behind the receptionist desk with her head resting on one hand. A
large display of fresh flowers was placed on a table just beside her
desk. She raised her head, yawned, and then sighed. Her eyes
flicked toward the display and moved across the delicate rose petals.
Saoirse plucked a red crayon from a box and began coloring the
petals of a flower display she sketched. When she finished, she held
the sketch underneath the desk lamp and made a face. Coloring her

sketches with crayons was simply inadequate, but they would have to do for now.

Saoirse had tried painting once before. Her family had left her home and promised they would not return until nightfall, presenting her the perfect opportunity to try her new watercolor set. Her model had been a simple one: a bowl of fruits. But it had been difficult to perfect. She had struggled on one sheet of paper after another, but in each one, the colors were somehow not right. The more she pushed, the more the voices had laughed, assailing her with words that dug into the most fragile parts of her inside. Still, she had continued, persistent and relentless like a man walking through sand dunes pressing on and on until—until something in her finally snapped. In a wild and crazed rage, she had screamed. She had screamed and screamed and screamed. When the voices giggled at her deranged anger, she had lashed out, digging her nails into her skull and into the soft flesh of her face, neck, legs, and arms, ripping the skin she could catch. The parts of Saoirse she could not tear, she threw against walls, against desks, and against chairs.

And then, she spotted the mirror. The large hand mirror on her desk where she saw not her own reflection but the reflection of her mother. Saoirse had shrieked like an angry, stuck pig as she smashed her fist into the mirror again and again. The broken glass had split her hand open, but even as blood gushed from her open wounds, she felt no pain. Saoirse turned instead to the colorful sheets of paper, ripping, slashing, and tearing at them. She threw them like a child flinging dead leaves into the air and then fell in a crumpled heap, crying as the bloodied shreds floated back down and settle on her tired, broken body. Only then did the voices finally leave.

The phone on the desk buzzed, startling her. Saoirse picked up the phone and recited the company greeting with feigned enthusiasm. She looked through the name list, asked the caller to hold, transferred the call, and hung up. She turned back to the display and studied the textured colors of the leaves. She searched through the box of one hundred, plucked four crayons, and began a trial run on a separate sheet of paper. She studied each color intently and settled on the first crayon. Then, she hesitated. Saoirse looked back at the leaves in the display and considered the possibility of mixing a little yellow with the chosen green to give a more accurate portrayal. She could just imagine Billie's response if she saw her now with the box of crayons.

Though Saoirse did carefully omit the specifics, Billie knew that she had sworn off painting forever because of her failed attempt with watercolors. Billie had ridiculed her apprehension and pointed out that it was only her first attempt, but she had only shrugged. Secretly, Saoirse knew using crayons justified the imperfection of her artwork. She could only blend the colors so far to match reality. And the knowledge that the imperfection was not due to her own failures gave her some relief. Saoirse was glad she had perfected her drawing skills while she was still young. She remembered the basketfuls of failed attempts, the mounds of eraser shreds, and the boxes of pencil stubs she collected as a child. She was more tolerant of her childish attempts then. She didn't remember when she had become so unforgiving of herself.

"Religion is why you're so screwed up. Religion, people at your church, your parents—they made you into what you are," Billie had said hotly, "You're a sock puppet. The hand opens, the mouth of your sock opens. The hand closes, your mouth closes. Follow the lines, Saoirse, follow them perfectly like you follow your parents. If you're perfect, you'll go to heaven. And if you screw up, God'll zap you straight to hell. My God Saoirse, look at yourself. You don't want to paint because you can't reproduce the colors perfectly? News flash. You're not perfect and you won't ever be."

In the end, her secret had been exposed anyway. Billie saw right through her sketches and into her soul. Saoirse remembered how her tongue had lashed out at her friend like a leather whip and how

Billie had screamed back and missed church for a month just to avoid seeing her. She didn't know why she had screamed at Billie. Everything she had said was true.

The phone on the desk buzzed again. Saoirse picked up the phone and recited the greeting. She asked the caller to hold, transferred the call, and then hung up. She sighed. Already, she was weary of the day's work. In the year she had worked in the office, she had grown even wearier of living. Saoirse felt a sudden urge to smash the flower display against the wall. She squeezed her eyes shut and rubbed her hands over her face. She wondered what was happening to her. She wondered why she seethed with rage. She glared at her abdomen.

The new corset was poking at her again. The sturdy material held the creature so firmly against her she could barely breathe. But even so, her parents and she herself noticed that her midriff was protruding more conspicuously than before. Fortunately, the excuse that she had been born with a defect held the few questioning observers at bay. As she tugged at the corset, a voice spoke huskily over her shoulder.

"That's a nice sketch you got there."

Startled, she spun around. A man stood at the receptionist desk entryway with an arm perched on the desk. His eyes lingered with amusement on her bewildered face. Saoirse frowned. Though she had worked at the office for more than a year, she could only match a few faces to the employee name list. "Is there something I can help you with, sir?" she asked, whipping her arm out as she stepped from the high swivel chair. Her arm struck the box of crayons, scattering the tubes across her desk like billiard balls.

"Great," she muttered.

The man took a step towards her, plunked his forefinger down, and stopped a rogue crayon as it rolled across the desk.

"It's a pity you're using crayons instead of paint," he said.

The man's sea blue eyes glinted in the dimly lit room. Rich chocolate brown hair swelled like wild waves around his face, a face that was handsome, open, and inviting. The young man moved easily in a wrinkled shirt, faded jeans, and black Converse shoes, a stark contrast from the suited employees. Saoirse guessed that he had probably gotten off on the wrong floor and was in need of directions. Still, his intrusion into her private corner and the closeness of his body to hers disturbed her. She took a step back.

"May I help you?" she said with annoyance.

"Straight to business. My father would appreciate that."

Saoirse crossed her arms over her belly.

"I'm surprised you don't recognize me. You must have at least seen me in passing a few times this year. After all, the only reason I come to this office is to see you."

She blinked.

"You don't look familiar. Is there someone you have a meeting with today?" she asked.

The man continued to gaze at her. *He could see your mother in you, Saoirse. He knows.* Saoirse averted the man's eyes and tried not to notice that her heart was fluttering like a frightened hummingbird. The man pulled a wallet from his back pocket, removed a card, and presented it.

"Rhett Haas. Proof I'm not here to go postal. I just wanted to admire you up close for a change," he said, slipping the card back into his wallet.

"Okay," she replied.

Rhett chuckled, stepped back from the desk entryway, and circled around up front.

"Let's start from the beginning. My name is Rhett, and aside from the fact that I enjoy just watching you, I'm here to see my father, Carl Haas. Will you ring him up for me? I'm meeting him for lunch."

Saoirse relayed the message to the president of the company and then hung up. "You can have a seat now, Mr. Haas will be right with you," she said.

Without another glance, she stooped over and began collecting the scattered crayons. The man, however, remained standing before her, his eyes moving across her face and the pale skin of her neck. She wondered if her mother ever felt as she did now, eager and yet disgusted at her own weakness.

"I'll be dropping by the office more over the summer. We should get together. Maybe watch a movie or take stroll on the beach."

"I can't," said Saoirse

The man smiled. "I figure you'd say that. But I'm not giving up you know. You're worth my persistence."

Rhett weaved his fingers underneath a rosebud, closed them around its stem, and pulled the flower smoothly from its display.

"I don't think you're allowed to do that," she warned.

Rhett laughed. "I see you've taken on the charge to shift my moral compass," he said with a smile. He held the rose beneath his nose and breathed deeply. "Don't worry, Saoirse. I'll put it back," he said, giving her a reassuring wink.

A squeaky voice called from the entryway. "Rhett?" Rhett turned. "It is you! Back from San Francisco, I see. How are you?" cried a squatty man as he scuttled toward them with Mr. Haas walking comfortably behind. The young man placed the rose on the receptionist desk.

"I'm doing well, Joe. I was just getting to know the new receptionist. Hey dad."

Joe Banders glanced at Saoirse and pushed his glasses up his face. "You mean Saoirse? Saoirse's been with us for more than a year. I got her this job. She's a member of my church."

"Saoirse was seventeen when she started. I had my doubts, but I think she's doing well," said Mr. Haas.

"You're eighteen then," said Rhett, "didn't you have to go to school?"

"Saoirse was homeschooled. Her schedule was flexible, so she filled in part time when Rose wasn't working. But she's done with school now and not going to college," said his father.

"And don't you worry. I will personally be keeping my eye on her. Her father wanted someone dependable to watch over her, so of course, with me here, this job fit perfectly. So rest assured, Rhett. I am the human resources manager after all," Joe said with a chortle.

Rhett rolled his eyes toward his father.

"I think we're ready for lunch now. I'll get back with you later, Joe," said Mr. Haas.

"Sure thing boss. Nice seeing you again, Rhett," Joe said eagerly before walking off.

Saoirse stood alone with the rose still lying on her desk. Its petals had wilted and bruised in the cold air. She picked up the rose and placed it in the wastebasket. A moment later, the phone buzzed.

34

During the summer months, Rhett Haas spent long hours in the office and often included Saoirse in his projects. His father allowed them to work together as long as Rhett supervised the work and as long as the work could be completed at the receptionist desk. Saoirse, however, continued to rebuff Rhett's invitations to breakfast, to lunch, to dinner, to coffee or to any other activity located outside the office walls. But every time he asked and every time she declined, her heart sank a little more. She wondered whether the prickly pains in her chest meant she was making a big mistake. She wished Ms. Goodman and Billie had never moved away. Billie understood boys, and she understood men. She missed her best friend.

Saoirse scribbled back and forth on a sheet of paper with her head propped on one hand. It was raining when she had arrived for work. Though there were no windows in the lobby, the knowledge that it had been raining made the room seem grey. She sighed.

"Hey there, hot stuff," a man whispered.

Saoirse scowled and looked up. Her eyes met Rhett's curious gaze, and her cheeks felt the warmth of his breath. She stopped breathing.

"Oh, it's you. Back for winter break?" she said. Her stomach did a double flip, but she returned to her paper and continued scribbling systematically.

"Is that how you greet an old friend?" he teased.

"Didn't know you were my friend," she said with a slight smile.

He grinned. "Ouch." Rhett pulled his head back and leaned coolly on the desk. "What is it that makes you so distrustful of me."

"I'm not distrustful."

"You're not? You could have fooled me. I was under the impression that a friendly face did not possess..." He studied her face. "A furrowed forehead. Flat, stern lips. And though very beautiful—menacing emerald green eyes."

Saoirse's lips twitched as she stifled a smile.

"There you go. That's more like it. Why so gloomy? You should be happy this time of year—only a few more days 'til Christmas. That is the birthday of your Savior, isn't it?"

Saoirse stopped scribbling and forced a smile.

"You don't have to smile because I said so."

"I didn't. I smiled because it's almost Christmas."

"Wow. You're making me feel down now. What's wrong?"

"Nothing. It's just, my best friend moved to Alabama, but I haven't heard from her for a while."

"Ahh...You'll make new friends. I'm your friend."

Saoirse gave him a slight smile. Her heart did ache so much for a companion.

"Back for Christmas?" Joe called from the lobby entryway.

Rhett turned. "Yeah," he replied.

The squatty man shook his head. "Time flies," he murmured before scurrying off.

Rhett exchanged a look with Saoirse. "As I was saying, what you need is company. Why don't you and I have lunch together this weekend. Out in the open. With everyone around us. I promise you I'll be good."

"I can't go out on a date with you. My parents will know."

"What. Your parents won't let you date? You're eighteen."

"My father never said I couldn't. He just doesn't trust me because my mother—" She bit her lip.

"Okay, so it's okay then. Then let's have an early dinner, on a workday, I know you don't go straight home. I've seen you in your car eating what your mother packed."

"I pack my own meals," she retorted.

"All right. You pack your own meals. That means you do sometimes eat before you go home, so why not have dinner with me? I assure you, it'll be much better than eating alone."

She hesitated.

"Come on, it's the holidays. Loosen up a little."

"I have to work until six," she protested weakly.

"I have the patience to wait an hour," said Rhett, "We can have an early Christmas celebration. Just you and I."

35

Saoirse rested her head against the driver side window of the forest green Chevy truck. It was late, more than two hours past the latest hour she had ever returned home from work. She flipped the flashlight on again and popped her eyes open. The red in the whites of her eyes had dissipated. Her face was still slightly flushed, but she no longer looked like the red beet Rhett had compared her to.

She had agreed to join him in his convertible for a short ride. When they had parked on a cliff and he had offered her a glass of wine, she had declined. But Rhett had been persistent, coaxing her until she acquiesced. It took only a few sips for her heavy heart to grow heavier still. And yet, she had reached for the bottle again and again so that her sipping turned into gulping and her gulping turned into a desire to drown in a sea of hysteria as she laughed and cried at the city lights below. There was a secretly sweet perversity to drunkenness: a perversity of self-flagellation for her ineptitudes as a human being. God knows she deserved what was coming her way for what she was doing. And so she drank more.

"Whoa, Saoirse, slow down," Rhett had said, "You're redder than a beet, and I doubt your parents would appreciate me dropping you home." She would have rather drunken herself to death than face her parents. Indeed, she would've drunk herself to death earlier if she weren't as naïve about getting the job done. Billie was right. She was not ready for the world.

Saoirse stepped out of the truck and closed the door. As she walked towards the house, the front door swung open and Alice stood at the entryway with her hands on her hips.

"Where have you been? Do you know what time it is?" she demanded.

Saoirse lowered her face, hoping the night shadows would hide her secrets.

"Look at me when I'm talking to you," her stepmother hissed.

Saoirse looked up at Alice who studied her and then smirked. "I knew Billie's truck was trouble. Give a little freedom to a person and you'll see what she's made of. You train her to be a holy vessel, but a sinner and a whore she'll always be."

Alice moved aside and hissed, "Get in here."

Saoirse followed her stepmother into the living room where her father was already seated in the black leather arm chair. A reading lamp threw a sickly glow on his face as he followed her with dark eyes. He frowned when she lingered in a corner. "Don't be stupid," he growled. Saoirse bowed her head and moved closer while Alice circled around and stood by her husband.

"Where have you been?" he demanded.

"I was out having dinner."

"You were out having dinner," said William. He looked up at his wife and said, "She was out having dinner." Alice smirked. He turned back to her. "What kind of drink did you have with your dinner?"

Saoirse blinked. She didn't think her parents could see the effects of the alcohol anymore. "Wine," she murmured.

William exchanged a look with his wife, gazed at Saoirse in disgust, and then moved his head slowly side to side. "You must have had a friend with you then. Can't be Billie. Who were you drinking with?"

"A person at work."

"A person at work," he said, "A man?"

Saoirse did not reply.

"Did you have more than good food and wine with this man of yours?" William sneered, "Did you do anything with him?"

"I—he kissed me."

"He kissed you. I guess that means you didn't kiss back."

"Did you have more than a kiss?" asked Alice.

"I—I'm not sure I understand."

"Don't play with me, Saoirse. You know perfectly well what I mean," she snapped.

"You're very good Saoirse," said William, "Very good. Almost as good as your mother."

"I am not my mother," Saoirse retorted.

William stood up in a flash, took two quick steps, grabbed her arm, and squeezed. Saoirse shrank back, frightened and confused, but his grip kept her restrained. He shoved his face into hers and snarled, "I raised you. Don't you dare speak to me with that voice. Not when hell freezes over, not ever."

Afraid that her father would strike her, she turned instinctively. William jerked her back, so she tumbled towards him, but then thrust her forward, nearly snapping her arm. He peered down at her frightened face.

"I am your father. To you, I should be like God," he growled, shoving her away.

Saoirse tumbled backwards and remained sprawled on the ground. Tears welled up in her eyes as she looked up at her father.

He glared at her and hissed. "Don't you threaten me with those eyes. You don't scare me. I know what you've got, and I can assure you, my God is bigger than that demon of yours."

Yes. Good. Feed me. Let me sink deeper. Deeper into her core.

Underneath the corset, the creature dug its fingers into her flesh. A few blockages in its blood vessels burst open, allowing Saoirse's blood to flow through. Her blood fed the creature, strengthening it, giving it life, and then returned to her for more. The creature's eyes popped open and then gradually closed as it enjoyed the sudden rush of ecstatic pleasure. Saoirse was unaware of what was happening. Instead, her eyes lingered on her father as life drained from within. She remained on the floor, wishing she was dead. A teardrop slid down her cheek like a drop of thick, viscous blood.

William watched the teardrop fall. It pleased him. He needed it to know that his words had pierced her like a knife in all the right places. He needed it to know that she had repented for her sins. He returned to his armchair, sat down, and placed his arms on the armrest. He gazed at her with satisfaction as another teardrop fell. He waited for more. He found a sense of righteous fulfillment, even pleasure at what he saw. Nothing was more gratifying than tasting the repentance of a sinner. When enough tears flowed, he spoke firmly, but with a trace of sympathy.

"I care for you Saoirse. Whether you believe it or not, I do. If I didn't, I would have let you run wild. Addiction and rebellion ran in your mother's blood, and now it runs in yours. That is why you are drunk. And that is why you draw so many men. I was naïve about your mother. I trusted her, so I married her. I cannot change the choices I've made. But I can correct the product she has created. That is why I am so hard on you. Because I care for you."

William turned and exchanged a look with Alice who nodded and spoke as genuinely as she could. "Your battle with your mother's demons will be difficult. It may take years. Maybe even a lifetime. But God will help you. We will all do our best to help you."

The word years and lifetime echoed in Saoirse's mind, bouncing off the skin that imprisoned her soul. *If you're really, really good. You'll be free. But you'll have to try really, really hard. A lifetime of keeping that demon of yours reined in.* Saoirse thought about all the years she had tried to be good. She had tried her best. She had done all the right things. She had prayed daily, she had read her bible consistently, and she had attended church regularly. She had tried to be good, but the anger, the deep bottomless pit of hatred and rage kept growing and spreading, devouring her soul like demons. Yes. Like Legion. Demons she could not purge herself from. What more did God require before she could be free from them. What more. As her tears continued to fall, she thought only of her fatigue and the great aching pain in her spine, the pain that had been growing from the weight of the creature she lugged around her belly. Someone help me, she screamed inside, save me, please.

36

Alice stood beside the leather armchair with her purse hanging on the crook of her arm. Across from her, Saoirse sat on the couch with her hands placed neatly on her lap. She was dressed in a black ensemble of a blouse, a loose cardigan, and a skirt that fell to her ankles, and she and her mother were both waiting for Mr. Churcher.

William adjusted his steel cufflinks as he descended from the stairway. He smoothed his hands over his suit and tie and then exchanged a look with his wife.

"The Stantons say we can leave Darren at their house as long as we need to. I left him with a few books to keep him busy," said Alice.

William grabbed a set of keys from a nearby shelf. "Tell her to get up. We don't have all day." Alice tried not to smile as she urged her child to rise.

The moon trailed after the black station wagon as Saoirse stared somberly out its rear window. A dark, sinister foreboding hovered over her like an impending death. She knew her parents had scheduled a meeting with the pastors, but she did not know what the meeting was for. When they arrived at the house, the senior pastor's wife answered the door and seated the women in the living room. Then she led William down a long hallway, knocked on the double doors of a room, and announced his presence.

"Let him in," a voice replied.

The old lady opened and then shut the doors behind William. The three men in the spacious room arose and greeted him.

"I appreciate you gentlemen for meeting me at such an hour. And thank you, Pastor Kirklin, for opening your home after such short notice."

"This house is your second home. You are welcome any time, especially if the matter concerns your family." The old man urged the men to be seated, leaned forward, and then continued, "Now. What is this urgent matter?"

William glanced over at Henry and then at Rick. He was sure that Henry would support him in his concerns, but he doubted that Rick had the maturity or the experience to understand what he was about to discuss. Rick and his wife Cheryl tried too hard to relate to the youth. They were too much like a pair of Labradors, too eager to please with their tongues lolling about but with hardly a speck of credibility as watchmen. He was annoyed that the young man was even permitted to join them.

"This meeting concerns the disturbing progress of Saoirse. I had initially believed that it was best to keep the matter hidden because I did not want to bring her shame. But now, I feel I have no choice," said William.

The senior pastor and Henry nodded while Rick looked at the others in bewilderment.

"You all know about her mother's affair. And yet, I took Saoirse in without contesting her paternity because I believed it was the right thing to do. I believed that under my watchful eye, I could prevent what happened to my ex-wife from happening to Saoirse. I believed I could prevent the human propensity to sin."

William leaned back and placed his hands on the armrest.

"When I took Saoirse in, I was informed she was born with an abnormality, a parasitic twin. But when I saw the creature, I knew this growth could not be explained by science alone. The Lord showed me that the parasite that hung from her abdomen was the result of her mother's transgressions. That it contained her DNA of sin."

Rick's face furrowed.

"Can it be surgically removed?" the senior pastor asked.

"No. They share too many vital organs. Its removal would result in Saoirse's death."

"I've read about parasitic twins, what makes you think it's not what the doctors describe it to be?" asked Rick.

William's eyes narrowed. "I kept Saoirse's abnormality hidden for years because I was unsure. The parasitic twin was small, about the size of a fetus. So I had a corset specially made to keep it hidden. Saoirse had been obedient when she was young, but she has changed considerably for the worse lately, so I'm sure there's something more to this creature."

The senior pastor leaned back and exchanged a look with Henry. "Henry and I have noticed this, too. Saoirse has always been so polite and respectful. But lately, I sense defiance in her spirit, a growing independence that carries with it a flame of hatred."

"Yes. Yes. And I notice—I mean, my wife and I notice that she has been turning the heads of young men at church. Saoirse has a natural beauty which draws a person—at least from what my wife has told me. But lately, she tells me the color of her clothes is much brighter and reveals more of her skin. Are these changes you or Alice have made?" asked Henry.

"I allow Saoirse to keep the money she earns at work. Her new outfits were bought without our approval."

Rick's sudden laughter startled the men. "I'm sorry, William, but I'm not sure how brighter clothes and simply being attractive is relevant to the parasitic twin, which, as you say, is the root of an inborn sin. Aren't we being a little superstitious here? Saoirse is eighteen. Defiance and volatile emotions are normal for girls her age. She's far more behaved than the teenagers out there."

You damn punk. William's face reddened, but he smiled at the young pastor. "I raised this child. Your lack of knowledge is understandable when it comes to matters that involve Saoirse. Defiance and volatile emotions are unnatural in my household, Rick. I have my son and I have Saoirse. Both were raised under the same roof by the same parents. My wife and I have given Saoirse more time and discipline than we've given our own child. Yet, Darren has given us no reason for concern while Saoirse grows more rebellious by the day."

"Yes, but Darren and Saoirse are completely different from one another. And more nurturing wouldn't necessarily ensure that both children would turn out to be twin angels," Rick argued.

"He's right," said Henry, "My sons are very different from one another. Though, of course, I don't have the same kinds of problems you have with Saoirse."

"Allow me to finish then," William said steely, "As I said, the parasitic twin was the size of a small fetus. The doctors had reassured me that the twin could not grow much and that it had no independent life of its own. One night about a month ago, Saoirse admitted she had gotten drunk with a man from work and kissed him. I had her resign from work immediately. This morning, my wife called me at work. She was distraught and asked me to return home at once. Saoirse had approached her about getting a new corset. She had torn two of her four corsets, which had not been made very long ago. When I returned home, my wife showed me what had been bound underneath. I was shocked. The creature had nearly tripled in size. And what the doctors had once said could not possibly move for biological reasons now moved."

The men looked at one another.

"Saoirse claims she did not commit fornication with the man she kissed. But even as a woman looks at a man with lust in her heart, she has committed the sin. I sense that Saoirse has become deeply impure. And I believe that this is what has given the creature life."

Rick looked incredulously at the men as they contemplated these words. "You're not actually serious about your conclusions are you?" he blurted, "This—this theory of yours sounds like it came right out of the Dark Ages or a bad horror story. I mean if what you say is true, then most teenagers would have these little critters crawling all over them. Saoirse is a healthy teenager with sexual urges. She just needs to be taught to control them."

William flashed the young pastor a look of contempt. Then he arose and walked to the fireplace. He fed a piece of wood to the fire and watched as it licked the edges and then consumed the kindling whole. He turned and smiled grimly.

"Mr. Darton. You are the youngest and the least knowledgeable of our pastoral team. I have seen things beyond your years and understanding. But I can hardly blame you for not believing spiritual realities you've not encountered. I can't blame any of you for having your doubts. That's why I brought Saoirse. I brought her so you may all see whether the creature is an abnormality of the flesh or is really a depravity of the spirit."

As he walked towards the men, the pastors rose instinctively. He smiled grimly. "If you will wait here, I'll call my wife and Saoirse. There is enough light by the fireplace for all of you to see. Please excuse me."

****

Outside, Mrs. Kirklin entertained her guests with stories of her grown children as she sipped tea. Alice smiled and nodded while Saoirse sat quietly with her arms folded close. She shivered as her eyes roamed through the high ceilings and the tall windowpanes of the house.

"You look pale, Saoirse. Are you cold?" asked Mrs. Kirklin.

"I'm fine. Thank you," she replied, catching Alice's frown of disapproval.

The old woman continued with her stories but stopped abruptly.

"William. You've finished so soon."

Saoirse turned to see her father towering over her. "The meeting hasn't ended yet, Mrs. Kirklin. I'd like my wife and Saoirse to accompany me now."

"Oh, of course. I'll just boil another pot of water for some tea. It's getting chilly in here."

"It is," William agreed.

The women followed William as he walked through the dark corridor and opened the double doors of the room. The men inside arose.

"Good evening, Alice. Hello, Saoirse," greeted the young pastor.

Saoirse mumbled a greeting as she approached the men with her arms wrapped around her belly. She could feel their eyes moving across her body, studying the bulge beneath her breasts.

"Stand in front of the fireplace," William ordered.

"Is she comfortable with this?" Rick whispered, but William ignored the young man.

The men trailed after William's lead and then formed a semi-circle around Saoirse while Alice circled around behind her.

"Remove your cardigan and lift your shirt just below your breasts," he ordered, "Alice will remove your corset when you're done."

Saoirse fought back tears as she unbuttoned the cardigan and drew her blouse up beneath her breasts. Alice snapped on a pair of latex gloves, unfastened the corset, and then slipped it off. The men stared in horror at the naked beast. Its long, sinewy arms and legs clung to Saoirse like a feasting parasite. Its head was pressed against her heart, and its body rose and fell in rhythm to her breaths. Saoirse hung her head as the men continued to stare.

For your viewing pleasure, gentlemen.

The eyes of the creature opened.

"God help us," whispered Henry. Then a voice that sounded like his own echoed in his head. *Henry.* Henry took a step back. He prayed silently for God to protect him but kept his awareness of the voice to himself. Only sinners hear from the devil. And he certainly wasn't one of them.

Beside him, Rick was hearing a different voice. He was hearing the voice of a woman he had once been intimate with, a woman he had met before his wife and before God. The voice echoed in his head, calling out his name. *R—ick. I miss your body.* His face grew pale. He wondered if anyone could hear what he was hearing. He looked over at the senior pastor who appeared to be listening intently to William.

"I hope you all believe me now. When we first saw the beast, it was only skin and bones, and it dangled, instead, like a dead branch. With the corset on, no one could even tell it existed. But Saoirse puts the corset on herself, so neither my wife nor I have noticed much of a change until now," said William.

Rick took a step back from Saoirse.

"Tests show that the creature was not biologically capable of moving on its own. But as you can see, that's no longer true. And…" William frowned. "Rick, are you listening?"

The young man stared wide-eyed at him.

"Rick," William said with impatience.

The senior pastor clapped a hand on the young man's shoulder, but he pulled away and screamed, "Get away from me!" Rick stared at the old man in bewilderment and then his cheeks colored. The sound of his own voice had awakened him.

"I'm—I'm sorry. My mind is playing tricks on me." He placed a hand on his forehead. "I need to sit down." The young man sank into an armchair and covered his face with his hands. Then he peered at Saoirse from between his fingers. Her shirt was still lifted, and shadows danced across her naked skin. *Tempting isn't she.* Rick quivered from the rising convergence of lust and revulsion. He wanted to run. He was familiar with such temptation. And he hated Saoirse for reminding him of what he once was.

"You were right, William. You were right," he muttered.

"Is she possessed?" Henry asked.

"I don't believe so. Saoirse is baptized, and I've poured holy water on her but she hasn't responded as those who are possessed. I believe she's tormented, though."

"How do you know?" asked Henry.

"You can't hide sin from me. I can see it in her eyes."

Alice called out. "Is everything all right?"

"Yes, tell Saoirse to put on her corset and clothes," said William. He placed a sympathetic hand on the young man's shoulder. "It's common for young pastors to be unaware of spiritual realities. You'll learn in time."

Alice walked over to her husband and tossed her gloves into a trashcan. "She's dressed," she said. The old pastor looked over at Saoirse who stood alone by the fireplace. "William may not be a pastor, but he has walked with God for many years," he said.

Rick shook his head. "But why would God punish a child for her mother's sins?"

"Sin can be generational like a curse passed from father to son. Generations of drunkards, drug addicts, sex addicts, members of a family line that all seem to have a tendency to commit suicide or repeat some violent act. They're all the same, cursed from the sins of their forefathers. Of course, not every family member will inherit such a disease, but as you can see Saoirse obviously has," said William.

"But the chain can be broken," the senior pastor added, "We can keep her pure. If she obeys our rules, it's possible to break the chain."

"My wife and I have tried that, Pastor Kirklin. It didn't work. That's why we're here today. We need to begin disciplinary procedures."

"But has she sinned to require such judgment?" asked the old man.

"Saoirse claims she didn't have sex with the man she had gotten drunk with, but I have my doubts. She can't go unpunished for her drunkenness either. The church must know that I've given my all as a father and a spiritual counselor. My hands are clean."

"I agree. We'll disclose to the congregation her sin and deformity this Sunday. The shame will be enough to break her."

"What about Saoirse? Will you let her know your plans?" Rick asked.

As William looked up at his daughter, their eyes met. He turned and said, "She already knows."

37

The night sky was illuminated by a full moon. The bright, silvery moonlight made her especially nervous. The plan was to sneak out with two duffel bags and a backpack without waking her parents. This might have been easier if her bags were packed more lightly so she didn't have to make a second trip, but it was too late for should-haves when she was already climbing out her window. Saoirse leapt off, but her foot caught on the frame, and she plunged head first to the ground below. She picked herself up, permitted a few tears, and slipped her fingers across her teeth. No cracks, but still, mistake number two. It was not until she tiptoed to the truck with her first duffel bag and backpack that she realized how much Billie's words rang true. Saoirse stared dumbly at her truck. She was running away from home, but she had no clue what she was doing.

Saoirse snuck back to the house with her duffel bag and backpack, hoisted the three bags into her room, and climbed back up the window. She huddled on the floor in the dark and cried at all her getaway blunders as she wiped at the sweat on her forehead. When her tears finally dried, she comforted herself with one thought: at least she didn't fire up the old truck. The truck would have awakened the dead. She would have no second chances if she botched this one. She wished Billie had been there to help. Two more days. She would have to come up with another plan soon. Fortunately, she got her lucky break the next day.

The Churchers had gone to dinner with friends and left her home. Seconds after their departure, she sprang into action. Saoirse lugged her bags and backpack quickly into the car, left a note for her parents, and then locked the front door of the house. She slid the key underneath the door and then took her first steps into the world alone.

The Churchers had returned home tired and satisfied after enjoying a well-made meal. They did not notice that the old Chevy truck was no longer parked beside the road. They had gone straight to bed, forgetting completely about Saoirse.

The next morning, William entered the dining room with Saoirse's note.

"She's gone," he said.

Alice stopped soaping the frying pan while Darren continued munching on his sausages.

"Who? Saoirse? She's gone? Are you sure?" cried Alice.

William handed her the note. "Most likely right after we left. I would've heard the truck if she tried to leave while we were home."

A flurry of mixed emotions rose within Alice. She was relieved that Mara's child was finally gone. She had waited so long for this moment, a moment she was not sure would ever occur. And yet, she felt a tinge of guilt that she had secretly harbored such loathing. Alice comforted herself with the awareness that she did try hard with Saoirse. She had provided her food, shelter, clothes, and an education. And she had tried to raise the child with a fear of God. Her relief and guilt suddenly turned into fear. What would everyone think of her as a mother? Would they blame the child's insolence on her? Her fear escalated into anger.

"Should we call the police?" Darren asked sleepily.

Alice slammed the frying pan into the sink. "We should. We should have her locked up for being so selfish. How could she embarrass me in front of the congregation? And what will everyone think? They'll say I was the evil stepmother, that I did the beautiful princess wrong. No one will know how much I've put into this child. No one," she cried, "I hate her. I really, really hate her."

Her husband's eyes flicked at her with annoyance. "We're not going to report this."

"But everyone will blame us, William."

"The truth will redeem us. Saoirse couldn't face her sins, so she ran away. The pastors will be our witnesses. And we have this note to prove she left on her own. Saoirse will be nineteen soon. She has a right to leave this house. If she won't take her punishment from us, then she can take it from the world. The hand of the world is a lot harder than ours."

The Sunday service proceeded with the announcement of Saoirse's departure and rebellion and commenced with a sermon about turning from debauchery. At the conclusion of the service the senior pastor approached William and placed a sympathetic hand on his shoulder.

"Don't blame yourself," said the old man.

"I know. We tried our best," he said

"May God save her soul from the hell she has stepped into."

38

Muted sunlight lay veiled beneath the grey layers of dawn. Saoirse gazed undecidedly at the row of mailboxes. Every day after work, she checked for mail, but lately, she had been wrestling with the temptation to make a morning round. She knew the mailman probably didn't make any late deliveries after she returned home, but she couldn't help it. She unlocked her mailbox. Again, it was empty. Her heart sank. For the fifth time in a row, Saoirse promised to check her mail only once from tomorrow on.

"She knows," she muttered as she stepped into her truck, "she knows."

The time on the receptionist phone flipped to the next minute. Saoirse sighed and looked around the expansive building of the company that had hired her only months ago. Unlike the glittery high rise of her first job, bricks lined the interior walls of this building, giving it a raw appearance of rough city streets. Sunlight flooded through steel-framed glass windows that lined its upper walls. Behind her desk, employees ascended and descended a staircase that spiraled to the second floor.

Though she didn't much care for her new job, Saoirse was glad the company had hired her. Her first job at Eddie's Diner, a roadside eatery whose patrons rarely left more than loose change for tip, paid much less. After leaving home, Saoirse had driven through cities and towns searching for work. The money she had saved was used only for gas or food. Fast food restaurants served as rest stops and washrooms; and at night, any well-lighted parking lot served as a secure campsite. She prayed in her desperation for a job, forgetting that she didn't actually believe in a god. And to her surprise, she got one two weeks after she left home.

Eddie Franco didn't hesitate to bark at anyone who stepped into his eatery without the sole purpose of purchasing a meal. But he had been understaffed for months when Saoirse walked in. The portly man grumbled about the bump on her belly and about her inexperience in waitressing, but hired her "only until a real waitress could be found." For a while, Saoirse bumbled about and Eddie growled at her, but Dolly's threats that she would quit if he fired the new waitress kept his mouth in check—that, and the knowledge that he was paying Saoirse a dollar less than he was paying Dolly.

But Eddie never stopped grumbling about the size of her belly. The frequency of his complaints increased when the material of her old corsets began to loosen over time. The diner's regulars chided him to stop being an ass, but Eddie was more concerned about the reactions of his new patrons who often stared wide-eyed at her irregularly bulbous belly. Saoirse's explanations of the defect elicited no compassion, however. After bearing with her for three years, Eddie finally let her go. Saoirse had grown a thicker skin and a sharper tongue hanging around the tough crowd. So when she was let go, she was ready to move on. Still, even with the new waitress hired, Saoirse was kept on staff for a month while she searched for a job, which, according to Dolly, was a real miracle.

The time on the receptionist phone flipped again. Six o'clock. Saoirse looked over sleepily, pressed a few numbers on the phone, and logged herself out for the day.

The Chevy truck rolled past rows of dilapidated buildings and parked in front of an apartment complex. Saoirse got out of her truck and walked to the row of mailboxes. She checked her box. Again, there was nothing. She trudged up the stairs gloomily, unlocked her apartment door, and flipped on the light switch. There were only a few pieces of furniture in the small room: a table, a lamp, a rusted folding chair, and an old mattress placed on the floor below the window.

Saoirse dragged herself towards the window, heaved herself onto the mattress, and buried her face in the pillow. When the air in her lungs dwindled, she turned her head aside and stared at the sketches and photographs taped on the wall. The man in both sketches stared back. Saoirse had xeroxed both versions of the mysterious man and then posted them on her wall, keeping the original sketch tucked safely in her purse. Then, she made a hundred copies of the more accurate portrayal, posted the copies all over town with a contact number, and purchased an answering machine. But Saoirse never received a single lead.

Beside the sketches, photographs of her friend were also taped on the wall. She had caught Billie in one photo looking sadly out a window as she fiddled with her best friend's camera. Billie had developed the photo and given it to her along with another photo that Ms. Goodman had taken of the two girls smiling. They were the only photographs Saoirse possessed of her friend. She propped her head up with one hand and spoke to her smiling friend.

"You were right. I can't find him. What am I supposed to do?" she asked. Saoirse waited, as if inviting Billie to reply, and then complained. "Why won't you call or write?"

The stocky girl in the photograph simply smiled.

"Fine. If you won't come to me. I'll just have to go to you. And you can't say no, because I've already got the ticket."

Billie had moved out on her own soon after the Goodmans moved to Alabama. Her best friend never settled in a city or town for long, so Saoirse mailed her letters to Ms. Goodman's address. But Billie hardly ever wrote back. "I'd rather call," she had explained, "but keep writing. I still drop by mom's sometimes." But Billie hardly ever called either.

Billie had changed somehow, too. Her voice sounded different over the phone, dragging at times in a low and slow pace and rambling nonsensically at others. On the days she was coherent, she was easily angered or annoyed. When Saoirse had tried to get her friend's contact number, Ms. Goodman had replied gloomily, "I don't even know where she is, Saoirse. She drifts from place to place, staying with whomever will lend her a couch or floor. She hardly ever calls, and she just doesn't listen anymore."

And then, she heard no more.

At first she waited patiently, but when Billie had not written or called after almost a year, she grew increasingly concerned. She had left multiple phone messages at the Goodman home, but she had received a return call only once. And that had been six months ago. The message on the answering machine had been vague: "Hi

Saoirse. This is Ms. Goodman. I'm sorry I took so long to call. Things have been hard. Billie is home now. She's sick, but she's been improving these days. She knows you've been calling. She says she'll call when she feels better." The voice paused and then continued. "Everything will be all right. I'm sure. Okay. Hope you're doing well in California. Goodbye." The message had bothered Saoirse enough for her to start saving for a plane ticket.

Saoirse sat up and crossed off another day on the calendar that hung beside the photographs. Ten more days until her first plane ride. Neither Ms. Goodman nor Billie knew of her plans to visit. She was afraid they would dissuade her from going if they knew. Besides, she had already bought the ticket. Billie was her last hope of something good. She may even consider moving to Alabama if the trip went well. Her eyes locked with her friend's smiling eyes.

She has forgotten you. Saoirse frowned, but remained silent. *She's not your friend anymore. She hates you. That's why she stopped calling you.*

"You lie," she said underneath her breath.

She doesn't even know you, Saoirse. She doesn't even know the real you. The voice laughed. *Only the Churchers and your mother know who you really are, and you remember how they love you. You're a freak.*

"Be quiet," she cried.

You can't run from me, Saoirse. I know everything about you. Every dirty little thought. Every dirty little act. I'm waiting for you.

"I said shut up," she growled. Her chest constricted as angry tears covered her trembling face. "Shut up! Shut up! Shut up!"

A voice that sounded like her own echoed with laughter, fueling the fire. Hatred and fury flowed through her veins like hot lava. The laughter accelerated into a piggish squeal. Saoirse cocked her fist back at Billie.

I hate you.

She cursed hysterically at the stocky, dark-haired girl. *You should hate her, Saoirse. You've suffered so much. You—* The light bulb in the room crackled, and flickered back on. Saoirse blinked and then waited. Her body slackened, and then her arm dropped. The tears that burned her now covered her with shame. *It's back again, and it's winning.*

Saoirse peeled her shirt back, revealing a crudely-sewn corset stained a urine-colored yellow. She had sewn her corsets herself, but they were both inferior in material and needlework so that they only kept the creature from flopping about rather than being hidden. Saoirse had been afraid she would be unable to find a job because the shape of her deformity was now as plain as day. But she discovered that people were willing to believe the beast was a biological defect as long as it remained partially unseen.

She unhooked the metal clips and pulled the corset away, exposing the naked beast underneath. Its body had swelled to the size of a corpulent child. Fat folds of firm, lumpy flesh hung like sacs of tumors around its belly. Long, sinewy arms and legs snaked through with pale bluish-grey veins secured themselves on her back with elongated fingers and toes. Behind her, bruises and bloodied crescent-shaped indentations speckled her skin. The creature's head was pressed against her chest with a smile across its face. Its eyes were closed, but Saoirse was not deceived. It had taken her a while to figure things out, to know whether it was a friend or foe, but she knew now. It was sovereign. And it wanted total and complete control.

Fresh tears fell as she watched its peaceful demeanor. She hated it. And she hated God for plaguing her with it. But Saoirse supposed this was God's way. It was God's way to plague a prodigal child until he or she either returned home or crumbled back into dust. He was a jealous God after all. One who hated sin. A God who demanded strict obedience or meted out swift punishment and even death. A God who was always disappointed and rarely ever pleased. A God very much like the Churchers. Though she had once known God differently, those days had long since scattered like the ashes of the dead over a deep sea. Saoirse hardly remembered what her mother looked like. And she had already completely forgotten Luz Ekklesian. She knew God no other way now. And because she always, always fell short of Him, she was to be forever plagued until she returned to dust and her soul sentenced to hell.

A crazed giggle pierced the air. Saoirse did not know whether she or the beast had laughed. She looked down at the creature confused, angry, and afraid.

Kill it.

Her grief spilled over her eyes and dripped onto her hands.

Stop crying and kill it.

The fabric of her mind stretched. Whipped, crazed horses snorted and pawed as they heaved at all four corners of her mind and sanity.

If you hate it, kill it. Kill it now.

Threads of fabric ruptured. She opened her swollen eyes.

"If you remove the parasitic twin, Saoirse will die. Their fates are inextricably linked," a voice whispered.

Another voice slipped through, angry and impatient. "Why should we be afraid? What's more glorious than to die for God, to be with such evil would be the greater death."

Alice is right you know.

Saoirse hugged her legs and rocked back and forth, scanning the room. Her eye caught the glint of a silver blade. She rocked and rocked, staring at the short and wide paring knife. She stood up and walked to the kitchen.

Kill it.

"Kill it," she murmured.

Saoirse raised the knife, studied its fine, razor-sharp blade, and then looked down at the creature cuddling close. She walked to a table, sat down, and then pried the beast from her body. She studied its serene features. Then she pressed the blade on the juncture where she and the beast were joined as one. The knife sank into the wrinkled grey flesh like it would into a slab of soft butter. The creature's eyes shot open, but its crooked smile remained. For a moment, Saoirse was lost in its green orbs as they bore into the aperture of her eyes and drew her in. She leaned towards the beast in a dazed stupor. Below, the tip of the blade burrowed deeper. Then, pain slapped her ruthlessly awake.

Pain. Pain. Pain. Saoirse dropped the knife, and blood spilled everywhere as she rushed to the sink. She filled a cup of water and poured it over the open gash, but the crimson flow continued to spread down her abdomen and leg. She hobbled into the bathroom, tore out a wad of paper towels, and placed it over the wound. Then she grabbed a first aid kit from the bathroom sink drawer and began clumsily dressing her wound. As she did so, the eyes of the creature closed, but its smile still remained spread across its face.

You couldn't do it, could you. You couldn't kill me even if it would save you, even if it was for God.

Tears rolled down her cheek as she dressed her wound. It was true. She couldn't do it. The pain was too severe. And she was too afraid. Though she had been baptized, she was not sure where she would go after she passed.

When Saoirse finished dressing her wound, she remained sitting at the table for a long time.

39

The morning sunlight pierced through the cracks of her curtains. It was Saturday, so she was still in bed. Though Saoirse was awake, her eyes were closed, and her face and hair were wet with tears. She was trying to capture all the pieces of a dream that had scattered like frightened birds. Laughter floated through her window again. She was very much annoyed. The laughter was what had pulled her from her dreams.

The mysterious young man had appeared to her again, but she did not remember why she had cried. The laughter and chattering below grew louder still. She frowned. Saoirse rose from her bed and peered at the streets below. Just as she had thought. A group of young adults were congregating on the streets again. Saoirse scanned the young adults and found a familiar face. She was hard to miss with her bright toothy smile, freckled nose, and fiery red pony tail. Saoirse had caught a glimpse of her chocolate brown eyes as she introduced herself as Julie McNeil and then shared the gospel of Jesus Christ. She remembered how she had brushed the girl aside saying, "Don't waste your time. I know Jesus," before she walked off.

The voice of an older woman echoed. "Okay kids. Let's gather 'round to pray."

Saoirse pushed the curtain aside and watched as the group gathered and bowed their heads. The older woman dressed in a t-shirt, jean shorts, and white tennis shoes looked vaguely familiar. Silvery hair curled around her aging face, but she bore a youthful sturdiness to her presence. "Amen," they concluded. The woman opened her eyes and smiled. Saoirse followed her as she walked over to Julie, paused, and then suddenly turned and looked towards her. Their eyes met before Saoirse spun quickly behind a wall. A moment later, the woman spoke.

"We'll meet back here at three. Did you bring any hats, Jules?"

"David's got 'em," the girl replied.

The voice of a man echoed. "Hats. Oh yeah. They're in the car. Sunscreen, too. I'll get 'em." As the exchange continued, Saoirse slid back towards the window and peeked from behind the wall.

"Good. We don't want to find cooked lobsters when we get back. We'll head out first then," said the woman.

The young adults said their goodbyes and then the woman and half the group crossed a street and disappeared around a corner. At a distance, a boy with fiery red hair jogged towards a car and then bobbed in and out of the vehicle. As he jogged back with a bag in hand, his facial features suddenly became clear. Saoirse gasped.

"That's—that's impossible," she whispered, "He's got red hair."

He was the man from her dreams. Saoirse had always seen the man in black, white, and shades of grey, so she had assumed that the man had black hair. When he rejoined the others, the man offered a bright toothy smile, the same smile she had seen in her sleep.

"All right, everybody. You guys ready to go?" said Julie. The group replied in unison.

The time was now or never. She had waited so long for this moment. She had to make sure that the man below was who she thought he was. Saoirse fumbled through her purse, grabbed the original sketch, and rushed out of her apartment. She dashed down the flight of stairs and then walked briskly towards the young man. As she reached out to him, she felt a hand rest on her. Saoirse spun around, startled. It was the red-haired girl she had snubbed.

"Hey there. How are you?"

Her heart stopped. She stood stiffly in front of the girl, staring at her.

"Do you remember me? I'm Julie. We met a few weeks ago."

The girl extended her hand. Saoirse stared at her hand and then looked down at herself, horror-stricken. She had run out of her apartment without her corset, and she was wearing what she had slept in: a large baggy shirt and sweatpants. The creature was clinging tightly to her body, but the shape of its lumpy mass was visible underneath her shirt. She blushed. The young man and three others had already turned at the sound of Julie's voice. Saoirse waited warily for a snide remark about what god-forsaken monster lay underneath her shirt as they gathered loosely around her.

"Hi," said the young man, "My name is David. I'm Julie's brother. And this is Ted, Arthur, and Amanda."

Saoirse stared at him. David was unquestionably the mysterious man in her dreams. She moved her head slowly side to side. This had to be a mistake. David was too young to be her father. Her mind raced through a number of possibilities. She ignored the young man's greeting and fumbled, instead, with a piece of paper. Saoirse looked down at the sketch and then back at the man.

"It is you," she said, "But—it can't be you."

David and the others looked at the badly creased paper.

"Wow. That looks exactly like David. You know my brother?" said Julie.

"No, but I've been looking for this man for a long time." Saoirse shook her head. "This doesn't make any sense."

Then, her eyes brightened.

"Do you have pictures of your father? A family photo maybe?"

David exchanged a look with his sister. "Yes, I have one in my wallet." He pulled out his wallet, flipped it open, and handed a photograph to Saoirse.

"My mom, dad, Jules, and me. We took this photo last Christmas."

Saoirse studied the features of the older man. Except for his chocolate brown eyes, the man looked nothing like his son. His black hair was thick and wavy, unlike David's straight, fiery red hair. And unlike his son's strong, angular jaw, his face was small and oval-shaped, and his smile reserved. A toothy woman with fiery red hair stood beside the older man.

"Are you sure this is your biological father?" she asked.

The young man's forehead wrinkled. "I'm positive."

Her heart sank as she returned the photograph. "I made a sketch of this man from a dream I had, thinking he was my father. The joke is on me I guess."

"You're looking for your father?" said Julie.

Saoirse crumpled the sketch. "I was looking for him."

Julie exchanged a look with her brother. "What's your name?" she asked.

"Saoirse."

"Saoirse, it is pretty remarkable that your drawing looks so much like my brother. Maybe God is trying to tell you something."

Saoirse smirked. "God doesn't speak to people like me."

"God speaks to everyone," said Julie, "God loves you."

She lies.

"You lie. You don't even know me."

"You're right. I don't know you. But God does."

He certainly does. The rage in Saoirse bubbled underneath her skin. "Yes he does. And you want to know what he knows?" she said, taking a step towards Julie.

"He knows my mother cheated on my father and gave birth to me. He knows her sin courses through my veins, so he created a beast in me. You have no idea what I look like, do you, Julie."

Her head throbbed as she took another menacing step forward. Underneath her shirt, the beast released its hold and laid back. Julie, David, and the young adults watched in horror as arms, legs, and a humanlike mass struggled underneath the baggy shirt. Saoirse continued on unaware of the beast.

"My mother tried to kill us both but was only successful in killing herself. My mother's husband was a devout Christian man. A godly man who later married a godly wife. They raised me but were repulsed with the very thought of me, and you say God loves me? You lie."

The creature's body popped out from underneath the shirt. It grabbed a hold of her shirt outside, climbed back onto Saoirse, and clung to her like a pregnant spider.

"My God," said Ted, taking a step back.

Amanda tugged at Julie's shirt. "Let's go. It's none of our business."

Saoirse followed Amanda's horrified gaze to the creature on her body. Then she looked up at her and grinned.

Julie opened her mouth. "We can help...."

Suddenly, her face turned bright red and she bent over and heaved. The young adults surrounded her, their eyes wide with fear.

"Julie! Are you all right?" cried David.

Julie raised a hand to signal she was fine. Then she opened her mouth and heaved again. When she finished, she squatted down and quivered.

"Julie?" Amanda whispered.

Julie wiped her mouth. "I'm fine. I just need to sit for a moment."

"Ted, can you run and get Luz?" said David.

"Don't. Really. It's something in the air. A choking smell of some kind."

David looked at the others hovering over her. "We didn't smell anything. Are you sure you're not sick?" he asked.

"Maybe you're dehydrated. Here drink some water," said Amanda.

Julie took the water bottle and drank deeply. When she finished, she looked around and said, "Where's Saoirse?"

David stood up. "She was here a minute ago."

"She must have slipped away when you were throwing up. She probably went back to her apartment," said Arthur.

"We should look for her. I think we can help her," said Julie.

"I don't think she wants us to," said Ted, "We can try to find her, but the tenants probably won't be too happy about us knocking on their doors."

"You're probably right. We should tell Luz though. I think that sketch of hers is more than just a coincidence."

"You did see that thing on her, right?" said Amanda.

"Yes. I did."

David looked back at an open second-story window. He did not know Saoirse, but he felt the same inexplicable feeling as his sister that somehow he and the girl were destined to meet.

Upstairs in her room, Saoirse stood beside the window with her back against the wall.

Stay away from her, Saoirse.

Saoirse slid down the wall and hugged her legs tightly. She thought about the words "God loves you" as tears covered her face. She grabbed two fistfuls of hair.

All lies.

"Help me," she whispered, "Help me."

40

Swollen clouds covered the grey skies over the airport. Outside the tall glass windows of the terminal, a vehicle below pulled carloads of luggage towards a plane. Saoirse sat quietly in her seat with a duffel bag and backpack nearby. Her eyes flitted apprehensively between the grey skies and the small man in the vehicle below. An elderly man who sat on one side studied her beneath bushy eyebrows. "First time for you to fly with your baby?" he asked.

Saoirse crossed her arms over her belly. "First time for me to fly," she said.

The man furrowed his brows and said, "Don't worry. God will take care of you," before he returned to his book. Saoirse's eyes flicked to the elderly man and then returned to the small man below. She took a deep breath and released it.

41

The rental car drove by expansive, untouched lands. Trees and wild grass undulated like emerald green waves. A few houses dotted the lands where the trees and grass were shorn. Cows and horses observed from behind white picket fences. With a map in hand, Saoirse continued down long, winding roads. She made one last turn before she faced her point of destination: a two-story house with a sagging roof and a swing on the front porch. Saoirse slowed the car to a crawl and then parked beside a Chevrolet. She checked herself in the rearview mirror and then straightened her corset. She chuckled. She didn't know why she was fixing her corset. She had come this time to just be herself. She wanted her friend to know anything and everything about her. She needed to know that Billie was her friend regardless of who or what she was. Saoirse, after all, had accepted Billie just as she was. She took a deep breath and let go. She grabbed her backpack and duffel bag and slammed the door shut.

The grass on the lawn had not been mown for a while. Saoirse listened to its swishing sounds and then clomped up the front porch. She slipped her backpack and duffel bag off, looked around the dusty floor, and then pushed the doorbell. The bell inside echoed, but no one answered. Saoirse persisted, growing increasingly anxious, until a voice shouted, "Go away, damn you, we don't want anything here!"

"Ms. Goodman?" she cried, "It's me. Saoirse. Saoirse Churcher? I'm not here to sell anything, Ms. Goodman."

She waited in silence. Then the voice spoke. "Saoirse?"

"It's me, Ms. Goodman. I flew all the way here to see you and Billie. I thought I'd surprise you both, so I didn't call."

A moment later, the door cracked open. Ms. Goodman peered through the crack and then opened the door. "Saoirse, my god, sweetheart, you're here."

Saoirse's eyes widened. She had never seen her friend's mother in such a disheveled state. The portly woman was wrapped in a faded bathrobe. Her watery, blood shot eyes appeared listless and her cheeks sagged like jelly-filled sacs. Her hair, normally curled and dyed an auburn brown, gathered in tangled clumps and faded to grey at the roots.

"Oh my god. Are you pregnant? What happened?"

"I'm not pregnant, Ms. Goodman. It's a medical condition that has just gotten worse."

"Oh, God. Thank God. That's—that's wonderful. I'm sorry, I just haven't had a visitor for ages. Come on in," said Ms. Goodman as she ran a hand over her tangled hair. Saoirse stepped into the house with her bags and closed the door. "We can sit in the living room. Are you hungry? Do you want something to eat or drink?"

"I'm fine, thank you."

Ms. Goodman placed a hand on her shoulder. "Let me at least get you something to drink. Make yourself comfortable. I'll be right back."

Saoirse set her bags down and looked around the living room. The curtains were fully drawn, and the room was dark. It was orderly and looked nothing like the Goodman's living room in California. She wondered where Ms. Goodman had placed Billie's paintings. She wondered if Billie was home.

Saoirse walked over to the mantel where framed photographs were displayed. She picked up a picture frame and squinted at the photo. A girl in pigtails stood at the edge of a cliff with both hands raised high. Behind her, a metal railing stood between her and a land of tall mountains, deep valleys, and a tangled maze of trees. Saoirse loved the way Billie's hair looked before she dyed and straightened it. She smiled as she walked to a window with the photo and pulled aside a curtain. Sunlight blinded her as it flooded into the room. A film of dust rose from the disturbance and drifted in the stale air. Saoirse turned aside and coughed. When she looked around the living room again, she saw a layer of dust blanket the room like it would a catacomb.

Ms. Goodman walked into the room and squinted. She placed a plateful of cookies and a glass of milk on the coffee table and walked over to the windows.

"I haven't used this room for months. The dust bunnies always know where they won't be disturbed," she said as she pulled aside the curtains and threw open the windows. She wiped a tear from her eye and muttered, "For God's sake, pull yourself together, Martha."

As Saoirse returned the picture frame, Ms. Goodman said, "Is that the one with Billie's hands thrown wide open?"

Saoirse nodded with a smile.

"That's my favorite picture of her. Haven't seen her smile like that forever," she said, "Come and sit with me on the sofa. I want to get a good look at you."

Saoirse sat beside Ms. Goodman who pushed aside a strand of hair from her face.

"I'm sorry. I didn't mean to cut you off back there, sweetheart. I've just had so much happen, I've been absentminded. Now tell me, did a doctor take a look at that?"

"The doctors say I'm fine. It has just grown bigger these past years."

"Are you sure?"

"I'm sure."

"That's good."

Saoirse glanced up at the stairway. "Is Billie home?" she asked.

"You miss her, don't you."

"I'm sorry, Ms. Goodman. I didn't mean to be rude."

"No. No. You're fine," she replied, staring down at her hands. "I'm sorry I haven't called. I told myself I would when she got better."

"Is Billie sick?"

Tears suddenly poured down Ms. Goodman's face. She covered her face with trembling hands as her body shook with guilt. Saoirse handed some tissues to Ms. Goodman who wiped at her face but could not bring herself to look at Saoirse.

"Billie passed away five months ago."

Saoirse stared at Ms. Goodman.

"Billie and I got into a fight after we moved here. I found some—some drugs in her room, so I told her she couldn't see her friends. She moved out the next day. The police said there was nothing I could do. I tried to get her to listen, but she—" Her voice choked. "A friend of hers called about a year ago, she told me to come get her soon and that if I didn't, she'd die. I hardly recognized her when I saw her, Saoirse."

Saoirse remained silent.

"I tried to give her the best medical care, and she started looking a little better. Her face had more color and she was able to move around slowly, so I was sure the worse was over. I brought her breakfast in bed one day, and she said she was tired but wanted me to stay. I held her hand for a while, but—but then I left. I left because I wanted her to rest, to get strong. I didn't know her heart would give up on her, Saoirse, I didn't know."

Quiet sobs rose in Ms. Goodman's throat. She wiped at her face again and said, "I'm sorry. I should have called you. I'm sorry."

Saoirse felt a hand close over her heart and squeeze, but she said nothing. The house was already weighed down from the pain of death. She couldn't allow herself to add her own. She waited until her pain and sorrow settled.

"Billie must have been happy to have had you by her side," she said.

Ms. Goodman raised her head slowly.

"You love Billie. I can see that. I think Billie saw that, too. Whatever happened, she died knowing that you've always loved her."

Tears welled up in Ms. Goodman's eyes. "Oh Saoirse," she croaked.

The tired woman clasped her in her sturdy arms and sobbed. Saoirse stiffened but allowed her to cry. The last time she remembered being embraced was when she saw the Goodmans off at the airport. It was the only hug Billie had ever given her. She felt the familiar strength of the embrace. Ms. Goodman pulled away and laughed.

"Look at me, blubbering all over you. I've made you a complete mess."

Saoirse smiled a little. "It'll dry."

"I'm so glad you came, Saoirse. Except on the days I dragged myself to work, I kept myself locked up at the house. But I did need someone to come. I did." Ms. Goodman took her hands. "I hope you'll be staying with me while you're here. The guest room hasn't been used in ages."

"I actually do need a place to stay."

"Then it's settled. Let's get you to your room."

Ms. Goodman picked up the duffel bag while Saoirse swung her backpack over her shoulder and followed her up the stairway. As they passed the first room, Saoirse caught a glimpse of many colors. She wanted to stop, but continued on.

"This is the guest room. My room is downstairs. There's a bathroom the next door down," said Ms. Goodman. She dropped the bag down and pulled aside the curtains. "I have to dust your room first," she said between sneezes. Saoirse lowered her backpack.

"Did Billie continue painting after she left home?" she asked.

"I don't know. She only had a backpack when she came back. But she did paint at home. Would you like to see it? You've always understood her language better."

"I would love to."

Saoirse followed Ms. Goodman out into the hallway. As she stood in front of the partially opened door, memories of her introduction to her friend flooded into her mind and lingered as she entered. The paintings in the spacious room were neatly displayed. The familiar collage of license plates and photographs hung on a wall. A plate for California and Alabama had been added, but only California had a photograph attached to it. Splinters of pain pierced her as she remembered the anger and hatred she had felt against her friend days earlier.

She steadied her voice. "I remember this display."

Ms. Goodman smiled. "Billie loved to travel. She always added a plate whenever we moved to a new state. I'm sure she's lived in many more since she left home, but she never added any plates or photos after she came back. She still has that sketch you made of her, too."

Saoirse walked over to Ms. Goodman and studied the framed drawing. Billie had practically ordered her to make the sketch. "This is perfect," her friend had said, "My next birthday gift from you will be a painting. I'm telling you, a little color in your life will make you happier." Saoirse wished she had learned how to paint earlier. Billie had so much color in her life, even though most of the colors were harsh or dreary. Saoirse had envied the freedom she thought her best friend had enjoyed. She wanted so much of what Billie had had. She wondered what had happened.

"I placed all of her old paintings in this corner," said Ms. Goodman.

The grief and seething rage called out to Saoirse from its corner, but she looked away. Now is not the time to let go.

"Billie made one last painting after she came back. I told her not to strain herself, but every time I left the room, she would be up again painting. In a way I was glad she didn't listen," said Ms. Goodman.

In the painting, a small brown-haired girl in pigtails was surrounded by trees that bent over her. The girl appeared to be walking in a valley where shadows of a tumultuous night pressed in on her and would have swallowed her whole except for a light that enfolded her.

"Billie. It's how she looked in the photo," said Saoirse.

Ms. Goodman nodded.

"I think she was speaking to us. I think she was telling us it didn't take everything of hers. The darkness. It didn't win. Maybe Jesus appeared to her in her sleep and she took his hand," mumbled Ms. Goodman. She looked hopefully at Saoirse. "I don't know much about art, but you think I'm right don't you? That I'll see her in heaven?"

There is no heaven. Billie is dead.

Saoirse did not want to think about God let alone heaven and hell. Her best friend was gone. The mystery man she had dreamt of had not been her real father. And she no longer knew of a reason for her to live. She just wanted to be left alone. Saoirse forced a smile and nodded.

42

Luz Ekklesian stood below the apartment window where she last saw the mysterious girl. A still, small voice had told her to look up. She had had many years of experience filtering out the voices that clamored for her attention. The voice that spoke to her that day, Luz knew, was one she needed to listen to. Their eyes had met only briefly before she vanished from the second-story window. Luz didn't recognize the girl, but something told her that the fleeting moment should not be dismissed. Julie's report confirmed this.

"Her name is Saoirse. I don't know her last name, but she has something attached to her. Something that had the body parts of a human being, but—"

"But looked like a monster from a horror movie," interjected Amanda, "The thing also moved on its own apart from the girl."

Luz was sure that this was the same Saoirse she knew from years ago. She had tried to file a missing person's report on the day Mara had disappeared with her daughter, but the police had waved her off. The circumstances had indicated that they left by choice. Moreover, the police had said, Luz was only a friend. There was no reason they should search for and detain the mother and child. Not long after, Luz sold her home, moved down to southern California, and joined a local church. Despite her age, she became involved with the church youth group and was well-loved. Still, with all the changes in her life, she had never stopped praying that she would one day be reunited with the woman and child she had taken in so long ago.

The news about Saoirse excited her but also brought a quiet unease. According to Julie, the parasitic twin had grown and even appeared to possess an independent existence, a fact doctors had said was not biologically possible. Its physical appearance and size, its ability to move and climb, and the strange stench all troubled her. In the seven years Saoirse had stayed with her, Luz had never once noticed any growth or movement of the creature. She wondered what had given it life.

Luz counted the number of windows to the window she last saw the girl, ascended the stairway, and then counted down the number of doors. She stood in front of a door, said a short prayer, knocked, and then waited. She knocked again, but no one answered. On her third attempt, the door next door opened, and an elderly woman peered out at her.

"You looking for Saoirse?" she asked.

"Yes. Is this her apartment?"

"It is. But she's in Alabama. Won't be back until, well, I don't remember, I think a week from now. You can check back in a week and a half to be sure."

"Thank you. If I hadn't known she was on vacation, I might have thought she didn't want any visitors."

"I wouldn't be surprised of that. Saoirse keeps to herself. I haven't seen anyone visit her since she moved in."

"Thank you, Mrs…"

"Mrs. Stone," said the old lady who smiled, nodded, and then closed her apartment door.

43

Saoirse heaved her backpack and duffel bag onto the passenger seat of her truck, slipped into the driver seat, and slammed the door shut. She was tired, drained from her stay with Ms. Goodman. She had kept a smile on her face for the sake of her best friend's mother for four long days. All she wanted to do now was to go home and sleep. It was Tuesday. Saoirse was scheduled to work the next day, but as soon as the plane landed, she had called in sick. A severe case of stomach flu, she had informed them, and she likely won't be in until next week. The office had taken the message and then she was free to be alone with her grief. When she arrived home, she jiggled her key on the stubborn lock and cursed. A door cracked opened and an old lady peered out at her.

"Saoirse. You're back. I thought you'd be gone for a week."

"Hello, Mrs. Stone" said Saoirse. The lock turned. "My trip was only for four days."

"You had a visitor yesterday. A lady with silvery hair. She looked to be in her sixties."

Saoirse paused. "Did she give you her name?"

"I'm sorry dear. I didn't think to ask."

"Door-to-door sales probably."

"I don't think so. Sales people have a certain look, and they talk a lot. This woman made no attempt to sell me anything. And when we were done talking about you, she left. She did say she'd be back in a week or so."

"I'll wait for her then. Thanks."

Saoirse stepped into her apartment and then closed and locked the door. With the curtains drawn, she finally felt safe to let go. She let her backpack slip from her shoulder and dropped her duffel bag. Pain slowly bubbled up from her chest and settled in her throat. She took a few indifferent steps, kicking aside books and clothes. A glass cup popped and splintered underneath her shoe. Saoirse clicked on a lamp and then stared at the light. No light. She did not want to see any light. She seized its neck and flung it across the room. Then she fell on her knees with tears spilling over her face and chest. They drenched her until her consciousness departed, leaving her in black.

44

The soft glow of sunlight around the edges of the drawn curtains was not enough to awaken her, but her stomach growls did the job nicely. Saoirse opened her eyes in a dizzy stupor. Dark rings encircled the emerald green discs like black holes, threatening to swallow the life within. Saoirse licked her dry, cracked lips and tasted blood.

Sleep. You'll feel nothing when you sleep. It'll all be over soon.

Her eyes rolled back up as she closed them. She had not eaten in the past four days and had not taken any fluids in the past three. In the past two days, she no longer rose to relieve herself. Urine and defection drenched her bed. Saoirse uncurled herself and lay on her back. Her spine throbbed and ached like that of an old woman. Her slender frame had shrunken to the hollow remains of a desiccated corpse. Threads of blue veins pulsed feebly beneath her pale, almost translucent skin. Only the gentle rise and fall of her ribcage indicated she was still alive. On her belly, the creature was still fastened to her like a tick feeding on its host. In her starvation, the creature remained bulbously large and sturdy.

Soon, you will have peace.

The black. Saoirse needed the black to return. She looked forward for it to take her back into its familiar drunken oblivion. She had faced death once before, locked in a pantry room, alone and dying from starvation. History had repeated itself. Only this time, she's willing. She had closed the door, secured the chains around herself, and thrown away the key.

It's what you deserve, Saoirse. You should have died years ago, but you refused. Now you're back to where you belong. You deserve no mercy or grace this time.

"No mercy," she whispered.

William and Alice had said so. Her own mother had done so. The people at church, the people on the streets, and maybe even Billie if she had known the truth. All of these by their words and actions had rejected her, hurt her, and even tried to kill her. Even God. No, God especially had wanted this. She knew, because he had taken away her every hope of reuniting with those she loved and those who might have loved her. If there was a God, he could see her. And if he could see her, then he knew that she was a girl who did not love God. She was a girl who had broken God's first and foremost commandment. Thus, death was her reward. She had tried hard. She had tried very hard. But it was impossible. It was impossible to love a God who hated you, who found you utterly repulsive.

Sleep my child.

And so she slept.

45

No one responded to Luz's knocking.

"I saw her come back," Mrs. Stone reassured, "And I can see her truck in the parking lot from my window. She must be home."

Luz was troubled by the lack of response. Though Mrs. Stone had advised her that Saoirse would not be back until much later, Luz had felt a persistent urge to drop by the apartment earlier. When she knocked on Saoirse's door yesterday, Mrs. Stone had opened hers and reassured her that Saoirse was back and that she had not heard her leave since then. "The walls are very thin. I can hear more than I'd like from my neighbors," she had said. But no one had answered the door. Luz returned home with an unease that urged her to persist. But both she and David had called out to her for twenty minutes now and still, no one responded.

"Please open the door, Saoirse. It's me, Aunt Luz," she called.

"Do you think I should leave?" said David, "Maybe she saw me through the keyhole. She didn't seem too happy when she found out I wasn't the man she was looking for."

"I don't think that's it, David. I think she might be in trouble."

Luz returned to the window by the door. The curtains were drawn across, but the window was cracked slightly open. David had already peered through the cracks of the curtain but saw nothing. Luz bent down, prayed, and then waited until a gentle wind drifted by. She caught a glimpse of an overturned lamp and shattered glass before the curtain returned to rest.

"We need to get this door open. See if you can find a manager on site," she said.

David turned and sprinted down the hallway.

"This is making me nervous. I'm going to call the police," said Mrs. Stone.

Luz pounded on the door. "Saoirse! Are you in there? Saoirse!"

Inside the room, Saoirse's eyes slit open but saw nothing.

David returned moments later.

"Is the manager coming?" Luz asked.

"I couldn't find one."

"We need to get to her now though."

"I can cut the window screen and pull open the window."

"All right," she said.

David punched a hole in the mesh and ripped aside the screen. He reached through the gap with both hands and pulled at the window with all his strength. The window shivered but did not budge.

"There's a lock on it," he said, "Let me see if I can move the curtain."

David stuck his fingers through the gap and pushed at the curtain. The fabric swayed, allowing him to catch quick bursts of the room. Broken glass. A broken lamp. Then, a pair of emaciated legs appeared and disappeared. David gasped. "Saoirse! Open the door, Saoirse!" he shouted. He flicked at the curtain again, but the legs remained still. Adrenaline coursed through his veins as he jerked the window again and again, but it was no use.

"We've got to help her. Step back," he ordered.

"Shouldn't we wait for the police?" said Mrs. Stone.

"No. It might be too late."

Luz stepped away from the window while Mrs. Stone hid behind her apartment door. David took a step back and pounded his foot through the window once, twice, three times. The glass split into a web of a thousand pieces and then, after another pounding, shattered through. David reached in through the hole and yanked the curtain aside. In a corner of the room, the skeletal body of a woman lying on her belly was sprawled over the mattress and across the floor. The flies that had been waiting for her scattered and then circled above. David smashed the glass edges of the window, climbed into the room, and hurried over with Luz following behind him. Gently, he rolled the body over. The creature remained affixed to Saoirse with its fingers and toes clutching the flesh of her back. Saoirse's lips parted and her throat whistled as she sucked in the stale air.

"Thank God. She's still alive," Luz murmured as David pulled a blanket over her.

"The police and ambulance will be here soon," cried Mrs. Stone.

Though he barely knew her, David knew somehow, by divine intervention, their paths were meant to cross again.

"Stay with me, Saoirse," he croaked, "Stay with me."

46

The heart monitor beeped while Saoirse lay peacefully on the bed in the dimly lit room. Tubes ran into her arms and snaked across her body. Luz and Julie sat nearby while David stood by the door. It was late and both Luz and Julie had fallen asleep waiting for the doctor. A quiet knocking startled him. He opened the door, looked back at the sleeping women, and stepped outside.

"I'm sorry about the delay, Mr. McNeil. We've had to do a few more tests than we anticipated," said the doctor. "I have some bad news. Saoirse's weak from starvation and severe dehydration, but she might have recovered if those were her only concerns. The tests, however, indicate a large cancerous growth on the parasitic twin."

David frowned. "Can't you remove it?"

"Saoirse and the parasitic twin share too many vital organs for a surgical procedure to be safe, and unfortunately, the cancer cells have already metastasized into her body."

David rubbed a hand over his tired face.

"I'm sorry," said the doctor.

David nodded. "I'll let Luz and Julie know."

The doctor turned and then walked briskly down the hall.

David sat outside the door, letting the news sink in. "God, we need your help," he cried underneath his breath.

Inside the room, Luz's sleep was filled with troubled dreams. Her mind flitted with images of herself as a child. A woman that looked like Mara had placed her into a room and then closed and locked the door. She could hear the metal chains clinking as the woman secured the door from the outside. Luz turned the doorknob, pushed, and then pounded on the door, but no one responded. Tears fell from her eyes as she watched her little body waste away in the darkness. Beside her, the desiccated creature lay limply on the floor. Luz watched as droplets of black, viscous liquid seeped in through the dried veins that connected the creature to herself. The liquid leached into her bloodstream, slithered up her body, and pumped into her heart. An exchange occurred and her heart pumped fresh blood back out. Blood filled with life and nourishment pushed at the dried veins until they gave way and then fed the desiccated cells of the beast.

"No," Luz whispered, but her childlike body had already faded into black.

Luz awoke in her dream to the faces of strangers with glowing white crucifixes emblazoned on their chests. The grim images of a tall, broad-shouldered man with emerald green eyes and the man's wife and child flitted across her mind. An old lady loomed over her with gloved hands that held a threaded needle and scissors. Then, she became the center attraction of a circus freak show.

She watched as hands lifted her shirt and exposed the beast on her belly. Dark eyes ogled and crooked teeth gnashed at her in disgust. She saw the corners of people's mouths twitch and tremble at her deformity and sin. Gloved hands shoved her from one person to the next. Voices pummeled her, beating her on her head, neck, back and chest. *"What's more glorious than to die for God, to be with such evil would be the greater death,"* *"Don't touch me,"* *"Just like your whorish mother,"* *"She deserves to be punished,"* *"Selfish, ungrateful bastard,"* *"Should have let her die,"* *"She's got sin in her blood, sin in her blood, sin in her blood."* Though she did not recognize the family, Luz could feel herself crying out to the green-eyed man and his wife as a child would her parents, pleading with them to save her. But the couple had stood there unmoved, their faces grim. She was overwhelmed by a deep humiliation that seeped into the marrow of her bones; she burned with rage; and she sank in an abysmal sorrow from the death of a close friend. More of the exchange occurred: black, viscous poison for fresh crimson blood. The voices and faces surged like a crescendo of discordant notes until Luz felt her body would burst from the harsh, cacophonous vibrations. And then, there was silence.

Luz lay in a crumpled heap in the dark, her body broken and bruised. She opened her eyes and looked down at herself. She was in Saoirse's body. It was a youthful body that had grown pale and emaciated and ached as one who faced impending death. Approaching footsteps echoed. The body she was in cried feebly for help as it propped Luz up with an arm. She peered into the darkness where the echoing arose. A young woman, strong and healthy, emerged and stood over her. The woman took another step from the shadows.

"Saoirse," Luz whispered, squinting up at the woman.

The woman looked down at Luz with disdain and spoke.

You disgust me, Saoirse. You should kill yourself.

Luz wanted to shake her head, but she could not. Though she was inside the body, she was not in control of it. "Don't say that," she cried, "It's a lie. God loves you." But the emaciated body did not hear. Despite her pain, her hand reached out with its remaining strength and grabbed at the strong and healthy woman. Bony fingers sank into the image, clawing and ripping at the woman who stood before her. "Saoirse, no! You aren't what they say you are. You aren't what you think you are. Stop, before it's too late," Luz screamed.

She felt the powerlessness of her words. With bitter hatred and rage, Saoirse lifted her unwilling fingers and stabbed them again and again into the figure that towered over her. Luz could no longer watch herself destroy the woman she was trying to save. Saoirse was killing Saoirse. She screamed. "Get me out of here, God. Please, help me!"

A large hand rested upon her shoulder. She pulled away and awoke, gasping for air.

"Luz, are you all right?" asked David.

Luz trembled as she looked confusedly around the room. When she found Saoirse still lying on the hospital bed, she covered her face and breathed a sigh of relief.

"I was dreaming," she said.

"I'm sorry. I didn't want to wake you, but Doctor Parnell stopped by."

"What did he say?"

"The parasitic twin has cancer. And the cancer has already spread into Saoirse."

Luz looked over at Saoirse. "This isn't over. Saoirse is struggling with bitterness and hatred. Voices have been implanted in her mind. Voices that want her dead. She thinks the voices are from God, but she doesn't know that she's blocking him out of her life. She thinks the solution to her suffering is death, but she doesn't know that it's not her that's pushing her towards it. It's the darkness that she has allowed to take over. We've got to pray for her."

"Should I call the others to pray?" asked Julie.

"Yes. Call them. God wants her to live, but she has to want to live, too."

47

The wind whistled shrilly in her ears, penetrating into the corner of her mind where she hid. It whirled around her, seeping through her skin and muscle and stabbing at her rickety bones. Saoirse quaked in the cold but kept her eyes tightly shut. She was too afraid to open them. She was afraid of what she might see after having died and gone to hell.

A still, small voice whispered. "Saoirse."

At the sound of her name, her eyes popped open. She found herself squatting on the ground, clutching the tattered rags she wore. Her body was weak and emaciated, exactly as she had last seen herself before her mind was pulled into the black. She raised her head and peered into the darkness. The hell she was in was a vast piece of dry, desolate land. An eternity of wandering alone. A grey mist suddenly sped towards her and whirled around her like a pack of hungry wolves. No, she'd rather not wander. She would rather spend an eternity in hell, huddling close to the ground. The voice spoke quietly to her again.

"Step forward, Saoirse."

Did she hear right? Or was the insanity of hell settling into her mind. She waited for the voice to speak again, but it did not. The grey mist moved and pulsated like a live wire, coming close to her, threatening her, but never touching her. If she took even one step forward, she would be electrocuted, her flesh stripped away from the rushing train of grey or afflicted with even more sinister evils. Man could not possibly fathom the depravity of hell, their minds were too limited. When Saoirse considered her fears a little longer, she almost laughed. She was in hell. The dead cannot protect themselves here. It made no difference if she listened to the voice. Saoirse closed her eyes. She remained squatting there for a long, long time.

"Saoirse," said the voice.

Saoirse opened her eyes. Who was calling her?

"Hello?" she called out tentatively. Her thin legs quaked as she rose. "Hello?"

The grey mist began to move and to pulsate more wildly. Saoirse stood with her knees slightly bent, uncertain as to whether she should risk torment out of a hope that she was not alone. The voice spoke her name once more.

"Saoirse."

Saoirse raised her leg with eager anticipation, but before she could complete her step forward, the wind stopped. The grey mist that raged and encircled her contracted, distilling itself until it formed bones, muscles, sinew, skin, and then finally stood before her as a human being: a woman. Saoirse stared at the woman, stunned, but also troubled by a fear deep within.

"Who—who are you?" she stammered.

The woman laughed. She flipped her long, wavy hair back. Her eyes glittered like emeralds set in ivory. A healthy glow radiated from her face. The woman stood straight and tall, a perfectly proportioned human being with no beast that clung to her abdomen.

"*Don't be silly, Saoirse. You know who I am. I am you perfected,*" said the woman.

Saoirse looked down at the rags that covered her weak and emaciated body. Her own skin was dull, and wrinkles lined her face. She stooped over like an old woman, and the creature still clung to her with its bulbously large body. Its eyes were open and fiercely alert.

Saoirse pulled her rags close and peered at the woman.

"What do you want from me," she said.

"*Saoirse, I'm surprised. You seem... afraid of me,*" said the woman.

"I'm not afraid," she lied.

"*You do know that I'm only here to help,*" the woman reassured, "*But I can understand if you're afraid. So many people have hurt you. Your mother, the family that took you in, strangers, even God. I can see why you question my presence. You have the absolute right to be bitter and angry. The absolute right.*"

Saoirse did not reply, but she placed her foot down. She waited for the woman to continue.

"*Why don't you sit down? I'd like to talk to you and help you,*" said the woman.

Saoirse could feel her limbs with the cessation of the numbing wind. She suddenly became aware of how faint and weary she was. Her body had been reduced to an empty shell with a feeble pulse of life beating within. She wanted so much to sit down, not because the woman had encouraged her to, but because she wanted so much to sleep. To sleep forever in eternity.

"Am I in hell?" she asked.

The woman appeared mildly amused.

"*In hell? No, honey. This is hardly hellish I would think. It's much too cold.*"

"Then, am I dead?"

The woman gazed intently into Saoirse's dull eyes as if she were trying to read her thoughts. "*No,*" she replied carefully, "*Why would you ask such a strange question?*"

"I'm not? Then—then how do I get out of this place? I want to get..."

The woman suddenly shrieked and writhed with pain. Her joints and bones moved in ways that were inhuman in the sack of ivory white skin. Saoirse crumpled to the ground in terror. The shrieking continued, assailing her until the woman suddenly ignited in flames. The spirit that had masqueraded as a youthful, healthy Saoirse had failed. Roaring flames consumed its beautiful exterior as skin and burnt flesh melted into a black viscous liquid. Another figure stood in the midst of the fire: an emaciated woman with a creature clinging to her belly. The woman was an exact replica of Saoirse who now cowered like a frightened child on the ground. She stepped away from the fire and the flames subsided. The woman did not open her mouth, but Saoirse could hear her own voice speaking to her in her mind.

God hates you. Do everyone a favor and kill yourself.

"No, get away from me," whispered Saoirse.

The voice that sounded like her own metastasized into the voices of Legion.

Do it Saoirse. You've been doing it to yourself slowly all your life. Finish the work or we'll do it for you.

Saoirse cried. "God, if you're really there, help me. Forgive me for hating you, but I beg you, please, help me."

A drop of black viscous liquid trickled down the corner of the woman's lips. The voices disappeared. Saoirse suddenly realized she could only hear the sounds of her own weeping. As her crying subsided into quiet sobs, she uncovered her head and raised it slowly. The emaciated woman still remained before her, but she had crumpled to the ground like Saoirse. She did not speak, but Saoirse could see fear in her green eyes. A voice spoke gently, but firmly.

"Arise."

The still, small voice she had heard earlier had changed. It was now clearly audible and there was an inexplicable familiarity to it. Saoirse no longer questioned the voice. She rose from the ground.

"Walk forward," said the voice.

Saoirse took a tentative step forward, and then another. As she drew near the woman cowering before her, the voice spoke again.

"Walk forward. Do not walk around it."

Saoirse hesitated. She did not want to step on the woman. She didn't even want to touch her. But she obeyed. She took a step forward, but before her foot could strike the woman, the woman dissipated into a black mist and parted. Saoirse watched as a burst of fire burned the mist mid-air until it disappeared. Before her, she could now see a thick, wooden stake towering over her.

Saoirse stepped forward, reached out, and touched the pole. The wooden stake seemed vaguely familiar like an old piece of furniture that had been stored in an attic because of years of disuse. In the vast desolate land, she felt strangely relieved of its presence. Her eyes tracked a crimson flow that trickled to the ground, joining a puddle of fresh blood. Grey clouds gathered in the skies above, and thunder cracked, sending her to her knees. A torrential rain began pouring over the land. Saoirse bowed her head with one hand still leaning against the wooden stake. Tears of fearful reverence and sorrow ran down her cheeks. She trembled as she wept. She knew that the wooden stake was not just a stake, but a cross.

"I'm sorry, God," she whispered, "Forgive me for my sins."

Blood trickled from the wounds slashed opened by a crown of thorns and mingled with a teardrop from the man that hung above. Heavy rain pelted down on Saoirse. But when the drop of salty blood fell on the palm of her hand, she knew it came from the man above. As the precious drop rested in her hand, she felt the strange, long forgotten feeling of being loved. She waited until it permeated her skin.

A fiery hot sensation suddenly lit her belly. The creature opened its mouth and screamed. The landscape began to quake, crumble, and fall away. Saoirse tumbled back as the earth shook. But she got onto her knees and crawled fearfully back towards the wooden cross. She hugged the thick pole with both hands and looked up for help, but the man was already gone. From within, she heard a voice speak.

"Fear not, my Saoirse, for I am with you."

The beast screamed again. The force of the scream flung her back from the cross. She looked down. Its bulbous flesh was quivering and rapidly shriveling. A white light glowed and burned at its base. The glowing light spread through the creature like a maze of tributaries, reaching the tips of its claw-like fingers. The creature released its grip from Saoirse as it writhed. It cried out to her, pleading.

Saoirse, help me. Tell him to stop. Please.

Saoirse wished the light would burn more quickly. She didn't care about the pain. She only wished she could no longer hear its cries. The beast read her thoughts through her eyes and hissed. *If he kills me, you'll die. I won't leave without taking you with me. And even if I die, others will come. I promise you.* The creature made one last effort and lunged at her with outstretched claws. Saoirse shut her eyes and raised both hands to protect herself.

A voice shrieked.

48

Saoirse jerked and shook underneath her blanket in the hospital room. Then she lay still. Her eyes flitted back and forth in their sockets without her awakening. Luz, David, and Julie stared dumfounded. They had been praying for more than four hours now. In the last fifteen minutes, they had watched Saoirse jerk and quake in short, quick intervals. Now, only the creature underneath the blanket moved. David drew the blanket aside. All three watched as the beast writhed. Its green eyes bulged from their sockets, and its mouth was stretched open as if it were screaming silent screams. Julie shivered at the grotesque distortions of its body as it thrashed about.

"Keep praying," said Luz.

All three continued as the creature writhed and thrashed as if fire were consuming its body. They watched in horror as it shriveled, its flesh somehow being sucked dry by an invisible source. The creature's mouth moved silently, but this time it seemed to speak rather than scream.

"It's dying," Julie whispered.

Then suddenly, the beast turned towards Saoirse with fiery rage. Saoirse lay at rest on the bed, but her eyes continued to flick beneath her eyelids. The creature lunged at her, making one last attempt to kill her.

Luz shouted. "No!"

The base where the creature had been attached to Saoirse snapped off. A white light burst in the room, and Luz, David, and Julie were hurled back by a powerful force. All three struck the hospital walls and fell on their faces, unable to move and too afraid to speak. Only the beeping sound of the heart monitor assured them that Saoirse was still alive. Though they could not lift their heads to see, they were suddenly aware of a weighty presence in the room.

49

When Saoirse opened her eyes again, she found herself lying on the floor of a lush, green forest. As she rose, her bones ached and complained like a rickety chair, but her astonishment at the beauty of her surroundings eclipsed her pain. The wooden cross was nowhere to be found. In its place, green, leafy trees towered over her and covered the vast landscape. Saoirse gaped wide-eyed at the magnificent old oaks, the rows of swaying coconut trees, and the towering green pines. Grape vines curled around low-lying tree branches, heavy with clusters of plump concord grapes. On the forest floor, honey bees danced about henna and lily blossoms.

As she stared, Saoirse reached out to scratch an itching, burning sensation but winced and pulled back her hand when she touched moist flesh. Black blood. Saoirse held up her fingers to avoid staining the pristine landscape. She looked down at herself. The creature was gone and splotches of black blood stained the fabric around the hole where the creature once jutted through. She made a face. With her stained hand, she pinched the fabric of her shirt together and winced as it chafed her wound.

Where was she? This place was too filled with life to be hell, unless—unless it was a mirage. She breathed in the air. The fragrant fusion of wild flowers, rich soil, and an assortment of forest woods was intoxicating, more beguiling than any manmade perfume. She listened to the soft gurgle of water. Saoirse licked her dry lips and moved toward the source, weaving through tufts of wild flowers and trees. In the deep forest, she found a long, winding brook. Water. They have water here. Saoirse hobbled quickly toward the brook and squatted down. The water shimmered like pristine diamonds and seemed too beautiful to consume. She dipped her hand in, but black blood leached into the slow-moving water. Saoirse snapped her hand back, feeling guilty and ashamed, but the black blood did not move downstream. She watched as the dark liquid remained still in the moving water, floated into the air like smoke, and then disappeared. The forest was not a mirage but neither was it the familiar surroundings of what she knew of earth.

Her thirst returned when the shame passed. She submerged both hands in, scooped up the water, and drank deeply. The water was delicious. Saoirse let her tongue roll in the liquid and then allowed it to trickle down her throat. The water refreshed her aching muscles and bones. At this, she abandoned all human decorum. Saoirse shoveled one handful of water after another into her mouth, but the process was still too slow. Frustrated, she knelt on the ground, plunged her head into the water like a horse, and guzzled.

When she lifted her head, she gave it a little flip and giggled. This wasn't hell. She was having way too much fun for it to be hell.

The sound of her laughter echoed in the woods for a long time. Saoirse cupped a hand over her mouth. That was really loud and almost wild. She had never laughed as much as she did just now. The muscles on her shoulders suddenly tightened. She was afraid someone would hear. She listened and heard soft, melodic voices. People did hear, and they were coming her way. Saoirse wiped her mouth with the back of her hand, scuttled around the forest, and slipped into the hollow cavity of a tree. She listened as the voices weaved perfectly with one another, creating a harmonized tapestry. Soon, the voices were hovering all around her; and yet Saoirse saw no one singing. She could only see the rocks and shrubs vibrate and she could only feel the cavity of the tree quiver with the sound of music. Suddenly, the singing stopped and the rich voice of a man, deep, strong, and yet gentle, spoke.

"There is no need to hide from me."

The voice sounded familiar to Saoirse. A voice she recognized yet could not quite identify. Saoirse squeezed herself out of her hiding place and peered from behind the tree. A man with kind emerald green eyes stood by the brook, waiting for her. Though there was an inexplicable familiarity to the man, she did not recognize him. The stranger was dressed in a white robe overlaid with a brown burlap coat. He was aged but tall and broad-shouldered. He smiled and said, "Hello."

Saoirse stuck her head out. "Hello," she squeaked.

She coughed and cleared her throat, and then she blushed at the thought of a twenty-two-year-old woman hiding behind a tree. She stepped away from the tree, looked down at herself, and then blushed again at the sight of her ragged clothes. She clutched the fabric of her stained shirt and stood in front of the man in awkward silence.

"You're hungry. I've made food for you at home," said the man.

Saoirse was not as interested in food as she was with knowing where she was and who this stranger was before her.

"It's all right, sir. I'm not that hungry," she said. Her stomach disagreed vociferously. "Well, just a little."

"You have many questions, and I promise to answer them. But for now, it would be wise to feed your hungry friend. You are welcome in my house. Will you come with me?" he asked.

Saoirse looked around hesitantly and then nodded.

As they walked beside the gurgling brook, she stared wide-eyed at her surroundings. There was an inexplicable perfection to the forest as if each tree and each plant was meant to be where its seed had settled and buried its roots. The order was not contentious like that of a forest where the wild plants and trees vied with one another for sunlight and fertile soil. But neither was it cold and calculated like that of a farmland where the fruit trees stood in straight immaculate rows with only fruit trees of their own kind. There was perfection to the order. There were flowers that filled the forest too, only a few of which she recognized. Birds and animals of all kinds moved about. Not a single one took flight or skittered because of fear.

A cool breeze blew over her. She closed her eyes. There was such peace in this forest. She could stay in this place forever. She didn't even care if there was a house to live in. She could live here out in the open under the warm sun.

As they approached a clearing, a house built with stone and thick planks of acacia wood could be seen at a distance. A chimney stretched from its roof into the sky. The architecture of the home was unlike what she had ever seen, ancient and yet not of the world she knew. As the man approached the house, the double doors parted. Saoirse followed behind him, gaping wide-eyed at her surroundings. The man walked into the living room and turned, catching her unaware. She snapped her mouth shut and stammered out an excuse for being uncouth.

"Your home. It's—it's beautiful. Sometimes beauty can feel cold or distant, but it doesn't feel like that here. It feels like home—a home, your home I mean, sir."

The man gazed at her with kind, emerald green eyes. He looked at her like a father who for so long had been denied the opportunity to lavish his love. An unrequited love. Deep in the thick, protected cavity of her chest, a voice whispered.

You were right the first time. This is your home, too.

Saoirse's chest tightened as if bracing for a storm. The flood of emotion was too much. She turned away from the man and choked down her tears. She was silly, crying in front of a stranger. Hadn't she learned from her gaffe with David? Stop being needy, she lectured herself silently. This man is not your father, and this house is not your home. You'll just have to accept that you'll never find your father. Saoirse did not turn to face the man. Instead, she took a deep breath, stepped away from him, and pretended to admire the room.

"You have a beautiful living room, sir," she said.

The man looked sadly at Saoirse but said nothing. He would wait. He had waited for this long already.

"Thank you, Saoirse. It would delight me if you explored this house as you would your own. When you're done, you can come to the dining room. I'll be waiting for you there."

Her face wrinkled. The man knew her name. How did he know her name? Saoirse was silent. She waited until she could no longer hear his footsteps on the hardwood floor before she turned around. When she saw that he was gone, she wiped her angry tears with the back of her hand, sat down on a couch, and stared out the window.

The living room was a room of great beauty. Tall, glass windowpanes were built into the stone walls of the room. Saoirse could see the expansive backyard outside. The land was covered with neatly-trimmed grass. Stately trees provided rest spots of shade even though the weather and temperature outside did not require such reliefs. A lake sparkled under the sun like deep blue sapphires just beyond. Inside, the living room was beautifully furnished with plush couches and intricately carved furniture. A stone fireplace was set in the far corner. Saoirse had always wanted a fireplace in her house. In her younger days, she had often daydreamed of cuddling with her imaginary parents in front of a fireplace on wintry nights. The fireplace in this room had been built exactly as she had once imagined.

Despite the magnificence of the house, its beauty did not hold her attention. Her thoughts still lingered on the man's kind eyes. Who was he and how did he know her name? Saoirse surveyed the room, looking for clues that might tell her something about the man. Anything. On a table beside the couch, she found two picture frames and a photo album. Saoirse looked over her shoulder and then picked up a hand-carved picture frame. The photograph was taken of a baby with outstretched arms and a wide open mouth. A snapshot of a hysterical giggle. Saoirse smiled sadly. The man did have a child after all.

Saoirse put the picture frame down and picked up the one beside it. The photograph was one of Saoirse as a normal child without her deformity. She was looking sadly at a dog outside her window. Saoirse wrinkled her forehead at the impossibility. The picture was taken in the privacy of her bedroom. From what she could recall, her father had entered her room only once. This stranger couldn't possibly.... She threw a nervous look over her shoulder and put the frame down. She picked up the photo album and flipped it open. The pictures were all of Saoirse. Each photograph brought back living, moving memories of people she had completely forgotten or had come close to forgetting. Her mother. Luz Ekklesian. Tony and Betty Silvan. Ellen Hong, Mrs. Chen, and Charlie Strong. There were pictures of Saoirse in her most private moments when she was sure she was all alone. And there were pictures that captured every part of her: her tears and sorrow, her ecstatic joy and laughter, her raging uncontrollable anger, and her hopes and yearning desires all the way from her birth, her childhood, her teenage years, and even unto her present age. As long as the album was open, she was brought unrestricted by time into any period of her life. What perplexed her even more was that she did not see the creature in any of the photographs. Not even one. She closed the album.

The house had many more rooms for Saoirse to explore, but she no longer desired to do so. She wanted only to know the identity of this man and how he captured every part of her life without her knowledge. Saoirse placed the album down and rose. She meandered through several rooms as her nose tracked the aroma of a lavish feast that was already set on the dining table. The man had not called on her to assist him in its preparation. Her parents would have scolded her for being selfish. She felt a tinge of guilt spread within like an ink drop in pristine waters. The man stepped into the room holding a pitcher.

"I'm sorry. I should have helped you set the table," said Saoirse.

The man smiled. "I've been waiting for you for a long time. This is a time of celebration. It's more important to me that you eat and are fully restored."

Saoirse was bewildered by this response, but her stomach responded wholeheartedly. The man placed the pitcher on the table and laughed.

"Come. Let's sit down and eat."

Saying a prayer before a meal was a habit of hers regardless of whether she believed in God. Saoirse interlaced her fingers, threw a few curious glances at the man, and bowed her head. She had planned on saying a short, perfunctory prayer, but instead, her chest swelled with inexplicable sheer joy.

Joy filled her like helium would a deflated balloon, egging her to pop a summersault, dance a jig, or belt out a gospel tune. Saoirse squeezed her eyes to concentrate. No. This is serious. This is prayer time not play time. She opened her mouth for prayer. Words of sincere and heartfelt gratitude tumbled from her lips. She tried to stifle a smile and to remain as somber as she could, but it was hard. It was hard not to laugh and to giggle with joy. When she finished with a hallelujah amen, she opened her eyes, a little shocked. What was that?

She had vague memories of being loved once. And she recognized the similar delightful feelings of bliss, but this—this was infinitely greater in intensity, infinitely greater and entirely pure. She was sure she was being loved, though she knew not by whom. It had to be love, because it was only because she was loved that she could pray to God with such love. It was only because she was filled that she could overflow like the pure waters of a spring fountain. She felt suddenly almost young again. Almost childlike in her mind.

"That…was…really…strange. I feel different," she said.

The stranger smiled. "These are all your favorite foods. They were made just for you."

Saoirse did not recognize any of the dishes, but she scooped some of each entre onto her plate and was glad that the man was filling his own plate generously as well. Saoirse cut a small piece of meat and forked it into her mouth. The soft, tender meat was absolutely delicious. Her stomach whined like a famished puppy. Saoirse ate at an accelerated pace that still relatively complied with the rules of etiquette. But every time the man looked away, she would shovel food quickly into her mouth, not thinking that her scheme would only leave her with both cheeks bulging uncouthly with food. The man was right. There was nothing on the table that was not her favorite. Saoirse chewed the food she stored in the sacs of her cheeks like a sprightly chipmunk.

"This is ree ree dericious," she said enthusiastically, "I mean ree ree dericious."

The man looked very pleased. His eyes and smile reminded Saoirse of the pleasure of her mother when she had complimented her as a child. She remembered the goodness of her mother before her mind had gone awry. Her mother did once love her. Saoirse had simply forgotten after all these years. She did miss her mother after all.

"You'll be tired after such a heavy meal. I've prepared everything you'll need upstairs. You'll have a new change of clothes in your room, and you can take a bath to soothe your muscles," said the man.

Saoirse washed down the food with a glass of fruity drink and wiped her mouth with a napkin. "Sir, when can I ask you my questions?" she asked timidly.

"They'll be answered soon. Your body needs to be restored first with food and rest."

"All right," she said.

50

Saoirse curled comfortably underneath the comforter. The curtains of her bedroom were drawn so she did not know whether morning had arrived, but her body told her it was time to get up. She kept her eyes closed a moment longer. Opening them now would only erase the wonderful dream she just had. She remembered the house with the tall glass windows and the sparkling blue lake in its backyard. She remembered the exquisitely delicious food with just the right flavors and textures. And she remembered the stranger with the kind, emerald green eyes. Saoirse sighed. Like all happy and fantastical dreams, this too must come to an end. She opened one eye. And then another. She rubbed her eyes, but it made no difference. Saoirse sat up on the king-sized bed and looked up at the high ceilings of the room. The house, the forest, the food, the stranger. This was no dream. This was real.

She popped out of her bed, unbuttoned her nightgown, and looked down at her abdomen. Small splotches of black blood soaked through the bandages she had bound across her wound. She peered at her wrist watch. The watch was ticking, but none of its hands moved. Saoirse padded to the adjoining bathroom and closed the door. She let the water in the sink run.

"Just gotta clear my head, that's all," she reassured.

Saoirse cupped a handful of water, splashed it over her face, and repeated the process twice. She pulled a towel off a nearby rack and wiped her face. Then, she stared at her hands.

Her hands seemed peculiarly small. So did her feet. She also felt shorter somehow. Saoirse looked at the mirror. "What in the world…" She spun around to look at the full length mirror behind her. A girl that looked exactly like Saoirse when she was twelve stared back at her. Saoirse poked her face with one finger. The girl in the mirror did likewise.

"This must be an ongoing dream. It has to be. Either that or I'm really going crazy."

Saoirse washed her face, brushed her teeth, and dressed her wound quickly. Then she rummaged through her bedroom closet, put on the first dress she found, and rushed outside her room. She padded quickly down the stairway, stepped calmly down the last step, took a deep breath, and walked to the dining room. An extravagant breakfast was already set on the table, but the stranger was not there. In one corner, a reddish-orange light undulated like waves of fire in the midst of shimmering, varicolored lights.

Her voice trembled. "Hello?" The colors continued to shimmer undisturbed. She tried again. "Who are you?" Still, no reply. She wondered if the being understood English. Then, as if in response to her thought, soft giggles floated into the air.

"I'm looking for the owner of this house. Do you know where I can find him?"

A chorus of harmonic voices replied in unison. "You'll see him soon, soon, soon!"

Saoirse watched as the being flittered into separate, smaller forms and then disappeared. She stood dazed until the sound of distant knocking startled her. The front doors had opened by themselves when she and the man first arrived. She wondered who was knocking.

"Coming! I'm coming," she called, "Who is it?"

Saoirse peered through the window beside the door. It was the man with kind eyes. She looked for a door lock but found none. She turned the knob and opened the door.

"Good morning, sir. I didn't mean to check on you through the window like that. I mean, this is your house. I just didn't think it was you that was knocking, because...I thought you'd just like...like walk in. I swear I didn't lock the door. I swear."

"I know, Saoirse. But I prefer to enter when I'm welcome. Did you sleep well?"

Saoirse nodded and said childishly, "Mm—hmmm."

She imagined how silly she must look nodding and speaking as she did. She had never done so with her own father. What was going on with her?

"I mean, I slept very well, thank you sir," she said, "Please come in."

The man stepped into the house and she babbled on. "I'm sorry, sir. My watch was broken, so I didn't wake up in time to make breakfast. But when I got downstairs, breakfast was already made. I saw this rainbow-colored light that laughed and even spoke to me. Honest to God, sir. Were you here earlier? Did you see the lights?"

Saoirse did not want to be called a liar, especially not by this man. She felt her anxiety rise as she listened to the absurdity of her own story. The man rested his hand on her shoulder, and instantly, she felt peace.

"I had breakfast made, and yes, I did see the lights. Come. Let's sit down and eat. We can talk over breakfast."

Breakfast was just as delicious as the dinner Saoirse had thought she enjoyed in her dreams, if the meal she enjoyed could be called dinner that is. Saoirse didn't remember ever seeing the sun set. The light had always been present. Before she slept, she had simply drawn the curtains. She did notice, however, there were only curtains in her room. She wondered why this was so. She took a few more hungry bites, swallowed, and cleared her throat.

"Sir, um, do you see anything different about me?" she asked.

The man's eyes twinkled. "Yes. You look healthier. I'm glad to see you recovering."

Saoirse looked down at herself. She saw that in addition to her youth, her arms and legs were fleshier and emanated a healthy glow.

"Oh yeah. I didn't notice that. Thank you, sir," she said, "But, I mean—do you see anything else that's different?"

"I do. You now look as you did when you were twelve."

Saoirse was astonished at the man's ability to so accurately determine her age. She could no longer hold back her words as they spilled over like a waterfall just after a storm.

"Yes! I mean, Yes. I'm like not twenty-two anymore, even though I have all my memories up until I was twenty-two. And what's weirder is I don't remember the sun ever setting. And then there was that red-orangey thingy with rainbow colors. You seem to know so much about me, too. Your photo album. I'm sorry, but I peeked and saw pictures of my whole entire life. And…and…did I say how strange you seem to know so much about me? I hope that's not rude, but I don't even know who you are, or where I am. Am I still alive?"

The man laughed. "You have a lot of questions, Saoirse. I'll answer them, but continue eating. I want you filled."

"Okay," she replied, watching the man intently as she shoveled food into her mouth.

"You are alive, Saoirse. Your physical body is very weak. But as you are restored here, your body on earth will be restored as well. Your body will continue to grow younger in this realm until you recognize who I am. I desire also for your mind to be restored. It has been hurt by others and by what you have chosen to believe. The things that you see here are strange because you're not on earth, though your physical body remains there. I'm here to help you. I'm here to help you see the truth."

"But who are you?" she asked.

"I can tell you now, but I'd much rather you discover who I am as you walk with me."

Saoirse thought for a moment. "Okay. I can wait."

"But I'll tell you this. I am an artist. Painting is a great pleasure for me."

"You are? I've always wanted to paint. I've just been too afraid."

"I know," he said.

After breakfast, they cleared the table and washed the dishes together. Saoirse chatted about her curiosities and about her likes and dislikes without any restraint. She felt a strange freedom with this stranger, and an overwhelming sense of peace. A sense of tranquil assurance that she guessed someone who was fully accepted and loved might feel. It was a strange but blissful feeling.

"I've got a surprise for you," said the man, wiping his hands on the kitchen towel.

"Ooo, I love surprises. Should I close my eyes?"

"Only if you trust me enough to guide you to the back yard," he said.

"Cool, okay," said Saoirse.

She closed her eyes and felt a hand rest on the back of one arm. The man guided her with his voice out the kitchen, through the maze of furniture and rooms, and out the front door.

"You can open your eyes now," he said.

Saoirse opened her eyes. Centered between the blue skies above and the green grass below was a painting canvas, a high chair, and a table with painting paraphernalia. A vase of exotic flowers was placed on a high chair in front of the canvas. A sparkling sapphire lake rippled just beyond. Above the canvas, varicolored sparkles shimmered around reddish-orange waves and then disappeared. Saoirse did not see the strange lights. Her mind was completely focused on the blank canvas before her. The canvas brought back memories of a past she had hoped she would never remember. Her smile faded.

"Thank you for your surprise, sir. It's wonderful, but I don't know how to paint."

"Every artist began where you now stand. Everyone who has ever tried to paint," said the man, "Everyone including Billie."

"Billie? You know Billie Goodman?"

"I do. She's in a good place," said the man.

"How do you know?"

The man did not reply, but Saoirse already knew. This place was too perfect. It couldn't be anywhere else but heaven. And if this man knew Billie, then she must be somewhere here, too. Who was this man? In the second that a million thoughts flickered through her mind, something within her clicked. Dad. This man was her father. Her real father had met a premature death and was now reaching out from heaven to help her. She gazed intently at the stranger. Dad. Should she ask? No. She remembered her embarrassing mistake with David. She would keep the revelation to herself until she knew with absolute certainty.

"But I'm afraid I'll mess up, sir," she said.

"I promise to guide you. Will you trust me?"

Saoirse wanted to paint. She wanted to so badly. But she was afraid of herself. She was afraid of the craziness that would arise from deep within, a dark and bloody rage that would blight this perfect world. She was afraid after seeing her for who she really was, this man would leave. Her own father. Well, possibly her own father. Or worse yet, the man might tell God that he had made a mistake about Saoirse, that she was not supposed to be in heaven and that she should be sent instead to hell. She searched the man's emerald green eyes. The kindness in them comforted her turbulent heart. The kindness in them gave her courage. She'd risk it.

"I'll try," said Saoirse.

The man smiled and handed her a paintbrush and an artist's apron. She put on the apron and turned to him.

"What do you see on the table before you?" he asked.

"Purple and red flowers in a vase."

"Good. What else do you see?"

"I—I don't see anything else," she said.

"Keep looking. A friend will help you to see," said the man.

Saoirse turned back and studied the vase of flowers. She expected this unknown friend to tap her on the shoulder when he or she arrived. As she waited, she began to feel a great sense of sadness with such beauty. She felt the wildness of the large heart-shaped petals and the thorny vines that curled around the vase. She saw the pearl-like beads of white nectar on the fragile petals where the roguish vines had pierced them. She saw the blend of colors that formed the matured royal purple flowers, and she saw the purple bleed into the still-budding petals of crimson red. Colors she never would have imagined could complement one another began to merge before her. She could see everything. And she could feel everything. This was Billie before her. And this was Saoirse. She knew this flower well. Without hesitation, her hand began to move, blending the paint on her palette with a paintbrush and then dancing across the canvas like a ballerina. There was no uncertainty in her hands. No fear of error. There was just a need to pour the life of Billie and herself into this wildly beautiful flower.

When she finished the final stroke, the need to release herself into the painting lifted like a soft morning mist. Saoirse stepped back and took in the colors, shapes, and movement as one. She could not believe her own hand was capable of such beauty.

"It's beautiful," said the man.

Saoirse turned and saw that the man had been standing beside her all along. Her cheeks colored. He wouldn't understand what she had created. The completion of this painting was not at all like her usual artwork. It was painted with the joy, sorrows, and pain only Saoirse alone could understand.

"I'm sorry. I didn't paint your flowers exactly how they're supposed to look."

"It's you," said the man, "I see you in this painting, and it's beautiful."

51

Doctor Parnell walked down the hallway studying the clipboard in his hand. He was tired from the sudden influx of patients and was looking forward to getting off from work soon. He only worked three days a week now, so going through such a long and busy workday tired and annoyed him. He looked up from his clipboard as a nurse walked by.

"Nurse, give room 12B his meds. And make sure you check if he swallowed."

"Yes, doctor," said the nurse.

"Don't see why we have to keep him going if he won't take his damn meds," he muttered.

The doctor looked at his clipboard again. Final stop, room 4A. This one won't take long. The patient was as good as dead. There were a few medical possibilities, but he found no reason to prolong such a life. The doctor pushed open the door and took two brisk steps into the room. He caught a glimpse of a thick cloud before a quick and powerful jolt flung him aside. His body struck a wall and then dropped hard onto the floor. The doctor wanted to squeal like a frightened child, but he did not. He lay on the ground silent and unable to move. His eyes flitted around. He was aware that he was not alone. Three other bodies lay sprawled on the ground. He did not try to help them nor did he try to call out. He was too afraid.

"It's all right. We're not dead," a woman whispered.

The doctor's eyes rolled nervously. The voice came from the body nearest him. He wondered if it was okay to speak. Whatever had thrown him against the wall had not killed the woman. He would try finding a way out of this alive.

"Wh—What's g—g—going on?" he whispered.

The woman did not reply. No one did. This was a good sign he had better stay silent. He tried to recall what he saw before he was thrown against the wall. A cloud. A thick, white cloud near the ceiling and hazy mist underneath. Was the patient still on the hospital bed? He didn't see. But he did see what looked like a glowing figure in the mist. Or was that just a part of the mist? He wasn't sure. It had all been a blur. Whatever it was he saw was definitely not of this world. He didn't have to see what it was. He could feel the weight of its presence even on the ground. A presence of fearful, unearthly proportions.

Though the doctor had been a card carrying atheist since he started his freshman year at college, he prayed hard now, repenting for every sin he could remember.

52

Saoirse trusted this stranger: this secret father of hers. She would go anywhere with him after what he had done for her, and she told him so. The man had helped her to paint. Something her best friend had not been able to help her do. Something not even Saoirse herself was able to do in the privacy of her own bedroom. She felt somehow free to feel now, liberated from the lines and curves of the black and white sketches: the black and white commandments, the rules, and her parents' and church's demands and expectations she had tried to mindlessly follow so that she might be good, so that she might serve a God she did not know, a God who knew her recurring failures and thus despised her very soul.

It had been hard to be good. But everything has changed now. She no longer was a puppet pulled by man's strings. What she did now came from the heart, even God's commandments and rules, they were not mindless instructions to obey. They were safeguards she would gladly follow, because somehow, she felt that God might actually be real and that just maybe, God did like her and wanted the best for her.

God did at least like her enough to send her what she had been waiting for all along: her father. Even if it were only for a short time in heaven, it would be enough. Because her father, this man with kind emerald green eyes, loved her. She could tell. This man who had committed a horrible sin with her mother had still made it to heaven. If that were the case, then maybe God would be just as merciful with her. Maybe God sent her father to help her to follow the right paths. Maybe God actually liked her and wasn't as repulsed with her as the Churchers were with her.

Saoirse blinked and then found herself standing in a dimly lit room. The man held her hand as she looked tentatively around. She could see a couch with the cushions arranged in an orderly fashion, a coffee table with a bible, and a black leather armchair. Her muscles tightened as her eyes lingered on the armchair. Then, she remembered. She shook her head slowly, jerked her hand away from the man, and then looked up at him in disbelief. He had betrayed her.

"Why'd you bring me here?" she whispered hotly, "What if they see me?"

"Your parents are not home," the man said quietly, "They have gone to church."

"It doesn't matter. I want to go now. Please."

"You've been searching for your father for a long time. Are you sure you want to leave?"

"What do you mean my father? I thought...."

Her mind grew clouded. She felt as if her heart had been pierced through with a sword. He was not her father. The stranger had invited her into his home, cared for her, and given her rest and a taste of freedom, but he was not her father. She wanted to cry. You've done it again, Saoirse. You've become too needy. You must stop this now. She was not a twelve-year-old child. She was a twenty-two year old adult, a rational human being. She had been searching for her father all her life. The Churchers were not home. So, yes, she was willing to experience some discomfort to know the identity of her real father. She swallowed her tears and spoke steadily.

"If I can find the true identity of my father here, I'll stay."

The man offered his hand to Saoirse, but she looked away. The stranger never said he was her father. He had merely acted like one. Still, the loss of such hope was unbearably painful. The man lowered his hand.

"Though you will not be able to see me, I will always be with you," he said.

The man placed his hand over her eyes. When Saoirse could no longer feel his touch, she opened them. The man was gone, but she was not alone. A young woman was sitting on the couch in the room, her body translucent and glowing like a ghost. Her face was worried and her hands were clasped together as a dark vaporous energy encircled her belly. Frightened, Saoirse drew back quickly but tripped over her foot. As she lay sprawled on the ground, she noticed a pair of shoes beside her. She looked up gradually at the ghostly man that towered over her. Above her, large square glasses shielded the man's clam-shaped eyes.

"How can you do this to me, Mara," said the man.

Saoirse looked back at the woman. The woman looked almost as young as she did at twenty-two. She whispered in disbelief, "Mom."

"And to discover this from a 'client' of yours," the man continued.

The woman rose anxiously to her feet. "But William."

Saoirse withdrew slowly from the man. She was still very much afraid of her father though he appeared to not be able to see her. The woman stepped towards the man.

"Don't," he warned.

"I tried to tell you, but you said let the past stay there. I had no options, William. I had no money, no food, nowhere to go. It's horrible I know, but you don't understand. Please. My heart belongs to you and only you. I would never do anything to hurt you. I love you."

"You were a whore. Do you think I would've said that if I had known? You lied to me with your prim and proper dresses and your phony piety."

Tears ran down the woman's face, but she said nothing.

"There's nothing you can say now, can you. You lied to me without words. You're nothing but a liar and a whore."

The woman fell to her knees and crawled towards the man. "Don't say that, William. Please. I stayed pure years before I met you. I've always been faithful to you. I'm carrying your child in me...Our child. I swear to God, William. I swear."

The man bent close to the woman's ear. "You don't have a God." He rose and turned to leave, but the woman lunged at him, grabbing his shoe.

"Please," she cried.

"Don't touch me."

"But we have a child together. Doesn't that matter to you?"

"I said don't touch me," he growled.

"William."

The man bent over, grabbed the woman's arms, heaved her up, and flung her back.

Saoirse cried. "No!"

The woman fell to her side, and the vapor around her belly buzzed like a swarm of angry hornets. Shocked and angered, Mara lashed out.

"How dare you! What I've done is mine. But this child is innocent. If there's anyone that doesn't have a God, it's you. You!"

Saoirse was astonished at her mother's protective ferocity. The memory of what her mother had done in the small, abandoned house had completely eclipsed the memories of her mother's love. But seeing her now reminded Saoirse that her mother had once loved her. It was a time her mother had forgotten her past, everything about her father and all the vicious words he had used to assail her. In her sanity, her mother had loved her.

The woman recoiled as the man drew near.

"You should be thanking me for not divorcing you. You've made me the laughing stock of the church. But still, I let you stay so you could provide for that bastard of yours. But God is a righteous God, Mara, and he will judge you. That child will be cursed because of your sins."

The woman's lips quivered. "This—this is your child. We can take a paternity test to prove it. It's not completely accurate, but in a few years, they'll come up with better tests. Then we'll take it again, and you'll know that I'm speaking the truth."

William paused as if these words had awakened him to a possibility of uncovering the truth. His lips did not move, but Saoirse heard everything that went on in her father's mind.

You've ruined my name, Mara. A righteous man with a whore like you. Not even my pathetic mother was a whore. If you force me to admit that a child birthed from a whore came also from me, I'll make your life a living hell.

"I am not taking that test unless you plan on destroying this marriage," he said.

"But why? Everyone in church thinks I've betrayed you. Don't you want them to know the truth? What about our child? The child will be branded for life."

"If you force me to go through a paternity test, our marriage is over. If you speak with anyone about what happened today, our marriage is over. This is a family affair. I won't have you dragging my name in the gutter anymore."

"But you're the one who told everyone at church about my past. And then you told everyone I cheated on you. You destroyed your own name without verifying the facts, and now you won't take the paternity test? Why?"

"The announcement was the truth. You are twisting the truth. If you say you love God then you won't drag my name down with you. You'll take responsibility for your sins, or you'll leave this house."

When the man walked away, his ghostly apparition dissipated. The woman remained sprawled on the floor with tears streaming down her face. Voices continued to echo in the room.

Don't touch me. You've ruined my life. You did this to yourself. You.

The woman covered her ears with her hands, but the voices continued to drone in her mind. The dark vapor around her abdomen began to slither in and through her. "Stop. Stop," she cried. Mara's body began to waste away as if time were passing in a rapid pace. Her face withered and her skin sank into the hollowness of her skull. Saoirse watched in horror as the voices sucked both flesh and life from her mother. She could hear the voices as they whispered and crooned to her mother in her own voice. Only her still, unmoving lips indicated to Saoirse that it was not her mother who was speaking. Mara curled into a ball and began rocking back and forth, muttering to herself.

"Did I do anything wrong, God? Help me. Help me to remember," she rambled, "Maybe it was…It was in a moment of weakness…with a passing stranger. It might have been the way he looked at me. And… the way I looked at him. Yes. Yes. It's coming to me. But how would he have looked like?" Mara continued rocking, thinking, and imagining. "His hair…his hair would have to be wavy. I've always liked wavy hair. And…and it would be black. Black like the raven, like the Song of Solomon. And his skin would be milky white."

Mara stared into space at the epiphany. She touched her belly as her face twisted in horror. "My God, William was right. What have I done? What have I done?"

The dark vapor began to slither and weave through her body until it reached her brain. Saoirse shook her head. "No. Don't believe it. It's not true." She crawled to her mother, forgetting her fear of ghosts, forgetting her mother was already dead. She reasoned with the apparition, hoping her mother would hear so that the course of history could change.

"Mom. Listen to yourself. You're making this all up. Don't you see? Dad lied to you."

The ghostly apparition suddenly dissipated.

"Mom!" cried Saoirse as she swiped at the air.

The apparition reappeared in a far corner. Mara was standing now. Her hand was perched on an imaginary doorknob, and she no longer looked youthful. Her mother looked exactly like the last and only memory Saoirse had preserved of her. Vacant eyes, disheveled hair, gaunt, and dying. Quiet voices whispered in the air. Mara looked sadly down at the empty space before her and spoke. "I'll see you soon, Saoirse love."

The woman closed the door. Saoirse could see her mother's ghostly hands weave the invisible chains as they jangled outside the door. The click of the lock echoed in the house. Mara walked a short distance and then fell to her knees.

Her husband had spoken the truth all along. She had sinned, and Saoirse had been the product of her sin. The birth of a demonic curse on her illegitimate child. William had moved her to the room downstairs, and they had lived in the house as strangers. She had repented relentlessly, and even secretly bludgeoned and cut herself, but she knew she could never be forgiven. She had seen this truth in her husband's eyes and in the eyes of everyone else in her life before she ran away. The birth of the creature had confirmed her belief. No child born with such a curse and no mother who birthed such a child can live and be pleasing to God. Mara had remembered why she had run away. She had run away to die.

"I remember now, God. I remember what I'm supposed to do." The voices began to whisper like a cloud of angry hornets. With tears streaming down her face, she turned to the imaginary door. "I'm sorry, Saoirse. I love you, but I see no way out. Please forgive me."

Saoirse crawled to her mother's side. "Mom, I love you, too. Don't do this."

Her mother picked up an imaginary jar and began to drink.

Saoirse shrieked, "Don't!" She leapt at the glowing figure, but fell through. Her mother did not change course. She lay down, and then moments later, she dissipated.

For years, Saoirse had forbidden herself to think of her mother, to even cry. She had buried both the life and death of her mother deep in a cavernous hole, thinking they would be gone forever, hoping they would be. Now, she let the pain deep within permeate into the salty fluid orbs as they rose to the surface, shimmered, and then tumbled over.

"I don't want to hate you anymore, mom. I love you, and I forgive you," she whispered.

In the dimly lit room, a bluish-white light burned. The light had been glowing subtly, but Saoirse had been so caught up with her mother that she did not notice its presence. Now that she was alone, she could see rays of light pierce through her dress.

Saoirse wiped away her tears and unbuttoned the mid-section of her dress. The light had already burned through the bandages as it singed the edges of her wound, causing a vaporous smoke to rise. Warmth gradually saturated her skin and permeated into the depths of her body. She watched in astonishment until the glow around the edges of her wound faded, leaving her in the darkened room.

Saoirse rose from the floor, walked to a window, and pulled aside the curtain. The wound circumference had shrunken and the black blood dried, but a dark scar still remained. Saoirse felt her shoulders lighten and her spine straighten from the lifting of an unseen burden. Her forgiveness had brought her healing.

She watched as a butterfly flew in through a window crack and settled on the family portrait. Saoirse met her father's cool gaze below. He was seated in the center of the portrait, composed and unsmiling. A ruby-encrusted cross hung over his grey suit. Darren, a tall and broad-shouldered boy who looked more like a man than an eleven-year-old child, stood behind him and across from his mother, also unsmiling. His hand rested on his father's right shoulder just as his mother's hand rested on his left. Saoirse quivered at the sight of her family staring disagreeably down at her.

"I wish you were here, sir," she whispered.

At these words, she suddenly felt a presence. Saoirse spun around, terrified she would find her family glowering at her from behind, an intruder in their home.

"It's me, Saoirse," reassured the man.

She clutched at the man's arms. "Oh God, sir. Thank God. I'm so glad it's you," she cried. Saoirse found herself still clinging to his sleeves, afraid that he would leave. She blushed and released him reluctantly.

"My parents…Is it true William had been my father all along?"

"Yes, Saoirse. It's true."

Her own father had destroyed her mother without casting a single stone. He had lied without using words, and he had lived a lie as if it were the truth. He had not wanted to be seen as united with a former prostitute, so he made sure the truth would never be discovered by anyone, including himself. Was this omission a sin? Because it sure seemed wrong in her eyes. But he was a man of God. He was a man who prayed daily, read the bible daily, and dedicated his life to the church and to obeying the commandments of God. A man who had never given in to the temptations of the world as she had seen so many, even in the church, had done. A man who unlike Saoirse had done all of this willingly. She was the one who didn't believe God existed. She was the one who resented God all her life for his anger and his eagerness to punish. She would make a point to ask the stranger later, because she was sure that if the man beside her was not her father, then he was definitely an angel.

"You know where we must go next, don't you," said the man.

"To see my father I suppose. I'm not gonna be able to forgive him, but I'll go."

The butterfly fluttered from the portrait and landed on her shoulder. When the man offered her his hand, Saoirse smiled at him and took it. When she opened her eyes again, she found herself standing in the woods that encircled a white, windowless building. A large cross towered above its steeple. Rusted air conditioners droned at a distance, circulating the stale air within. Saoirse remembered the countless times her peers had tormented her within its four walls. She remembered the reproachful eyes of the congregation and her father's promise that he would expose her to the church before she ran away. There was too much pain in this place. She released the man's hand and withdrew.

"Did it have to be here? In front of all these people. In front of God?" she cried, "God wants to shame me, doesn't he. He wants to get me for being bad."

Saoirse began to sob. She was a twenty-two-year-old soul sobbing with the hot, angry tears of an eight-year-old child. The man looked as if her words had pierced him through, but he let her cry. He didn't smite or burn her into a thunderous crisp as she expected an angel would after listening to a mere human accuse the God of the universe of being mean. The angel didn't even give her a little whap over the head. He just held her and waited until her sobbing subsided.

"God doesn't want to get you, Saoirse. God loves you," said the man.

"That's not true, sir. I've read the bible over at least ten times. He does smite people."

"Just as the sun rises and the rain falls, sin always brings destruction and decay. Sin brings destruction to even those who have not committed the sin, just as a single disturbance in a lake creates ripples far beyond. Unfortunately, many do not understand that they are the ones who have disturbed the waters. Yes, God does require judgment for sin. But he is long-suffering and he is always good. His desire is to reconcile with man, not destroy him. He wants you to know him, not by your misunderstanding of him, but to know him for who he really is."

Saoirse wiped her runny nose with the sleeves of her dress and rubbed her swollen eyes. If God is really that good, then maybe she didn't know him after all. The angel, at least, had been good to her, better than anyone she had ever known. She had expected an angel to be more like her father or Alice. But is it possible that she didn't know God even after she had read the bible so many times?

"But if I go in, they're gonna kick me right out. They will, sir. If they didn't want me around when I was there, they're not gonna want me back after I've run away."

"No one will recognize either one of us when we walk in. Your face will be slightly changed. And anyone who sees you will assume you are my child."

"Are you sure?" she asked.

"I'm sure," said the man.

Saoirse bit her lip as she considered these words. The man had not let her down so far, so she stretched out her hand. She noticed how small her hand had shrunken, and how it looked like that of a young child. The man smiled and folded his hand protectively around hers. Together, they walked out of the woods, across the lawn, and up the church steps. The man pushed opened the heavy double doors, and Saoirse stepped in.

The church building looked exactly the way it did before she had left. No one was there, not even her family. As Saoirse walked tentatively toward the front, she suddenly felt as if she were being followed. She peered over her shoulder and then whirled around.

A familiar pair of emerald green eyes looked down at her and then at the angel whose hand rested protectively on her shoulder. Her father had aged. His thick, black hair had thinned through the years and was now peppered with grey. His forehead was lined with deep grooves and his face sagged so that he looked as if he were perpetually frowning, even when he smiled. But still, her father towered over them both like a wall of unbending firmness. William offered the newcomers a frowning smile.

"Good morning. You're both early. We're usually the only ones here at least for another twenty minutes or so," he said.

Saoirse withdrew and hid behind the angel's leg.

"A little shy are we? I won't hurt you. I promise," he said as he waited for the child to shake his outstretched hand. When she did not, his face darkened. He straightened himself.

"My name is William. My wife and son are usually here with me, but I've sent them out on an errand just around the corner. They'll be back before church starts. Are you visiting?"

"We are. I am Avi- 'Ad, and this is my daughter, Saoirse," said the man.

Saoirse looked up at the man in surprise. Avi- 'Ad was a strange, foreign name, but she wasn't bothered by the name as much as she was with the angel calling her his daughter. She was shocked, absolutely astonished that this angel had lied. She had assumed that any angel who lied would instantly be dashed into the pit of hell or be struck by lightning or by whatever weapon God used to smite angels, but nothing happened. She waited a little longer, almost afraid to stand too near to this Avi- 'Ad. Still, there was nothing.

"I see you're not from around here, though I am familiar with the name Saoirse," said William. A vaporous form that had been camouflaged against his black suit suddenly detached itself and slithered around his neck like a small garden snake. Saoirse waited for her father to yank whatever it was that slithered around him, but he did not. Her father's eyes flicked aside.

"Where's your wife?"

"I was never married," said the man.

William stiffened.

"I see. Have you come to search for spiritual truth?"

"I've brought my daughter here so she might know the truth."

"Yes, we should train our children to follow the ways of God, but we must know God first as parents. Do you know the Lord Jesus Christ?"

"I know him well. And you?"

William's face darkened. He didn't trust this man. He had a bad feeling because he felt fear, a fear that warned him not to trifle with this man. It had been a long time since a man was capable of troubling him, and this stranger had done it by his quiet gaze alone. William reached for his crucifix and ran his fingers across it. The head of the slithering vaporous form split into two.

"I've been a member of this church for more than twenty years. My grandfather and father both served God, and I've dedicated my life to serving him. Though I am not a pastor, I'm respected by the leaders here and by my congregation. That's why I keep the keys to these doors. What is your business with our church today. Have you come to attend our service?"

"I have a few questions to ask," said the man.

"Well, you may ask me if you like," said William.

The man gazed at him. "Do you know the two most important commandments of God?"

"The first is to love the Lord with my whole being; then I'm to love my neighbor as myself."

"What does it mean to love a sinner as oneself?" said the man.

William's eyes narrowed. He could smell a trap in these questions.

"We must love our neighbor, yes. But God hates sin. Simply put, a sinner must accept Jesus Christ as their savior and repent. When I say repent, that means they're never to commit the sin again. But there are those who time and time again return to their own vomit of drugs, alcohol, dirty women, and greed. These hypocrites sin by night and make worthless promises of repentance by day, never able to have any kind of self control. And what's worse, some continue to attend church day after day. It's a mockery."

"Without God's presence, it is impossible to break from sin," said the man.

"I assure you, these never change. Sermon after sermon, discipline after discipline, they continue. It would've been better these were never saved," William argued.

"Without God's presence, it is impossible to break from sin," said the man.

William scowled faintly.

"What is the purpose of a church then?" said the man.

"The duty of the church is to redirect those gravitating towards hell just as we are exhorted to correct our children, to even beat with the rod. For the rod does not kill, but hell does. To love God is to obey. Disobedience demands church discipline. This is true love. This is how my father loved me, and this is how I love my child. God does not take sin lightly. Neither should we," said William.

"God is love. And love's desire is to reconcile man with God. After all, those who receive Jesus Christ as their Savior become sons and daughters of the living God. Discipline is a part of love. A father who loves understands this. But discipline and even sacrifice can be done without love," said the man.

William's scowl deepened, but the man continued.

"Love is so much more, William. Love is not an equation. It is fluid, specially tailored for each person. A person would only know how to love a sinner so that he or she might be reconciled to God if the person knew the ways of God and was guided by him and not by man or by his experiences with his earthly father."

The vaporous form, which had split its head into six tentacles, suddenly plunged one of its limbs into William's skull. William exploded. Saoirse shook with terror as the black form snaked around his body and then weaved in and out of his brain. She discovered then and there that it was possible for a person with the body of an eight-year-old child to want to throw up from pure fear.

"How dare you instruct me! Are you saying I don't know how to love? I've dedicated my whole being to God, and I've read the bible more times than the years underneath your belt. I may not be a pastor, but I have everything it takes to be one. I was made by God to be one. I know what you're thinking. You're thinking why in the world am I not then? You want to know why? You want to know why? Because people are afraid. They're afraid that if they made me a pastor, they would be exposed. They're afraid that I would put my finger in their sinful, festering wounds and dig up all that gunk. Oh, be sure, they'll hurt and bleed, but I do it, because I love God. And I assure you, I know how God loves more than you. So damn you. You and that illegitimate child you've spawned."

Saoirse could not stand looking at her father any longer. She was sure that if she did, she would throw up right in the middle of church. She peered at the man beside her, trembling with anxiety and fear. The man was at rest. His face did not twist in anger or resentment at her father's tone. Instead, his emerald green eyes held compassion, the kind of compassion a father would have for an angry, shrieking child who had been tormented at school.

The silence in the church was deafening. Blue-tinged veins had popped out of her father's pale forehead and forked into a throbbing V. William could hardly speak as his hands shook with rage. When he could finally breathe again, he spoke in a low, trembling voice.

"Get out of my church. Get out of my church right now. Or I'll throw you out."

Saoirse waited for the man to explain himself, to at least give some kind of apology to alleviate her father's fury, but the man did not. Instead, he wrapped her hand with his and said, "Come Saoirse, it's time for us to go." Saoirse could feel her father hovering over them as they walked. When they approached the entrance, the double doors suddenly flew open. Saoirse and the man stepped outside. William was taken aback by the doors, but only until the stranger let go of Saoirse's hand and turned to face him. He folded his arms and looked down at the man who gazed at him and then spoke.

"I forgive you, William."

William stared at the man as if he had just been slapped across the face. He was stunned, shocked to a degree that he could not utter a single word.

It seemed like an eternity that the men stood facing one another. Then, rays of light gradually blazed through the door from outside. Saoirse squinted and looked over her shoulder. Fear suddenly gripped her soul.

Two gigantic feet greater in size than ten logger trucks parked bumper to bumper stood beside her pulsing with reddish-orange waves that shimmered with varicolored light. Saoirse moved her wide-eyed stare upward, taking in the gigantic legs, hips, arms, chest, head, and two folded wings that towered over her. Her spindly legs quaked so badly they knocked against one another. She turned slowly around, gazing open-mouthed at the expansive lawn.

She had not seen them when she stepped outside the church, but now, she could see. Hundreds of angels of different shapes, sizes, and colors stood on guard across the church lawn. Hundreds of thousands of others hovered in the skies above. Flanked on the left side of the man was another angel just as gigantic as the one that stood beside Saoirse.

Saoirse pawed blindly for the man's hand, too frightened to look away.

"Dad," she whimpered. When her hand closed around the hand of the stranger, she suddenly knew. She had been mistaken all along. The stranger was not an angel sent by God. And he was not an earthly father who had died and gone to heaven. He was her Heavenly Father, Abba. She looked up at the man beside her with wide-eyed astonishment. She was suddenly aware of his patience, his kindness, and his long-suffering in this world. She was aware of his command of all the power beyond the universe to utterly destroy those who hated him. And she saw just how much God did love the world through Jesus. Saoirse turned to her own earthly father in amazement, wondering if he could see what she saw.

Time seemed to have slowed in the moments she had this epiphany, because her father was still staring at the man in fury and disbelief and his hands were still folded across his chest. Saoirse wondered why he could not see. And then, she understood. This encounter was hers. She needed to forgive her father. She needed to stop hating him for never loving her the way she needed to be loved, to stop hating him for destroying the lives of her mother and herself, to stop hating him for believing that he was blameless and pure, and to stop hating. She needed to stop hating and to forgive as God had.

Saoirse looked at her earthly father with different eyes. She took a step toward him and spoke with a quiet assurance.

"I needed so much for you to love me, dad. I wish things were different between us. Maybe they will be someday. But even if they never change, I forgive you," she said.

William was flustered by her words. Suddenly, moist, scale-like pieces peeled from his eyes and fell. And then, he saw Saoirse. He saw Saoirse as a beautiful eight-year-old child. She was exactly as he had seen her when he first met her, except the creature was no longer a part of her. The wound on her belly had been glowing fully and brightly blue.

"Saoirse," he murmured, "But—but that's impossible. You're grown."

William backed away slowly from Saoirse and the stranger.

"Goodbye, dad. God be with you," said Saoirse.

She turned around, took the man's hand, and disappeared in a bright light. Then, as if hundreds of thousands of angels suddenly took flight, the trees outside swayed and the old building groaned from a whirlwind that swirled about the church. William clung to the doorframe of the church, bracing himself. He suddenly felt sick, sick with a feeling that told him he may have just done something wrong, something very, very wrong.

53

When Saoirse opened her eyes again, she found herself standing alone by the lake in her Father's backyard. She had taken his hand before the white light had consumed them. Where was he? She spun around and came face to face with the man with the same emerald green eyes as her own. He was still with her as he had promised. She was glad God had still appeared to her as a man. Anything more glorious would have frightened her. She smiled a wide toothy smile. Saoirse had to fight the urge to dash towards her Father and pounce in his arms. She was, after all, a twenty-two-year-old adult. And he was, after all, God. She felt the discordant twang of envy when she considered the eight-year-olds who still possessed their childlike minds. They would not have reined themselves in. For a moment, she wished once again she was a child in both body and mind.

The man squatted down and held his arms open. "You are my child through my Son Jesus," said her Father.

Saoirse let her spindly legs fly and then threw her arms around her Father's neck. He laughed and she giggled. Tears of joy, laughter, and love left a wet, messy trail on her cheeks. She straightened herself and wiped her runny nose with the back of her hand and then wiped her hand on her dress. She laughed at how disgusting this must seem to God.

"I'm sorry for being angry at you all these years, Abba. I didn't know you really cared. I mean, I read your word, I prayed, I was baptized, but I thought you hated me because I was always making mistakes. I thought you didn't want to have anything to do with me. But you aren't what I thought you were. You're nothing like what I imagined," said Saoirse.

"I cannot love you while hating you. And I do not love you one moment and then hate you the next."

"But I could never hear you while I was on earth, Dad. All I could hear was that—that creature and my own voice. Sometimes I couldn't even tell the difference between the two. Why was I born with it?"

The man took her small hands in his and squeezed them gently. "The creature was not my plan for you. Evil has a voice, a voice that brings destruction and decay. One of its most vile schemes is to manipulate the very people a person trusts the most to destroy that individual. The other is to destroy a person by manipulating his or her own hands. Evil's greatest deception is to do so without the person suspecting that it even played a role. The world could see the evil one on you, but the evil that haunts many are not visible to others or even to themselves."

Saoirse thought of Billie. Then she remembered the dark vaporous shapes that weaved in and around her mother's abdomen and her father's brain.

"My parents," she whispered. "But it can't be. My father is a man of God."

"The sins of your parents shaped you while you were in your mother's womb. Your father's pride and hatred and your mother's bitterness and shame imprinted themselves on you while you formed."

"My father sinned?" she echoed.

The man's kind eyes gazed steadily at her. "Except for my Son Jesus, no other man is God, Saoirse. Only I am."

Saoirse allowed the words to sink in. "But my father said. So my father's belief that the creature was a result of my mother's past—"

"Is not the truth," the man said gently, "The creature feeds on sin. It feeds on the venom that comes from hatred and unforgiveness. The creature was weak when you were born. It would have died if you were continuously loved, nourished, and disciplined in a healthy Godly way, and also if you had made the choices to come to know, to trust, to love, and to obey me, not as a mean taskmaster, but as your Father in heaven who loves you and who instructs you because he watches over you."

"Then… it was my hatred against my parents and the people who've hurt me…it was my misunderstanding of you that fed…."

The man gave her a gentle squeeze of assurance.

Tears welled up in her eyes. "I'm sorry, God. Will you forgive me?"

The man rested a hand on her cheek. "My child, your sins were wiped clean when you first asked me to forgive you." She met her Father's gaze hopefully.

"White as snow," he reassured. Saoirse smiled a crooked smile and squeezed the man's large palm with her small hands.

"As you walk with me and as you heed my word, you will know my voice, my ways, and me more and more. You will know me for who I am and not by how others misrepresent me. You are my child, Saoirse. I love you more than you will ever know."

As he spoke, the man began to glow. Then, he rose to his feet slowly.

"Where—where're you going?" she asked, trying to quell the frantic rise in her voice.

"I'm not going anywhere, my child. I will always be with you. But you must go back. You still have many years to live and to share my love with those around you."

She clamped her fingers down on God's hands. "No! You can't leave me. I don't want to go back. I'm scared. And I don't have any love to give anyone."

The man bent down again and met her emerald green eyes with his. "You won't be alone. My Holy Spirit is with you. He taught you to dance on canvas and will teach you much more. It's true that human love is never sufficient. But my love never fails. And I will fill you with me as you walk with me. We will meet fully again one day in heaven."

She gazed into the man's kind eyes. She didn't want to go. Nothing down there appealed to her. There had been mostly only pain and sorrow where she had come from. But God had promised that he would be with her. She would go back because she loved him. When Saoirse took a step back from the man, her face glowed.

"Goodbye my child. I will always be with you," said God.

"Bye Dad," said Saoirse, "I love you."

54

The four bodies had lain quiet and still on the hospital floors long after the misty cloud had lifted. They were waiting for a voice of either God or man to let them know they could arise. Saoirse's eyes had stopped moving underneath her lids. Gradually, the muted beeping of her heart monitor swam slowly from the depths of her mind to the surface. She stirred and then her eyes fluttered open. She looked groggily at the tubes and wires that connected her to various machines. She was in a hospital. She knew that much. Saoirse propped herself up with her elbows and peered around the dim room. She caught a glimpse of feet on the hospital floor, and tilted her body aside. "Hello?" she called, squinting at the person on the floor.

Doctor Parnell remained still as his eyes rolled nervously upward. "It's God," he whispered, "I'm gonna die. I'm gonna die. Oh God, I'm gonna die."

She called out again. "Are you guys okay?"

Luz lifted her hand. It was no longer stuck to the ground. Slowly, she rolled to her side and looked up at Saoirse, who was looking curiously down at her. David and Julie began to stir, gradually lifting their aching bodies from the ground. Seeing that it was now safe, the doctor rose as well. Luz limped stiffly towards the hospital bed.

"Are you all right, Saoirse?" she asked.

Saoirse's memories were still filled with what she had seen in her time with God. She stared hard at the strangers, trying to retrieve their identities as they stared back at her in astonishment. The memories of a distant past floated toward the surface like air bubbles from the depths of the sea. The red-haired boy, Saoirse remembered to be…Don. Dillon. David. Yes. David was his name. And the red-haired girl who stood beside him was most certainly his sister. She remembered. David and Julie. The two young evangelists she had met outside her apartment. The man wearing the white coat with the stethoscope around his neck was likely a doctor. And the silver-haired woman. The silver-haired woman with the bright blue smiling eyes….

Luz whispered her name. "Saoirse?"

Saoirse murmured in astonishment. "Luz."

Luz's eyes welled up with tears. She had waited so long to see Saoirse. She couldn't believe how they would be reunited in such a miraculous manner.

The silent bond they shared briefly was interrupted.

"That's impossible," cried the doctor, "Look. Look at her. Is anyone looking at her body?" The doctor stepped forward with breathless excitement, "Excuse me, I'm Doctor Parnell. You were brought in a few days ago. We performed some tests and found a malignant growth in the parasitic twin attached to you. Can you do a visual check? Because from here, it looks like the twin's gone."

The memories of the days leading up to her hospitalization returned. She remembered Billie, and she remembered how she had stopped eating and drinking. She had wanted to die. But her arms looked nothing like the emaciated limbs she remembered them to be. They were now healthy and strong. Saoirse pulled aside the blanket and touched her belly. Then she pulled the neckline of her gown open and looked down. Her belly was smooth and the skin unblemished. Not a single trace of the creature remained.

"It's gone. My belly. It's normal," she marveled.

"I'd like to do a few tests to see if any malignant cells still remain if that's all right," said the doctor.

Saoirse nodded and then turned to Luz. "I saw God, Luz, I saw God. He's real, and He healed me."

"Hallelujah, Amen."

55

A cool breeze drifted through the open window and warm summer sunshine filled the room. A vivid brilliance of paintings, sketches, and pottery pieces colored the room. In its midst, Saoirse moved her paintbrush in small delicate strokes across a canvas. A knocking echoed.

"Come in," she called.

Luz popped her head into the room. "Aren't you going to the movies today? The girls are waiting for you downstairs. Oh, and David, too," she added mischievously.

Saoirse blushed and looked down at her watch. "Oh my gosh. I'll be there in ten minutes. Thank you, Aunt Luz," said Saoirse, removing her apron hurriedly.

Luz nodded and closed the door.

Saoirse couldn't help thinking how wonderful her life had become in the last few months since she recovered. Luz had welcomed her into her home. She had made a whole new circle of friends at church. She had started looking over college brochures with the hopes of attending an art college. And her boss had given her a second chance, allowing her to keep her job. For the first time in a long time, she wasn't wondering if life could possibly be happy. She was happy.

Saoirse brushed her hair quickly in front of the dresser mirror, dabbed on some lip gloss, and then smiled at the woman in the mirror. Then she darted back to her painting to admire it one last time. A man with kind emerald green eyes was gazing down at a girl as they walked hand in hand. He held her with his gaze as an adoring father would. A warm glow of love suddenly filled Saoirse's heart.

'The whole thing was a lie, Saoirse. You were dreaming,' a voice whispered.

Her smile faded. Had she just heard what she heard correctly?

'He's forgotten you.'

Her heart trembled. The voice brought confusion in, rocking what she knew. She felt herself recoil, but then, something deep within arose: a bubbling of anger against what had taken so much from her.

"He would never do such a thing," she cried, "God loves me. And I love God."

She looked back at the painting of the man with the same emerald-green eyes as her own. The man in the painting looked as if he were beaming with pride at his child.

"Thank you, Abba," she whispered.

Saoirse opened the door and exited the room. In the corner of her room, varicolored light sparkled around reddish orange waves.